To the Rea[der]
Magical ...

Hidden Places on Earth
by Darcus Wolfson

First edition 2013

Thanks to Rebecca Jones, Steve Johnson
and Katherine Noon

Cover art by Danielle Mellor

Darcus xx

Contents

Hidden Places on Earth	1
The Final Testimony of Christopher Morell	29
The Waster Troy	44
The Angel of Fogwin	70
The Steve McQueen Story	102
Mother Astra	123
What he saw on Knightsheath	161
The Special Monster	190
Frozen	220
Devourer of Men	244
The Perfect Gift	263
Jellyhead	274

Hidden Places on Earth

My battle with the forces of darkness began on May 4 1979, the day Margaret Thatcher became Prime Minister of Great Britain. The Tories were not the greatest evil I had to endure, there were institutions far more demonic and ancient at work on this damp little island and they too would grow fat on the wholesale slaughter.

Excerpt from the journal of Ray Weaver, volume one.

*

Ray woke up and groaned. He realised that he was nearly frozen to death and numb with pain. He could hear birds singing. He opened his eyes and saw a canopy of leaves above him. He was naked and not in his pyjamas as usual. He was lying on the ground in a forest and not at all in his bed with his wife. He strained to keep his eyes open, the daylight burnt them. His tongue felt like it no longer belonged in his mouth. There was a harsh salty taste at the back of his parched throat. As he rose to his feet, Ray made more alarming discoveries. His naked body was covered in dirt and bruises and what was that dark stuff? Blood? He inspected himself more carefully, squinting and whimpering with self-pity. He felt an immediate need to remove the snail from his scrotum. He was not completely naked, however, as previously suspected. He still had one sock on. One soggy sodding sock. *So this is what it's like to get drunk,* thought Ray.

*

The coast was clear. Ray scanned the back garden again to make sure. There was a nice little shed with curtains in its nice little windows, a well regimented flower bed and a vegetable patch. There was a circular pond in the middle of the lawn where a pair of gnomes looked optimistic about catching some fish. There were starlings flitting in and out of a tiny wooden birdhouse nailed to a tree, joyfully at ease with the presence of a naked man. He saw no humans. Ray had his eye on a pair of trousers and a jumper hanging out to dry on the washing line. They looked like a grubby old man's clothes but after wandering around in the woods for the last hour, fighting off hyperthermia, they looked like attire fit for a king. Ray had stumbled across this row of houses but he still had no idea where he was. It had taken him a while to remember *who* he was. He irritated himself by continually looking at his wrist and finding only the white skin of his watch imprint. His Rolex had gone with everything else. He took a deep breath and leapt over the fence. The barrier was a good four feet high and the involuntary nudist had to scramble ferociously up its rough, splintery surface to get over it, landing on the other side like some hairless gibbon. He was down suddenly amongst the petunias and cabbage. It suddenly seemed brighter as if someone had thrown a spot light on him. There was no turning back. He made a dash for the clothes. His fingers were frozen and he struggled to unhinge the plastic pegs that were holding the trousers and jumper in place. He heard what sounded like a back door opening followed by the more recognisable noise of a woman screaming. No modest scream either, more the cacophony of a thousand anguished cats. The deafening wail gave speed to Ray's unyielding digits and he made good his escape with the clothes. He bounced back through the flower bed and splashed through the pond, kicking a gnome in the process and breaking its ceramic fishing rod. He chanced to look back at the banshee. She was stood, framed by the back door of the house; her hag-like face frozen with terror, her hair in curlers. She stopped screaming and put a dainty hand on her chest, melodramatically.

'Aren't you Ray Weaver?' she asked.

'Not me, luv,' said Ray Weaver and leapt back over the fence.

*

Thankfully, Iris had taken the kids to nursery school by the time Ray got home. His wife, however, was not at work as he had hoped. He stood on the front doorstep. She looked at him up and down with disgust. Ray looked at himself up and down with disgust. The ill-fitting old man's trousers and jumper and absence of one sock drew attention from everyone he encountered. His twelve-mile journey home was populated by sweet kids, adorable puppies and kindly old folk, all staring at him with horror. It was like a waking nightmare. The rest of the world seemed impossibly bright and happy and wholesome, like an advert for washing powder in which he was not welcome. It was not until he looked at his reflection in a post office window that Ray noticed that his face was burnt black. His eyebrows had been completely erased. He barely recognised himself. He looked like Yosemite Sam after a backfired attempt to explode Bugs Bunny. At one point, a police car passed him and Ray, now a thief, was forced to hide unceremoniously behind a bus shelter. He was ready to weep at the sight of home.

'Where have you been all night? What happened to you? What in Christ's holy name are you wearing? What happened to your face? Have you been in an accident?' Iris was nearly in tears too.

'Which one of those questions would you like me to answer first?' asked Ray, his head swirling.

'You stink,' stated his wife. Her scarlet locks and rosy cheeks accentuating her rage, as always.

'I smell like a charity shop,' Ray sniffed at his newly acquired jumper.

'You smell of drink,' she whimpered. 'What happened to you, Ray? You never drink. What would Jesus say?'

Ray looked around, self-consciously, not ready yet to take on the son of the Almighty. 'Can we do this inside?'

'I'm not letting you in.' Iris crossed her arms defiantly.

'The neighbours will see us,' suggested Ray, his wife's fear of "what the neighbours will think" strategy deployed. He was dragged inside. His feet actually left the ground like he had been seized by an enraged orangutan.

Ray stripped off slowly and handed Mrs Weaver the three items of clothing that had sustained him on his walk of shame. She took the rags and put them into a plastic bag. She lifted each item up with her marigolds and inspected it, crinkling her nose up in revulsion and then dropping it into the bag like it was nuclear waste. Ray's wife had a penchant for the theatrical when she was cross. She could not, for example, just throw the clothes in the bin. Iris had to make a meal of it. Ray usually found this habit excruciating but he was glad to be home. He looked around at the mundane features of his kitchen with delirious consolation. He wrapped himself tighter in the towel Iris had handed to him. Warmth returned to his abused body and he suddenly felt drowsy. Coherent thoughts were casually slipping away from him like guests from a boring dinner party.

'Aren't you going to work today?' barked Iris, cruelly snatching him away from the embrace of a welcome oblivion.

'In this state?' pleaded Ray.

'Archie rang. He says he wants the dog story.'

'Dog story? What dog story?' Ray scratched his head, striving again to remember anything from the previous twenty-four hours.

'I don't know, do I? That's just what he said. He sounded angry.'

Ray buried his head in the towel and mumbled; 'well, I'll have a bath and drive in.'

'You can't, I'm taking the car today. We've discussed this already,' Iris explained.

'That's right,' Ray looked up at her, suddenly fierce, 'because I obviously haven't done enough walking today, have I?'

'You're in no position to make demands, Raymond Weaver!' Iris' Glaswegian slur was now dripping with venom.

Ray backed off quickly. 'Okay, fine, don't worry about me.'

Ray was reluctant to say anything more. He was far too bewildered to argue with her. Even when at his best, Ray rarely won their squabbles.

Iris finished disposing of the nuclear waste and gazed at him. 'You really don't remember anything, do you?' Her tone softened a little as she closed in to put some cream on his burnt face.

Ray gazed back at his wife and shook his head, tears finally rolling down his cheeks.

*

I have tried to make clear from the start that all I ever wanted was an ordinary life. On the chessboard of existence, a steady career as a pawn would have sufficed but the gods had me chalked up for something else. My upbringing in north-east London was normal enough if belonging to an alcoholic mother with nine kids could be described as normal. What I mean is that my childhood was unremarkable. I vaguely remember my dad from when I was very young or, at least, I remember the feel of his knuckles as they struck my face. Despite the odds, I did very well at school, with the exception of the occasional playground scuffle or three. English was my strongest subject and I left at age 16 for an apprenticeship in journalism. Three years later, I moved from Hackney to an infinitely quieter place in the countryside called Fogwin. I continued to do well there and got a job with the local rag, quickly getting a reputation for quirky news reports. By the time I was 24, I was mortgaged up to the eyeballs and married with two kids of my own. I strived to give them the happiness and attention that had been denied to me. It is my biggest regret that my life did not stay that way. I was content with my lot. Then we got our first female Prime Minister who went and opened the door for all the lunatics to come in.

Excerpt from the journal of Ray Weaver, volume one.

*

'Where the hell have you been? You're late! You look like death. Where's the fucking story?'

Ray could deal with his angry wife. He could deal with his angry boss. He could not, however, deal with his angry boss' moustache when it was provoked. It formed a malign existence of its own. The silver monster with the tobacco stain bristled at him. Ray handed Archie the office swearbox at arm's length, keeping his eye on that dreaded top lip.

Despite his fury, Archie pulled out some change from his trouser pocket and deposited a coin. 'You and that damn box!'

'Keep 'em coming.'

'Oh, what? Come on! "Damn" isn't swearing?'

'It's a profanity.'

'For Christ's sake!'

Ray could have busted Archie for 'the Christ' but he did not want to push the moustache too far. It looked ready to leap from Archie's face and seize him by the throat.

'So, where's the ... erm ... story?' the editor calmed down a bit.

Ray held up his hands, defensively. 'Listen, Archie, I've had a rough night. You're gonna have to help us out a bit, mate, what story are we talking about here exactly?'

'The fucking dog that drinks!' the moustache shuddered with rage again.

'Oh, that story,' Ray gestured to the swearbox. 'Well, Archie, me old mucka, as soon as I remember what happened to me last night, perhaps I'll remember the story.'

'So what you're saying is that you've missed your deadline because you got pissed as a fart? Oh that's alright then! Pardon me for speaking out of turn!' The moustache was getting sarcastic. It completely covered Archie's mouth. Ray speculated that his editor did not actually have a mouth, it was the moustache that spoke.

'Archie! You know me better than that, you know I never touch the stuff.'

'True,' Archie nodded in fairness and leant back in his leather chair. 'However, you were off to do a story about a dog in a pub in the company of a notorious pisshead, so what am I supposed to think?'

'Magical Garry was with me?' Ray was stunned. His mouth dropped open just to show the moustache how stunned he was.

'Yeah, and he hasn't fucking showed up today either!'

A slow, cold tingle crept down Ray's spine at this revelation.

'Your notebook, Mr Weaver,' Doris suddenly appeared next to him. In the receptionist's outstretched hand, sure enough, was Ray's notebook. It was tattered and stained but it was his tome, nevertheless. Ray snapped out of his daze and began leafing through the pages just to make absolutely sure. He had made notes on the last couple of pages concerning the peculiar habits of a dog called Toby. Doris moved on to hand some letters to Archie.

'It was in with the post this morning,' she explained as she left the office.

'I don't suppose my wallet, clothes and watch got put through the letterbox as well?' queried Ray.

Doris vaguely shook her head at him.

'Would you tell me if they had though, Doris, eh?'

Ray was just playing with the receptionist but the humour was lost. She merely waddled away, taking all seven of her backsides back to reception.

'Do you have to tease her, Ray? She suffers from depression you know?'

'Well she needs some cheering up then, don't she? Besides, things are looking up, it looks like I've got your precious shaggy dog tale.'

Archie cocked a curious eyebrow at Ray and the reporter held up the notebook with his first smile of the day, it had been a long time coming.

'Good, it seems you've got a guardian angel, Weaver.' Archie's moustache seemed to relax a little too. 'Get it typed out this afternoon. I need you up at the Tory Club right now.'

Ray was deflated. 'Not those bastards?'

Archie pushed the swearbox back towards him. 'They'll sort this country out, you'll see.'

'Not you as well? Isn't this more Mark's sort of thing? I do the funny stuff, remember?'

'You missed the funny stuff that happened early this morning.'

'Oh yeah?' Ray was strangely afraid all of a sudden.

'Some naked bloke pinched some old dear's washing,' the moustache had a little chuckle. 'Mark's gone up there to investigate.'

Ray made himself scarce, covering the Conservative Club's celebrations suddenly seemed like a good idea.

*

A few days passed in which I decided to do as I was told. It seemed to make everyone happier that way. I had ventured a step out of line and tiny little step though it was, it was enough to shatter my world. I fed the kids, bathed the kids, told them stories, cuddled my wife, took the bins out, said my prayers, mowed the lawn, serviced the car, paid my taxes, documented small town life and anything else that put a smile on someone's face. My good friend Magical Garry did not show up to work, however, nor did he reappear at home or indeed anywhere else. The Police began making inquiries and my total memory loss of the night in question was not making them go away. My notebook had been returned to my office by a mysterious benefactor but this only compensated for my amnesia as far as my general whereabouts. These were journalist's notes and therefore only concerned with details of stories for the paper and not of my exact movements. More worryingly still, I was having bad dreams; nightmares that were making me sob in my sleep which, in turn, was freaking out Iris and the nippers. I had no choice. I had to go back.

Excerpt from the journal of Ray Weaver, volume one.

*

The rustic interior of the Bull and Hook in Raven Holes did not jog Ray's memory but it seemed to bring some comfort to him. It was tall and narrow with oak beams and an open hearth fire. It looked like some Viking drinking hall of old. It smelt organic, like freshly dug earth. Attached to the beams and walls were a myriad of objects that would have made a museum curator dizzy with excitement. There were antique firearms and weapons jostling for space with agricultural implements of ambiguous purpose, pretty bottles and lamps, oddly shaped hats, stuffed creatures, ornate plates, timepieces and other things too wild and bewildering to take in all at once. The pub's daytime clientele seemed to be a strange assortment too but they all seemed congenial enough. They merely flicked him a casual glance. Ray went up to the bar and ordered himself a lemonade. It was a warm day and he loosened his tie and took off his jacket. He sat down at the bar next to a miniature Dachshund that was lapping black liquid from a saucer.

'Alright, Toby?' Ray asked the dog.
'I'm sound as a pound, yourself?'

Ray nearly screamed then realised that it was the old man to his right that had answered the question, not the pooch.

Ray glared at him. 'I was talking to the dog.'

'Sorry,' the old man tipped his cap, apologetically. 'My name's Toby as well. I thought you were talking to me, happens all the time.' The old man scuttled away with a mischievous smirk on his face. There were a few quiet chuckles from elsewhere in the room.

Ray sipped his lemonade and ignored the punters. He noticed a woman behind the bar looking at him.

'Back again?' she asked.

'You recognise me?'

'Even without your eyebrows,' she laughed. There were more sniggers in the bar. Despite being well into her fifties, the woman was attractive. She was worn and wrinkled but still had her curves, cleavage and long blonde locks. Her eyes sparkled with an inner youth and despite her rural surroundings, she was dressed glamorously, like some fading dame of the silver screen.

'Barbara Clement?' asked Ray, plucking her name from somewhere. Perhaps it was because she was the only woman in the room and had to be the landlady mentioned in his notebook. Ray also had the vague feeling they had already met.

'Yes,' she said.

'So I've been here before?

Barbara Clement nodded. Ray noted that everyone in the pub now seemed to be watching him and smiling.

'You boys had quite a night,' she added.

'A little geezer with a ponytail and a big hooter was with me?'

Barbara laughed again, as if recalling some amusement. 'Yes.'

Ray looked around. 'Can I talk to you in private, luv?'

*

'It's my mate, Garry, he's missing,' explained Ray in the more confidential confines of Barbara's rear parlour.

'The man who was with you?' she said, lighting a cigarette.

'Yeah, he came up here with me and no one's seen him since and I can't remember a thing. The Police are looking for him. We're all looking for him.' Ray felt no need to mention the fact that he had woken up naked in the woods.

'Well, it doesn't surprise me that you can't remember anything,' Barbara offered Ray a fag.

'It doesn't? No thanks.'

'Sure, you boys were guzzling Old Bob all night.'

'Didn't Old Bob mind?'

'It's a local beer, you big silly.'

'It is?'

'Sure, Ned Weatherly from up the road brews it himself. I've seen big strong men drink a few pints and finish up like babies. I usually only open up the barrel on special occasions, but you and your friend were very special guests.'

'We were?'

'Sure, we all read your wonderful stories in the paper, Mr Weaver, and Magical Garry's horoscopes. We were so thrilled that you'd come to do a story about our little Toby and our little boozer.'

'You were?'

'Sure, and you were such wonderful guests, after finding out all about Toby, you decided to stay for a drink and you were both so entertaining, especially after drinking Old Bob. Garry did some tricks for everyone and you performed your dance of the flaming sock, or at least, I think that's what you called it.'

Ray scratched his head in bemusement but the landlady's words did seem to hold some kind of truth. 'And we left together for home?'

'You left together but not for home,' she said ominously.

'No?' Ray peered at her, suddenly reluctant to know the truth.

'You wanted to drink some more of Ned Weatherly's brew. He was here, in the pub. You left with him.'

'To where?'

'Just up the road to his place I suppose.'

They fell silent. Ray faced another blank episode in his memory.

'I think I will have that fag, luv.'

*

Ray finished his cigarette and lemonade back in the bar. It was now mid-afternoon and Toby and most of the humans had left. A cool shadow settled across the room and Ray perched on a stool and looked out across to the other end of the pub. He composed himself and tried to recall being there. The cigarette assisted his concentration. He gazed around and fragments of memory slowly fazed back into his mind, images and sensations from a drunken reverie swimming back to him like phantoms. He could hear himself and Garry and others laughing raucously and could see a kaleidoscope of leering drunken faces spinning around him. He could hear the echo of one of Garry's old Irish folk songs. He felt the motion of hopping on one foot as the other one burnt and lots of people laughing hysterically. He saw Garry pull a bunch of flowers from the landlady's cleavage, much to the throng's delight. Barbara's information had unlocked some of his booze sodden remembrance and Ray relaxed. So he and Garry had gotten drunk in a nice old country boozer? So what? Archie had been working him hard recently and going home only brought fresh demands from Iris. It occurred to Ray that he had vented a little bit of steam here. Garry had been a good friend to Ray, joining him on his investigation, it was only natural for the two of them to have a blow out together.

'There's another thing,' said Barbara from behind him.

Ray turned around and looked into her sparkly eyes.

'I returned your notebook.'

'Thanks for that, Barbara, you've been great.' Ray kissed her hand.

'Think nothing of it. I just hope you find your friend.'

'So do I,' said Ray with a shrug.

'You and him can come back anytime,' Barbara gave Ray a curious wink and left the room, leaving Ray to ponder its true meaning.

*

Ray meandered up the road, which was little more than a dirt track, and wondered how far away Ned Weatherly's place was. He realised that Barbara had been vague about the distance and his troubled memory was still miserly. It had grown chilly for May and the open fields did nothing to shield Ray from a damp icy breeze. He pulled up the collars on his jacket and hunched down inside it, making what little effort he could to continue the hunt. He hobbled a little. His feet were still a mess from the long walk home. The nails on both of his smallest toes had consequently turned black. It was impossible to walk fast without aggravating them. Ray gritted his teeth with pain and strode into the countryside. This was not some whimsical report for the Fogwin Enquirer but a personal mission to find his missing friend. Gone was Ray's customary jocular approach to his work. It was with a grim resolution that he pursued his man.

He looked at his somewhat out of place reflection in the panes of a red telephone box on the edge of the village as he limped past. He saw his sharp grey suit and tie against a backdrop of endless fields reflected in the glass of civilisation's last beacon. He looked distinctly out of place and he mused on how a boy from the city had wound up here. He began to wonder if people like him died in places like this, alone, strange and uncertain. Did the laws of society exist this far out in the sticks? Surely the permanent occupants of a tiny village like Raven Holes had their own laws and customs, their own way of dealing with nosy strangers? Ray shuddered and tried to put potential horrors out of his mind. After all, the locals in the Bull and Hook seemed affable enough. Not the sort likely to drag strangers out in the middle of the night to sacrifice them to old gods, just a giggle at his expense to go with their beer. The landlady actually seemed quite sophisticated. The only sense of unseen menace in the pub was the one in Ray's own mind. Despite telling himself this, Ray felt the need to look back at the telephone box for reassurance. The scarlet bastion was still there and not that far away. He was glad that there were no tortoises around to show him up.

*

Half a mile along, Ray encountered a different variety of misery. Gnarled old trees appeared by the side of the road with increasing frequency and the rolling fields were replaced by thick woods. The foliage defended him from the wind but Ray was still desperately cold. The trees were so closely knit that they seemed to capture the damp chill and hold it there. The gloom slowly closed in and Ray felt oppressed by the vale of silent sentinels on either side of him. It was hard to see more than a few feet into the trees and a dreadful silence hung between the clammy limbs and boughs. It was spring and he expected to hear birds singing but there was nothing, only the occasional crack of a twig or muffled plop. At moments, Ray felt the peculiar sensation that he was being watched. It was if something was moving around quietly in the woods alongside him, something that did not want to be seen or heard. The shivers that ran down his spine made him quicken his pace and he breathed laboriously with the effort. His injured feet protested at every step but Ray just gritted his teeth and willed himself onward. Stuck out there alone, absurd fears became tangible. Ray repressed recollections of old horror films that his brothers forced him to watch when he was a kid. These sadistic sibling rituals had given him an unforgettable knowledge of screen monsters and his ease in dismissing them as harmless hokum was growing difficult. It was as if he had stumbled onto the set of one of those films. He occasionally dared a glance into the murk, half expecting to see a pair of inhuman eyes glare back at him. Ray breathed a deep sigh of relief when he turned a bend in the lane and saw it open out into a farm, the trail into a hive of crude buildings which were alive with the sounds and smells of animal husbandry. He could see half a dozen men working and they were an earthly sight amongst the dark fairytale trees. The grey cloud that hung over Ray dissipated and he almost laughed at himself for being so ridiculous.

'Ned Weatherly?' Ray asked the first man he got to. The man shook his head and thumbed to a fatter, older colleague getting out of a tractor in the farmyard. Ray did not have to ask again. The other man addressed him first.

'Mr Weaver? Come back for some more of my brew?' Ned Weatherly grinned, revealing missing teeth. His face looked so ruddy it was if the blood vessels were trying to burst forth from his cheeks. His sweaty copper hair was also trying to vacate the premises.

'Er … yes … er … no,' said Ray, floundering for words. He glanced into a nearby barn and saw a large wooden barrel perched sideways on a framework stand. A pair of large Dobermans bounced playfully up to him from the other direction, shifting his attention. They barked and sniffed at him.

'Then what can I do for you?' asked Ned, amused by the attention from the dogs.

Ray was not so delighted, he put a friendly hand out to one of the canine guardians and it nipped at him. 'I'm looking for the man I was with … Garry.'

'He's gone missing?' Ned said immediately.

Ray's eyebrows arched in surprise as he looked at him. 'You know?'

Ned scratched his ginger chin. 'No, but I told you not to go into the woods at night, didn't I?'

'You did?'

'Of course, it's what I tell everybody. I've lived here all my life and I've learnt a healthy respect for all the legends.'

'The legends?' Ray felt the chill from his walk through the trees return to him.

'People have been vanishing around here ever since my granddad's granddad ran this farm. Others have seen strange lights and heard noises in the trees. I told you all about this the other night.'

Ray fell silent. He wandered across the farmyard to look at the demonised wilderness beyond. He tried to suppress a sick feeling that was rising in his gut by hugging himself.

'When I was a boy, there was an ugly old woman that lived in the woods who everyone called Mad Bess,' said Ned, trailing after him and adopting the tone and posture of a seasoned storyteller. 'She was a harmless old crone who just wanted to be away from other people but Lord knows why she chose this place. She would go down into Raven Holes once a week for things but when she didn't turn up for a while, a search party went up for her and she was nowhere to be seen. They just found her little house with a meal still uneaten on the table.'

Ray shivered and continued to stare solemnly into the trees.

'Well publicised that was, as was little Jonny Sewell's disappearance ten years back. You'll find it in your paper's records if you go digging,' Ned added.

'Little Jonny Sewell?' And you let us go in there?' Ray snapped at the farmer.

'You were determined, Mr Weaver.' Ned fumbled with his flatcap, nervously. 'You said you were going to launch an investigation into the unknown. You said that it would be a natural direction for your work. Your funny friend, Garry, well, he agreed with you. That Old Bob of mine can give a man a certain inspiration. I've seen it happen many a time. Most lads won't go into the woods at night though. I'm not sure that ...' Ned hesitated to say more.

Ray was glaring at him. 'What?'

'I'm not sure that you took my heeding seriously, being from the city and all.'

Ray recalled his nude awakening the morning after the night in question and remembered the filth and the blood on his body. He looked around at the men working on the farm. He noticed that all of them resembled Ned and had an odd ape-like gait to their movement, as if evolution had not quite got round to them yet. They were casting unusual glances at him. It suddenly occurred to him that perhaps the incident had a more plausible explanation.

'Perhaps you and your clan decided to have a little fun with me and my mate and you're making all this rubbish up?' Ray walked over to Ned menacingly. 'Is that it, eh?'

The farmer just looked at him, his face becoming redder. He opened his mouth but no words came out.

Ray could no longer hold down the tumultuous feeling building in his gut. His wrath spat forth. 'Come on! Let's have the truth! You ... you ... rapist!'

Before Ray knew it, he was taken down by a pack of farmhands and dogs. He was suddenly on the ground, amongst the straw and dung, being grappled, kicked, punched and bitten. They pinned his limbs down and one of Ned's men pressed a shotgun to his face. The metal felt cool on his forehead. The mutt that had already taken a dislike to him had Ray's knee gripped in his jaws. It was a swift and efficient defence.

Ned looked down at him from behind the wall of leering, snarling faces and grinned. 'Now, now, Mr Weaver, let's not get excited shall we?' I told you and Mr Garry not to go into the woods. We had a nice friendly drink and shook hands goodbye and that's all there was to it.'

'Yeah! And now my mate's gone missing!' groaned Ray miserably from under the mob.

'Get him up!' shouted Ned. The men and, somewhat astonishingly, the dogs responded to his order instantly and Ray was brought back to his feet with one combined jolt. Ned looked at him with a little pity and picked a few bits of straw from his jacket. 'If you want, we'll take the boys and the dogs and go have a look for him?'

Ray looked at him with a resentful sneer on his face. 'No, thanks.'

He marched away, picking the remaining straw off his jacket himself. He stomped back down the road, his frustration and fury overrode the dread he had of the woods. *This isn't like you, Ray, you're losing it*, he thought. He had only half an hour to wait for the bus on the village green.

Ray never went back to Raven Holes ever again.

*

Feeling a Bit Woof
Story by Ray Weaver, published in the Fogwin Enquirer 6.6.1979.

It is often said that a dog is man's best friend but the bar staff at the Bull and Hook in Raven Holes never expected one to pop in for a pint. Toby, a four year old miniature Dachshund likes a daily tipple and for the last two years has been served by landlady Barbara Clement and her somewhat bemused employees. Toby not only calls in for his half pint of Guinness but takes the bus to get there. Regular drivers of the number 28 from Fogwin have become used to stopping at the end of the lane in Lungston Parish where the tiny four-legged boozer waits patiently at 12.10pm every day. The doors open and young Toby climbs on. He takes his usual seat on the floor just behind the driver's booth. The bus gets into Raven Holes ten minutes later and unperturbed by the astonished looks of his fellow passengers, Toby gets off and crosses the village green to his favourite watering hole. The canine quaffer is greeted by the other locals and is given pride of place on a stool at the end of the bar. He is then treated to his half of the black stuff in a saucer and the occasional sausage or streak of bacon. When Toby has drank his fill and caught up on the day's events, he makes his way back home across the fields to owner Simon Grant. 'The vet says Toby has a rare blood condition' explains Simon; 'this causes a slight iron deficiency which he compensates for by having a daily Guinness. I don't drink myself but I don't mind Toby sneaking off for one if it keeps him healthy. I know that Barbara and her staff treat him with kindness. How the dog knows what's good for him and how to go about getting it is a mystery.'

*

Ray awoke, his swollen eyelids swivelling open like an iguana's. He stared into the blackness of his bedroom. He wondered why his brain had decided to wake him at this hour. Then, there was the noise. There was something in the room. He could hear its rasping breath at the bottom of his bed. His heart thumped so hard that he could feel its vibrations in the mattress. Ray wanted to budge, he wanted to yell, but his body would not respond. There was just his sticky iguana eyes and his pumping heart. The rest of his form barely seemed to exist. He heard the intruder's tiny talons scraping at the wooden frame of his bed as it climbed up and plopped itself onto the mattress, near his feet. Ray willed his legs to recoil from the threat but there was no feeling, not even a tingle. He felt like a corpse that was not quite dead yet and about to be defiled. The prowler crept up between his legs and climbed up onto his frozen buttocks. Its wheezing became louder and more excitable and Ray's nostrils were filled with its fetid breath. Ray could just about see the duvet bulging upwards out of the corner of his eye. The thing crept up his spine and kissed his neck. The scream finally came.

Suddenly, Ray was staring into the face of his frightened wife. He was still in the bedroom and it remained dead of night but he could now move at will and he was drenched in cold sweat. He looked around. There was no sign of the interloper. He saw his children poking their faces around the door. They too looked afraid.

'You need to see a Doctor, Ray,' stated Iris.

*

Transcript from a psychiatric session between Dr. Ishmael Neuter (IN) and his patient Raymond Weaver (RW) 19.8.1979.

IN   Your fear of clowns originated in your childhood?

RW   Well, my dad leathered me when he was dressed up as one.

IN   And you didn't realise it was him?

RW   No, not until afterwards. Turns out he'd got a new job.

IN   As a clown?

RW   Yeah, he went and got legless to celebrate. I was only about five. I just thought that a friendly clown had come to see me. It was my birthday.

IN   How sad; and your phobia has returned?

RW   I don't think so. I got over the clown thing. This is something new.

IN   A fresh trauma?

RW   Possibly.

IN   Tell me about the nightmares.

RW   They feel real, like I'm actually awake except I can't move. My mind is awake but my body isn't. There's something in the room, something that creeps slowly into my bed and then onto me. I'm panicking but I can't respond.

IN   What is it?

RW   I don't know because it stays out of sight. I can't even move my head to see it. I just know that it's something nasty; something that wants to hurt me.

IN   I see. How interesting,

RW Interesting? Are you taking the mickey, Doc? I could lose my family because of this. I wake up screaming blue murder every night. Even the neighbours get woken up.

IN Sorry, Ray. From a professional point of view, your condition is intriguing but perhaps not entirely remarkable.

RW No?

IN It's not covered by mainstream psychology, or at least, not yet. There are studies into sleep paralysis but they exist only on the fringe, unfortunately.

RW Sleep paralysis?

IN "Old Hag" as it's sometimes known. Different cultures have their own name for it. References to it can be found from all over the world dating back centuries but they all have common features, a feeling of being awake, the threat of attack from a malevolent presence but the inability to move. Sometimes it's an actual old woman but the manifestations differ. Fuselli's famous painting "Nightmare" is considered to be an artistic interpretation.

RW So it's common?

IN No, it's actually quite rare. That's why it's a fringe study. Sleep paralysis is regarded by most of my peers in the same way as flying saucers or the Loch Ness monster.

RW Great! So what do I do?

IN Don't worry; I fully intend to help you, Ray. This might be my own personal chance to bring the condition into the light of the twentieth century. I suspect that your brain is having difficulty waking.

RW You're saying there's something wrong with my noggin?

IN I'm saying that your conscious mind wants to take over but parts of it are still asleep and vulnerable to the demons of your dreams. Tell me more.

RW Well, there is something you should know.

IN Go on.

RW A few months ago something happened to me.

IN Yes?

RW I got drunk.

IN I see. This is unusual?

RW I don't usually touch the stuff, my missis is very religious. Then there was my dad as well, he sort of put me off for life. What is weird is that my mate Garry disappeared on the same night.

IN Disappeared?

RW Yeah, he's not been seen since. I think something bad happened to us.

IN And you don't recall anything at all?

RW A little bit. I went back to the boozer where we got drunk and remembered being there. It's in this little village a few miles out of town. Turns out the woods there have got a reputation.

IN A reputation?

RW People going missing, strange lights in the sky, ghostly noises in the woods, that sort of thing. The place is straight out of an old horror film.

IN And you think that you and your friend fell foul of … something?

RW I'm coming round to the idea, yeah. It seems more likely to me than my dad coming back to haunt me. These nightmares started soon after that night in the boozer. I woke up in the woods; bruised and naked and Garry, he's gone. Something definitely happened to us, wouldn't you say, Doc?

IN It would seem that way, yes. I'm not sure about the lights in the sky and the ghosts. I would suggest that the incident has a more earthly origin.

RW You just mentioned those things yourself.

IN In the context of sleep paralysis being regarded as a phenomenon. We're talking about dangers of the real word now. Have the police become involved?

RW Yeah, but they're just as clueless as I am.

    PAUSE.

IN Perhaps I should refer you to a contact of mine. This seems to be more his field of expertise.

RW You're going to pass me on?

IN My aim is to make you better, Ray, and Cedric might be able to help you more than I can.

RW Cedric? What kind of nonce name is that?

IN His name is Cedric Hamilton Montague. He's quite a character. Most people just call him The Professor.

*

Ray lurched through the rain soaked streets of Soho and regarded its sleazy occupants with disdain. The constant downpour seemed to make it even more hostile than he remembered. He hated London. He loathed its grey uncaring world where the lost roamed and were preyed upon. It was the cradle of grime that had made his upbringing so miserable. He was one of the city's children and he felt no gratitude. Samuel Pepys once said 'when a man is tired of London, he is tired of life' but Ray thought the opposite; 'when a man is tired of life, *he* moves to London.' He wondered why he had been pulled back here. It was like the city had a hook in him and it would not let him go. He hoped, with some sense of futility, that this would be the final time. He could go home with his demons firmly exorcised and everything would be normal again. He longed to be back with Iris and the kids, back in the green leafy embrace of simple small town life. Ray could hear their joyful laughter in his mind but it was not enough, he wanted it to be real.

Ray checked the bit of paper Ishmael had given him and looked at the building again. It confirmed "The White Hart". He was in the right place. At least it was a pub. Ray would be able to calm his nerves with a drink. He had promised Iris not to, in light of the last disastrous consequence, but his beloved was not here and the embrace of alcohol seemed not just appealing, but vital. He went inside and ordered himself a pint and a chaser before making any attempt to find the man he had arranged to meet. It was only when he had sipped firmly from both glasses that he looked around. The interior of The White Hart was dark. The clientele were obscured by shadows. They lurked within the gloom and whispered to each other and seemed content to do so. Ray noted that they were all men. One patron sat by himself reading a newspaper. He was immaculately dressed, sporting a tweed suit and a bottle-green waistcoat. He wore a golden cravat and a pair of horn-rimmed spectacles on the end of his nose. His trimmed black hair was finely combed across his skull. He looked out of place in a back street Soho pub yet gave no signal that he was uncomfortable amongst the scum. The man seemed too young to bear the moniker of The Professor yet somehow, Ray knew it was him.

'Cedric?' queried Ray, stumbling over.

The man looked up at him over his perched glasses and cocked an eyebrow. 'You can call me The Professor. Mr Weaver I presume?' His voice was loud and confident.

'The name's Ray.'

The Professor's handshake was genteel, like a woman's. He gestured for Ray to sit down and folded away the paper.

'Bit weird, innit? The Professor?' said Ray, looking at him and sipping his pint.

'If you say so. How may I help?'

'I was hoping you'd tell me that.'

'Ishmael told me that you had a strange experience?'

'You could say that. Almost as strange as meeting a geezer called The Professor in a Soho dive.'

'This is just one of my hangouts. It pays to be discreet in my line of enquiry. I'm afraid I don't have an official practice. I'm not a medical man, more an academic, you might say. An expert.'

'An expert on what?' Ray half-dreaded an answer.

'Ghosts, poltergeists, telepathy, U.F.Os, vampires, spontaneous human combustion, holy relics, teleportation, sea monsters, man-beasts, witches, fairies, mutations, conspiracies, feral children, the afterlife, mind control, spoon bending, zombies, penis thefts, that sort of thing.'

'Penis thefts?' Ray looked around, self-consciously, wondering why a Harley street psychiatrist had arranged for him to meet with a complete lunatic. No one was paying attention, however, and Ray looked back at The Professor. He noted that two men were going to the toilet together, holding hands.

'Anything that exists on the peripheries of science, philosophy or religion is of interest to me. Ishmael has a more conventional reputation to consider. That's why you've been referred to me.'

'And what about your reputation?' asked Ray.

'Sullied many eons ago, I'm afraid. Besides, someone has to deal with the damned.'

Ray's brow became as furrowed as a ploughed field. He felt perplexed and frightened. His mind became hazy again, like the morning when he had woken bare and ruined in the woods. This Professor character had reeled off a list of bizarre notions with a completely straight face and Ray fought the urge to just laugh at him and run away, yet this was not some meths-sodden madman ranting from a gutter, Cedric was well spoken and seemingly genuine. Also, Doctor Neuter had spoken quite highly of him and the only alternative was to go home with his nightmares intact. Plus, Ray felt his journalistic curiosity kick in.

'So you think you can help me?'

'The woods of Raven Holes are known to me though I've not had the chance to investigate that particular window myself.'

'Window?' Ray drained his chaser.

'A term we give to an area of vibrant supernatural activity. Some places seem to attract it like a magnet. They exist all over Britain, all over the world infact.'

'I wasn't looking for supernatural activity. I'm a newspaper reporter. I deal with facts. I was there to do a cute story about a dog.'

The Professor leaned forward, his eyes wide with conviction. 'And yet it found you! That's usually the way. You've encountered something that you cannot explain, something that you cannot deal with. If you do not confront it, it will tear you to pieces. You will try to lead a normal life but it will haunt you and you will slowly go mad. You've been chosen, my dear man!'

'But I want a normal life,' grumbled Ray, staring stubbornly into his beer.

'That's not for you to decide.' The Professor leaned back into his chair and rubbed his chin, thoughtfully.

After a few moments of contemplative silence, Ray looked up at him. 'So how do I go about confronting it?'

'We could try hypnotic regression?' The Professor arched his fingers.

'What?'

'I'll put you under hypnosis. We'll try to unlock the part of your memory that has shut down.'

Ray looked around suspiciously again. 'This isn't some elaborate scheme, is it?'

The Professor seemed confused. 'I'm not sure what you mean.'

'Well, you're not some kind of wufta, are you?'

'Wufta?'

'I've noticed there aren't any women in here.'

'I am a homosexual, yes, but I am trying to help you, not entrap you.'

Ray sighed. 'Okay, well, where do we go?'

'I have an apartment upstairs. We can begin straight away.'

*

'Are you sure you're not trying to bum me?' asked Ray as he peered around The Professor's apartment. Ray expected the place to be posh, like the man, but it was quite bare and dilapidated. The furniture and curtains were shabby and soiled. There were no books or trappings associated with his academic status. Ray could not shake off his sceptical instincts.

'I'm not much of a housekeeper, I'm afraid, and this is one of my lesser used abodes,' explained The Professor, mincing round the room and drawing the curtains. 'I'm not interested in the contents of your underpants, Mr Weaver, though if you don't trust me you are perfectly welcome to leave. I am doing my best to assure you.'

'Why should I trust you? I don't know you,' Ray drank more of the pint that he had managed to sneak upstairs with him. He tried to stand in the most manly and defiant way that he could.

The Professor looked at him and stated with sincerity. 'It's come to the point where you have to trust someone, hasn't it?'

Ray could think of nothing else to say. He had come to London to be treated but he did not expect it to happen in a dingy flat above a Soho pub. However, Ray knew that The Professor had a point. His predicament was bizarre and perhaps the solution would be equally so.

'Please, lie down, try to relax.' The young scholar gestured to a scruffy leather couch in the middle of the room.

Ray obliged and took up position. He placed his beer on the floor next to him, reassured a little by its close proximity.

The Professor went off to rummage around in an old chest of drawers for a while and then returned clutching a tiny silver charm on a chain with some indication of purpose. He pulled up a purple velvet stool and sat next to the grubby couch. He held out the charm in front of Ray's eyes and began to swing it gently from side to side.

'Watch the charm … stay focused on it … feel yourself becoming sleepy … sleeeeepy …' The Professor's tone became slow and soothing.

Ray had seen this routine in a contrived melodrama on telly once and felt silly. He could hear glasses clinking and muffled voices coming from the bar downstairs. The Professor continued to swing the charm and Ray noticed a curious light reflected in the silver.

'Sleeeeepy … back, back, through the mists of time …'

Despite his reluctance, Ray gradually felt his body lighten and ripples of warmth ebbed through his damp limbs. His eyelids became heavy. Ray desperately clutched at his sense of logic but as he watched the twinkle of light from the charm, that part of his mind became elusive. The noises from below grew fainter. The twinkling filled his consciousness. Soon, he was somewhere else …

'Come on, Raymondo!' cried the voice.

Ray opened his eyes wide but he could not see anything, just darkness. 'Where are you?' he shrieked.

'Over here!' bawled the voice from nowhere.

Ray spun round but his body did not respond too well to his brain's request. His legs buckled. He suddenly felt hard ground beneath him and damp leaves on his face. A wave of pain rippled through his body, followed by one of nausea. *So this is what it's like to get drunk*, thought Ray.

'What you doing', Raymondo?' said the voice but it was no longer calling to him from oblivion, it was now stood right over him, close enough for him to smell the booze on its breath.

Ray twisted his head to look up and saw the leering, leathery face of his friend, Magical Garry. 'Just having a rest.'

'Good stuff that Old Bob?' cackled Garry, reaching down and seizing him.

'No!' protested Ray melodramatically. 'Don't try to pick me up, leave me here!'

'I'm not leaving you out here in the middle of nowhere, you dipstick!' groaned the smaller man as he heaved Ray to his feet. There was a titanic struggle as the two sozzled friends uprighted themselves and stumbled to and fro, clutching onto each other like awful tango dancers. One of them tripped and both of them fell. They tumbled down a vast embankment, clown-like, hitting unknown objects in the dark. Ray remarked to himself that it was a surprisingly long amount of time before they came to a halt. They lay there and groaned and sniggered for a bit, astonished at their lack of injury.

'You alright, Raymondo?' gurgled Garry.

'No,' murmured Ray, feeling the liquid in his stomach move around like it did not want to be in there anymore.

An owl hooted from somewhere above.

'You can get stuffed!' shouted Ray at the bird.

'Now, now!' Garry sat up and began rifling around in the pockets of his leather jacket. 'This is Mr Owl's home, you should have a bit more respect, mate.'

Ray sat up too, albeit more slowly and painfully, and looked at him. 'What is this? Wind in the fucking Willows?'

'Your language!' scoffed Garry. 'What would your missis say?'

Ray glanced around as if expecting to see Iris. Despite being drunk, his eyes were growing accustomed to the dark and he could make out the ghostly shapes of trees all around them, but no wife.

'Where the dinkins are we?'

Garry pulled out what looked like a monstrous badly-rolled cigarette. 'In the haunted forest, aren't we? You said we were going to launch an investigation into the wotsit ... the unknown.'

Ray looked at his luminous Rolex with horror. 'It's three in the morning!'

'Don't tell me that, this was your idea, you could still be having it off with that saucy landlady.' Garry lit up the article. He pulled deeply on it and breathed the smoke out slowly. He passed it to Ray, 'Here! This'll sort you out.'

'I don't smoke,' stated Ray weakly and found himself taking the thing anyway. Garry chuckled at him as he dragged on it. The smoke tasted thick and sweet, but not unpleasant. Ray glanced around again and thought he saw traces of wild colour in his monochrome surroundings. He had another puff and tried to pass it back but the astrologer was now staring at something in the opposite direction.

'Hello! What's going on here?' muttered Garry.

'I dunno,' said Ray, not really looking.

Garry was clearly perturbed, however, and sprang up like a startled chimpanzee. '*It is* Wind the Willows! I don't believe it!'

'What?' mumbled Ray as he staggered to his feet to have a look. It first appeared to be a river moving past them but as Ray peered closer, he could see that it was not made of water, but of animals, lots and lots of animals.

'Hedgehogs! Rabbits! Weasels! Foxes! Toads!' cooed Garry with wonder as the wildlife procession went by.

The two revellers watched, dumfounded, as more critters scurried or hopped past. They seemed unperturbed by the presence of the humans. A massive badger even scrambled between Garry's legs.

'Where are they going?' Ray scratched his head.

'Perhaps we've woken them up?' Garry speculated.

Suddenly, a beam of white light shot out from deep within the woods, providing them with a more rational explanation.

'Christ!' yelped Ray as the beam swept passed his face, blinding him.

'Quiet!' hissed Garry, his voice dripping with panic. 'Fucking lampers!'

'Eh?' Ray put his hands over his eyes.

Garry grabbed hold of him and whispered harshly in his ear. 'Poachers with lamps! We might get shot!'

Ray pushed him away and screeched in the direction of the light. 'Don't shoot! Don't Shoot! We're not rabbits! We're journalists!'

Garry stood next to him and put his hands up in mock surrender as the beam hovered back over them. There passed what seemed like an age. They stared into the brilliance. Eerily, there was no answer. The light explored them.

'Raymondo?' queried Garry.

'Yeah?'

'That farmer?'

'Ned.'

'Yeah. He told us these woods were haunted by strange lights didn't he?'

'Some hooey like that, yeah.'

'Like that one?'

'Like that one.'

The beam did have a unearthly quality to it, not like a torch or a lamp, but like a funnel of mist that was impossibly bright. Ray and Garry continued to talk to each other but as the source of the light moved menacingly and slowly towards them, their voices dipped to inaudible mutters. Ray experienced some vague instinct to run away but felt rooted to the spot. Garry's warning about lampers seemed absurd but Ray now found himself hoping that it was some nocturnal hunting party. Perhaps they could have a drink and a laugh with them as they had done with the other locals.

Garry looked up at him. 'It's been a classic night, Raymondo!'

Ray looked back at his friend but he could not manage anything more poignant than 'yeah.'

Ray could see the glimmer of tears in Garry's eyes and caught a faint whiff of shit. Ray turned to see a huge white egg floating through the air towards them and he too vented his bladder and bowels. The beam of light was coming from the front of the floating egg. It halted in mid-air and the beam transformed, fluid like, into an aura around its bulk. A seamless hatch opened out on one side and a mob of creatures poured out. They were everywhere quickly, like one entity spreading out across the ground. They seized a few of the animals who were too old and slow to get away and dragged them back to their craft with remarkable efficiency. Again, Ray felt an elusive impulse to flee but the scene unfolding before him was too compelling. Soon the creatures were upon him and Garry like a wave of ants. In their drunken, hypnotised stupor, they were easily overwhelmed. Ray felt tiny claws grab hold of every part of his anatomy as the creatures climbed all over him and dragged him down. He thought he heard his friend screaming but he could not hear him over his own wails of terror. Tree roots and stones dug into Ray's spine as he was heaved along the ground towards the giant egg. He could see the beings more clearly now; they were tiny humanoids with spindly limbs, the biggest no more than twelve inches tall. They wore white suits and their long silky hair and skin were the same colourless hue. Their miniature faces displayed no emotion or indeed any obvious feature to do so with, only lidless eyes which were black and shiny like buttons.

Ray felt the surface beneath him turn flat and hard and he realised that he was now inside the egg. The interior was a sort of charcoal colour but they were countless lights on the curved walls and ceiling. It was too dazzling to see anything clearly. His inhuman captors did not seem to suffer the same handicap, they lifted Ray with combined effort onto a slab. They did this without making a sound or any other apparent method of communication. There were hundreds of them but they all seemed to know exactly what to do. Ray was released from their grasp but still felt unable to move of his own free will. It was as if the slab he was lying on was a magnet and he was made of metal. He could just about see out of the corners of his eyes. Garry was lying to his right and to his left was what appeared to be a deer. Some of the creatures climbed onto the slab and started poking and molesting him, again, with no sentiment. Random lights and bits of ambiguous equipment descended from the ceiling above him. He had an absurd impression of being at the dentist's. A multitude of metal arms and tentacles reached down and joined the examination. It suddenly dawned on Ray that he was naked and every part of him was now being freely violated. Somehow, his clothes had vanished. He thought that he could feel the presence of one sock, however.

'Get off me, you bastards!' Ray cried, but it came out as a mere whimper.

One of the creatures loomed over him. It was identical to the others but twice as big. It looked right into his eyes but Ray could still not detect any emotion in those black, lidless orbs. Curiously, its head split apart like a hatching egg and something black and slimy quivered from the newly exposed brain pan. The thing moved and started to climb out. Ray decided it would be a good time to lose consciousness.

... suddenly, he was back on The Professor's couch. He looked up at him. The professor had a grave expression on his face and seemed older somehow.

'Welcome back. All has become clear.' The Professor handed Ray what remained of his pint.

'I think I need something a bit stronger, don't you?'

*

Ray looked out over Soho from the doorway of The White Hart. The rain was falling even harder and there were less lowlifes wandering the streets.

'Sure you won't stay the night?' asked The Professor.

'No thanks,' said Ray. 'I want to be at home with my family.'

'I understand.' The professor nodded and the two men shook hands.

Ray gazed out into the streets again and despite what he had said, seemed hesitant to leave. He turned back to The Professor.

'Shouldn't we tell the Police or the Government or something?'

The Professor smirked. 'What would you say?'

Ray shrugged his shoulders.

'The authorities already know and have known for quite some time, especially this new government of ours.'

'Really?' Ray's eyebrows raised but he felt that he could believe anything now.

'The ruling class have been in league with demons from other worlds since England was named England.' The Professor explained.

'And there's nothing we can do about it?'

'I didn't say that.' The Professor handed Ray a card and gave him a wry smile.

Ray looked, it simply said "The Professor" with a telephone number underneath it.

'Myself and a few others are waging a war against the forces of evil,' said The Professor, somewhat theatrically. 'If you need our help, don't hesitate to call.'

'Thanks,' said Ray. 'But I think I'll try and get back to normal.' He ventured out into the street, waving at The Professor as he left. Ray felt himself pocketing the card. Loathed as he was to admit it, he had the feeling they would meet again.

*

I never saw my good friend Magical Garry again and the nightmares have never really stopped. Through sheer will and determination, my life did return to normal for a few months but later that year, my troubles really began.

Excerpt from the journal of Ray Weaver, volume one.

The Final Testimony of Christopher Morell

I clearly recall the day the ship arrived and it is with some confidence that I begin my testimony. I knew not the time of day, nor which day. As it transpired, not even the month nor the year were known correctly to me; so long had I spent on that tropical coast. The first I heard were the words of my companion, Henry Bagshaw, waking me rudely from my slumber.

'A ship! A ship! A ship! A ship! A ship!' he squealed, over and over again.

From my hammock I opened one eye and squinted. Henry was running around in a circle with wild excitement, caring not a jot for his calloused feet. With his perpetual helmet of palm leaves, he appeared to me as some peculiar jungle creature in a state of madness.

'Henry!' I roared. 'Quit your shrieking!'

He stopped running in a circle and bounced on the spot instead, unable to contain himself. I would have thought such energy impossible for a man on such a limited diet but I suppose the prospect of salvation was spur enough.

'Look, Chris! Look!' He extended a bony finger out to sea.

I removed myself from my hammock with difficulty; I had bent to its shape and I could not share the vigour of my companion. The sun was at its zenith making it hot and bright. I had taken to sleeping in the daytime when existence was at its most difficult. The cacophony of the forest was tenfold in darkness and it made any half-sane man cautious of attack so I chose these loud cool dangerous hours to be awake. I stumbled over to where Henry bounced and peered out into to the azure oblivion. The hillock that we called home was encircled by trees like a crown on a bald head. There was a narrow gap afforded by the thicket where we could look out onto the beach and the sea beyond. Despite the partial view I saw the object that inspired my companion's animation; a black speck bobbing on the horizon. I cursed the absence of our telescope, we had ruined it to use its lenses to make fire but it was no matter. I blinked and stared with my bare eyes for a while and there was no mistake; the black speck was indeed a ship.

'We're not seeing things?' Henry turned to me to ask, his voice quivering with doubt.

I shook my head. 'No, my little friend, we are saved. Let us light a fire!'

I joined Henry in jubilation and we set ourselves to the task. So rehearsed were we and so furious was the sun above us that in next to no time we had produced a column of thick black smoke. By no method would the passers-by miss our signal. We gathered what few possessions we had and wandered down to the beach.

'What of Alfonse and the Baptist?' I asked as we went.

'They're in the jungle, widening each other's arseholes,' explained Henry with disdain.

I took his meaning but was not so happy to leave the third and fourth of our party to their fates. I took a moment and turned to yell for them.

Henry and I waited. After all, the tide and wind were out and there would be good time before the vessel reached our shore. I called out some more and Henry joined in, raising our combined voice to the very heavens until we could so no more. Despite this, The Baptist and "his wife" did not appear. We cursed and muttered against the fools. So deep were they in depravity that they were going to miss their rescue. Perhaps they would be more content to be left here, I mused, trying to make myself feel better about it.

Henry offered another eventuality. 'They've been gone since yesterday morning. I reckon they've gone too deep into the jungle.'

My companion conjectured with venom. I believe that he was jealous of Alfonse and the Baptist. They were both men but they accepted each other as lovers and were genuinely happy whereas Henry was alone and miserable. I must confess that I too was tempted by the forbidden at times, appalling as that may be to the sophisticated reader. Let me tell you this; my friend Henry was as ungainly a creation as any spoiling God's Earth but even he became appealing to me in the long absence of any women or any other form of healthy distraction. However, I remained doggedly focused on the soft whiteness of the female form and I convinced myself that I would look upon its wonder again one day. This prospect was unlikely but, as it turned out, correct. Henry and I would leave this land unbuggered.

'Leave them!' said he and walked further towards where the water lapped the sand.

I did so with greater reluctance. Henry could have been right, perchance they had wandered too far into the forest? At first, eight of us had been marooned on that coast but within days we fell to four. Something that hated us lived in those trees though whether it was man, creature or force we knew not. The only certainty was that it was safer to stay on the edge of the jungle and not go dwelling within. My fears for Alfonse and the Baptist were soon replaced by a trepidation of the arriving ship. As it grew closer, we could see that it was no ordinary rover. I have served aboard some kingly vessels in my time but this was a frigate of a size and majesty that I have never laid eyes on before. It was black too and it creaked and groaned so much that we could hear it above the immense clanging of its bells and the roar of the sea. It was a whale's coffin of a ship.

'What you reckon?' I asked Henry, unable to tear my gaze away from the abomination. 'It must be a 500 ton? 30 guns?'

No opinion was forthcoming from Mr Bagshaw. I looked at him and he was pale and even more flabbergasted than I.

It became obvious that the denizens of the black warship had spied our smoke as they headed straight towards us. The dark infernality of the monster robbed the blue sky of its cheeriness as it sliced through the waves. Henry and I lost the joy from our hearts but we had little choice other than to wait. A return to the jungle could only have meant certain death for us both. We had waited so long for rescue but neither of us could have anticipated that it would come in such a bleak form. I felt a curiously horrible mixture of hope and regret and I knew that Henry shared it.

The anchor was dropped and a rowing boat soon appeared to replace its advance. We could just about see half a dozen men clamber into it. A certain comfort was found in these two facts and we found fresh smiles as the boat skipped over to meet us.

Henry finally found some words. 'I can't believe this is happening. It's like a dream!'

I glanced at him and saw tears sparkling in the sun on his cheeks. I felt sentiment rising up in me too. To think of all those days, scraping by like animals in the muck and sand; barely surviving. I placed a sturdy hand on my companion's shoulder. 'It's all over, my little friend, it's all over, I shall be happy just for the plain notion of never to hear your damn snoring again!'

Henry stared at me, as if hurt, then his wet face softened and we laughed so long and so loud that our rescuers must have thought us lunatics. By the time we had become silent they had crashed through the water and stood before us. The biggest of them waded through the last laps and cast his impressive shadow across us. He and the others appeared normal enough, at least to our eyes. They were mixed European, all darkened by the sun and they all wore the loose and colourful attire of sailors. They stank heavily of damp wood, tobacco and sweat, as you would also expect, and their long hair and beards were tied and decorated. They wore their battle scars proudly too, along with the weapons that could cause them. Some had teeth and body parts missing. The big man set his blue eyes upon me and revealed a wide set of sharp pointed teeth.

'We're here for Christopher Morell,' he announced loudly in English.

Of course, I was astonished. How could they know my name? Surely no one had knowledge that I was out here on the edge of the world? I left my family behind so long ago that it was like a different life entirely. I had no close friends who still breathed other than Henry who was marooned with me and I had always been just a nameless nobody to everyone's navy. The only likelihood was the man who had abandoned us here in the first place but why would he send someone back to get me after all this time?

'Who?' I asked with my head spinning.

'Christopher Morell,' repeated the big man with the teeth.

'That's him!' Henry, the fool, jabbed his thumb in my direction.

'Henry!' I cried and glared at him with anger.

The shark-mouthed giant looked me up and down in disbelief. I realised that I must have looked a pitiful sight. My skin was stretched over my bones like leather and there was hardly anything left of my clothes and boots to hide it. I was so thin you could see my heart beating just under the surface of my flesh. 'You're Morell?' he challenged. His shipmates laughed.

I looked at him and nodded.

The big man narrowed his eyes at me. 'The same Christopher Morell who served under Stede Bonnet and Edward Teach?'

This I was not so happy to admit. 'I think you're getting me confused with someone else,' said I.

The big man smiled and nodded. 'That's a pity,' he said. 'We've come to recruit the Christopher Morell who served under Bonnet and Teach.' And with that, he and his shipmates turned their backs on us and plunged back into the shallows.

Henry and I were at once agitated. The prospect of being abandoned in this steaming hell hole again drove us to panic. 'Wait! Wait!' we cried.

The large sailor and his brethren stopped and looked at us, laughing heartily.

'I am the man you seek, though I am only half of what I was,' I explained. 'Admitting to an association with such notorious pirate lords is not something that I make a habit of. For all I know, you could be privateers sent to bring me to justice?'

'I understand,' chuckled the big man. 'And we are privateers of a sort but we're not here to drag you to the gallows, my friend, but to offer you a place in our crew.'

'And you are the Captain?' I asked.

The men guffawed at this too. 'Nay, lad,' said their spokesman. 'I am the Quartermaster and I go by the name of Razorbill and I am an Englishman, such as you, though not one of your education I fancy.'

'How do you know of me?' I pried further.

'Our Captain knows of you,' explained Razorbill.

'And who is your Captain?' was my inevitable question.

'You'll find out soon enough, lad,' was his queer reply.

'Is it Blackbeard himself? The bastard that left us here?'

This caused a stir amongst the rescue party and Razorbill shook his vast head. 'Nay, for Blackbeard is dead.'

'But you follow The Code?'

'The Captain has his own code,' he added.

I nodded but I was puzzled.

'So what say you?' Razorbill scratched his head and peered at me. 'Are we going to stand here all day, chattering like ladies or will you return with us to the Accamus?'

'She's a mighty vessel,' observed I, looking out to the ship and shivering at its aspect.

'And you can be aboard before the sun's over the yardarm,' grinned the Quartermaster. 'Eating your first meal in many a moon and doing what you were born to be which is be a pirate!' The offer was accompanied by Razorbill's men who gave a little cheer.

I shrugged my bony shoulders. This was no choice at all. I nodded my agreement and pausing only to look back at the jungle one last time, picked up my things and followed them into the water.

Henry followed my suit but Razorbill frowned at him. 'Sorry, lad, the offer is only to Mr Morell.'

Never have you seen such disappointment in a human being, dear reader. All the colour drained out of poor Henry. He opened his mouth to speak but naught but silence came out.

'Henry is an able seaman!' I protested on his behalf.

'The Captain is very particular,' explained one of Razorbill's companions. The Quartermaster himself was already trampling through the tides, back to his boat.

I turned to look at Henry and tears were glistening on his cheeks again.

'You can't leave me here!' he sobbed. 'Find the heart to take me as far as the next port at least!'

The men from the so called Accamus showed no interest in my companion's plea. I could hardly believe it myself. Choosing to take only one of two marooned companions amounted to nothing less than cruelty. My decision had become much more complicated.

Henry gazed at me with his wet piggy eyes. 'You won't leave me here, Chris, after all we've been through together?'

'Sorry, my little friend,' was all that I could find to say. I patted him on the shoulder and left. All the way to the ship, I could hear Henry wailing in despair but I could not bear to look back. A wave goodbye from me would only have served to mock him.

I know that it is shocking that I hardly hesitated to make up my mind but it is impossible to understand unless you have been in that scenario. Try to picture what it is like to be stranded in a wild and hostile land where there is little to drink or eat, barely anything to do at all, except listen to the incessant ramblings of the jungle and my oafish friend. As it turned out, we had been marooned there for over a year, and if I had been there any longer my murderous hands would have surely found poor Henry's throat.

*

And so it was that I felt the heave of the sea beneath my feet again, though I did not dare to dream it. Relentless waves I could still hear but they crashed against creaking timber and not that accursed beach. A reckless grin grew on my face as soon as I was on deck and the dogs that waited there greeted me with likened expression. Nothing other than a stinking and mutilated horde would have matched this vessel and I was not disappointed. There were dregs from all nations, flourished with tattoo, silk, jewellery, pistol and cutlass. It was less the aspect of their trappings that gave them away but more the glint in their eyes; here were men that had travelled the troubled seas for so long that they knew little else. For me, Razorbill remained the biggest and most fearsome amongst them and that was saying much. The Quartermaster forced a way through the curious throng, took me below deck and commanded his cooks to put the flesh back on my bones. At first I was given only gruel but this tasted like a dish worthy of a King compared to the coconut and fish that had sustained me for so long. The feed was too foreign, however, and my stomach was unaccustomed. I charged back up to the deck to vanquish it into the ocean. Anchor had been weighed and a few toiling sailors were amused by my bout. As the cooks knew, decent food would be wasted on me for a time. After I wretched I chanced to gaze back to land but it was already just a shadowy slip on the horizon. I felt queer and glad but little did I suspect then that my rescue would fit that description poorly. Henry, infact, had been the lucky one.

For a full cycle of the moon, life aboard the Accamus was agreeable enough. I was provided with fresh clothes and a choice from the armoury. I was given a few days to replenish my strength and then I was put to work with the four hundred strong crew, half of whom laboured by day and the other half by night so the formidable frigate kept progress around the clock. I expressed my interest in the hours of darkness as I had become comfortable with these. The only times when I met my counterpart were once in the morning and once in the evening, when we exchanged hammock for duty and vice versa. I never even knew his name. I must say that I enjoyed my work more than my rest. After all, the toil meant the freedom of the decks; seeing to the masts and rigging and assisting with the navigation (unlike many, I could read and write). My fellow sailors were mostly fine, with the odd exception, and we exchanged tales, songs and jests almost constantly, with the cool night breeze blowing through our shirts. As I first suspected, there was not a novice amongst them. Each man I conversed with seemed to have at least a decade of seafaring under his belt and claimed to have served under at least one Captain of ill repute. Some of them had sailed alongside Bonnet and Teach, like me, and I already knew them to some degree. The time below deck, on the other hand, was substantially more awful. Picture if you will two hundred sweating, unwashed bodies swinging in hammocks with rarely a moment where a shipmate was not snoring, groaning, coughing or spitting. I can curse my time marooned a thousand times over but at least I slept alone in the open air. Of course, we did not just slumber, there were games too, but these consisted mostly of cruel and dishonest gambling that I quickly lost any fascination with.

There was one peculiar facet of service aboard the Accamus that became an obsession for me: The captain, or lack of. It was customary to meet the master of a privateer ship upon joining and a contract would be agreed, yet even after a few weeks I still had not been given as so much as a name. I made enquiry to many but all I got was an answer similar to the one Razorbill had originally given me: 'You'll find out soon enough.' This was often accompanied by a knowing smirk or laugh, as if it was a joke I was not allowed to share. Either this or the shipmate was as equally uninformed as me, being new to the vessel. It seemed that only the longest serving crewmen held the privilege of knowing their captain. After a while, I became irritated and found one who shared my feeling. He was an old Jamaican who had been picked up two months previous to me and his name was Colker. We often shared look out duty together and he was a source of fantastic wit and fancy.

'I know nothing like it,' he said to me in a hushed voice one night. 'I've sailed to the four points of the compass on a hundred different rafts (this is what he called all vessels). I've seen things you would not believe; women with eight arms, sea serpents, mountains made of fire, lands of ice …'

I chuckled as I recalled these wild notions from stories he had already told me. All I could see in the blackness were Colker's eyes and they stared at me with grave sincerity. I sobered myself and he continued.

'… but I've never served on a ship with no captain!'

'I'm on the verge of marching up to his cabin,' I confessed. 'I'll force my way and demand to see him.'

It was Colker's turn to laugh, adding teeth to the eyes. 'I wouldn't if I was you.'

'Why ever not?' I questioned.

'For a start, he's always surrounded by his most trusted mates, you know, big bastards like Razorbill, and they don't take too kindly to a lack of appointment. I've tried it myself.'

Knowing Colker, I was incredulous. 'You have?'

'Aye, and I'll tell you what I saw if you swear to keep it yourself?'

'Colker! We're friends are we not?' I leaned in closer.

'All I caught was a glimpse into the Captain's quarters but the sight was enough to haunt me.'

'Why?' I asked, feeling a chill all of a sudden.

'It wasn't normal within,' Colker's voice trembled with fear and fell to silence.

'What do you mean?' I urged him.

'I don't know,' he shook his head. 'The walls inside were dripping wet but it was hot like fire and there were fat flies buzzing around, you know, like those that feast on a corpse, and it stank and there was a laugh … a laugh like thunder … I don't know…'

It was less Colker's description that appalled me but more his aspect. Here was a seasoned storyteller who had divulged to me many terrors in a composed manner but this episode had obviously shaken him.

'But you didn't see our Captain?'

'Nay,' he said. 'But I've got a feeling we're about to.'

'Why?'

Colker grinned at me. 'Haven't you heard, Englishman? We're going to raid a fort on the Spanish Main.'

*

This brings me to the most alarming episode of my testimony, dear reader, though you may scarcely bring yourself to believe it. I myself relive the experience every night, waking rapidly from my sleep with my mouth agape in a silent scream. It has become the very fabric of my nightmares. All I can do is give what I consider to be a truthful account of the night in question. It is your privilege to judge the validity of my words.

As Colker had told me, we attacked the Spanish. There was a new port, twenty miles east of Porto Bello and its defences were untested and, as it turned out, inadequate. The place was so new no one had even named it yet and we would turn it into a grave before anyone had chance. Such monstrosities sprung up like anthills all along the coast because the Spaniards could not export the treasures of their new land quick enough. Of course, in the face of so much piracy their navy had become formidable. Nearly all of the infamous captains that plagued The Main had been finished. Infact, the feeling amongst many of my shipmates was that their time was over and a more civilised age begun. Yet, like some vengeful leviathan of the deep, the Accamus bided its time and returned to remind the Spanish of what they truly feared.

The assault was perfection: Looming out of a starless night, the infernal frigate gave the fort a full broadside before they could spy us. Colker and I watched from a deck full of men and we all jerked in unison from the recoil of the cannon. With so many crafty seamen aboard, the ship was turned swiftly and they gave the fort a second fusillade with the other side. Within three minutes, the nameless fortification had been pounded by thirty-two cannon, reducing it to little more than smoke and ruin. My friend and I kept silent as the fort lit up with flames. There was shouting and screaming from within and some of our fellow buccaneers answered by crying out with murderous delight.

'Leave no man alive, lads!' Razorbill yelled above the din. 'Children we'll take for slaves! Women we'll take for sport!'

The Quartermaster's instructions excited the slavering horde and they could barely wait to occupy the shore boats.

'Hark! Our Captain joins us!' proclaimed Razorbill, dousing the furnace of their frenzy.

As I had yet to lay eyes upon the Captain I was compelled to turn, as were many of my shipmates. What manner of man the Captain was I cannot say, if man at all. There was a tremendous presence all of a sudden and some of the crew were forced to make way. I saw some of them gasp and wince. There were those that even made the sign of the cross; a gesture rarely witnessed in such wicked company. There was a thudding, as if heavy of foot, and a snorting, as if a full-grown bull had wandered onto deck. I strained my neck above the crowd to get a glimpse but I did not have to; the creature was twice the size of our biggest lads. Two legs he walked on but they more like ancient oaks than mortal shanks. His waist was slim but his chest protruded like a barrel. From his mighty arms swung axe and sword that no other man could have lifted. The man-thing's head was merely a dome of what seemed like scar tissue and all of his bare flesh was smoky grey, only the eyes seemed visible, glowing like smouldering coals.

The Captain raised his weapons into the air and a maw dropped open to bellow: 'Follow me, my devils!'

This whipped up the mass into rage. Colker and I were swept along. We had not been aboard as long as some and they were like carnivorous beasts uncaged. I could see their wild eyes in the red glow from the shore and I pitied any of our victims that still lived. Our queer Captain needed no boat, I saw him merely plunge into the ocean and propel himself to shore with his unnatural limbs. The rest of us followed him as fast as we could but there was madness in the rush and two boats collided with each other in the dark, spilling their passengers into the ocean. Those that could swim lived and those that could not drowned. Even those of us who managed to stay afloat faced peril. The occupants of what was left of the fort assembled a hasty defence. It became clear that they still had a cannon or two of their own, despite the battering they had been given, and a few balls came our way. I swear that one whistled straight past my head. Whatever god that had granted me mercy still looked over me and the projectile hit the party behind us instead. Their boat smashed into driftwood and more pirates were cast into the black surf. There was an unseen guardian with a long arm musket too, and a keen eye to warrant it. Poor Colker lost most of his head and the rest of us were showered with his brains. Instinctively, we pushed his body overboard and I caught a glimpse of him floating away. 'You'll be telling no more tales, my friend,' I commented to myself.

The boat I was in was one of the last to reach the shallows. Most of the Accamus crew were already swarming up the beach towards the flaming ruin and those in my boat were eager to join them, they leapt out of the boat and it lurched wildly. I lost my balance and toppled backwards into the water and no one remained to give me a hand up. My pistols were soaked. I would have to rely on my rapier. I picked myself up, drew out the blade and rushed after the mob. I noticed a corpse or two had already washed ashore but these were nothing compared to the ruin that lay within the fort. I stumbled over sand first and then over a carpet of bodies though whether this was the result of the broadsides or the ensuing battle I could not tell. Parts of men lay amongst the rock and fire and the stink of freshly spilled guts and burnt flesh was cloying. I raised my neckerchief about my mouth and nose and found a spot to survey the scene. Even with watery eyes, I could see that a reckless fight still raged in the centre of the wreckage. Though their walls had been reduced, the Spanish still had plenty of men and they looked as desperate and as fierce as we. There was an exchange of musket and pistol and scores of men on both sides dropped to the ground. Their shots spent, my shipmates waded in, wailing like lunatics and I was obliged to join them. Many a skirmish I have participated in but it had been a while since my last and I had forgotten the terror. Razorbill found me faltering.

'Lost your appetite, lad?' said he.

I shook my head.

'Then let's get stuck in!' he cried.

I charged with the giant. The defenders had formed a line of bayonets and some of our shipmates had fallen before it. Others were still striving to penetrate the barrier and the Quartermaster and I joined the struggle. I danced to avoid the bayonet that was thrust towards me, as did Razorbill. Our rapiers were much shorter and they had us at an advantage. We did not need to worry too much, however, the Captain loomed out of the darkness and he went down the line, hacking and chopping with his vast implements. Our opponents despaired just to look upon him but they did not cry for long; the Captain made short work of them. I watched with wide eyes as he cut many of them in two. We, 'his devils,' were compelled to step back, lest we get caught in those awesome swipes but we were not far enough to avoid getting coated by waves of gore. The Captain single-handedly despatched the defenders in a few heartbeats and then he turned to us and laughed till the ground shook. Razorbill and the others shared his glee but I had to feign mine. I actually felt sick. The mighty Captain paused to lick the blood from his blades with a lengthy forked tongue, like that of a serpent. As he did so, he was shot. A crack rang out from above and a musket ball was blasted downwards through his meaty neck. I anticipated him to fall. Even a formidable brute such as he could not weather a shot to the throat? But I was wrong; he just gazed up and cackled again, bloody drool dripping from his dreadful maw. I stared upwards too. One tower of the fort still stood and was being occupied by a marksman, perchance the same one that had killed Colker.

'With me, Mr Morell!' ordered Razorbill.

I ran behind him to the base of the intact tower. The only way in appeared to be a bolted door and we had to find two others to help us barge it down. Some of our shipmates were shot in the meantime. The man in the tower clearly had his pick of targets and the pirates, in their exhilaration, had not the sense to take cover. Once we had battered down the door, the Quartermaster instructed me to go first. I nodded in compliance and lead the way, skipping up a spiral staircase all the way to the top, gripping my sword tightly as I did so. In the higher most nest we came upon our quarry. He looked to me little more than a boy, barely filling out his uniform. He glared at me with fearful eyes. I took pity on the youngster and suggested to Razorbill that he would make a worthy addition to the crew, with his marksmanship and all, but the Quartermaster just slowly shook his head. The boy made one last gesture of defiance and swung his rifle butt at me but I merely stepped out of the way and gutted him like a fish. I doubt very much that I will ever forget his eyes. They stared at me as the life drained from them. Nor will Razorbill's pointy-toothed smile ever leave me. The fiend watched and grinned as I butchered the boy.

So I participated in the mass murder, upon the Quartermaster's insistence. I had killed my one and only 'man' that night. By the time we had descended back down the tower, the battle had been won. Only women and children remained, cowering in the shadows. I often wonder if it would have been the same outcome without the Captain. The ship's cannon had destroyed the fort but most of its soldiers had survived and they were courageous and disciplined whereas we were nothing more than a shambolic rabble. We owed our victory to the monster.

The holds of the Accamus were filled with booty. We took everything the Spanish had and there was plenty; weapons, silks, sugar, spice, tobacco, gold, slaves. What remained of the night was spent drinking. Not even the time to bury the dead was spared. We rejoiced and sang and danced amongst them. And of the womenfolk that we captured? I shall spare you any illustration of their torment though I will confess that I did participate. Many moons I spent marooned but this is no excuse for my awful deeds.

*

'The Captain wants to see you.' A long shadow darkened the deck.

Those were the words I had come to dread. I quit scrubbing the timbers and peered up at the owner of the silhouette. It was Razorbill. There was nothing in the Quartermaster's aspect that offered a reason why my presence had been requested. I simply nodded and got to my feet. Outwardly, I was composed, but within I was terrified. I had seen the Captain once and that was enough. Pausing only for a glance out to sea, I made my way to his mysterious cabin. Winds were calm and the ocean was placid, as were my shipmates. We had been back at sea for a week but the attack was still recent enough to mollify them. This is the usual mood for pirates in my experience. They spend a long time waiting for an opportunity and their will to murder, steal and rape builds until they are barely contained. After they have vented their unhealthy desires there is a curious aftermath where the crew are at peace, almost docile. The retribution of the Spanish navy was a concern, of course, but there was no sign of an armada yet. Some of the buccaneers regarded me as I passed them but their faces were as blank as that of Razorbill.

The deck around the Captain's cabin was clear. I knocked on the door and there was no answer from within. I was glad of this and turned to walk away when I heard the door open behind me with a loud creak. I had little choice but to accept the ominous invitation. I began to shiver as I stepped inside though it was from dismay, not cold. Infact, the interior was searing; like when you step into a smithy, yet I saw no furnace. The furnishings of the cabin were simple; it was fringed with shelves crammed with candles, bottles, boxes and the occasional skull or trophy. In the middle was a table, coated with maps and navigational pieces, as you would expect. I recalled Colker's description and he had not lied to me, despite the temperature everything seemed damp and the air was thick with the buzzing of flies. Slouched in a chair that could only have been built for him was the beast that I last saw cutting men in half and laughing off a shot to his neck. He was as monstrous as I remembered him but his glowing eyes were more meaningful at close quarters. I could see an ancient intelligence burning back at me, years if not centuries. I tried to stop shaking but the more I strived the worse it seemed to get.

'Thank you for joining me, Mr Morell,' was his unexpectedly civilised greeting. His voice was like a ship grating against rock.

'The privilege is mine,' I stuttered with the opposing volume of a mouse.

'Won't you close the door?' he asked.

As I did so, the cabin filled with darkness and those dreadful eyes became even brighter in the gloom.

'Razorbill tells me that you were somewhat reluctant in our little venture?'

I decided to answer him with honesty. 'A year marooned has given me opportunity to reflect on my life, Captain.'

'You are a learned man?'

'I was educated at Oxford, sir.'

'Guilt is the curse of the scholarly.'

I swallowed and nodded.

'How come you to be amongst us vermin?'

'I wanted to see the world,' I explained. 'I discovered that it is easier to take what you want than toil for it. That's the short version of my tale anyhow.'

'There is a pain in your soul? The death of a loved one perchance?' His observation was accurate and unsettling.

'My fiancée was killed,' confessed I.

'May I ask by whom?'

'Me, sir.'

He laughed at this and I swear that my ear drums almost burst.

'I like you, Mr Morell,' said he eventually.

I felt no more relaxed and he went on.

'The battle has left my crew depleted. The bosun is dead. I am told that you fulfilled such a role on the Queen Anne's Revenge?'

'Only when the proper bosun was too drunk to stand.'

Again the Captain laughed and again my ears endured.

'Nevertheless, you have some knowledge and practice and that will suffice for now.'

I could hardly believe that this brutish creature was so eloquent and here he was offering me such a prized position in his crew.

'Who are you?' I blurted out.

He paused before his answer; wetting what passed for lips with his snake tongue. 'I think you already know who I am, Mr Morell.'

'And what is our destination, sir?'

'I think you know where we are going.'

I found myself sobbing. 'But I am tired of this life.'

'So I see,' said he. 'But it is much too late to repent, my friend. Your crimes against your fellow men are numerous and terrible. Places on this ship are reserved for those of a notable disposition.'

I took the meaning of his words and I ran. I bolted out of the door as fast as my shanks would carry me and all the way down the ship. A few men tried to stop me from climbing into a boat but I was so frightened that I was manic and they could not bond me. I even knocked two of them senseless with an oar. I cut the boat loose and dropped into the sea. I rowed furiously away from the Accamus. I kept my head low as I expected musket shot but there was none. I could not breathe easily until the infernal vessel was out of sight. Within a few minutes she became just a speck on the horizon as when I had first laid eyes upon her. I had given my resignation.

*

Though I have escaped I must declare that I should have done so with more guile and preparation. Here I am in a small rowing boat with only an oar and a knife as possessions. I have no food, water or protection from the glare of the sun or the wrath of the sea. I have doomed myself to a slow and lonely death. I imagine that my shipmates must be laughing at me but I can take some comfort that I would not be on board the Accamus for its final journey 'home.' How long I have spent in this boat I cannot tell you. Days and nights have become minutes. I attach myself to the bottom like a limpet and my existence feels like one long fevered dream. I fear I shall soon be nothing and I have carved my final testimony into the wood of this boat with my knife. It is my hope that one day some soul will find it and perhaps these words will make any reader think again before choosing the road that I have taken.

God have mercy on my soul,
Christopher Morell

The Waster Troy

The man gasped as the thing emerged from the plughole. He noticed it first as a black speck and watched through shampoo-stung eyes as it grew in the gap between his feet. Its body was tiny yet bloated. Its hair twitched and prickled with the effort of its ascent through the swirling water. He gagged back a scream as his most intimate and treasured of rituals was violated. He retreated to the other end of the shower, clutching his oyster-shaped sponge for consolation. The distance was not enough to console him and he panicked, leaping sideways out of the shower. Only his beaded floor mat saved him from a blunder. Through the steam, he peered again at the hirsute intruder but it had yet to venture further from the plughole. It remained there and shuddered, as if unsure of its new surroundings. The man waited for a few moments while it made up its alien mind. The soapy water drained away and the vapour cleared and the true origin of the trespasser was revealed. The man bent down to confirm his suspicions. The scream was finally vented, but it was born of rage, not fear.

*

'Did you hear something?' quizzed Eddie as he sank into his armchair and scratched his belly like a lethargic baboon.

'What? Like a scream?' suggested Troy from the comfort of the nearby sofa.

Eddie looked over at him but Troy did not return his gaze. He was entranced by the colourful and seductive images on the television screen. 'Yeah, like a scream.'

'No.' Troy offered no more insight. The telly had taken him.

'Are you okay, babes?' yelled Eddie into the kitchen instead.

Ruth appeared, her cheerful smile sandwiched between rosy cheeks. 'Yeah, why?'

Eddie shrugged a shoulder. He wanted to shrug both but the other one hadn't woken up yet. 'Thought I heard screaming.'

'Well it wasn't me,' she said.

Eddie watched television for a minute to see what Troy found so compelling. It was a shopping channel. The white-toothed presenters were gushing over a deluxe bread maker. Eddie didn't get it. He grew bored. 'I'm ready to break my fast,' he announced at an obnoxious volume.

Ruth walked in, putting on her uniform. 'Zip me up.'

She plonked herself in between Eddie's legs and he strived to do up the zip with his clumsy man fingers. 'I said I'm ready to break my fast,' he repeated, breathless with frustration.

'What does that mean?' asked Ruth.

'It means I want some breakfast,' explained Eddie.

Ruth fidgeted into her outfit and got up. 'You'll have to get your own. I'm late.'

Eddie's face became a whirlpool of disgust. 'Get my own breakfast? What the fuck?'

Ruth removed her bag from the detritus on the floor and made for the front door. She turned before she left. 'And don't forget to take Troy to the Doctor's.'

Eddie's discontent grew. 'What about my goodbye kiss?'

His goodbye kiss was a blast of cold wind from the street outside as she left. Eddie contemplated her instructions. 'Get my own breakfast? After what I did for her last night?' Eddie's objection was voiced at Troy but it was a waste of time; the furry Welshman was focused on the specifics of the bread maker. Alone in his cause, Eddie pushed himself out of the abyss of the armchair. He shuffled like an old man to the gloom of the kitchen. The refrigerator opened with a creak and it was followed by the lively crunch and spurt of a can being opened. Eddie shambled back in and returned to the embrace of his favoured chair, the minute beginnings of joy materialising on his face. He slurped at the can with gasps of satisfaction.

Troy blinked into life suddenly. 'Where's mine?'

'Only lagers left,' explained Eddie.

'Bollocks,' scoffed Troy. 'I bought eight ciders last night.'

'You drank them.'

'I don't remember that.'

'That's because you drank eight ciders.'

Troy opened his mouth to say something more but the impulse left him. He looked like how Einstein must have looked when relativity first started to bug him.

Eddie just beamed back at him like a bastion of established logic and lit up a half smoked fag from an ashtray on the chair arm.

So occupied were they in mutual reflection of the night before that they failed to notice Paul's entrance. He stomped in, dripping wet and naked except for a meagre towel wrapped around his vitals.

He glared at them and held up a small furry object betwixt his finger and thumb. 'What in the love of god is this?' he rumbled with theatrical disgust.

Troy and Eddie sensed his menace. They glanced up at him and then at the object of inquest.

Eddie pouted. 'Is it a spider? It looks like a spider.'

'I don't like spiders,' added Troy.

'I don't like shafting spiders either!' roared Paul, transferring his glare to Eddie to Troy and back again. 'I'm a diagnosed arachnophobe!'

'Ah! I thought I heard somebody scream,' Eddie smiled and sank into his chair with satisfaction like a detective solving a case.

'Thing is: It's not a spider, it's another one of Troy's shafting hairballs!' explained Paul, his face red with the effort of being furious.

'Well, what's the problem then?' Eddie scratched the fleshy island in the middle of his dreadlocks. 'You thought it was a spider. It wasn't. Panic over.'

Paul snorted like an outraged horse. 'I was having a nice hot shower, before I go to work, at my job, which I go and do before I go to uni, the one I do to pay for the rent on this house!'

'That reminds me,' said Eddie. 'Can you get us some bread and milk and can you get Troy some ciders?'

'I won't be back until tonight. I won't be back for ten hours.' Paul furrowed his brow.

Eddie sucked in some air and shook his head at Troy. 'Ooh, ten hours. Can you wait that long, mate?'

'Hell no,' replied Troy, wide-eyed with anxiety.

'This has got to stop!' Paul shook the hairball at them.

'I agree entirely.' Eddie looked at him. 'You've got to get booze faster than that.'

'Why don't you get your own shafting booze?' bellowed Paul.

'Because you're an employee,' reasoned Eddie. 'You get discount.'

The semi-naked man put his hands on his hips in defiance. 'They're starting to think I'm an alcoholic at that place.'

'You're a student, same difference.' Eddie blew out a rational cloud of smoke.

'Don't you think that it's about time you two went to a lecture? Got a job perhaps?' Paul danced from foot to foot with agitation.

'Steady on now,' Troy coughed.

'Yeah, be reasonable, Paulo,' added Eddie. 'We'll try to do something about Troy's hairballs, alright? But less of the going outside talk. It's cold and scary out there.'

Paul scrunched up his lantern jaw and nodded, as if he had gained a small victory. 'And another thing ...'

'What now?' Eddie rolled his eyes with annoyance.

'Can you keep the noise down a bit at night, please, Eddie?'

'What do you mean?'

'You know what I mean.'

'Do I?'

'You and Michelle.' Paul tried not to blush but it happened anyway. 'I can hear everything, you know. The walls are paper thin.'

Eddie sniggered like a badly-oiled machine gun. 'Aw, shit! Sorry, mate.'

'That's alright.' Paul looked away. 'Just keep it down.'

'Or don't keep it up, you mean?' Eddie mused.

'Quite.' Paul fumbled coyly with his towel. 'It sounds like she's crying. It's really disturbing to listen to.'

'It's Ruth now anyway,' stated Eddie. 'Michelle's gone. Ruth's a bit quieter.'

Paul nodded. He scanned the room. 'Where's the bin?'

'Over there in the corner,' indicated Troy with a feeble finger.

Paul stepped over all the rubbish on the floor. He deposited the hairball in the bin. Another parade of disapproval marched across his face. 'Do you know that this bin is entirely empty?'

Eddie and Troy gave him blank expressions.

Paul snarled. 'It's the cleanest object in the room for god's sake. The shafting irony!'

Paul held it up with his meaty paws. 'You do know what this is for, right? It's for putting rubbish in. It's called a bin. Say it after me: B-I-N. Say it!'

Troy and Eddie repeated it like a remedial class on a Monday morning. 'B-I-N.'

Paul nodded with satisfaction. 'Get all this crap up off the floor. I want to see the carpet again by the time I get back,' he stomped out of the room with one final glare.

Troy looked at Eddie, his eyes trembling with concern. 'Is he serious?'

'I think he's had enough, mate, yeah,' Eddie stubbed out his fag.

'So let me get this straight: I've got to go and see the Doctor and my tutor and get my own ciders and tidy up?'

'It's looking that way, yeah,' Eddie scratched his bald patch with regret.

'Flaming doomsday!' exclaimed Troy, finally budging.

*

The woman's breasts hung like white grapefruits. Troy could see the central clip on her bra straining. He thought he could see the borders of her nipples, rising like two pink suns.

'So?' she said. What can I do for you … erm?' She frantically searched the documents that coated her desk. 'Tray Batty?'

'Troy Botting.'

'Oh, yes, that was it.'

'I need some extension time on my essay, please, Carol.' Troy passed her a grubby, screwed-up Doctor's note.

The woman called Carol took it like she had been handed a rat corpse. She placed a pair of spectacles on her nose and studied the medical scribbles carefully. Troy felt the oppression of silence. Best focus on her breasts, he decided, don't look at her evil, craggy face. He stared at the milky behemoths again and wondered what they would be like pressed up against his mouth. He felt the crotch on his trousers tighten. Could such a wonder ever take place? Did this stuffy middle-aged biology professor have a sex drive? Would she feel a wild and impetuous urge for a tiny Welshman with an in-growing toenail?

'I don't know about this,' Carol tutted. 'How does this stop you from writing an essay?'

'I can't walk to the library to do the research,' explained Troy. 'Too painful.'

'I'm not sure,' Carol shook her head with indecision. 'I've just granted an extension to a girl who's just found out that she's pregnant and before that, to a young man whose mother has just died. This toenail pales in insignificance, wouldn't you say?'

'We've all got our crosses to bear, Carol,' Troy attempted to state with confidence but this meant looking into her venomous, bespectacled eyes and he was, at once, intimidated. He returned to the valley of wonder below her neck.

'Are you sure you're even in my class?' she asked. 'I don't remember ever seeing you before.'

'I may have missed one or two,' suggested Troy.

'One or two?' Carol sighed, glancing through her attendance register. 'I don't see your name here anywhere and it is very noticeable.'

'Sometimes I go by the name of Danny Trenchard,' clarified Troy.

'Don't bullshit me!' Carol snapped.

Troy was torn away from the solace of her bosom. He had been so happy there; the curves and undulations were so smooth and white and flawless, like a perfect skiing holiday. Now he was at her face; scowling, wrinkly, cross.

'I know who Danny is, he's an excellent student and you're not him.'

All Troy could muster was a slight nod. He had seized up in fear.

'Masquerading as another student!' she scoffed. 'Do you really think you could get away with that?'

Troy managed a meek shake of his head.

'You're being foolish, Mr Botting,' she went on. 'How am I even to know that this Doctor's note is bona fide?'

Troy gulped so loudly that he was convinced that it must have been audible. He could no longer handle the tits, let alone the face. He stared down at his own corduroyed lap. His penis had gone soft. It was in danger of vanishing into his body, along with his balls.

'Very well,' the formidable hag decided. 'I'll make you a deal. Get this essay to me by this time next week and attend the rest of my classes and we'll see what's what.'

Troy was astonished. Perhaps his terrified gerbil act had won her over. He forced himself to look up and say 'thank you.'

'Now get out of my sight,' she instructed.

Troy got up and reminded himself to limp painfully out of the office. He snatched one last eyeful of the soothing boobs as he negotiated the door.

Eddie was waiting outside for him. He was sat on the wall, smoking a fag. 'How did it go?'

Troy limped over to him, keeping up the facade in case Carol was watching him through her office window. 'I've got another week.'

'A week!' Eddie beamed. 'From Carol Jennings! Good work! Let's get wrecked!'

Troy frowned at him. 'Did you hear what I just said?'

'Yeah, you said you'd got another week.'

'Another week to write a three-thousand word essay on the peculiarities of the biochemistry of the box jellyfish that I haven't even started yet.'

'A week's loads of time,' reasoned Eddie.

Troy sighed deeply. 'Come on then.'

*

'Imbibe,' ordered Eddie.

'Me? Again?' Troy was outraged.

'Imbibe, motherfucker, you haven't even drunk the last one.' Eddie snatched his glass and filled it up under the table.

'How much are you putting in?' Troy tried not to show any fear in front of Ruth and her friend Nerys.

Eddie passed him the glass back and grinned like a maniac. It was twice as full. Some of it had splashed onto the table and was stripping the varnish away.

'That's loads, you tosser.' Troy sniffed his drink; the vodka overwhelmed the smell of the coke. 'It's supposed to be a finger's worth.'

'What can I say? I've got big fingers,' Eddie displayed his monstrous digits.

'He's looking a bit pale,' commented Nerys.

Troy looked at her and found that she too was grinning at him. 'You lot are trying to get me wrecked.'

'Come on, you pussy!' laughed Eddie and loaded the bong.

Troy exhaled noisily and strived to digest more of the chemicals. As soon as he had done so, Eddie handed him the bong. He accepted it with shaking hands. Eddie ignited the little metal bowl with a lighter and Troy took in a lungful of the acrid smoke. He blew it out again a few seconds later like a little hairy dragon and the girls twittered with astonishment as the smoke from his lungs filled the room. They even clapped their hands as though it was some perverse magic trick. Eddie dealt out the cards again and Troy blinked as they flew around the table. Remnants of ice cubes brought some chilly comfort to his protesting innards but that was all. His head felt like a merry-go-round. The other players picked up their deals but Eddie halted them with a raised hand.

'No mercy,' Troy predicted what he would say and with a gurgle he slammed down an empty glass.

Satisfied, Eddie gestured for the game to resume. Play passed round the table like wildfire, interrupted only by chuckles. Troy noted that Ruth in particular was smirking unashamedly; fortune keeping her cool. She had yet to imbibe once, sipping a can of cider at her leisure. Troy suspected a conspiracy. He glanced around the lounge but it looked fuzzy and grainy, like a video taken on a cheap mobile phone. It was familiar and yet unfamiliar. He decided it was best not to move his head too much and concentrate on the game.

'It's your turn, Troy boy,' said Nerys suddenly.

He squinted at her shiny painted face through the haze and then at the others. How long they had been waiting for him was not certain. They were sat there, staring back at him with collective amusement. It was as if they were all moving ten times as fast. Troy leered at the sodden cards in his fist and with an elusive logic, selected one to throw down. The gang seemed content with his move and they all responded with a Mexican wave of cards and euphoria. 'Imbibe!' they cried as one.

Troy was stunned at the speed. He slowly peered around at everyone's hands and sure enough he was the only one holding any cards. He threw them down in disgust. They soaked up the wet table. 'You cheating wankers!'

'Imbibe,' repeated Eddie and grabbed his glass again. Troy's only consolation was a glimpse of an almost empty bottle. Eddie handed over the glass. With bravado, Troy chucked the liquid down his throat. Everyone laughed.

'I need another lager,' announced Eddie.

'I need to shake my lettuce,' added Ruth, rising to her feet.

'We need another bottle too, babes,' said Eddie, waving the empty one at her.

'What did your last slave die of?' she challenged.

'I shagged her to death,' he explained. While Ruth was gone, Eddie replenished the bong and scrutinised her friend. 'So what is it you're studying again?'

'I'm at nursing college with Ruth,' Nerys replied.

Eddie nodded, feigning interest. He passed the contraption to Troy.

There was silence while no one could think of anything to say. Troy took his hit and leered at Nerys like he was going to say something but keeled over to one side suddenly, the sound of his skull colliding with the floor, the fetid water of the bong spilling across the carpet.

'Alright, mate?' asked Eddie.

The Welshman sprang back up into an upright position. 'Feeling a bit wonky‘, he explained. He did not realise that a discarded yoghurt pot had now stuck to his hair.

Nerys burst into laughter.

'I thought you'd gone then,' Eddie shared the hilarity.

Troy looked at them both with bewilderment. 'I could play all night long me.'

Ruth returned, cradling various bottles and cans in her arms. 'I think we should play something else.'

'What?' protested Eddie. 'This is just starting to get good.'

'He's looking a bit pale,' Ruth glanced at Troy with concern. 'I'm not sure he's even supposed to drink with them pain killers.'

'You're alright aren't you, mate?' Eddie asked him.

Troy nodded his head and grinned like a happy infant.

'This is so funny,' added Nerys, still guffawing at Troy's new hair accessory.

'Besides,' said Eddie. 'His luck will even out. The aim of this game is to get us all wrecked, not just Troy.'

'And what then?' enquired Nerys with a mischievous smile.

'We go upstairs and have a no-holes-barred sex orgy,' Eddie glanced at her and winked.

Nerys' eyebrows arched playfully as she giggled. 'I see.'

Ruth did not share their joke. She plunked herself down in between them. 'Come on then. Deal!'

Eddie gathered up the sodden cards and distributed them accordingly. Behind them, there was the heavy thump of the front door opening and closing. 'Here comes the fun police,' muttered Eddie under his breath.

The girls turned to look but Eddie and Troy did not. Paul marched in, carrying two full shopping bags in each hand, seemingly without toil. There was a cold aura about him as if he had brought the outside chill in with him. He glanced around the room like a nervous predator.

'Hi,' said Nerys, staring at him with bemusement.

'Hello, Paul,' ventured Ruth.

Paul ignored them. The bags dropped to the floor with a clamour that shook the floorboards.

'Did you get me ciders, big man?' asked Troy, trying to focus on his hand.

Paul continued to be silently furious.

Eddie couldn't take it anymore. He glared up at him. 'What's wrong, you melodramatic prick?'

'I tell you what's wrong!' Paul barked so loudly that all they jumped out of their skins, even Eddie. 'I've been out all day working! I ask you to one thing in my absence; one tiny shafting thing!'

'The tidying up?' Eddie nodded.

'Yes! The tidying up!' Paul clenched his teeth and his fists. 'It's even more of a mess than it was this morning!'

'Change of plan,' Eddie sparked up a fag. 'We decided to have a party instead. There's no point in tidying up *before* a party, is there?'

At once, Paul seemed defeated by Eddie's shield of logic. He merely stood there in his huge black overcoat and fumed, his spilt shopping indistinguishable from the leftover products on the floor.

'Ruth and her mate came round,' Eddie continued. 'We have to entertain the ladies now, don't we? Don't we ladies?' He turned to Ruth and Nerys for support.

The girls nodded and huddled together, cooperative but fearful of the scary man in the big coat.

'That's not the point,' grumbled Paul. 'You never do anything, Eddie, but at least you pay your share of the rent. He's not even supposed to be here.' Paul stabbed an accusing finger at Troy.

'He's my mate,' Eddie puffed. 'And he's got nowhere else to go, have you, Troy?'

It seemed to take all of his effort for Troy to nod his head in agreement.

'He lives here for free and he turns it into a shit tip!' bellowed Paul, some weird froth emerging from the corners of his mouth. 'What's that wet patch next to him? Has he pissed himself?'

'It's just bong water,' explained Eddie. 'What do you want me to do? Throw him out onto the streets?'

'Yes!' cried Paul.

'He can come and live with us,' Nerys suggested, excitedly.

'I think Matron might have something to say about that,' Ruth said.

'He could live in your cage with the guinea pig,' guffawed Eddie.

The girls laughed.

'He deserves to live in a shafting cage!' sneered Paul, turning the jest ugly.

Everyone turned to Troy. He returned their attention with a broad imbecilic smile. He then opened his mouth wider and ejected a tsunami of puke. It hit everything; the table, the floor, the walls, the cards, the drinks, the attractive female guests, Eddie's phone, Paul's shopping. It reeked too; a blend of vodka, cider, strawberry milk shake and Sainsburys Chicken Korma for One. Very little was untouched by Troy's stinking gush of vom.

'Sorry,' Troy managed to say before he passed out.

*

She had been following him for weeks; always just in sight. Troy would glimpse the girl over his shoulder but when he turned fully she would vanish, like a pesky ghost. The first few times he put it down to coincidence. After all, he saw her mostly at university and it was not unusual to be in the same place as another student on the same course. However, Troy caught sight of the girl increasingly off campus; out on the streets, in the shops and pubs. She had a problem remaining discreet: Her hair was so blonde it was almost white and despite her oriental features, she was distinctly pale. From far away, her hair and her face became one, like a pallid blur on the top of her body. The impression reinforced her ethereal status. Troy was too shy to confront her but, as it turned out, he did not need to.

'What are you doing?' was her first question as she approached him.

Troy looked around at the narrow confines of the passage they were in. It must have looked weird and it was going to be hard to explain. 'I'm gimmelling.'

'What's gimmelling?' she asked, unfazed.

Troy struggled for a few moments. By way of attempted explanation, he showed her the map on his clip-board. 'I mark out all the gimmels in town and review them,' he said, perhaps a little too quickly.

'What's a gimmel?' she pried further, peering at the map.

Troy looked into her eyes and was lost for a second. He almost expected them to be pink to conform with her albino-like appearance but they were amber coloured; equally as strange.

'You know …' he floundered again, '… a gimmel. It has different names in different places. Some people call them gennels or gunnels. It depends on where you're from.'

The girl was blank.

'An alleyway?' ventured Troy.

She laughed harmoniously. 'Oh, I see! And where is it you're from?'

'The Valleys,' stated Troy.

She seemed perplexed again.

'Wales,' he clarified. 'You're not from round here either are you?'

'No,' the fluty titter again. 'You could safely say that.'

Troy shuffled nervously. He inspected his map and fidgeted with his pen. He wanted to proceed with the gimmelling. It felt much cosier than conversing with a female.

'So, is this a project for uni?' the girl enquired.

It was Troy's turn to be amused. 'No, no,' he said. 'It's just a hobby.'

'Haven't you got lots of work to do?' she said, suddenly concerned.

Troy shrugged his shoulders. 'I have, yeah.'

The girl nodded and bit her lip slightly.

Troy felt awkward. She was so well-turned out. Her clothes and hair and skin were immaculate. In contrast he was grubby and scruffy and spotty. What would a passer-by think if they saw them talking to each other? The pale oriental princess and the mucky little Welsh boy? In the absence of imagination, he decided to tell the truth. 'I needed some fresh air. I was a bit … erm … poorly last night.'

'I see,' she said. 'So how does this one rate?'

'Oh, quite highly!' proclaimed Troy with sudden animation. 'It's long and it's got two corners that form a classic Z-shape and the wood panelling is a smart feature. It's well kept, probably because it's out in the suburbs.' He pointed out the characteristics of the gimmel as he spoke. He then wondered if the girl was taking the piss and he looked at her. To his surprise, she seemed genuinely interested.

'Have you got any more to explore?'

'Perhaps just another one,' he replied. 'It'll be getting dark soon.' Troy peered up at the wintry sky. It churned in response to his foreboding.

The girl did not say anything and Troy felt uncomfortable again. Instinctively, he began to wander away, deeper into the passage.

'Can I tag along?' she asked.

Troy spun round and looked at her, those sharp amber eyes catching him off guard again. 'Sure,' he stuttered.

She beamed and leapt the distance between them. 'My name is Cassandra. Cass for short.'

'I'm Troy,' he said.

'I know,' she giggled and much to Troy's astonishment, took him by the hand.

*

'That's amazing!' proclaimed Troy as he scanned the lofty privet hedges. In the failing light, they seemed so formidable and dim, as if they were guardians for the entrance of another world.

'I shouldn't be letting a guy take me down a dark alley,' joked Cass nervously as he led her further into the shadows.

'It isn't even on the map,' sniggered Troy and shook his head at his clipboard.

Her attempt at humour lost, Cass snuggled down into her fur-lined overcoat and said 'perhaps it's a new one, you know, built since the map.'

He cocked an eyebrow at her and there was a glint in his rheumy eyes. 'Or an old one? A gimmel that's been forgotten?' He took in a nose full of air. 'There! You can smell its age.'

Cass sniffed the icy air too but all she got was a cold nose.

'Come on!' beamed Troy and his enthusiasm carried them further down the passage. She had no choice but to walk behind him. It was too narrow for them to walk side by side. Troy lead her for quite a distance, down to the bottom of the gimmel where it opened out onto the pavement of a smart suburb. Troy looked around, his eyes wide with the joy of realisation. 'We're here? Wow!'

Cass breathed deeply with relief as she emerged from the tunnel. 'That was very long and narrow. Not as nice as the last gimmel.'

Troy nodded at her. 'Yeah, it was a bit freaky. Sorry.'

'It's alright,' she smiled. 'It's just getting dark.'

'We'd better be making tracks I suppose,' he agreed. 'Where do you live? Do you want me to walk you?'

'I live near you. Are you going to ask me back for a cup of tea?'

'Erm ... yes,' Troy was hesitant. He thought of the pigsty in which he lived. The one that he had redecorated with sick the previous night.

'It's alright if you don't want me to,' said Cass. 'I'm sure we'll see each other around.'

'How about tomorrow?' ventured Troy, finding some assertiveness from somewhere.

She looked at him. Her eyes turned shiny black in the gloom. 'Okay, perhaps we could plough through our research methodology papers together?'

Troy was temporarily stumped. 'Research methodology?'

'The class we're both in?' Cass explained.

'Oh, yeah,' he chuckled. 'I knew that.'

There was a pause. Troy peered back up the gimmel. 'The quickest way back to our part of town is back up there I'm afraid.'

She shrugged her shoulders. 'I'll be alright as long as I'm with you.'

'How do you know I'm not a werewolf?' he grinned.

'Do they have werewolves in Wales?'

'Oh, yeah,' said Troy. 'It's werewolf central. Lots of sheep to eat.'

'It's not a full moon anyway,' Cass peered up at the sky.

Troy turned to look and he too saw the spectral crescent behind the billowing clouds.

They watched it together for a few moments and with silent agreement, meandered back up the gimmel.

*

Eddie felt the mattress bounce beneath him like an undulating wave as Nerys stirred next to him.

'Put the kettle on, babes,' he murmured in response.

'I think I should put some clothes on first,' she said as she got up.

Eddie always took a little time to wake up. He liked his passage from fugue to reality to be an unhurried, gentle transfer. He would examine the stains on the ceiling for a while or even just the inside of his eyelids, whatever he focused on first, unless there was a naked woman to look at, of course.

'What?'

'I think I should put some clothes on first' she repeated.

Eddie had already turned round, his eyes popping out of their sockets.

Indeed, Nerys was starkers; her bold and curvaceous form outlined in the pale winter light. A veil of twinkling dust particles cloaked her like a holy aura. Eddie was not unaccustomed to the vision but this girl was new.

'Carved by god's own chisel.' Eddie ogled in wonder. 'Aren't you cold?'

'I don't really feel it,' she said and caressed her pointed nipples playfully. 'I'm a farm girl, remember?'

'I thought you were a nurse?'

'I was brought up on a farm, you dick,' Nerys mocked.

'Oh,' said Eddie and yawned. 'Well, yeah, put some clothes on. You'll give the boys heart attacks if you go downstairs like that.' He pushed himself up onto his elbows to get a better view of her form as she hunted for something suitable from the piles on the floor.

'Haven't they seen a woman naked before?' she asked.

'Those two?' Eddie wheezed and spluttered violently with laughter, so much so that Nerys paused to see if he was alright. 'Aw, shit, that's a good one!' He calmed down again and wiped the tears from his eyes.

Nerys slipped on one of his t-shirts. 'Troy was with a girl earlier.'

'What?'

'I got up this morning for a drink of water and Troy was with a girl.'

Eddie peered at her. 'Are you sure?'

'Yes,' she said.

'Shagging?'

'No just talking.' Nerys opened the door. 'She's still here. You can hear them.'

Eddie scratched his dreadlocked scalp and frowned as he listened. Sure enough, Troy was audible from downstairs and another voice; quieter and more melodic.

'This I gotta see!' he leapt from the mattress excitedly.

'There's my fucking knickers!' exclaimed Nerys.

'Oh! Sorry.' Eddie took them off and gave them back.

*

It was a double shock for Eddie. Not only was his friend with a member of the opposite sex but he also appeared to be doing some work. Troy and the girl were sat together on the sofa, divided by an oasis of papers and books. Eddie stood and stared. No explanation was forthcoming. So deep were they in mutual concentration, they did not even appear to notice him. Eddie opened his mouth to say something but Nerys came in and dragged him through to the kitchen by his longest dreadlock.

'Leave them be,' she whispered. She took a lager from the fridge and shoved it into his hand.

Eddie accepted the drink. He even managed to open it and slurp some of it down but he kept staring back through into the lounge as he did so, seemingly mesmerised.

'What's wrong with you?' laughed Nerys as she put the kettle on. 'There's someone for everyone, you know.'

'I just thought he would have needed my help,' explained Eddie. 'If it ever happened at all.'

'Don't be so arrogant,' Nerys whined. 'You haven't got the keys to the entire female species.'

Eddie winced at her, his trance broken. 'What are you talking about?'

'Troy has pulled,' she said. 'All by himself. I think it's sweet.'

Eddie glared back into the living room. 'She's quite fit. Do you think she's a prozzy?'

'Helping him out with his coursework?' she ridiculed.

'Maybe it's some strange new backstreet service for students? Essay and a hand job?' Eddie scratched his chin, ponderingly.

'That's ridiculous,' she shook her head. 'Besides, Troy hasn't got any money.' She turned to look at Eddie but he had lurched back into the lounge, his curiosity bettering him.

'Wotcha,' he said to the girl, plonking himself in his chair opposite her. 'I'm Eddie.'

'Cass,' she replied, glancing up at him for a split second. 'I'm not a prostitute.'

'What?' Eddie coughed.

'I could hear you in the kitchen. You were wondering if I was a prozzy, as you put it.' Cass carried on reading and writing as she talked.

'Oh,' said Eddie. 'What are you then?'

'I'm Troy's study buddy,' she explained.

'Is that what they're calling it these days?' Eddie guffawed dementedly. He was alone in his amusement, however. 'You didn't tell me you had a bird, Troy?'

Troy looked up at him. 'Leave it out, Eddie, you heard what she just said.'

Eddie sat and puffed and bothered them no more. He then looked around with sudden awareness. 'Somebody's tidied up!'

*

'So, have you nobbed her yet?' quizzed Eddie as soon as they got into the car.

'Who?' replied Troy, wrestling with his seat belt.

'Forget it, it's fucked,' said Eddie. 'Just pretend.'

Troy held the seat belt across himself.

Eddie ignited the engine. 'That weird stuck-up chinky chick. Have you nobbed her?' The mini shuddered into action and shot off into the night like an eager puppy waking from a deep slumber.

'It's not like that,' explained Troy. 'She's a study buddy.'

'What kind of gayness is that?' Eddie propelled the tiny automobile along, while fiddling with the radio and lighting a fag. 'Get it nobbed.'

'She's helping me with my research methodology. I'm not interested in … you know.' Troy was pale with terror. He hated Eddie's contraption and the way he drove it. It was like pelting around in a tiny coffin. He looked out of the window at other vehicles and all he could see was their wheels.

'Do me a favour,' snorted Eddie. 'Are you telling me if that bird got her kit off and got into your bed, you wouldn't do the nasty?'

Troy was silent for a few moments as they sprang through a red light and narrowly avoided being pancaked by a juggernaut. 'I don't know,' he muttered when his heart had started beating again.

'What do you mean you don't know?' exclaimed Eddie, seemingly unfazed by the close encounter. 'I know that I've got the copyright on scoring chicks at our place but when provided with the opportunity, I expect you and Paul to be hot-blooded beasts, just like me.'

'It doesn't happen very often,' said Troy, lighting up a cigarette of his own.

'Define often.'

'As in never.' Troy sank bank in his chair and exhaled the smoke with relief.

Eddie laughed like a gasket had blown. 'You're a virgin!'

Troy didn't share the joke. He just smoked and clutched his seat belt, as calmly as he could manage. 'She's not a chinky anyway, nor is she stuck-up.'

'Weird though,' said Eddie, accelerating round a blind corner. 'You must fancy her. I think she's a bit of alright; in an odd sort of way.'

'I only met her yesterday,' added Troy. 'Haven't had time to think about sex yet. I'm not like you. Besides, she's sorting me out with my work and that's more important.'

'Nothing is more important than sex,' stated Eddie.

'Bollocks!' snapped Troy. 'Me passing this semester is extremely important. Otherwise, they'll send me back to the Valleys and I'm not going back there. No, sir! Not for anybody! No girls back there, just sheep.'

'You've got a point,' Eddie eventually nodded in agreement. 'Get the work done but if the opportunity presents itself, I'd be up there like a rat up a drain pipe.'

Eddie drove them into the Final Frontier; the rough estate. They both grew silent while they passed the run-down tenements and their run-down residents.

'How do I know?' asked Troy.

'What?'

'How do I know when the opportunity presents itself?'

'Ah, so you are interested!' Eddie purred with satisfaction.

'Just cogitating,' explained Troy.

'Well, it'll be some sort of signal, you know, the look in her eyes, something she says.'

'Like what?'

'Like "I'm cold."'

Troy grimaced. 'Doesn't that mean that she's just cold?'

Eddie chuckled. 'Women are more cagey than that. They hardly ever say what they mean. You've got to look out for the sign: The Green Light as I like to call it. Trust me.'

'And then what?'

'Fuck her.'

'Just like that?'

'Yeah, just jump on her and get stuck in.'

Troy became quiet again.

Eddie glanced at him and grinned. 'Stick with your old pal Eddie and you'll be alright!' He drew to a halt and slapped Troy on the knee.

They glared outside at their destination. There was a bunch of big men stood outside a dilapidated house. In the badly lit street they were merely gigantic silhouettes.

'Looks like all the boys are here,' observed Eddie.

'I'll stay here,' volunteered Troy.

They sat and peered around for a bit.

'I still don't think she's interested in me that sort of way,' mumbled Troy.

'Bullshit,' said Eddie. 'All bitches want the cock. They just pretend they don't. He opened his door to get out.

Troy tried to lock his.

'That doesn't work anymore either,' explained Eddie. 'Just sit tight. I won't be long. You might find something that you need in the glove compartment.' He slammed the door behind him.

Troy was left alone in the gloom. It wasn't long before boredom got the better of him. He opened the glove compartment. Inside was a packet of condoms and a gun. Troy was not sure which item Eddie was referring to. He plumbed for the jonnies.

*

'So this is the inner sanctum of Troy Botting?' said Cass, looking around.

'Well, it's the spare room,' explained Troy. 'I kip down here.' He gestured to a sleeping bag and a stained cushion on the floor.

Cass became interested in the formations on the wall. 'What the heck is this stuff?' She reached out to examine them, tentatively.

'I'm not sure,' he replied. 'I think that one's yoghurt and that one's milk shake ... maybe.'

She turned to him. 'A cultivation experiment?'

He shrugged his shoulders. 'Sure.'

They stood in silence and malingered for a few awkward moments.

'Shall we go back downstairs and get on with the assignment?' she asked.

There was a weird glint in Troy's eyes. 'I thought we might relax for a bit.'

She giggled nervously.

Troy got down on his makeshift bed and stretched out with a fake yawn. 'It's been all work and no play.'

'That's because you've got the best part of a semester to catch up on.' She stopped giggling and crossed her arms.

'Why don't you come down here and chill out?' He looked up at her and patted the space next to him.

She snorted. 'Are you trying to seduce me, Mr Botting?'

'Maybe,' he chuckled with just a hint of terror.

She knelt down and gave him a stern look. 'The assignment has got to be handed in tomorrow, Troy, we haven't got time for this.'

He seized hold of her suddenly and dragged her close.

'Troy! No!' she squealed.

'Come here!' he growled and slobbered like a starving wolf.

Cass was slightly bigger and stronger. She pushed herself away and slapped him.

Troy went limp and stared into space, tears forming in his eyes.

She was panting with shock. 'I'm sorry,' she said.

'I am too,' his voice trembled.

'I don't feel that way,' she explained.

'Then why are you here?' He sat up but he could not look at her.

'To help you with your work,' she explained.

Troy shook his head slowly. 'I don't understand. Eddie said ...'

Cass snapped before he had time to say it. 'You listen to that Neanderthal?'

'I love you,' stated Troy with feeling but he could still not meet her gaze.

'You don't know me!' she cried.

'It's always the same,' he grumbled and sobbed. An enormous tear escaped down his cheek.

Cass softened and put a hand on his arm. 'Listen, Troy, I really like you, just not in that particular way. You're kind and you're funny and you're intelligent ...'

'You just want to be friends?' he ventured.

'Yes,' she said.

'It's always the same flaming story,' he groaned and more tears of despair fell. 'I've got loads of friends! It's a blow job I want!'

She stood up and backed away. 'I'd better go. I'm sorry for giving you the wrong impression.'

Troy stayed motionless and wept.

Despite her words, Cass did not leave. She watched him for a while. 'You'll get that assignment finished, won't you?'

Troy flared up in anger and glared at her. 'Yeah! 'Cos I really feel like doing that now, don't I?'

She opened her mouth to respond but nothing came out.

'Why the hell do you care so much anyway?' he barked.

'I don't know what you mean,' she murmured.

'You've been haunting me for weeks,' challenged Troy. 'Pestering me to do my work like you're my mum or something! It's flaming weird!'

Cass sighed deeply a few times and crinkled up her handsome face like she was in torment. 'Okay, I'll tell you what's going on. I'm not supposed to but I'm running out of options.'

Troy looked at her, his emotions dwindling. 'What are you talking about?'

Cass found a chair to sit on and composed herself. She engaged him with her stern amber-coloured eyes. 'I'm from the future. I was sent back in a time machine to persuade you to finish your studies. In just over thirty years' time, ninety percent of the human race is wiped out by a killer virus. A cure is eventually found and it is based on the innovative thinking of a biology student who never graduated. A student that wasn't listened to when he should have been. A student from Wales at the end of the twentieth century. A student called Troy Botting.'

'I see,' said Troy.

*

'Prisoner Cell Block H!' exclaimed Eddie, plonking himself down in his favourite armchair, opening a can of lager and lighting a spliff, all in one movement. 'Amazing!'

Paul looked up from his book with disgruntlement. 'I don't know why you watch this crap. It's enough to make me leave the room.'

'A good enough reason in itself,' grunted Eddie.

Paul left the room.

Butch Australian women in dungarees filled the television screen. Eddie watched them with barely restrained delight. His other housemate could not share his enjoyment either. Troy was on the sofa, brooding like only a lonely Welshman can. Eddie glanced at him. 'You not drinking, taffy?'

'No,' said Troy.

'It's Prisoner Cell Block H night,' Eddie proclaimed. 'We always have a bevvy on Prisoner Cell Block H night.'

'I'm not in the mood,' whimpered Troy.

'Bea's decided they're gonna riot,' said Eddie, ignoring him. He watched the female prisoners negotiate the hastily assembled script and shaky cardboard set for a while but continued to flick concerned looks over at the furball of misery on the sofa. 'It's that bird, isn't it?' he asked when the adverts came on. 'What's her name? Cassandra?'

Troy did not answer. He just twitched slightly at the mention of her name.

Eddie nodded. 'I thought I hadn't seen her round here for a while. What's happened?'

Troy remained silent.

'Come on,' he coaxed. 'Tell your uncle Eddie all about it.'

'It's nothing,' Troy muttered. 'Just turns out she's from the future, that's all.'

'She's what?' Eddie coughed.

'She's from the flaming future!' barked Troy.

'Easy now,' said Eddie. 'What future?'

'Our future, you idiot!'

Eddie's monobrow shot up to the top of his forehead in surprise and hovered there for a moment like a caterpillar caught in an updraft. 'Calm down, little man, I've never seen you like this before! You're super pissed off, aren't you? She's told you this guff has she?'

'Aye,' grumbled Troy.

'What she doing here then?' scoffed Eddie. 'Of all the places in the world you could go if you had a time machine! You could go and hang out with Cleopatra on the banks of the Nile. You could go to Woodstock and take the brown acid. Hunt a T-Rex. You could go and see shagging Jesus for Christ's sake! Why the shitting hell would you pick this dump in this time?'

'Because it turns out that I'm the saviour of the human race,' explained Troy. 'One that's lacking a little motivation.'

'I've heard some excuses for not getting their knickers off before but that's a new one on me' Eddie shook his head in disbelief. 'You can pick 'em you can!'

Troy grimaced at him. 'What do you mean I can pick 'em? This is the first girl I've ever been involved with.'

'I knew she was bonkers that one,' Eddie mused.

'Thing is: I sort of believe her,' exhaled Troy.

Eddie tore his gaze away from the telly, even though the riot in Cell Block H had begun in earnest. 'Oh, come on! Surely you're not going to buy that? Chick's a fantasist, that's all. She's probably just some Daddy's little rich girl from somewhere weird who's taken too many drugs and developed a fixation with that film ... whatsit ... The Terminator.'

'She said it with so much conviction.' Troy shrugged his shoulders. 'And she looks so strange, like someone ...' Words failed him.

Eddie puffed out a big cloud of smoke. 'Like someone from the future?'

'Aye,' Troy nodded. 'I had a funny feeling about her, right from the start.'

'So did I,' admitted Eddie. 'It's got to be a load of old twaddle though.'

'Has it?'

'Well; as if you could save the human race,' he chuckled. 'You can't even wash your own socks!'

Troy thought about it and then laughed too. 'Aye, you're right.'

'That's better!' Eddie proclaimed. 'Now go and get yourself a cider and I'll take you up to the nursing college at the weekend and get you a new bird. After I've made my deliveries. Those girls don't get much spare time and they're mad for cock. It's a fucking fanny gold mine!'

Troy got up and ambled towards the kitchen with renewed eagerness.

'Get me a fresh one while you're at it,' requested Eddie.

'I'll just forget about her,' Troy stated, even though, deep down, he knew he could not.

*

He walked home, adjusting his coat collar and quickening his pace as the wind and rain found strength. Troy felt the chill on his unwell toe through the hole in his shoe. The cold grey streets around him were obstinately normal. A full day of investigation had not yielded any fresh revelation. He had visited the university where both he and Cassandra studied. He sweet talked the lady in Administration as much as possible but she was a tiny officious mouse of a woman who clearly lived for regulation and procedure. The snippets of information that escaped from her tight thin lips were just things that Troy already knew: Cass was a biology student. She was in her first year. She lived in private accommodation. That was it. No science fiction. The bursar was forbidden to divulge personal data and obviously liked it that way. He waited outside her office for nearly an hour until the bureaucrat left and then he snuck in and tried to look in her filing cabinet and desk but everything was safely locked. He did find a packet of Strongmints in her desk-tidy which he pilfered. Not exactly James Bond but at least the wait had not been completely in vain.

 Troy then went to Cass' house. He had walked her home a couple of times and even though he had never been invited inside, he remembered where it was. He peered in through the windows and startled a frumpy girl in a dressing gown. She came racing outside and asked him sharply what he wanted. Troy knew that she was a fellow student because it was mid-afternoon and she was still in her pyjamas. She told him that Cass did live there but she had not seen her for a couple of days. Again, Troy's meagre charm failed him and it was like pulling teeth. The girl just sneered at him and mumbled something about it being cold then shut the door in his face. Troy crept around to the backyard after she had disappeared but there was no sign of a time machine; just some washing hung out to dry on a line and a few potted plants. Troy swiped a pair of knickers, determined once more that his time should not be wasted.

 His final port of call was the park where, he hoped, he would find his target and ask her some stern questions. Troy knew that Cass liked to go there. She enjoyed feeding the birds and the squirrels and watching the children play. Troy concluded that in Cass' disease-ravaged future, perhaps such simple pleasures did not exist then he reminded himself that he and Eddie had decided that she was a mentalist. He mooched around among the trees for a while but there was no pale oriental princess to be seen, hardly any humans at all infact. It was too cold for anyone, including him. None the wiser, Troy headed home with his hands in his pockets.

'Eddie, you in?' he called out but the house was quiet. He kept on his coat and went through to the kitchen to put the kettle on. He managed to make himself a cup of tea, two slices of toast and roll a fag before he heard a thump from upstairs. Troy peered up at the ceiling as if willing it to become transparent. He knew that Paul was at work and concluded that Eddie was having a late rise. He munched on the toast and slurped the tea and there were more peculiar noises from upstairs. It was the thumping noise again it became more frequent and rhythmic and it was accompanied by vague cries and groans. Still in an inquisitive frame of mind, Troy took his refreshments slowly up the stairs. On the landing at the top, Eddie's bedroom door swung open suddenly and the girl he had been looking for strode out. She was naked and coated in sweat. Cass hurried straight through into the bathroom and was gone in an instant, seemingly unaware of Troy's presence. He dropped his toast and his tea and his jaw. Eddie emerged, also wet and nude. He was in less haste, however, and noticed the flabbergasted Welshman.

'Alright, mate?' he asked.

'You bastard!' Troy found himself saying and he sprang away down the stairs, not wanting Eddie to see him crying. He charged back out into the street. He did not care who saw his tears, as long as it was not him. He scampered down the road and it was the first time Troy had run in years. His chest heaved with the unfamiliar toil and his legs transmogrified into rubber but it was a while before he stopped.

*

'Troy? Is that you, mucka?' Eddie peered at a vague shape down the alley but it was so dark and obscure that he could not even tell if he was talking to anyone.

After two seconds of silence, however, came the reply. 'How did you find me?'

Eddie breathed a sigh of relief. 'Well, I figured you couldn't have got far.' He took a few steps into the gloom. 'Perhaps as far as your favourite gimmel.'

'How did you know this was my favourite?'

'Cass told me,' said Eddie. 'She said there was a posh one with a bench in the middle and that you'd spent the night here a couple of times. She decided not to come. I think she's a bit embarrassed.'

'I'm the one who's embarrassed,' grumbled Troy.

Eddie had to walk all the way to Troy to actually see him. It was almost pitch black in the centre of the passage. 'Don't be, mate, it's no big deal.'

'I spent all day looking for her and all the while she was at my house ... with you,' Troy's voice was different, he sounded floaty and vague, traumatised even.

Eddie cringed. 'Sorry, mate. She actually came round looking for you. I invited her in and made her a brew and she said she was lonely so one thing led to another.'

Troy snarled like a mad dog at him. 'One thing led to another? How does a cup of tea lead to a penis-in-vagina?'

Eddie recoiled slightly. Troy's uncommon aggression and plain talk was unnerving and it wasn't helped by the fact that Eddie could barely see him. He shrugged his shoulders. 'I don't know. Women just wanna do it with me.'

Troy did not comment on this or at least not one that was audible. He just gave a sort of quiet whimper.

'Birds these days say they want a man who's sensitive and in touch with his feelings and shit,' Eddie explained. 'They're just kidding themselves. It's a bloke like me they really yearn for, you know, the Alpha Male. All muscle and bad attitude. It's just the way things are. It's the law of nature.' Troy remained silent so Eddie went on. 'I'm a drug dealer. They like the danger.'

'So you've just come to tell me this, have you?' Troy snorted.

'I've come to take you home, you retard,' Eddie attempted a chuckle. 'You can't stay out here on a night like this, you'll catch your death.'

'Maybe I don't wanna live,' he sniffled.

'Don't talk shit,' said Eddie.

'I might go back to Wales.'

'Now *you are* talking bollocks.'

'Why can't I have sex? Just once?'

'You're not going to increase your chances by killing yourself or moving back home are you?'

Troy puffed, silenced by his friend's logic.

'Come home, mate,' Eddie pleaded. 'Paul said the other night he's moving out. It'll just be me and you soon. No toffee-nosed arse-wipe from Dorset busting our balls day and night: Just Eddie Ball and the Bottster. Me and you, kid! It'll be party central. We'll prey on fresher girls forever more!'

Troy did not say anything. He froze and Eddie wondered if he was talking to himself again for a moment. 'Come on, Troy boy!'

'Alright,' he grumbled and rose to his feet. 'Give me a fag, will you?'

Eddie laughed with joy and pulled out some cigarettes. He lit one up and gave it to him.

Troy took a couple of pulls. 'I can't go back if she's still there though. I don't want to see her ever again.'

'Don't worry,' Eddie put an arm round him and escorted him out of the shadows. 'I told her to sling her hook. Now what do you say we go and have a celebratory pint?'

'I've been crying,' sniffed Troy.

'You big gaylord!' laughed Eddie. 'Come on, the first round is on me.'

They reached the mini in the light of the street.

Eddie looked at him before he got in and chuckled again. 'Saviour of the human race!'

Troy shared the humour. 'Aye, ridiculous!'

The Angel of Fogwin

He woke up inside a metal pipe. He squinted at a sallow light as it flooded in. He closed his eyes again. He wanted to go back to sleep. He felt warm and safe in the metallic gloom. His mouth burnt and his head was sore and he was not in the mood for daylight. It was the wetness on his face that would not let him rest. He lifted his head out of the damp and peered at his reflection in the oily steel. An abused doppelganger gawked back at him. The impostor was pale and his eye sockets were black. More puzzlingly he was wearing an object he had never seen before in his life; a shiny blue tie. He chanced to glance down and saw that the rest of his clothes were ripped and filthy. His skin was bruised underneath. One of his shoes and the sock that was meant to be inside it were both missing, leaving a grubby naked foot that he could barely feel. The shiny blue tie, in curious comparison, was immaculate. *Not again*, thought Ray Weaver.

Coiled up in his arms like a baby was an object wrapped in a stained cloth.

'Oh, shit,' he gasped, remembering what it was. He wished it was a nightmare but he would not have that luxury. The demons of his sleep and his reality were one and the same.

His heart leapt a second time as something stirred in the light outside. Instinctively, he held the bundle tighter to his chest.

'Somebody there?' his parched throat voiced inadequately.

By way of response, the head of a monster appeared, blocking out the light. Its face was an ocean of fur and teeth.

'Fuck off!' squealed Ray, wriggling down the pipe away from the inquiring terror.

The thing regarded him with cold green eyes, It licked its slobbering jowls with anticipation.

'What do you want? I'm sleeping in here!' snivelled Ray as the thing tried to get inside the pipe. Ray kicked at it violently. It hesitated and withdrew, sniffing around at something outside instead.

Ray lay there for a few moments. He peered deeper into the pipe and contemplated a course of action. A distant mechanical rumpus erupted from the blackness as he did so. He mused on how long it would be before the tube displayed its true purpose. He decided that a voluntary exit might be preferable, monster or no monster. He wormed his way along and stared out into the dawn. The creature was still there but Ray could now see that it was a fox and not a monster. It was the biggest and nastiest looking specimen he had ever seen. Its flank was scarred and matted. It looked like the veteran and victor of a thousand fights, but just a fox.

'Alright, mate?' Ray greeted the beast with more congeniality.

The fox shuddered and panted at him indifferently as it sprayed some piss into the wind.

Ray scrambled out of the pipe and peered around. Vapours of mist swirled around pools of stagnant water and battalions of bulrushes. Scrawny crows called out from the twisted branches of skeletal trees. His bare foot sank into the icy sponge-like earth and his teeth started to chatter. It felt like Armageddon. It was warm in the pipe and he pined for its metallic embrace. He turned and saw that it fed back to a concrete railway bridge; a storm drain he guessed. There were no humans in sight and Ray wondered where he was and how far from civilisation he had ended up this time. His attention shifted back to his new friend. It trotted over to him, its business done.

'Yeah?' asked Ray.

With an unexpected speed that betrayed its bulk, the fox leapt up, snatched the cloth bundle from Ray's hands and sprang away, its weight nearly toppling him over in the process.

'Oi! That's mine!' protested Ray, righting himself. 'You can't eat that, you burk!'

The fox wagged what was left of its tail and looked at him, clutching the bundle between its wet jaws.

'Give it here you cheeky cunt!' Ray made a futile lunge to reclaim his possession but the creature leapt out of the way playfully, like a pup.

'I'm serious! Give it here!' Ray sprang after the fox again. It bounded away into the mist. He tried to give chase but it trod solid ground and Ray was not so fortunate. He took a few strides and sank up to his knees in a bath of chilly filth. He cried out to the heavens. The crows screeched with him and flapped away in alarm. There seemed to be thousands of them and they were soon gone; black specks squawking away into infinite white.

'Fanfuckintastic!' He wallowed through the soup to the other side. Breathless, he seized a diseased sapling and hauled himself out.

'Great! I'm gonna get killed by a bleeding fox!'

Ray rambled on, taking more care in between violent shivers. It was not long before he saw the lithe silhouette of his tormentor in the mist ahead. Ray stopped and stared at it for a moment, expecting it to scarper again but the creature seemed to be in distress. It had unwrapped Ray's package and was stood staring at its content. It whined horribly and its hackles were up.

'Not so keen now are you?' laughed Ray.

The fox looked up at him and said 'you bloody owe me one for this, Weaver!'

It then ran off.

It never became clear to Ray why the fox had chosen those particular words. In times to come, he liked to think that the animal had not spoken to him at all and that it was actually a hallucination brought on by trauma.

Ray examined his package; there was some bite marks where the fox had ventured a nibble. He wrapped it up again and soon found a discarded plastic bag nearby to cover his naked foot too. Things were looking up. He climbed the embankment onto the railway bridge with the thing under his arm. The exertion warmed him up a bit. He followed the tracks all the way to a place that turned out to be Norwich. He had many lonely miles to piece together the last few days.

*

There was a general feeling of optimism in 1980. The new government were spearheading England's rise to economic enormity and that meant Thatcher turning the working class into Tories. There was a feelgood buzz though. It was not just a new year but a new decade. Everything seemed to become colourful all of a sudden; people's clothes, their hair, their cars, their TVs, their houses. I remember the 70s in sepia. I tried to share the hopefulness. After all, why not? I was living in a nice little town with a beautiful wife and two loving kids and writing cute parochial stories for the local rag. Apart from my tiny hiccup the year before, existence was sweet. So why were my instincts telling me that all was not well?

Excerpt from the journal of Ray Weaver, volume one.

*

'What do you think?' asked Archie Deakin, the editor of the Fogwin Enquirer.

His two reporters, Mark Lyons and Ray Weaver, stared at the large framed photograph of Margaret Thatcher that he had just hung on the office wall. Despite their notorious skill as wordsmiths, they could find nothing to say.

Archie turned round and glared at them. 'Well?'

'It's ... nice,' offered Mark.

'Nice?' Is that the sort of response I pay you for, Lyons? Didn't they tell you to stop using the word "nice" when you got to fucking junior school?' Archie was disgusted.

Mark hung his head in shame.

'It has a certain majesty,' observed Ray.

Archie beamed with delight. 'A certain majesty! Thank you, Weaver.'

Mark flicked Ray a look of jealous contempt.

Ray stuck his tongue out at him.

Archie turned back to appreciate the portrait of his beloved Prime Minister. 'Exciting times, my boys, exciting times!'

'What have you got for us, Archie?' queried Ray in an attempt to entice his boss away from the witch on the wall.

Archie turned and looked at them with glazed eyes. It was a few moments before he joined them on planet Earth. 'Oh!' he cried and grabbed a piece of paper from his desk. 'Local resident has received a postcard that's thirty-seven years late.'

'We live in exciting times indeed,' snorted Ray, sarcastically.

Archie's moustache prickled fiercely at him. Ray had noticed recently a vein popping up on his editor's forehead when he got angry. He could not decide which was more disturbing; the hairy upper lip or the bursting blood vessel. 'This is a quiet town, Weaver. What do you expect? UFOs or something?'

Ray coughed apologetically.

'What about the Earthcom opening?' suggested Mark.

'What's that when it's at home?' growled Archie.

'The new industrial estate. There's some kind of official opening this afternoon. Lucy Springer is cutting the ribbon!' he panted.

'Lucy Springer? The Page 3 model?' Ray's journalistic zeal became aroused all of a sudden.

'Yeah!' smirked Mark, feeling some invisible tits with glee. 'Turns out her Uncle is some bigwig at this new estate. She usually does national papers. This is a chance to get her in our little rag!'

'Very well,' decided Archie. 'You get your arse up there, Lyons, take the photographer with you if there's going to be a pretty girl.'

'Aye aye, Captain!' responded Mark, thrusting his pelvis like some depraved ape.

'Hold on a minute! Hold on a minute!' Ray put his hands on his hips in protest. 'How come Mark gets Lucy Springer and I get Royal Mail delivery problems?'

Archie snarled. 'This isn't a fucking pick and choose, Weaver. This is a small town newspaper. We have to cover all aspects of life in a pond.'

'Well, why don't me and Mark both go up to Earthcom?' Ray shrugged. 'It's a big place, it'll be a busy afternoon. One reporter might miss something. Two reporters and you've got it covered.'

'I don't think any man can miss those knockers!' cackled his rival, fondling unseen delights again.

Archie groaned. 'Since when have I sent two reporters to get one story?'

'A postcard turning up late!' pleaded Ray. 'That barely even constitutes news!'

'This isn't a fucking democracy!' Archie's moustache dripped with froth and his vein throbbed. 'I'm the editor and I'm telling you to go and investigate! If it isn't a story, then you fucking turn it into one, that's what I pay you for!'

Ray sneered. 'So the most exciting thing that's happening in Fogwin all year: Lucy Springer comes to town and you're sending the bloke whose best description of Maggie Thatcher is "nice"?'

'Piss off!' said Mark.

'What will we get on the front page this week?' scoffed Ray. 'It was a *nice* opening. The new industrial estate is *nice*. Lucy Springer's knockers are *nice*.'

Mark was glaring at him, his face all red and puffy.

'Then I need my best man on the most boring story then, don't I?' reasoned Archie.

'I cack better stories than Ray!' proclaimed Mark with a melodramatic shriek.

'Only when you use your special crayons,' giggled Ray.

'I don't use crayons! Tell him, Archie!'

'Mark writes with crayons!' mocked Ray.

Mark's temper snapped and they started scuffling.

'Stop it! Oi!' yelled Archie as his two reporters pushed and kicked each other.

'Stop it!'

The two reporters ceased fighting.

Ray put his hands in his pockets and sulked for a bit.

Mark teased him by continuing to hump an imaginary Page 3 girl.

'Alright, alright,' grumbled Archie, his face now purple with fury. 'Why don't you flip a coin? The winner gets to pick his story?'

'That's not fair!' grumbled Mark. 'Earthcom was my idea!'

'I knew about it as well,' retorted Ray. 'You just said it before I did.'

'Flip a fucking coin!' bawled Archie. The colour drained out of the editor's face with remarkable suddenness and he dropped to his seat, gripping his chest with pain.

Ray and Mark both bolted over to him like grandchildren attending an elderly grandfather.

'Blimey, Archie! You need to calm down, old son,' said Ray.

The writers waited while Archie took a few deep breaths and flushed some colour back into his cheeks.

Ray put a hand on Archie's shoulder and turned to Mark.

'You know what? You go to the Earthcom opening. I don't give a toss.'

Mark stared back at him with disbelief for a second, as if suspecting a trick but when it dawned on him that Ray was serious he jumped up and down and punched the air with rapturous victory. 'Lucy Springer, here I come!' He ran to his desk and grabbed his jacket. 'See you! Wouldn't wanna be you!' Mark was out of the door like the place was on fire.

'Have a *nice* day, Mark!' Ray shouted after him. He sighed and busied himself with making Archie a coffee.

'You're a better writer than Lyons,' mumbled the editor. 'Let the moron do the moron's work.'

'I better go and have a look at this postcard then,' said Ray when he had made the drink. 'If you've finished having a heart attack, that is.'

Archie nodded. 'There's just one more thing.'

Ray put on his jacket and looked at him.

'You've got to wear a tie.'

'What?'

Archie shrugged his shoulders. 'The chap specified that you should wear a tie.'

'What for?'

'I don't know.'

'I haven't got a tie.'

Archie pulled open a draw and, from a bewildering myriad of objects, yanked out a shiny blue one.

*

A friend once described me as a "freak magnet." I'd never thought about it before but looking back on things, he was right. I've been all over the globe and every prize winning fruitcake in the entire world has latched onto me at some point.

Excerpt from the journal of Ray Weaver, volume six.

*

Ray checked the address again. The house looked normal enough. It was a smart bungalow in the quiet end of town. Fogwin was a serene place in general and its elderly residents were gifted with a part that was so peaceful that it could only be beaten by the grave itself. It was a cold January morning but the sun was bright and Ray took a moment to compose himself. The glossy red door opened before he was ready and Ray did not notice the little old man stepping out to scrutinise him.

'Can I help you?' The tone was firm but not unfriendly.

Ray cocked an eyebrow at the gent who was as smart as his bungalow. He sported a shirt and tie beneath his tweed blazer which was adorned with a folded handkerchief in the breast pocket. He wore matching slacks and slippers with gold tassels. What was left of his greying hair was combed over neatly. Like some Bond villain, his arms cradled a slumbering white cat.

'Oh! Erm … I'm from the Enquirer … Ray Weaver. I was just admiring your bungalow, Mr … erm … Stanley?' Ray checked his notes.

'Call me Peter.' The man beamed. 'Have you come to see my postcard?'

'You bet'cha,' said Ray.

'Would you like some tea?' Peter stroked his cat.

'That sounds wonderful, Pete.' Ray strolled up the flagstone path and followed him inside.

'I very much like your tie, Ray,' stated Peter, turning to admire it in the hallway.

'Erm … yeah, thanks,' said Ray, feeling a bit self-conscious as the old gent leered at his neck decoration. He closed the front door behind him and was at once assaulted by the odour of the interior; a potent blend of whisky, pipe tobacco and furniture polish.

'Come through,' instructed Peter when he had gotten over the tie. He proceeded into a small adjacent kitchen. Putting the cat down on the table, he filled the kettle and lit a hob.

'Cosy,' remarked Ray as he came in and sat down. He gazed around while his host made the tea. It seemed ordinary enough; net curtains over the windows, resplendent china on the shelves, brass rubbings hanging on the walls, today's newspapers and a pools coupon on the breakfast bar, stuffed cat on the table ... whoa!

'This moggy's fucking dead!' Ray nearly leapt backwards out of his seat and through the wall.

The old man turned round calmly and smiled. 'Tibbles has been "dead", as you say, for over a year.'

'Tibbles?' choked Ray, staring into the thing's glass eyes.

'I can't bear to be parted with him ... sugar?'

'One please,' replied Ray breathlessly and eased himself back into the chair, confronting the piece of taxidermy like it was a live cobra.

Peter stirred his visitor's cup and passed it to him with shaky hands. 'Are you a married man, Ray?'

Ray took it and noted the moat of tea in the saucer. 'Yeah, with two nippers. Yourself?'

'Not anymore,' answered Peter. 'Passed on into the next world many moons ago, I'm afraid.' He gazed at a framed photograph on the wall. Ray followed his look. It was Peter and a woman who was presumably his wife sat on a beach somewhere, looking happy.

'Sorry to hear that. Hope you didn't have her stuffed as well, Pete!' Ray chuckled, spilling even more of his drink. After tasting it, he thought it just as well; the brew was weak and strangely salty.

Peter did not share the joke. He just frowned at Ray and scratched his balding pate.

'Got any biscuits?' quizzed Ray, wiping a stray tear from his cheek.

'Do newspaper reporters like biscuits?' asked Peter, seeming a little surprised.

'They love biscuits,' explained Ray.

'Gypsy creams?'

'Especially gypsy creams.'

Peter opened a cupboard and dragged out a packet. He fumbled with it for a while and it snapped open suddenly so most of the biscuits fell on to the floor.

'Damn you, Tibbles!' Peter barked loudly, his serene and polite manner suddenly replaced by one of biblical wrath. 'He always makes me do that!'

Ray fidgeted uncomfortably and looked around for exits. 'Never mind, mate.'

Peter began furiously to scoop up the biscuit massacre with a dustpan and brush.

'So, this postcard?' requested Ray, taking the opportunity to tip some of his tea into a potted plant while his host was distracted.

Peter turned and glared at the stuffed feline for a moment. 'It's not funny, you little queerlord!' He rounded to Ray and softened. 'Just there.' He pointed to a rack of documents on the table.

Ray saw the scruffy postcard poking out of the rack straight away. He examined it. It had grown brown and yellow with age but the writing was still legible. 'Eighth of September nineteen forty-three? Wasn't that the War?'

'Indeed,' said Peter. 'My friend George sent it to me from Naples. We Brits liberated it from the Nazis, you know.'

'So it is addressed to you. You've lived here all this time, Pete?'

'Yes, Lord knows where's it's been all of these years.'

'Have you spoken to Royal Mail?'

'I had a word with the postman but he didn't know anything. He just charged me extra money for the delivery.

Ray coughed. 'Better late than never I suppose. Where's your mate now?'

'George? He died a few months later at the battle of Monte Cassino, poor fellow. Such a nice man. Never wanted to hurt so much as a fly. He wanted to be a painter.' Peter shovelled the broken biscuits into a bin and sat down, teary eyed. 'His last words to me on a postcard and I've had to wait nearly four decades to read them! I should have some sort of official apology! Some compensation!'

Ray could see Peter's gorge rising again. He reached out and put a sympathetic hand on his shoulder. 'Don't upset yourself, old timer, like I said; better late than never.'

Peter peered at him. 'Are you religious, Ray?'

'My wife is.'

'Yes, but are you? Do you believe in the Father, the Son and the Holy Spirit? The transference of the soul to a higher place?'

Ray shifted uncomfortably again and shrugged. 'Got to believe in something I suppose.'

'We found an angel, you see.'

'What?'

'George and I. We found an angel. Right here in little old Fogwin. I'd forgotten all about it until the other day when the postcard arrived. I feel that I should tell someone. I might not be here much longer.'

Ray drew out his notebook and tucked the postcard inside. 'Alright if I hold onto this for a bit?'

Peter nodded. 'Are you listening to me?'

Ray sighed. 'Look, Pete, I came here to talk about the postcard. I feel a bit funny about this ... spiritual guff.'

'Suit yourself,' grumbled the old man. He stood up and busied himself with clearing the tea things away. 'I was just trying to offer you something more interesting.'

Ray rolled his eyes with annoyance. 'Come on then, you found an angel? What did it look like? How big were its wings? Describe it to me.'

'I can do better than that,' said Peter, beaming. 'I can show it to you!'

*

Ray looked down at the tiny unmarked grave. 'This it?'

'Well, we had to bury it somewhere and where else but the churchyard?' explained Peter.

'Not a very big angel then?'

'No. It was very small.'

Ray sniffed. 'So I can't actually see it?'

'Not unless we dig it up,' suggested Peter, glancing at Ray with a maniacal glint in his eyes. 'I'd very much like to look upon it again. It was a beautiful thing.'

'I don't think that's allowed, Pete.' Ray scanned the churchyard, self-consciously. The place was empty except for another old man who seemed to have a hunchback. He was cutting grass with some clippers and he was so far away, Ray could not be sure. He did keep popping his head up and staring over at them. Ray could hear his clippers stop every time he did so. He felt some concern about being seen with a man carrying a stuffed cat. Peter had insisted on bringing the morbid artefact with him. 'So it died then? This angel?'

'After two days, yes,' explained Peter. 'It was very poorly when we found it.'

'Whereabouts exactly?'

'Out in the fields,' Peter pointed away in a vague direction. 'Where the new estate is.'

'Earthcom?'

'Yes. That used to be all fields at one time, you know. We tried to care for it as best as we could while we wondered who to tell. We kept it in my garage and George tried to feed it on bread and honey and milk but I honestly think that it didn't eat. We never got to make a decision. It passed away one morning. We brought it here. The priest at the time helped us to lay it to rest.' Peter's eyes were moist again. 'War broke out a few weeks later and I never saw George or the Priest again. Both went away.'

'I notice that you use the word 'it'? Was it a bloke or a bird, this angel?'

Peter shook his head. 'Neither I don't think, it didn't seem to be either.'

'Androgynous?'

'Pardon?'

'No sex.'

'It had a little suit on so we couldn't see if it had a winky or a woo woo.'

'Eh?'

'Yes.'

Ray scratched his head and wondered what to write down.

'It's not the same these days,' Peter twittered on. 'People think they've got it hard. Two hours it used to take me to walk to work and two hours more in the evening to get back. The smog used to be so thick that me and my wife walked straight past each other one morning.'

Ray looked at his watch. 'Listen, Pete, it's nearly lunch time and my missis and my boss both keep me on a pretty tight leash.'

'I understand,' said Peter, clutching his deceased pet tightly. 'Will you tell my story in your paper?'

Ray scratched his head. 'We might be able to do something with the postcard, mate, but I don't know about this angel malarkey. My editor's on the verge of a coronary as it is.'

'As you wish. I've told someone about it now. That was my duty.' Peter walked away and sat down on a bench. 'I'm going to stay here. Tibbles likes the peace and quiet.'

'Take care of yerself, Pete,' said Ray and took one last glance at the sad old gent before he left. He noted that the pruning hunchback was still watching them.

*

Lucy Reveals Large Developments
Story by Mark Lyons, published in the Fogwin Enquirer 23.1.1980.

Yesterday marked the opening of the brand new Earthcom Industrial Estate on Knightsheath Road. Cutting the ribbon was Britain's number one glamour model Lucy Springer. Gracing the pages of national newspapers such as The Sun and The Daily Mail, Miss Springer is no stranger to public attention. Some hundred local businessmen and dignitaries were gathered to sample Lucy's charm and view the new premises, which until now have been shrouded in secrecy.

Among them was Fogwin's own Mayor, John Dodge, who was the first to toast the future of the estate with a glass of Champagne. 'It's great to see high quality accommodation for business. This development will be the linchpin for the regeneration of the town, I'm sure, 'concluded the Mayor.

The 43,000 square foot high-tech unit is backed by over 3 million in private investment and an equal amount from its owner Roger Beign who says 'I'm very pleased with how the estate has turned out. The project has taken two years to complete and it hasn't been without it's hiccups but I'm confident that we are now at the forefront of Britain's corporate future and it's happening here, in this lovely green corner of the country.'

Extending the estate could potentially mean encroaching onto land that contains what are generally believed to be historic ruins. When asked about this controversy, Mr Beign merely commented 'Out with the old and in with the new and all that.' The next business to move to the estate, Roger hopes, will be an international company specialising in scientific research. 'I can't reveal who that is yet,' stated Roger, 'it's an idea still firmly in the pipeline but let's just say they're very cutting edge, they're into genetics and all of that. It's very exciting.'

Lucy Springer, who just so happens to be Roger's niece, added 'I'm not sure what genetics means. Is it something to do with water sports? I like water sports.' When asked if she would be visiting our nice little town on a regular basis, Lucy replied 'I'm sure I will be, I like to visit my Uncle Roger; he always make a fuss of me and gives me a special treat.'

*

'Can I have a story, daddy?' requested William Weaver.

'Of course you can, son,' replied Ray, scanning the book spines above the boy's bed.

William caught onto him. 'No! Make one up!'

'I'm tired, son, I've had a funny day.'

'Please, daddy, your stories are the bestest.'

Ray gazed down at his little golden haired cherub. 'Alright. As long as you promise to go to sleep like a good boy.'

'Yes!' The five-year old jerked around in his bed excitedly, almost kicking off his sheets as he did so.

'Calm down then.' Ray righted the bed clothes. 'Now, there was once a very brave young man called William.'

'That's my name!'

'Funny that.' Ray leant back against the wall, flattening the multi-coloured beanbag beneath him, and crossed his fingers. 'He lived in a small town where everyone was very happy but William always wondered what the rest of the world was like. But wonder as much as he could his dad would not let him go.'

'Why?'

'Because there was a monster.' Ray paused for dramatic effect.

His son became silent; the desired consequence.

'William's dad would say 'you must never leave the town, boy, anyone who wanders away into the countryside is never seen or heard of again.' William was not scared though, he would say 'I'm not afraid, dad of mine!' 'But you would be if you saw the monster,' his dad would answer. 'Why hasn't anyone tried to get rid of this monster?' William would ask. 'Some have tried,' his dad would explain. 'They go with swords and shields, spears and helmets, bows and arrows, but they never come back. The monster is too great.' One night though, William gets bored of living in the same town and plucks up the courage to go and see the world. Against his dad's wishes, he packs a bag and wanders out into the countryside. He sees trees and hills and rivers and lots of animals; lots of wonderful things that he's never seen before. He climbs to the top of a very high mountain and from there he can see the lights of the town in the distance. 'Here I am,' thinks William, 'I've left the town and there's nothing to be scared of!' It was then that a big shadow fell over him. William looked up and there was this large thing stood there. It was slimy and it had massive feet and massive hands with yellow claws. It had a mouth that was big enough to swallow a man whole. It smelled like dog poo and it had one big eye in the middle of its forehead. 'This is my land!' growled the monster. 'Anyone who comes here becomes my dinner!' William stood up and looked the monster in the eye. 'I'm not scared of you!' he said bravely but the monster just laughed. 'You can never hope to defeat me! Where is your sword and shield? Where is your spear and helmet? Where is your bow and arrow?' 'I don't need any of those things,' said

William. 'I'm going to just let you eat me!' The monster looked confused because it was expecting a fight of some sort. 'First though,' said William, 'I think you should eat some bubblegum.' 'What is bubblegum?' asked the monster, who didn't know anything about sweets. William produced a packet from his pocket. 'It's stuff that you chew and it tastes good. When it gets soft, you can blow a really big bubble,' he explained. 'I'm not interested in that,' grumbled the monster, 'I just want to eat people.' 'Of course only the strongest can blow really good bubbles,' said William. 'I'm the strongest that there is!' proclaimed the monster. 'Prove it then!' William challenged, offering it the whole packet. The monster looked a bit confused again but took the whole packet of bubblegum and threw it in his gob and began to munch away like a greedy guts. Our hero had to wait a long time for the monster to chew the gum properly but eventually it stopped and with one mighty breath it blew the gum into a huge bubble. William had never seen anyone blow a bubble so big before. It was about the same size as this beanbag I'm sat on. Suddenly, the bubble exploded and it splattered all over the monster's face. It stumbled around for a bit, unable to see. It started howling and crying because it was scared for the first time in its life. William saw his chance and he pushed the monster's legs as hard as he could. It toppled off the side of the mountain and with one mighty thump that made the ground shake, it landed and lay still.'

'Was the monster dead, daddy?'

'Yes, son. The people were safe. William had freed everyone from living in the town for all of their lives and he could go and see the world.'

Ray coughed and became quiet. He and William looked at each other for a few moments in mutual contemplation.

'Monsters aren't real are they, daddy?'

'No, son, of course they're not. It's just a story.'

Ray shuffled to his feet and tucked in his placated offspring.

'Daddy?'

'Yes, son?'

'Why do you and Mummy sleep in different beds now?'

Ray kissed William. 'Never mind that. It doesn't matter. Goodnight.'

'Goodnight, daddy.'

Ray switched out the boy's lights but left the door open as usual. He could see out across the hall into Posy's bedroom. His two-year old daughter was undergoing a similar ritual. Iris was perched on the edge of her bed. Mother and daughter murmured together, their heads almost meeting, their red locks almost merged.

'Now I lay me down to sleep I pray the Lord my soul to keep. If I should die before I wake I pray the Lord my soul to take.'

It was done. There was a well-rehearsed crossover: Ray going in to kiss Posy goodnight and Iris transferring to say the prayer with William. They met again in the hallway.

'Goodnight, Iris.'

'Goodnight, Ray.'

They went to their respective domains. For Ray, this meant the attic. He'd had it converted into a fourth bedroom and now found himself to be its first occupant. There was one skylight window, a sofa-bed and a desk. He paced around listlessly for a while with half an intention to work. He peered around at all the papers and books and junk and found that his eyes kept falling on the postcard Peter Stanley had given him earlier. He picked it up. Cogs turned.

'I'll get you a story, Archie, I'll get you a bloody story.'

Ray opened the window to see what the weather was like.

*

Ray knocked on the door, rudely interrupting a perfect silence. It was getting late and he cringed as lights flickered on inside the house and a dog barked irately from a neighbouring abode. He waited whilst numerous locks and bolts were undone and the door opened slightly.

One wide eye stared at him from the narrow gap. 'Yes?'

'It's me, Pete; Ray Weaver. I came round earlier.'

The eye continued to stare without recognition. At the back of his mind, Ray wondered if Mr Stanley was under the influence of some form of medication. It seemed likely. He spoke slower; 'from the Enquirer. About your postcard. Remember?'

The penny dropped. 'Oh, yes!'

'I know it's late, mate, but can I have a word?'

By way of response, Peter opened the door fully and allowed Ray in. Despite the invitation, he stroked his stuffed cat anxiously and said 'it's alright, Tibbles, it's alright, it's that nice man from the newspaper,' as if reassuring himself. The old man was in his dressing gown and pyjamas but sported the same gold tasselled slippers he had worn earlier.

Ray explained himself. 'Sorry it's so late, Pete, I was thinking about what you said earlier; about how you'd like to see your angel again?'

'Yes?' Peter nodded.

'Well, shall we take a look?'

The old man looked at his watch. 'At this hour?'

'I think it would be best done …erm, discreetly.'

Peter glared at him for a moment and then smiled. 'Make yourself comfortable while I get dressed. Would you take Tibbles?'

'Sure,' said Ray and accepted the taxidermied feline.

Peter trotted away into the rear of the bungalow.

Ray held up Tibbles and gazed into its glassy black eyes.

*

He struck the ground as hard as he could but the earth was solid and the shovel barely made a mark. He dug again in a different spot but the turf remained unyielding. *Maybe this wasn't such a good idea*, mused Ray. It was January and the soil had been reinforced by the freezing temperature. He straightened up and looked around the churchyard. He had already questioned himself about a thousand times while sneaking out of the house, fetching the shovel from the shed, jumping in the Cortina, driving round to Peter's house, driving them both round to the church, losing his nerve, driving back again, regaining his nerve, returning to the church, climbing the wall to get in and then forcing the rusty old gate open from the inside so Peter could get in. Ray's nerves were already shot. He was a reporter, not a solicitor, and he knew nothing of laws on grave-digging, but suspected that there must be some.

It was so black and hazy that night that Ray could barely see more than ten yards in any direction. There was a sort of foggy veil clinging to everything like a bad signal on a television screen. Apart from the distant hiss of the occasional car on the road, it was deathly quiet. If Ray could not see or hear a living soul then surely no one could see or hear him or Peter: Perfect conditions for the latter day Burke and Hare. He leant his shovel against a neighbouring gravestone and took a little nip on his hip flask. The hot liquor consoled his insides and with fresh vigour, he lifted the shovel and tried again. With a malevolent penetration that felt and sounded like flesh tearing, some turf gave way, and without pausing to contemplate any further, Ray dug furiously and continuously, grunting like a nasty pig. After a long half-hour, he rested a second time, his sweat turning cold and making him shiver. His hands were sore and chaffed and his back was aching from the unfamiliar toil. He needed another hit on the flask. He passed it to Peter.

'No thank you,' replied the old man, little more to Ray than a shadow in the dark.

Ray offered him the shovel. 'Fancy taking over for a bit?'

'I'm eighty-two years old, Ray.'

Ray nodded and lit up a cigarette. 'You are keeping a look out though, right?'

'Of course,' said Peter, looking around by way of gesture.

Ray inspected his excavation as he puffed away. He had only descended two feet and wondered if it was true that graves were dug to a six feet deep criterion. This was the first time he had violated a final resting place, after all. Ray glanced around again but the wintry fuzz still hung in the air to conceal his sins. For a fleeting moment, he thought he saw the misshaped outline of the hunchback he had seen earlier that day. It disappeared behind a nearby tomb.

He turned to his companion. 'Did you see that?'

'See what?'

'Never mind.' Ray sniggered at himself for being ridiculous, sucked the fag short and began shifting dirt once more. He had passed the point of no return now anyway. He just hoped that Peter Stanley was not completely insane and that there was some unearthly secret a few shovel strokes away. It was another grueling half-hour before the blade struck wood. Ray paused. He panted with exhaustion but smiled; it was more like four feet deep. He carved out the rest of the earth and revealed a tiny makeshift coffin that was barely more than a box. With trembling hands, Ray lifted out the article. It stank of age. He placed it on the ground and scraped away any muck that was still attached. His heart rate increased but it was not from exertion. The last time anyone had looked upon this thing, Hitler was vogue.

'How exciting!' commented Peter, taking a step closer, clutching his dead cat tightly.

Ray took out his torch and with a deep breath, tried to open the sarcophagus. To add to their suspense, Ray discovered that the thing was nailed shut. He had another few frustrating minutes with the shovel to rend it open. The blade cracked off the top of the box abruptly and without ceremony. Ray shone his torch within. He stopped breathing. He backed away slowly, his mouth agape in a silent scream. Tears fell down his cheeks.

Eventually he gasped. 'Oh, Jesus Christ!'

'My angel!' added Peter.

*

Transcript of a telephone conversation between Raymond Weaver (RW) and Cedric Hamilton Montague a.k.a. The Professor (TP) January 19 1980.

RW Professor?

TP Speaking.

RW It's Ray.

PAUSE.

TP Who?

RW Ray Weaver, the reporter, I came to see you in Soho last August.

TP Oh God, yes! I'm so sorry. My dear boy, how the devil are you? Have the nightmares stopped?

RW They did but they've just started again.

TP I'm sorry to hear that.

RW I've found one.

TP Found one?

RW One of the things.

PAUSE.

TP One of the things that took you and your friend?

RW Yeah.

TP Are you sure?

RW Positive.

TP They came back?

RW   No, this one was buried in the local churchyard. Some old boy told me about it. Total coincidence.

TP   You had the grave exhumed?

RW   Erm … not exactly.

TP   But it is one of the same creatures?

RW   Yeah, ugly little thing with white skin and hair and black eyes. It must have been buried for years but it hasn't rotted away. It's still perfectly preserved. I can hardly bring myself to believe it.

TP   I told you didn't I?

RW   What?

TP   That some of us are chosen.

RW   Chosen?

TP   To experience such wonders.

RW   This is no wonder, Prof. The old geezer … he described it as an angel but it's no such thing. These things are evil.

TP   Indeed. Who else knows about this?

RW   Nobody.

TP   And where is it now?

RW   It's with the old geezer.

TP   And what do you plan to do with it?

RW   I was hoping you'd tell me that.

TP   Do you want to go public?

RW   I haven't got the foggiest what to do, Professor.

TP	You're a journalist, old boy.
RW	I know but this is different. This is big.
TP	You realise what it would mean?
RW	The corpse of a creature from a different dimension? I think that might make the front page of the Fogwin Enquirer, yeah.
TP	I suggest we have a look at it before you do anything.
	PAUSE.
	Ray?
RW	Sorry, my missis is shouting me.
TP	Do you want me to take a look?
RW	That'd be good. You're the expert.
TP	Let me think: I'm tied up in London at the moment. Keep it secure and I'll get back to you.
RW	I'll try.
TP	Excellent.
RW	I'm gonna have to go, Professor, Iris is shouting.
TP	I'll be with you as soon as I can.
RW	Right, ciao for now … oh, and … erm … thanks.

*

'Where are you going?' queried Mrs Weaver whilst washing a cauliflower under the kitchen tap.

'Nowhere,' replied her husband whilst searching for his car keys.

'Who was that you were talking to on the phone?' Iris turned to survey him, the cauliflower dripping onto the floor.

Ray franticly frisked the kitchen. 'No one.'

Iris put down the vegetable, wiped her hands on her apron and then placed them on her hips. She narrowed her eyes at him, venomously. 'Things aren't going to get any better until we communicate. You remember what Father Daniel said?'

'What did Father Daniel say?' muttered Ray, desperately going through the pockets of every jacket he owned, even the ones he had not worn for months or years.

'That things aren't going to get any better until we communicate!'

Ray froze and puffed so hard that his fringe stood up on end.

His son, William, appeared and held out the keys.

'Good boy!' Ray sniggered with joy and took them. The fringe resumed its usual duty.

'In the toilet,' explained the infant.

'So you're not staying for dinner?' Iris folded her arms in another well practiced gesture of contempt.

Ray turned slowly and looked at her. 'This is important, Iris.'

'More important than dinner with your family?'

'More important than anything in the world.' Ray crossed the room to kiss her.

She recoiled. 'Go then.'

Ray looked at her but could find nothing more to say or do. He ruffled his son's hair before he left. William ran to the front of the house and climbed a chair in the living room so he could watch his daddy get in his car and drive away. His mummy charged out there before he could go. She handed him what looked like a sandwich through the car window and said something. Mummy came back in. Daddy left. He thought he could hear mummy crying but he was not sure.

*

That's weird, thought Ray as he pulled up outside Peter Stanley's bungalow; the old timer's front door was wide open. *Perhaps he's just security mad at night*, he concluded. Ray quickly changed his mind as he skipped across the garden. He saw a white fluffy object lying on the hallway carpet inside. He took a couple of slow tentative steps towards the doorway and stared at the object. There was no mistake; it was Peter's cat. On closer inspection, there were signs that the door had been forced open too. His heart sank to the bottom of his guts.

'Pete? Are you there, Pete? Everything alright, mate?' his voice quivered.

There was no answer. The odd solid silence of retirement land persisted.

Ray shook his head and stepped inside. He picked up Tibbles and in his mind the events of the previous night replayed like an old monochrome film. It was not the corpse of the cat that he picked up but that of a hideous pale gnome. The image was followed by a replay of the hunchback vanishing behind the tomb. Suddenly he felt a surge of anger and this spurred him onwards through the house.

'Pete? Pete?' Ray yelled as he stomped through the antiquated chambers. It was not a big place and he soon found the old man. He was slumped in an armchair in the sitting room and he seemed to be asleep though his head lolled at an awkward angle. Even more disturbingly, he was not alone; there were two large men in dark suits standing either side of him. They turned round and glared at Ray.

'What the fuck is going on?'

'Mr Weaver?' enquired one of the suited apes.

'Maybe,' Ray shrugged his shoulders at them.

A huge hand came flying towards him. In its outstretched palm was a white handkerchief that reeked of chemicals.

*

'Iris?' mumbled Ray as he awoke. He was lying on his side and a reservoir of foul-tasting saliva had collected in his slack jowls. He opened his eyes but his vision was doubled. It was too much and it made him feel sick. He closed them again for a while and waited for the nausea to pass. When at last he could focus he could see that he was in a hospital, albeit an unusual one. The walls and ceiling were little more than bare rock. It was only the whitewashed floor and equipment which gave away the place's medical purpose. Ray was in bed but he was still dressed. For some strange reason, one shoe and the sock underneath it were absent.

'What the hell is this?' Ray heard himself ask. His journalistic fascination had ebbed and he was now cold and frightened. He wanted to smoke. He noticed a familiar figure sat in a dark corner. At first he could not put a name to the old man slumped in the wheelchair. His neat comb-over was in disarray and his clothes were ruffled and grubby. One of his slippers was missing a gold tassel.

'Mr Stanley? ... Pete?'

The pathetic shape in the wheelchair did not look up. Ray could not tell if he was awake or even alive.

'Pete?' ventured Ray again but there was still no sign of life. There was a noise from behind him. Ray turned over and noticed that various parts of his body ached and throbbed though he suspected that the pain would be worse when the anaesthetic wore off. A large and burly man with a mop of ginger hair and freckles came in and checked his pulse. He was wearing white scrubs.

'Get your hands off me!' Despite his wrath, Ray found that he could barely move.

The ginger giant just sniggered at him.

'What is this place?' Ray gibbered, panic rising in his guts. 'Some kind of private hospital? What have you done to Pete? He's just a harmless old guffer!'

No explanation was forthcoming. The red-haired behemoth merely stepped back and looked away. Another nurse emerged. Like the other one, this one was heavily built but she was no man. Her long hair and enormous breasts were the only clues to her true gender. She was as massive and as muscled as her male counterpart. Ray could see a myriad of crude tattoos under her paper-thin white uniform. She regarded him with big brown crossed-eyes and Ray could not return the gaze easily. He found his own eyes going crossed too. His attention was drawn to the old man that she carried in her arms. At first, Ray thought it was an enormous baby but the white hair and stubble gave him away.

'Wotcha,' said Ray.

The old man turned his head and peered at him with squinted eyes. Ray gawped in shock: The methuselah's face was deformed. The left portion of his features looked like melted candle wax and there was a lumpy growth in the middle of his forehead. He also smelt bad; a stench of shit and puke poorly masked by disinfectant.

'You're the journalist?' croaked the creature.

'Call me Ray.'

The old man squirmed in the arms of the masculine woman. 'Put me down, Jenny!'

Jenny did as she was told. She took the old man over to a wheelchair and delicately laid him down.

'Christopher! Get me a blanket!' he yapped.

The big ginger nurse called Christopher swiftly grabbed a blanket from a trolley and crossed over to place it on the geriatric. He tucked him in affectionately. The nurses then hovered around, as if waiting on his every word. Ray was stunned. This was definitely his most bizarre encounter yet, discounting creatures from other worlds.

'Take me closer,' instructed the old man.

Jenny pushed the wheelchair towards Ray's bed.

The old man protested: 'Closer, you slut! I don't like to raise my voice.'

The female subordinate gave no indication that she was offended by what he had called her and wheeled him closer. Ray was well within the radius of the old man's stink and he gagged. 'What do you want?'

The crone wrinkled up his features, making his face even more repulsive. 'I need a drink!'

The nurses busied themselves putting a kettle on.

'I wouldn't mind a brew,' said Ray.

He was ignored. The old man ogled at him. 'Do you know who I am, journalist?'

'Haven't the foggiest.' Ray said. 'Someone who's old enough to know the value of good manners?'

'You think you're a smart arse?' the old man chuckled or choked slightly. Ray could not tell which.

'I know I'm a smart arse,' explained Ray.

'Your insolent tongue will get you in trouble,' the old man gurgled.

'It has done from time to time,' admitted Ray.

'You're here. You can therefore assume that you're in trouble. Serious trouble.' The old man made some menacing yet weak claw-like gesture with his hand.

Ray suspected that is was meant to be a threat but he was not fazed, just puzzled.

'Do you know why you're here?'

Ray shook his head and hazarded a guess. 'The pleasure of your company?'

'I take an interest in everything that happens in your little town,' explained the old man. 'Every single little thing. If Mrs Jenkins hangs out her washing on a Tuesday instead of a Monday, then I get to hear about it. I'm especially interested in the special visitors that you sometimes have. I think you know what I mean.'

Ray smiled and nodded. 'Well, I suppose it's a bit boring for a man of your age and good looks. Nothing else to do except be a nosy twat.'

The old man wriggled angrily in his wheelchair. The nurses turned and stared at Ray, goggle-eyed with disbelief. 'You don't understand, journalist. I'm in charge here!'

'Oh, I get what you're saying, old timer,' Ray looked around. 'I've done something to upset you and you've dragged me out here for an ear bending, is that it?'

'You're not as stupid as you look,' hissed the old man; 'but do you know what you've done?'

'Hung my washing out on a Tuesday?' mused Ray.

'Bring him to me!' screeched the geriatric, his tiny withered body shivering with rage.

Ray felt colossal hands grasp him from behind. He was thrust forward, out of the bed, and down onto his knees. Finger nails bit into the back of his neck. He gazed into the ancient malformed face, now just inches away.

'Listen here, you cheeky pisser!' Ray gagged from the old man's foul breath. 'You've dug up something very important. I've been waiting a long time for someone to unearth that secret and now it's mine. Am I making myself clear?'

'Why didn't you just dig it up yourself?'

'I wasn't sure where it was or who had buried it. There's been a rumour going around for decades and my friend has been watching for a very long time.'

'The hunchback?'

'It's been very difficult to maintain that man's service. He has, shall we say, an unusual method of payment.'

'I don't think I want to know.'

'He likes children.'

'I didn't want to know.'

'So now I've finally got my hands on one of the visitors I want you to go back to your pathetic life and forget any of this happened. Do you understand?'

'The words go fuck yourself spring to mind,' stated Ray defiantly.

The old man grinned and slobbered. 'Very well, journalist, you asked for it.' The growth on his forehead started to quiver with a life of its own.

Ray stared at the lump with an intense combination of horror, disgust and amusement. 'You wanna get some cream on that,' he managed to say.

The centre of the growth popped open with a slurping noise. Two lids peeled back to reveal an enormous eyeball. The old man's two regular eyes were now shut as if somehow to compensate for the dominance of the third. It was shot with red and Ray was compelled to look. Within moments, the dreadful eye filled his vision and became his entire world.

'You will obey me,' came the old man's voice but it was now detached and ghostly. 'You will heed my words. You will know me as master. You will be my slave.'

Ray heard himself say: 'I will obey you. I will heed your words. I will know you as master. I will be your slave.'

The old man's seductive tone added: 'I have the power to make your wife have sex with me and then kill herself and you will watch and be powerless to stop her. Do you understand?'

'I understand, master,' agreed Ray.

The old man's eye swivelled over to his nurses. 'Put him back in the bed and give him another dose. When he wakes again, get rid of him!'

Ray struggled and kicked as the gigantic servants put him back in bed and injected him but he had little strength in his body to fight. Seconds later he was unconscious again and his dreams were filled with that horrible eye.

*

When Ray came round the second time the ancient cyclops and his subordinates were gone. The lights were switched off and the hospital room was dark. This suggested that night had fallen though there were no windows to confirm the fact. Ray realised that he had been drugged twice and had no idea what time it was. Hours or even days could have passed. He waited patiently for his body to wake up properly. Infuriated and scared though he was, his emotions gave no vitality to his limbs. The chemical cocktail that loitered in his system was effective. It took a few minutes just to sit up and have a proper look round. He confirmed that he was alone; there were a couple of machines that flashed and bleeped at him from the shadows but that was all. Gone was Peter Stanley and Ray wondered if the old man had ever been there; reality had become a bit slippy. He hoped that the creature that he now knew as master was a feverish figment of his imagination too but the reek that lingered in the air told him otherwise. A year ago, Ray could not have believed that anything like that monster could possibly exist but his experience in the woods at Raven Holes had changed that. He had no idea who that man was or indeed if he was a man at all. The only certainty was that he had to get out of this place.

Ray looked over his shoulder at the doorway and saw that there was a dim light coming from the passageway beyond. He thought he could hear someone out there; a quiet and muffled grunting or murmuring. He imagined another patient in an adjacent room. He stood up carefully but at once lurched wildly and proceeded to stumble around the room like a drunk on stilts. He managed to stop himself by crashing against the wall. He narrowly avoided knocking a trolley of equipment over. He was determined not to end up back in that bed with a third dose of anaesthetic and it was his will alone that saved him. Ray suspected that his captors would not waste any more drugs and just kill him.

Slightly more steadily, Ray got moving again and popped his head round the doorway. Like his room, the walls of the passageway were made of bare rock that had been whitewashed and disinfected. Other doorways led off from the corridor but Ray's eyes were drawn to the far end where a metal gate was slightly ajar. The light shone from just past the gate and the animated shadow of two people was cast onto the rough wall of the passageway. The silhouettes appeared to be in some sort of embrace and it occurred to Ray that the grunting and murmuring noises he heard belonged to them. It looked like two people were performing an intimate act on each other and Ray spied his chance to escape while they were distracted.

He crept like a bad ninja down the passage. He chanced to look through some of the other doorways and was thankful to find that they were unoccupied. The purpose of each room was ambiguous; one seemed to house a large square bath or pool and another a gymnasium. One area held something of more interest to Ray. It was a lab and on the dissecting table was a familiar object. It looked like a malformed embryo. The thing lay there in a foetal position with its unearthly flesh glistening in the poor light. Ray identified it as the creature that Peter knew as angel and that he knew as demon. He saw an opportunity not just to escape the dreadful place but to steal back their discovery. The thought made him tremble but deep down he knew how much was at stake. Ray edged his way in and scanned the cluttered workbenches. He spotted the grubby old cloth he had wrapped the creature in originally; he replaced the wrapping and tucked it under his arm. Stumbling back out into the hallway Ray was glad to see that the sentinels were still at it. It was only the sound of their own carnal activity that prevented them from hearing his approach. Any movement had become agonisingly laborious for the journalist let alone one of stealth. He was virtually crawling down on his knees by the time he reached the gate at the end of the passage.

If Ray thought he had seen his last disturbing vision that night then he was wrong. Through the gaps in the bars he witnessed the two nurses he had seen earlier; the big ginger called Christopher and the cross-eyed butch tattooed fem called Jenny, and they were fornicating furiously. One of them was bent over a desk and the other was thrusting from behind. It was not the way round Ray had expected because it was Christopher who was on the receiving end and it was Jenny that penetrated, though Ray could not see with what. The male nurse had become scarlet in the face and had a cloth stuffed into his mouth to stop him from vocalising his pain as his rear end was ruthlessly pounded. Jenny seemed to be enjoying herself much more and was chuckling and smiling and whispering quiet obscenities to accompany the rhythm.

    For a few moments, Ray was transfixed; unable to tear away his gaze from the extraordinary sight. He had to remind himself that he had been granted a golden opportunity to escape. Plus the old man with the third eye had been alarming enough and Ray did not care to see any more of this freak show. Gritting his teeth, Ray crawled around the gate and through the office. He dared not to look as he passed through but he saw the couple's shoes out of the corner of his eye. He entered another corridor on the other side and left them behind. He felt a sudden urge to get up and run but Ray persisted with his slow creep. He did not want to ask too much of his tampered body. His gamble paid off; the brutes were too engrossed in their depravity to notice him. He soon came to the bottom of an old stone staircase and, wasting no time, climbed up and found himself in a vast corridor of a different kind. Ray took the opportunity for a deep breath. He ambled slowly along, inspecting the gilt-framed oils that hung on the walls. He drew aside some heavy embroidered curtains and looked out through ornate windows across the grounds of what looked like a mansion or palace of some sort. *Where the hell am I?* pondered Ray. He glanced back at the staircase and realised that the hospital must be just one part of a vast stately complex. When the warped old man he now knew as master had yelled 'You don't understand, journalist. I'm in charge here!' Ray could not guess to what extent. It was night yet the estate was lit well enough for Ray to see that the old man's house looked like Balmoral Castle. He reckoned that he was on the second or third floor. Just as Ray struggled with the splendour of his location a young man dressed as a cook appeared from the other end of the corridor and made his way towards him, a silver tray balanced in one hand. Ray briefly considered diving back down the staircase but it was too late, he had been spotted.

    'I'm not sure you're supposed to be in here,' the cook said, hesitantly.

    'Why not?' scoffed Ray, feigning confidence.

    The lad blinked. 'Guests are confined to the east wing.'

Ray still had his wallet. He pulled it out, enticingly. 'What if we had a little arrangement? You and I?'

The cook shook his head immediately and barged past.

Ray glared at him and took out a ten pound note.

The lad hurried for the staircase.

'Hold on!' protested Ray. He realised that the youngster was not going to play ball and bolted after him. They reached the top of the stairs and Ray attempted a rugby tackle. Manually, Ray had yet to recover and all he succeeded in doing was tripping the lad up and he tumbled down the stairs head-first, his bones crunching as he collided with every stone step, the tray and its contents adding to the racket. Ray stared with horror as the boy fell. It was like watching a rag doll and the sounds of his skeleton breaking brought a bit of sick up into his mouth. He peered down into the gloom. The cook was at the bottom of the stairs, motionless but still breathing. Better still, the commotion had failed to alert Christopher and Jenny. He could still hear the nurse's exploits. *That was lucky*, thought Ray. He did not want to kill anyone. Then again, he was not about to be stopped by some officious little shit from the kitchen. He should have taken the tenner.

Leaving the victim to his fate, Ray decided to move faster. He crossed the long expanse of the corridor and sprang down another stone staircase at the other end. A blast of heat rose up to meet him. At the bottom, Ray found himself in a huge kitchen that bustled with activity. He was suddenly faced with a hundred more cooks. Fortunately, the boy's colleagues had a more casual attitude to security protocol. They seemed more preoccupied with completing what looked like a banquet fit for a king. Lobsters were hauled out of pots by the dozen and a million vegetables were chopped furiously. Ray wormed his way through the labouring throng and grinned at any sweaty subordinate that gave him a glance. He applauded the efforts of the crew by clapping his hands and pretended that he had a right to be in there. He scanned for an exit and spotted several contenders. He saw that most led deeper into the house and opted for one that led outside. Before Ray could breathe, he had found his way out into the cool night air. The kitchen staff had left a fire exit open to let some heat escape and in doing so had let their master's prisoner do so too.

He weaved his way down the side of the building and out into what must have been the front courtyard. There was a gargantuan party of some sort in progress and a crowd of people mingled amongst the lawns, hedgerows and flower beds. The men wore dinner suits and the ladies regaled in fine gowns and waiters plied them with Champagne. Gentle orchestrated music drifted out from within. Ray decided his only course of action was to keep up his façade of certainty and just plough straight through them. He buttoned up his jacket to conceal his ripped clothes and lack of suitable attire. He hid his grubby hands in his pockets and swaggered with a sense of purpose, despite the fact that he only had one shoe on and a dead monster under his arm. He could not tell if anyone viewed him with suspicion anyway; the exterior lights of the place were so dazzling. He squinted into the brilliance and people moved around him like vague silhouettes. It was a walk of sheer faith. They guffawed and pontificated with excitement as they rubbed shoulders but seemed to pay Ray no heed.

Gazing sideways at the main doors to the mansion Ray noticed that the revellers were showing invitations to a smart young woman as they filtered in. The girl seemed amiable enough but she was framed by two large lantern-jawed men in suits who looked a hell of a lot more serious. Ray followed the flow for now and he kept up the act by smiling at everyone but inside he was panicking. He was getting sucked towards the entrance and its doormen. Out of the corner of his eye, he could see that they had spotted him. The guests were too juiced and giddy to care about Ray but the guards had noticed his shabby exterior and, to their sober and vigilant eyes, he stood out. He swam out of the river of people before it was too late. Just as Ray reached the peripheries of the horde there was a commotion and he nearly screamed. Peering around, he realised that the animation was not due to him. A big black Limousine had drawn up and judging by the partygoer's reaction somebody who was obviously very important got out. The fascination was too great and Ray allowed himself a moment to stop and look. The occupant of the Limousine was instantly recognisable but it still took him a few seconds to comprehend it.

'I don't believe it,' whispered Ray to himself. 'Margaret bleeding Thatcher!'

He turned his back on the Prime Minister immediately. He did not care for another glance. He had regained consciousness in a weird underground hospital populated by perverted misfits and sneaked out into the midst of a lavish gathering of society's elite where, if anything, his predicament was even more disturbing. The true nature of the cyclopean master was unfathomable and the journalist's mind reeled from the implications of all he had witnessed. Ray was certain, however, that it would all be in vain if he did not escape with his life. The arrival of the Iron Lady switched attention of the doormen from him to her. With renewed determination, he strode away from the palace. There were enough trees and shrubs between him and them now to mask his flight. Staying within the shelter of the bushes, Ray limped onwards. He crept from the shadow of one feature to another and soon he was amongst the dense trees that formed the boundary of the immense courtyard. The lights of the house had no jurisdiction here and, finding sanctuary in the dark, Ray came to rest. For one startling moment, the moon broke cloud and illuminated the face of the devil under Ray's arm. Its wrapping had come loose and Ray felt the urgent need to cover it again. He then relaxed for a while and even laughed at himself.

'Just you and me, mate,' he muttered to the dead thing.

Suddenly, a dog barked nearby. Ray nearly jumped. He had become complacent again. To his right he saw the outline of man and canine separate themselves from the gloom.

'What is it, boy?' The guard prompted his dog.

The creature sounded off again and strained on its leash. The barking was so loud that Ray stared over at the guests congregating at the house to see if they had been alerted. However, no one seemed bothered. They were too busy making their way into the mansion or fraternising with each other on the threshold.

'What is it, boy? You got something?' repeated the guard.

Ray scanned around. The bastards had come from nowhere. He dived deeper into the realm of the wild fringe. Behind him came the words he feared.

'Go on then! Go get him!'

Ray heard the leash being unclipped, the padding of paws and the panting of beastly breath as it closed in on him. Ray was in no shape to outrun a dog. He then found inspiration; the sandwich his wife had given him! It was still in his jacket pocket. The snack was all scrunched up and coated in pocket fluff but Ray guessed that the animal would not be so choosy. He had seen it work in films and just hoped that a dog's greed was not a Hollywood myth. He backed up against a tree and ripped the article from his jacket. He lobbed the thing on the ground in between him and the advancing predator. Ray pressed on. He chanced to look back. He was glad that he did; the guard was staring down at a huge wagging tail and he could hear the fervent munching of the dog wolfing down the sarny.

Ray nearly laughed. *Nice one, Iris, you saved my bacon, luv.*

'Come on! You greedy toe-rag!' The guard clipped the leash back on the beast and dragged it away.

Ray caught a glimpse of the dog through a gap in the foliage. He could not see enough to identify the breed but it was certainly large and shaggy enough for the job. It was almost half the size of the man and looked more like a wolf than anything. He put it down to his overworked imagination but promised himself to always carry a sandwich whilst escaping from a madman's fortress.

He then walked many miles across a vague wilderness. A few hours before dawn he found a structure of some sort, at the base of the structure was a circular opening. Ray ambled over and clambered in. It was warm and metallic inside and he quickly gave in to exhaustion. It was only a matter of time before they noticed Ray had gone. The men and their dog things could track him but he was too tired to care. He snuggled up like a hibernating animal and held the wrapped corpse close to his chest. Though it was dead of night, somewhere a bird sang. In response, Ray farted.

*

Third Class Mail
Story by Ray Weaver, published in the Fogwin Enquirer 23.1.1980.

It is said that the mail always gets through, though in some cases it may take time. For pensioner Mr. Peter Stanley this meant thirty-seven years. A postcard sent by his friend George Jones was posted on the 8th September, 1943 in Naples but arrived in Fogwin only a week ago. What makes the delivery more astonishing is that George was a soldier in the British army and had only liberated the Italian city two days before from Nazi occupation. The postcard is somewhat faded and tatty but a clear image of the Cathedral of Naples still graces the front while on the back, there are some words from Peter's friend. Sadly, George was to perish later at the notorious battle of Monte Cassino. His final message is short and succinct mentioning the wonderful Italian art, wine and weather and informing Peter that he is to be home soon. A spokesman for the Royal Mail said that late deliveries are rare but at the same time, not unusual. He was at a loss to explain where this particular item had been for so long.

The Steve McQueen Story

Foreword by Ray Weaver

Let me start by explaining that this isn't Steve McQueen the famous actor, star of films such as "Bullet", "Papillon" and "The Great Escape". This is an entirely different Steve McQueen. In fact, Steve, when I met him, could not have looked more different than the big movie heart-throb, with his balding pate and hairy arms, his big teeth and pot belly, his wide nostrils and uneven ear lobes. Make no mistake; the two Steve McQueens are poles apart. The only similarities are that they are both American and that they are both heroes, though the actor was a screen superman and my Steve was a bona fide one.

    I only ever met Steve on three occasions and the first time was at a Craps table in the Moulin Rouge Casino, Las Vegas in 1986. I remember it well: I was on honeymoon with my second wife, Angie, who had gone to scour the stores for a bargain, leaving me alone to try my hand at gambling. Romantic, I know! Steve, liberated of his own spouse, was immediately amused by my total lack of ability to play Craps. The man had one of those infectious laughs; a kind of relentlessly manic high-pitched guffaw. You know, where something isn't particularly funny but you end up laughing because Steve is laughing. There must have been a dozen players at the table and they were collectively irritated by my greenness but Steve soon had them all in hysterics. After I left the game penniless, he bought me a drink out of sympathy and we got talking. Later that day, he drove me out into the desert in a Dune Buggy and showed me places that were far more fascinating than anywhere in the gambler's oasis. The kindly yank was also a walking storybook and one of the first tales he treated me to was the one you are about to read. Steve and I kept in touch until his death a few years later and afterwards his wife Tammy posted me his diaries, which she could not bear to keep. Within those extensive tomes, I discovered the story again in greater detail, and now present it to you, virtually unabridged, in the man's own words.

    In my long career as a writer, journalist and investigator of the paranormal, I have amassed many bizarre and disturbing tales of my own but little to equal this one. I have left it to the reader's discretion whether they choose to believe it or not. All I can say in Steve's defence is that he was a pragmatic and earthly kind of geezer and not prone to flights of fancy. At the time of the story, Steve was the Sheriff of the town of Enterprise in Oregon State and the year is 1975. As a word of warning to sensitive readers; backwoods America in the 70s wasn't the most "politically correct" of places and times so you might want to give this yarn a miss. In the future, if I get the chance, I may attempt to publish more of Steve's experiences but, at the moment, this is *the* Steve McQueen story. Rest in peace, Steve, I've always missed your laugh.

R.W. 10.6.1998.

*

I pulled into Devil's Creek at about 6.10pm. I knew some calamity had occurred: There were countless vehicles and people, including a few of my own deputies and rangers. The turkey roast I'd been daydreaming about all day, it seemed, would remain thus. My most attentive man saw my headlights coming.
'What we got, Clem?'
'Missing girl, Sheriff. Some kind o' retard.'
I parked the Chevy and found the core of the pandemonium; a crying woman. My new female deputy, Tammy, was doing her best to comfort her.
'This the mother?' I asked, removing my dark glasses.
'Temporary guardian, Sheriff,' explained Tammy.
'Temporary guardian?' I enquired looking at the woman. She was young and pretty.
'My name is Julie. I work at Happy Camp,' she clarified between sobs.
'The retard place up the highway?' I said.
'We prefer the name Happy Camp,' interrupted a guy with long hair, beard and sandals. 'It sounds more positive, don't you think?' I noticed his bus, covered in painted flowers. It was crammed with upset-looking youngsters. I had met this guy before. I had been up to the camp several times over the years for various reasons. His name was ...
'Gnarls Alderman.' He held out his hand.
I shook it. I didn't want to. Gnarls smelled bad and I always suspected the beatnik bastard was overly friendly with the kids, if you know what I mean.

'How long has the girl been missing?' I asked him.

'Over two hours now,' he replied. 'She had a tantrum and stormed off down that track.'

I followed the hippy's point; it was the main dirt trail leading into Devil's Creek Park. It was a popular walk with tourists but also the boundary of a big wilderness.

'We tried to find her but I guess she took off real fast,' Gnarls added.

'It's all my fault!' Julie blubbered. 'She was spitting at one of the other kids and I yelled at her. I shouldn't have yelled …' she broke down into tears again.

'Now don't you upset yourself,' said Tammy putting her arm round her. Some of the boys had objected to me appointing a female deputy but I knew that they were good for this kind of thing and Tammy was shaping up fast. I had no regrets.

I smiled and turned back to Gnarls. 'Name? Age? Appearance?'

'Her name is Ginger. She's sixteen with red hair. Goofy smile. About five' six''. Skinny. White sweater. Blue skirt. White socks. White sneakers.'

'You go on and take your people out of here. We'll find her and bring her home,' I told the pervert. He made like he was going to argue with me but the rest of his party were crying and hollering from the bus and I guess he knew it made sense.

'I don't know what I'm going to tell her parents,' he said.

'Don't tell them squat. We'll have her back before you know it,' I reasoned.

We waited for the Happy Camp to leave and I got my men (and Tammy) in a circle.

'It'll be dark soon, it's gonna be hard to find jack shit out there,' Denny Crabtree the old time ranger voiced what was on all of our minds.

'We're not going to try,' I said. 'Clem and Randy, you're on patrol tonight? Keep sweeping the local roads. Maybe the kid will turn up by the roadside. I'm gonna stay here all night and light a fire up on the tallest ridge. If she's in a twenty mile radius, she'll see it and hopefully come on back. If she don't show by daybreak, we'll get out the dogs and horses. I could use some company. Any volunteers?'

Would you believe it, out of about twelve men, nobody volunteered. Me being such fine companionship and all.

'I'll stay, Sheriff,' offered Tammy.

The boys looked up at me, excitedly.

'Haven't you got plans for the weekend, Tammy?' I suspected that the girl was trying to impress me because she was new. A few weeks on and she'd be like all the others; all heart till her shift was done.

She shook her head and I shrugged my shoulders. 'Okay, but run back to the office and get us some supplies first, especially my rifle. It could be a long night.'

My men dispersed. I said one last thing to Tammy before she left; 'call me Steve.'

'Okay, Sherr ... Steve,' she laughed. Cute. I hoped this didn't have the boys talking.

*

It wasn't a particularly long night. Tammy and I cooked some baloney and beans on the fire and we talked for a while. We settled down to sleep and Tammy went out like a light. She snored like a piglet for a little while, much to my amusement. I slumbered too though I kept one eye open and a hand on Betsy, my best rifle. There's all sorts of menace out in the Oregon wilderness; cougars, coyotes, wolves, bears. Very rarely have I known one of these critters to come wandering into a camp, them being frightened of the fire and all but you can't be too careful. It was mid-March, food sources were still scarce and a hungry predator is a dangerous one.

At first light, Clem and Randy came to check on us. Sadly, Ginger had not shown up. I told them to get the entire posse together. There would be a full search today.

Me and Tammy drove back into town. I thanked her for her extra duty and I intended to drop her off but Tammy was keen on seeing the job through. So, we washed and changed into clean uniforms. By the time we returned to Devil's Creek an hour later, there were some fifty men looking alert; deputies, rangers and volunteers. There were also hounds and steeds. Clem and Randy had done a fine job of rounding up every available man and creature. I wanted them to get started as soon as possible so I kept my talking down to a minimum. They all knew what to do anyhow. This was a well-rehearsed procedure for missing persons. I insisted on things being that way. I watched as the various posses split up and marched out into the wilds. Soon, all I could hear was the eager baying of the dogs in the distance.

'We better go see the Happy Camp,' I said to Tammy.

'Never did care for this place much,' I told my new female deputy as we drove into the meadow with three run-down log cabins in it. This comprised the so-called Happy Camp.

'I suppose it's good for them to get out here into the country,' reasoned Tammy.

'And look what happens!' I said, pulling up and getting out. I felt bad saying this as I knew Tammy was kind of right. I didn't feel the need to tell her that I thought the head guy was a kiddy-messer.

'Please tell me she's okay!' hollered Julie, running towards us. She was almost crying again. Gnarls and a couple of the retards were hot on her heels.

I put my hands up. 'We haven't found her yet but she'll be okay, I guarantee it.'

'How can you say that?' The hippy deviant challenged me.

'She's been out there all night on her own!' Julie sank to her knees and began sniveling. One of the retards started weeping too. The other one laughed.

'No one has ever gone missing while I've been Sheriff of Enterprise,' I explained. 'We always find them.' I knew this was a lie. Four years ago a woman and her baby had vanished. They turned up three days later in the stomach of a bear.

'And what are you doing about it exactly?' Gnarls sneered.

'I got my fifty best men out looking for Ginger right now. We'll find her,' I said with confidence. I always find that it's best to take my dark glasses off when dealing with a sensitive situation. Let folks see the light in my eyes.

'Can I tell the girl's parents now?' asked Gnarls.

I nodded and he walked back towards the cabins. The two cooky kids followed him. We stayed a while longer with Julie. I watched her cry with a sinking heart, I have to confess. I had given these people a promise now. I had no choice but to find that girl. I knew the longer it got, the more chance that something awful had occurred. Sometimes the great American wilderness just swallows up folks whole and they are never seen or heard of again.

*

The day wore on and I grew increasingly anxious. I tried not to let frustration get the better of me but as the posses started coming back empty-handed and the sky began to darken again, it got real tricky. To add to my vexation, some of the guys told me that their horses and dogs were getting spooked in the woods, you know; they'd picked up the scent of something which scared the hell out of them and had refused to go on. This was something new to me. Despite living in these parts all my life, I'd never heard of the local steeds and hounds losing their nerve. They had a reputation for bravery.

I got my closest confidants together. 'What the hell have we got here?'

'Could be a cougar, a big one,' was the first suggestion from Stig Waltman, the trapper. 'We found some impressive paw prints down by the river.'

'When have you ever known a cougar drag a full-sized human very far?' rationalised Clem. 'We'd have found remains by now.'

'Big Yella could be back,' mused Ben King, my longest-serving deputy.

'The head of Big Yella graces my fireplace,' I reminded Ben. This made the boys laugh a little. 'Still, a big bad crazy bear is the only thing likely to spook the beasts I suppose, though it's still a new one on me.'

'Son of Big Yella?' said Ben.

'This isn't the goddam movies, Ben,' I said.

'She could have just taken a tumble down a canyon,' was the morbid offering from Ed Brunswick, the county's best horse tamer. 'We just haven't found the body yet. We need to look out for circling buzzards.'

'Bigfoot?' I didn't see who had made this suggestion at first.

'What? Who said that?' I didn't much care for stories of the local boogeyman. It seemed to me that Mother Nature had enough real dangers without having to invent any.

'Me,' admitted Lance Bakerfield, Chief Ranger at the creek.

'Lance! I'm surprised at you,' I said. 'Bigfoot isn't real and you know it. Can we stay in the real world, please?'

Lance scowled at me like I'd insulted him. 'The Indians believe in him.'

'The Indians believe in a whole bunch of horseshit,' I said.

'They say Bigfoot got a bad stench and that animals are frightened of him,' added Jamie Bakerfield, Lance's eldest son.

'There ain't no goddam Bigfoot!' I yelled. It was too loud. Everyone within the vicinity was now glaring at me, not just my inner circle.

'Sorry, Steve,' Lance and his boy apologised and I felt bad.

'Forget it,' I said. 'I'll find this kid myself, be it a cougar, a bear or some goddam Sasquatch!'

*

Night fell and I sat on the back of my Chevy and drank coffee, thinking on what to do next. Most of the search teams had given up for now and gone home to rest. There was some talk of venturing out to hunt in the dark but with all the weird speculations, it wasn't just the dogs and horses that were losing their courage.

Tammy came over. 'Are you starting to regret what you said to those people, Steve?' she asked.

'What people?' I said.

'The Happy Camp?' she said.

'Yeah, I suppose I am, Tammy,' I confessed. 'The only thing I can do to keep my promise is to go out there and find this girl myself.'

'Are you really going to do that?' she enquired.

'I have to,' I said.

'Then I'm coming with you,' stated Tammy.

'No,' I shook my head. 'You go on home and enjoy what's left of the weekend. You've done more than enough.'

'I really want to help,' she explained.

I leveled with her. 'You don't have to impress me, Tammy, I know you're gonna be a great officer.'

'It's not that,' she said. 'I feel attached to this, you know.'

I looked searchingly into Tammy's big brown eyes and could see her determination.

'Okay,' I said. 'But there are definitely gonna be some rumours!'

*

I decided to drive up to Eagle Cap Reservation to pick up some much needed help. This would come in the form of Leoty, the most beautiful Indian woman you ever did see in your life. She was built like a goddess, had shiny black hair that sank to her waist and her queer golden eyes could melt a man's heart at ten paces. Leoty also happened to be the best tracker in the county, if not the state, if not the whole goddam US of A. If she couldn't trace this kid then no one could. The boundary of the reservation was guarded by some of the younger guys. They'd had a lot of trouble recently with folks trespassing on their land; developers, tourists, trouble-makers. They were aggressive and armed to the teeth but when they saw it was me, they softened and let me through. A couple of years ago, I saved Leoty from getting raped by a bunch of local sleazeballs. That made me friends with the tribe for life and meant that Leoty owed me a favour. It was time to call it in.

'McQueen!' said Leoty when she saw me and threw her arms around me like I was a long lost member of the family.

I could see the surprise on Tammy's face and it made me smirk. 'This is the Indian tracker?' my deputy asked, open-mouthed.

We were invited into Leoty's log cabin. Most of the tribe had given up living in wigwams a long time ago. I was pleased to see that Twasimotokai, Leoty's father, was there too. He was a cunning old Indian brave that I was fond of. Many times had I lost track of time listening to his wisdom and stories.

'You are welcome, McQueen,' he greeted me as we came in and sat down on the floor with him. 'You are here because of the missing girl,' he said straight away.

I nodded. 'You've heard about that, huh?'

'The eagles told me,' stated Twasimotokai. Sometimes he would say weird shit like that. You know, funny, silly stuff, but always with a straight face. I was never sure whether to laugh or not. I speculated that he was perhaps being serious but not literal.

'You want my daughter to find her?' he queried.

'I'm desperate, 'Kai,' I admitted. 'My best men are clueless.'

We whiled some of the night smoking pipes, drinking coffee and talking about this and that. Uncanny tracker that Leoty was, I couldn't expect her to start a search in the dark. They let me and Tammy drift off to sleep in the cabin and we caught an hour or three of peace. Leoty woke us as the first beam of dawn speared over the horizon.

'It's time, McQueen,' she said dramatically and my heart began to race with anticipation of the hunt.

Before we left the reservation, Twasimotokai made one last remark to me: 'Some things are not meant to be found, McQueen.'

I wasn't sure what the spooky old buzzard meant but his words echoed around in my head as we drove in silence back to Devil's Creek.

*

There was a kind of early grey light as we reached the park and it was bitterly cold. Me and Tammy had to put on our fur-lined jackets and caps to stay warm. I remember thinking that if nothing else, then the missing kid had probably died of exposure by now. Leoty did not seem to feel the chill. She just wore jeans, boots, bandana and a denim shirt with cut-off sleeves, like it was the middle of summer.

The only equipment she carried was a knife. I was amused by Tammy's bewilderment at this.

I had arranged for Ed Brunswick to meet us there with three of his best colts.

'Take care of 'em, Sheriff,' he pleaded as we saddled up.

'Don't worry, Ed, you just keep that jug o' coffee warm, we'll back before you can whistle Dixie,' I reassured him. I knew he had genuine affection for his animals and I was reluctant to take them. However, it was now thirty-six hours since Ginger had vanished and we needed to cover some ground.

Getting on the horses proved to be a waste of time at first. Leoty had to examine the trail where the disappearance had occurred and to do this, she had to dismount. This seemed to take hours and she looked at every stone and blade of grass for a two mile stretch. Me and Tammy could do nothing except try to wait patiently on horses that were champing at their bits. Tammy's colt had a will of its own and this brought some light relief. Well, at least it did for me.

'I thought you said you were a farm girl.' I howled with laughter as her horse wandered this way and that.

'I am!' Tammy blushed and tried her best to rein him in.

It wasn't till mid-morning that Leoty made any progress. Me and Tammy were just about to pour out some coffee from a flask.

'McQueen!' the Indian girl proclaimed.

I went over to see what she had found. Leoty showed me some broken twigs on a huckleberry bush and some fresh footprints leading off the path.

'This is where she left the trail,' she explained.

Forgetting the coffee, we mounted and we were off. Leoty rode slightly ahead, half-hanging from the saddle to peer at the ground as she went. Unlike Tammy's steed, her beast was perfectly calm and obedient. I guess that even animals were susceptible to her charm.

Most people head for the creek in these parts. Either to admire its natural splendour or to fish or to canoe. If our missing girl had done the same, then she would have been easy to track. The ground round the creek is soft clay and she would have left prints that a blind man could have followed. As we rode away from the creek into the woods instead, it dawned on me why we hadn't found her yet. The ground here offered few clues. It was thick with scrub and brush and root. Only a tracker who was born into it like Leoty could find some semblance of a trail. Although she had to stop a few times, she seemed sure that Ginger had come this way.

Few folks with any sense wander into the woods. There are a few trails known to hunters and trappers but even the most experienced country man can get lost. Human beings are no longer top of the food chain in this territory. I was aware of this and I had Betsy on my lap now, fully loaded with the safety catch off. I had enough ammunition with me to shoot every critter in the park. To be honest, I have always loved nature and all of its beasts. I would much rather see them mosey freely in their own environment than shoot them. Don't get me wrong, I ain't no hippy but I have to confess that it pains me that so many men come here to end the lives of wonderful creatures and take home their pelts and heads as trophies. I had only one head on my wall but it was that of Big Yella, a bear with a distinguishable blonde mane who had turned man-eater. I had no choice but to put the bastard down. He tore a sizable piece out of my gut first and I spent two months in hospital because of him. The boys had his big old shaggy head stuffed and mounted for me while I was gone. I could have done without it. I had nightmares about the creep for a long time and the last thing I wanted was to see him staring down at me every morning while I was having my breakfast. My mutilated torso is reminder enough. I'm sure my boys meant the best.

 I followed Leoty closely. We rode further into the woods and soon got to the point where all we could see were trees in all directions. It grew dim under those gigantic conifers and our horizon became barely ten feet. My tracker had her eyes on the ground and Tammy, behind me, was still struggling with her wayward horse, so it was mainly up to me to keep an eye out for pouncing terrors. Encouragingly, Leoty told us that she could find traces of a wandering girl. Although we wondered between us what would possess a young lady to drift out here, it gave us hope that Leoty had not found any signs of a wild beast. In other words, it seemed that Ginger had meandered of her own accord rather than been taken by anything.

 The afternoon dragged on and the heat gathered under the trees. I myself began to feel a little drowsy and regular doses of caffeine were the only thing keeping me sharp. Every time I started to nod off in my saddle and the shadows began to blur, I called back to my deputy for more coffee. Our lives depended on it. In hindsight, staying up most of the night talking to Twasimotokai and smoking his pipe hadn't set me up well for a day's tracking. It didn't help that the going was slow and Leoty had to halt increasingly more and more to detect signs of the girl's passing. My horse seemed to be getting a little edgy, with the occasional whinny or snort.

Leoty noticed it too. 'The horses are nervous, McQueen.'

'Some of my boys experienced this yesterday,' I explained to her. I didn't feel the need to mention Bigfoot.

'Perhaps they need a rest, some water,' she recommended.

'Maybe we do too,' I responded.

We found a stream not far ahead and allowed the colts to calm down and drink. Me and Tammy had some more coffee and supplemented it with some donuts we'd brought along. I think my new female deputy really appreciated getting down off that animal. She stretched her cramped legs, rubbed her sore hands and massaged her aching butt. I laughed and wondered if she'd had any regrets about coming along but didn't want to ask just yet. I slurped my Joe and munched my pastry and gave her my best reassuring smile. Despite suggesting the break, my Indian guide did not participate. She continued to mosey around in the undergrowth, looking for more pointers. Suddenly:

'McQueen! Come quick!'

I damn nearly choked on my donut. I was across to Leoty like a shot, rifle drawn. Tammy too, with her revolver.

'Clothes,' said Leoty. She was stood over something, looking down.

Tammy and I rummaged through the discarded belongings on the ground. There was a white sweater, white socks, white sneakers, a blue skirt and some yellow panties. They were grubby but thankfully, not torn or bloody. It looked like they had simply been removed and left.

'These belong to the missing girl?' asked Leoty.

'They match the description,' I replied.

'Why in God's name would she take off her clothes?' Tammy asked the question on all of our minds.

I shrugged my shoulders. 'Sometimes kids like to go swimming,' was all I could think of saying and I looked towards the stream where the horses were slurping.

'That stream ain't nowhere near deep enough for skinny-dippin', Steve,' Tammy rationalised.

I knew she was right. 'Well, at least it's just clothes and not a body.'

'She'll have frozen to death without these,' contemplated Tammy.

We took what we believed were Ginger's clothes. Tammy put them in her backpack. All three of us looked around a little. I was worried about what we might find but I didn't want to show this to my two female companions. I knew that the women were probably looking to me for strength so I just kept on smiling and stayed hopeful. My optimism paid off: Leoty soon found a couple of dainty bare footprints leading away from the scene. It seemed that our quarry had advanced even further into the wilderness, this time, without so much as a stitch on. Picking up the trail again, we pursued as quickly as we could but things didn't get any easier. The great forest knitted thicker the further we went. Not only thicker but lower. It was impossible to ride the horses and their drink at the stream had done little to ease their anxiety. We seemed to be almost dragging them along. Tammy and I whispered encouragement to them but we were no horse tamers like Ed. I was starting to get annoyed. Our steeds were becoming more of a hindrance than a help. I was so preoccupied with keeping them moving that I had little opportunity to do what I should have been doing; keeping an eye out with Betsy. Somehow, Leoty kept track of Ginger. Her own particular animal was relatively well behaved and allowed her to do her job. Tammy and I couldn't tell what it was that she was whispering into its ear as it was in Indian. Whatever it was, it seemed to be doing the trick. I noticed that Tammy kept flicking fierce glances at the tracker. I reckon that maybe she was getting a little jealous of her talents. This made me smile but I cannot express my relief in words when the damn trees started spacing out again a few miles later. The ground started to rise and became rocky.

'Where the hell are we?' I muttered.

'The Wallowa,' answered Leoty.

'We're in the mountains already?' I said. I was genuinely bewildered. I was sure that we hadn't travelled that far.

'It's just the foothills,' explained Leoty.

I shrugged my shoulders. Being in the woods all afternoon had obviously ruined my orientation. I realised that we'd now followed this kid for nearly twenty miles!

We climbed up onto a long bony ridge and looked out across an ocean of tree tops. There was a big sky, as we say in America, and we could see as far as Idaho. I wiped the sweat from my brow and allowed what remained of the day's sun to warm my face. Tammy tethered her unruly horse immediately and sat down on a fallen tree trunk which must have seemed like heaven on her ass after hours in the saddle. She looked forlorn. Leoty didn't allow herself any respite at all, she began walking up and down the bare spine of the ridge, looking for the next clue.

Tammy finally voiced her frustration. 'Doesn't she ever stop?'

I laughed long and loud and then said seriously; 'I guess she really wants to find this kid.'

'So do I,' said Tammy, dejectedly.

I went over and put a hand on Tammy's shoulder. 'She couldn't have gone much farther. Let's have some more of that coffee.'

We perched our weary bones for a while and had a caffeine fix. I was concerned about the furrows on Leoty's brow when she finally stopped pacing.

'What is it?' I asked.

'The trail's gone cold,' she said.

I got up and strolled over to the edge of the ridge with her. The other side was a sheer drop. It fell at least a hundred feet into the depths of more woods. Me and Leoty peered down and looked at each other. We didn't need to say it.

'What are we going to do?' cried Tammy as we mooched back over. It was a good question.

I looked up at the sky for an answer. 'We haven't got much daylight left and the way forward isn't clear so I say we sleep on it.'

'We're gonna stay out here?' moaned Tammy.

'This is a good place,' I explained. 'We can do what we did the first night and light a fire. It's high enough up here for the kid to see it and maybe she'll come on over.'

'If she's still alive,' added Leoty, unhelpfully.

'We haven't got much choice anyhow,' I said. 'We don't want to be making our way back through that bush in the dark, trust me.'

I radioed back to Clem and, thankfully, he was still in range, though we must have been pushing it. I told him that we were spending the night and not to worry, as we occupied an elevated position. It didn't exactly test the combined skills of the three of us to make a fire. There was so much dry wood lying around that a city boy could have done it. Without much to eat or much to say, we laid out and tried to catch some sleep. I must confess that I felt a little lucky that night. It took me a while to drop off and I got thinking. Here I was, in the middle of nowhere, with the stars twinkling above me and either side of me, two of the most beautiful women in the county.

*

A scream awoke me. My eyes snapped open. I must have dropped off. I looked to my left and Tammy was gone. I turned to the right and Leoty was gone too. I shook the slumber from my head, grabbed Betsy and staggered to my feet. There was another scream but I couldn't tell who it was. My heart was hammering.

'Tammy? Leoty?' I hollered and peered out into the darkness. I couldn't see jack shit except for the fire and the tethered horses nearby and they too were in a state of panic. I called out again but there was just silence now. For the first time in my life I genuinely didn't know what to do. I have always enjoyed sharp instincts and like my daddy before me, and his daddy before him, my decisiveness in an emergency got me my Sheriff's badge. I stomped around for a while and shouted into the night. Before I could summon the sense to do anything useful, the ladies came out of the gloom, holding onto each other like goddam lesbians.

'What the hell?' I yelled. 'You nearly gave me a heart attack!'

'Oh, Steve!' sobbed Tammy. She ran over and threw her arms around me. She was shocked and I was shocked too but I held her lithe body close to me while she soaked my shoulder. I peered over at Leoty for an explanation but her perfect Indian features yielded nothing. I had to wait for my deputy to calm down.

'I had to go pee,' Tammy finally said.

'Jesus, Tammy!' I growled. 'You should know better than to go wandering off into the woods by yourself at this hour.'

'I'm sorry.' She wiped the tears from her eyes. 'A girl's gotta have her privacy.'

'Did you get a fright?' I queried.

She nodded and all she could manage to say was 'eyes …'

'Eyes?' I urged.

'There were eyes watching me,' she clarified.

'An animal?'

Tammy shook her head.

'A man?'

Tammy shook her head again.

'Not an animal? Not a man? Then what in the holy kingdom?'

'I don't know … just eyes … horrible …' Tammy started crying and wrapped her arms around me again.

'This isn't right, Tammy,' I said firmly and sat her down by the fire. I grabbed a flask of bourbon from my coat and offered this as an alternative means of comfort. She took it and sipped, then screwed up her face and handed it back to me. I took a gulp myself and allowed the firewater to dull me down. I turned to Leoty.

'Did you see anything?' I asked.

'I saw nothing,' she replied.

Tammy glared at her, resentfully.

I crouched down and put my hand on her shoulder. 'The imagination can do funny things out here, deputy.'

'I saw nothing,' repeated Leoty; 'but we are being watched.'

'What?' I scowled at her.

'We've been watched since the start.'

I stood up and looked into the tracker's strange yellow eyes. She was a tall woman and we were at equal height. 'Why didn't you say anything?'

'I wasn't sure,' she explained. 'I've caught glances of something through the trees; a stench on the wind, footprints here and there. I think your deputy has confirmed what I feared.'

'Then what in the shit and shinola is it?'

Leoty shook her head. 'I wish I knew, McQueen.'

That was pretty much the end of the discussion. Both women were spooked and, I have to admit, I was too. We stuck close to the fire till dawn and said little more. Twasimotokai's warning bounced around my mind: 'Some things are not meant to be found, McQueen.'

*

At first light, we rose and mounted the horses. The fire we had built was still smouldering and the smoke could be seen for leagues around. Despite this, no missing girl had come to us. Silently, with whatever hope we had left in our hearts, we rode down the ridge and onto the forest floor. It was a long and steep descent and it wasn't till mid-morning that we reached the base of the cliff where the trail had ended. It was morbid but I expected to find Ginger's body there. It seemed that a fall in the dark was the most plausible conclusion. We found nothing, however, not even any evidence that she had been there at all.

I could see the frustration mounting on Leoty's face long before she said anything. 'I have failed you, McQueen.'

'Now, I'll have none of that bullshit,' I replied. 'You're the best there is, Leo.'

'A bloodhound could have scented her as far as I tracked her,' she confessed.

'The goddam dogs turned tail as soon as they reached the edge of the woods,' I reminded her.

'We could ride a little further in.' A little optimism restored, Leoty gestured onward into the trees.

I turned to Tammy and saw the reluctant expression on her face though she said nothing. I too felt hesitant at the prospect of another night out in the wilderness. 'Maybe just for another hour or two,' I decided.

Just as we spurred the horses into the shadows there came an almighty hollering from deep within the woods; an unholy kind of whooping scream that pierced through the air. It was like nothing I've heard in my life. My blood curdled but the horses were the first to panic. Mine and Tammy's steeds both bucked us to the floor and galloped away in different directions. Leoty kept control of her beast but it danced and sprang around for a while, fighting the urge to copy its kin. The horrific scream was replaced by Tammy's cries of agony. I picked myself up and bolted over to her. She was face down and her left arm was bent at an unnatural angle. An inch of bone had speared through the skin of her elbow.

Before I could say to her 'don't look!' she looked.

'Keep still, Tammy, keep still!' I said and held her down.

Leoty's terrified horse nearly crashed into us. I tried my best to comfort Tammy until Leoty had regained mastery of the animal.

'That's it!' I determined. 'We're gonna have to turn back!'

'What was that noise?' questioned the Indian tracker as she joined us.

'I don't know,' I replied; 'but whatever it was it sounds super-pissed.'

'We have to go on,' said Tammy somewhat ridiculously from behind clenched teeth.

I shook my head. 'Tammy, you've broke your arm, sugar.'

'She's right, McQueen,' reasoned Leoty. 'That cry! It could be connected with the disappearance?'

'No way!' I said. 'Officer down! Tammy is priority now!'

Me and Leoty huddled around Tammy for a while. My deputy was obviously in a lot of pain and was losing consciousness. I couldn't contemplate continuing the hunt, at least, not with her. I made a fresh decision.

'Leoty? Can you get Tammy back to Devil's Creek on that horse?'

She nodded. 'I'll try my best. Why? What about you?'

'I'm gonna take a look at whatever made that scream,' I said and picked up my rifle with intention.

Leoty glared at me for a moment and then nodded. I helped her and Tammy to mount the remaining colt. My deputy sat at the front and the Indian girl saddled up behind her, wrapping her arms around Tammy to support her and take the rein. There was nothing more to say. Leoty looked at me with resolution and Tammy glared at me with fear, her eyes wet with pain. I smiled at them and they rode away.

*

So, I wandered alone. All I had was Betsy to keep me company. The woods were wild here and I wondered if I was the first man to grace them. Steps forward were tiresome, the ground was broken and uneven and the undergrowth was dense. Often, I had to make my way around a spot that was impossible to traverse. There were no signs of animals, not even a bird song; a fact that worried me. Sweat trickled down my spine and my breath was heavy. I had flashbacks to Vietnam but I doubted that it was the Vietcong lying in wait for me this time. In hindsight, it was a good job that the horses had gone and my thoughts frequently returned to the ladies. I would never forgive myself if anything happened to them now. These godforsaken woods could chew me up and spit me out, just as long as those two good women made it home safely.

It was mid-afternoon when I questioned my own sanity. It was already so dark under the forest that it might have well been night and the trees were so closely packed together, I was virtually unable to move. I stopped, wiped my brow and neck with a handkerchief that was already soaked, and peered around into the gloom. I was reluctant to advance any further. I could not track Ginger as Leoty had done. If that girl had walked all the way out here by herself, she was almost certainly dead by now and we would never find so much as a body to bring back. I truly hate to quit in any situation but I had met my match here. If I didn't turn around and head back to civilisation now, then I too, would become just another name on the missing persons register. It was then that I saw them: A pair of black eyes staring at me from the bushes. My heart skipped a beat.

I slowly raised Betsy. 'You better come out from there, asshole!'

I meant to say this with my usual authority but I have to confess, that my voice trembled. The eyes were so piercing and savage but, at the same time, filled with a human intelligence. I knew that these were the same peepers that creeped Tammy last night. They continued to glare at me.

'What the hell are you?' I muttered, half to myself. I was ready to fire.

'What the hell are you?' came the reply. I leapt out of my skin. I hadn't expected an answer. It was low and guttural.

I swallowed back my fear. 'You're gonna have to come on out or I'm gonna shoot!'

'You're in no position to make demands, Sheriff McQueen,' said the menace in the bushes in a tone that was loosening my bowls.

I didn't understand at first but there was a sound to the left of me and I saw what the thing meant; someone else was pointing a shotgun at me from the shadows. I turned to my right and there was another firearm aimed at my head. I was surrounded.

I nodded to the eyes in the undergrowth to show that I understood and lowered Betsy. Guardian of the law I might be but an idiot I am not.

'Very good,' growled the voice, mockingly. The undergrowth rustled as its owner revealed himself and the strangest goddam bastard I've ever did see emerged from that bush. He was short and wiry and a man of sorts. He wore trousers and jacket that were ragged and patched but I could see that the rest of his body was covered entirely in thick black hair. His head was a ball of fuzz from which those devilish eyes continued to stare. He looked like a giant monkey though his face was snout-like and resembled more of a wolf. My mouth dropped open and my rifle tumbled from my slack hands. He laughed at my horror and revealed a pair of pearly white teeth.

'What are you?' I asked.

'Just a man like you,' he said. 'You're out of your jurisdiction.'

'The hell I am!' I yelled, my anger replacing my fear. 'This is a national park and it's my goddam responsibility!'

'It's also our home and has been for many years,' the hairy man explained.

It was then that something clicked in the back of my mind. My granddaddy had literally hundreds of stories he used to tell me when I was a kid. One of those tales was about a local woman who'd given birth to a peculiar pair of twins; they were covered entirely in hair. She tried to bring them up for a few years but the attention and ridicule the wolf-children brought was too much and they were abandoned in the wilderness to fend for themselves. I always thought that my granddaddy's yarns were a royal bunch of horseshit but I was now being forced to review that belief. Here was a creature that had walked out of a fairy-tale.

'You're the wolf-children?' I said.

The man cackled again. There seemed to be genuine mirth in his laugh and it relaxed me a little. I hadn't actually soiled my pants yet and that was a bonus.

'My grandparents were called such a thing in your world I think,' he said eventually.

'And you've lived out here all this time?' I quizzed.

'It's not so bad,' he grinned. 'You couldn't expect us to live in normal society, Sheriff, except as some kind of circus attraction?'

I had to admit that he had a point. I dared to look to my left at the shotgun wielder. He had stepped a little closer and I could see that he shared the affliction. He was taller and better built and his hair was lighter yet he was still covered in the stuff. The guy to my right was not, however. He was a different kind of freak. In contrast, he was completely hairless and smooth but his eyes were bulging, so much so, that they looked like they were about to pop out completely. The original wolf-man caught my reaction.

'We're not all hirsute,' he stated.

'Hirsute?' I queried.

'The name given to our condition,' he explained. 'The only thing we have in common is that we're not welcome in normal society. Out here, we get left alone. No one knows we're here.'

'Until now. How many of you are there?' I asked, my incredulity stretched to maximum.

'A few,' was his ambiguous answer.

I puffed and looked round at them. 'Well, I'm looking for a missing girl.'

'Ginger?' asked the shaggy spokesman.

Despite the fact that I was surrounded by monsters with guns out in the middle of nowhere, my spirits lifted for a moment. 'You've seen her?'

'She's safe. She's with us,' he said.

I cringed. 'What?'

The wolf-man let out a cry. It was the same whooping scream that had panicked Tammy's horse earlier. Despite the fact that I now knew what made the noise, I was no less chilled. He seemed to direct it elsewhere into the woods. We waited in silence while some others responded to his call and came crashing through the undergrowth to join us. There was a big fat woman and a skinny teenage girl with ginger hair. They held hands like mother and child and wore tattered old dresses.

I looked at the girl. 'Ginger?'

She turned to the fat woman and then back to me and nodded. She looked happy, like this collection of oddballs were her beloved kin.

'What in tarnation is going on here?' I said, exasperated. 'Why did you leave her clothes?' I asked, looking at the filthy rag that the girl now wore.

'Throw the dogs off the scent,' said boggle-eyes.

'Ginger is one of us now, Sheriff,' said the wolf-man.

'The hell she is!' I sneered and bent down for Betsy but the two gunmen growled and closed in to remind me that they still had the advantage. I left the rifle on the ground and straightened up.

It was Ginger who spoke next: 'I want to stay!'

'You don't understand, darlin'' I said to her. 'You can't stay out here. There are people waiting for you. People who want you back.'

'I don't want to go back,' she said. 'The man at the camp ... he tries to hurt me.'

I felt wrath building up inside me. I always knew that beatnik deviant touched the kids.

'Then I'll take you back to your folks,' I said.

'But Daddy tries to hurt me too!' squealed Ginger and burst into tears. The big momma took her in her arms.

'We may look strange, Sheriff,' said the wolf-man; 'but the real monsters are the ones hiding amongst you.'

His words were meaningful and to this day, still stick in my mind.

'I understand,' I said; 'but there's a procedure for dealing with this. You can't just go taking other people's kids no matter how unhappy they are. How will she survive out here?'

'She'll be taken care of, Sheriff,' replied the big lady.

'I'm sorry,' I said. 'I can't let this happen!'

'We're not going to give you the choice,' the wolf-man grinned.

Something blunt and heavy connected with the back of my skull.

*

The next thing I knew was waking up in bed. My vision was blurred for a few moments and I could not identify the faces looking down at me. As they came into focus, I saw that it was surrounded by friends; my deputies Tammy and Clem, Ed Brunswick the horse tamer and Lance Bakerfield, Head Ranger at Devils Creek. I felt like I'd had a bad dream.

'How's your coconut, Sheriff?' asked Clem with a grin.

'Tender,' I said, aware of the throbbing pain in my head. 'Where am I?'

'County hospital,' explained Tammy. Her arm was in a cast and sling but she looked happy.

'How you doin'?' I asked her.

'It'll mend,' she said with a wink. 'Thanks.'

'And Leoty?' I asked, thinking of my tracker.

'She's A-okay, Steve. Back at the reservation. You've been out cold for two days,' she said.

'Your horses, Ed?'

'They came on back, Sheriff, eventually,' he replied.

'You remember what happened, Sheriff?' questioned Lance. 'My men found you unconscious, down by the Creek. We tried to bring you round and you did ... briefly, muttering some hooey about wolf-men!'

Everyone sniggered at this but my blood froze. Images of hairy gunmen and boggle-eyed freaks swam back into my aching cranium. I thought deeply for a moment and considered telling them about the peculiar clan but I also remembered what Ginger had told me. 'I don't know,' I smiled. 'I must have taken a tumble and hit my head on somethin'.'

*

That's just about the end of my story. As far as I know, no one ever saw Ginger or the people in the woods again and, until now, I never told anyone about what happened. My favourite rifle became just a memory too as they had stolen Betsy from me. The Happy Camp got closed down by the authorities and reports of child abuse by Gnarls Alderman started flooding in. The sick bastard was ultimately prosecuted. My cracked skull mended, as did Tammy's arm, and we returned to active duty. I suppose I should mention that five months later we were married. Leoty became the bride of her tribe's chief, Little Bear. She and Tammy became good friends and the four of us go fishing most weekends.

One night a couple of years ago, I was relaxing on my back porch with a cold beer, gazing out across the woods and mountains. For an instant, I thought I heard the dreadful cry of that wolf-man in the distance but I could not be sure.

Mother Astra

Tommy was weeding the garden when a rock fell from the sky. He heard it whistling through the air as it dropped to earth. He stood up with a fist full of dandelion and cringed at the sun. The smouldering object landed at his feet.

'Well, I'll go to the foot of our stairs!'

Tommy bent down and picked it up. It was both warm and cold. He frowned at the small smoking crater it had made in his lawn. He glanced over at the kitchen window. He could hear Astra singing but could not see her mop of curly brown hair. He went inside. She was emptying meat out of a tin into Jeff's bowl.

'Look what I've just found.'

Astra looked up and scowled. 'Where?'

'Outside in the garden. It came out of the sky.'

Astra marched outside and peered into the cloudless blue heavens, as if expecting to see more rocks fall. 'You're having fun with me, you old goat.'

Tommy followed her, still clutching his discovery. 'It plain and simple did! Here, look, it's going green.'

Astra snatched the rock from him and revolved it around in her frail hands, its black crust was breaking away, leaving it smooth and glassy.

'Ooh, it's heavy! I'd say it was more aqua coloured.'

'Aqua? Is that a colour?'

'Of course it is, like the sea, isn't it?'

'It looks green to me with bits of orange and brown maybe.'

'Are we looking at the same thing? It's aqua.'

'Aqua's not a proper colour.'

'It blooming well is, you nanna!'

Edwin came out into the garden. Astra spotted a potential ally.

'What colour would you say this is?' She held the rock out to him.

'Snoob,' said Edwin, adjusting both his huge glasses and false teeth.

'What about aqua?' Astra was not giving any ground.

'Aqua?'

'See, he doesn't know what it is either.' Tommy sniggered with triumph.

'Like the colour of the sea!' Astra slammed the rock into Edwin's hand.

'Careful, it's hot!' shouted Tommy.

Edwin shrieked and dropped it on the ground. Tommy bellowed with laughter.

Astra picked it up. 'He's playing with you!' she said and gave it back to Edwin. She sat down on a wall and lit up a fag while Edwin examined the find.

'Rubble bubble,' he said eventually and walked back towards the house.

'Where are you going with my rock?' Tommy glared at him.

He stopped and came back.

'It's mine!' Astra claimed.

'That's not fair, I found it! It landed at my very feet.'

'It's mine because I dreamst it,' Astra exhaled with satisfaction. Jeff joined them in the garden but seemed more interested in the flies that plagued Tommy's wheelbarrow than the meteorite.

'I blinking knew it!' Tommy shook his head.

'I did! Last night.'

'Why didn't you say something then?'

'When?'

'When I first showed you the rock? Why didn't you say that you'd "dreamst" it?'

'I was getting round to it.'

'How convenient.'

'Are you calling me a liar?' Astra was snarling and it was ferocious enough for Tommy to back off. He stumbled off to persecute more dandelions.

'Let's hope one doesn't fall on your head,' he muttered.

'I heard that!'

Jeff grew tired of snapping at flies and sank down next to Astra, panting in the heat. Edwin tried to pat him but Jeff shrank away and laid his head under the chair.

'He doesn't like to be fussed when it's warm,' explained Astra.

Edwin turned his attention back to the rock. He fondled every nook and cranny with his vast sausage-like fingers and freed it entirely from its black shell. He held it up in the sun and it glittered. He snorted with gratification.

'I saw the blue sky in my sleep and I knew it would be a fair day. I saw this thing drop from out of nowhere too and it was no surprise to me when it did,' Astra said to Edwin but loud enough so Tommy could also hear.

'So what?' commented Tommy, disappearing into his shed.

'Tumble crumble,' said Edwin.

'Meaning that if I dreamst it then it must be significant.'

'Blinking Nora!' said the voice from the murky interior of the shed.

'Pass it to me,' instructed Astra to Edwin. He did as he was told. She turned the object around in her palms. 'I'll have to remember the rest of my dream to know what to do with it.'

'You do that,' said the voice from the shed with sarcasm.

'You carry on mocking me, Tommy Coomber, see what happens!'

Suddenly Tommy emerged from the shed, lawnmower blaring. Waves of grass erupted from its metallic jaws in all directions. Edwin screeched and ran back inside, closely followed by Jeff. Astra's peace was ruined and she made for the house too. She exclaimed some profanities at Tommy but they were drowned out by the din of the machine.

*

The rock in the shop window was of the same material as the one that dropped from the sky. It was a slightly larger and more jagged lump, nestled amongst other mineral samples and knick-knacks for tourists. Astra and Tommy peered at it through the glass.

'See?' she said.

'Well I'll be a monkey's uncle,' he said, smoothing out his mighty silver moustache.

'I dreamst this one too.'

'It must be common then?'

'What?'

'This stuff?'

'No, it isn't, it isn't at all. It's come from the stars.'

'Well, one fell out of the sky this morning and now here's another in our local shop?'

'Just coincidence, my bunny rabbit. Let's buy it.'

'With what?'

'Your money.'

'I haven't got any money!'

'You have so!'

Exasperated, Tommy turned to Edwin who was stood behind them with an ice cream in one hand and Jeff's lead in the other. The neglected treat was dripping in rivulets down his knuckles.

'Will you be alright out here with the dog, Edwin?'

Edwin grinned by way of response. Jeff wagged his tail lazily in the heat. Tommy and Astra went into the shop. A young girl regarded them from behind a counter, her long golden hair blowing in the synthetic wind of an electric fan.

'That's the way to do it,' Tommy beamed at her.

'Sorry?' the girl looked confused and frightened.

'The way to keep cool.'

'You've got lovely hair,' observed Astra. 'Hasn't she got lovely hair, Tommy?'

'Aye.'

'Thanks,' said the girl, no more at ease. She found comfort by flicking through a magazine.

Astra and Tommy looked at things in the shop and twittered with excitement, working their way round to the rock in the window. Eventually, Edwin came in. He showed the shop assistant his fingers. They were dripping with ice cream.

'He wants to wash his hands,' explained Astra.

The girl recoiled somewhat melodramatically and pointed to the toilet.

Tommy glared at him. 'Where's Jeff?'

Edwin gestured back out of the door and slipped into the toilet, opening it awkwardly with his elbows. Tommy puffed with frustration and went to check that Jeff was tied up properly; he was and actually looked quite contented to be left alone. He turned his attention back to Astra who was craning her neck over some display stands to look at the rock in the window.

'Can we buy something, please?' he asked the shop assistant.

The girl looked up at him with annoyance. She threw down her magazine and stomped over.

'Earning some extra pocket money?' Astra smiled at her.

'What?' she said.

'Earning some extra pocket money?' Astra repeated.

'I'm twenty-three!' the girl quailed.

Tommy giggled.

Astra's cheeks flushed. 'You look young for your age.'

'It's good to look young,' chirped Tommy, still giggling.

The girl put her hands on her hips and looked at them both. 'What do you want?'

'The rock in the window, please,' said Astra.

'Which one?' the girl asked.

'The green one,' said Tommy.

'The aqua coloured one,' insisted Astra.

The chunk was hard to get to and the shop assistant had to scramble around in the bay of the window and shift a lot of paraphernalia. This did little to improve her mood and she took it over to the counter, cradling it in both hands, almost breathless with rage.

'Six pounds ninety-nine,' she said.

Astra looked at Tommy, 'I'm having one of me flushes. I'll wait outside.'

'You always do when there's money to be spent. Funny that.'

Tommy watched her leave the shop. Edwin emerged from the toilet at the same time.

'Anything you want?' Tommy asked him, taking out his wallet.

Edwin grinned, showing his vast impossibly-white teeth and grabbed for the nearest item which was a child's plastic cowboy hat with a silver star on it.

'Orifice sheriff?'

'You daft beggar!' Tommy shook his head and swaggered over to the counter.

'I want some fags!' shouted Astra as she left.

Tommy paid for the rock and the fags and a packet of mints for himself. The shop assistant still had enough decorum to put the goods in a paper bag. He thanked her and left, taking Edwin with him by the scruff of the neck. The girl settled down again, turning her fan up a notch and resumed her magazine. It was not long before she noticed a trickling noise and a pool of water spreading out from under the toilet door.

'Oh, for God's sake!'

*

They looked at the two rocks. They were placed next to each other on the garden wall at the feet of a stone cherub. It was late afternoon but the sun persisted and made the rocks dazzle.

'Happy now?' Tommy asked Astra, closing his eyes and leaning back into his deck-chair. It creaked in protest under his bulk.

She did not answer for a while. She gazed at the rocks, turning slowly from one to the other and rearranging them, pulling deep on a fag with intense concentration.

'I'll be happy when we've found the other ones.'

One of Tommy's eyes flicked open. 'What?'

'We must find the other ones.'

'What other ones?'

'There are other rocks the same. From the same star.'

'How many?'

'I don't know yet.'

'Where?'

'I don't know that either.'

'You can't be serious!' Both of Tommy's eyes were wide open again.

Astra turned and glowered at him; 'I've never been so serious in all my life.'

'Bloody Nora!' swore Tommy but shut his eyes again and folded his arms across his chest, determined to relax.

Astra glared at him for a while in silence and then watched Edwin and Jeff frolicking on the freshly-mowed lawn. Edwin stopped suddenly and walked towards Astra with a look of concern on his face. Jeff trailed behind him, looking up with expectancy at the rubber ball in his hand.

'Trouble muddle?' said Edwin.

Astra nodded. 'There's power in these rocks. Can you feel it?'

Edwin's bottom lip sank to the bottom of his chin and he nodded slowly.

'I thought you would. It's like a vibration? Like a noise?'

'Fuzzy buzz.' Edwin looked at the rocks and screwed up his eyes. 'Nasty ones … nasty ones … nasty ones …'

'Shush!' hissed Astra. A rogue cloud drifted in front of the sun and it was suddenly dim and cold. She shivered violently. Edwin whimpered and crouched down. He put one of his big paws on her curly mop. She took him into her arms.

'We'll talk about it later when the sun goes down and I've got a fire going,' she muttered.

Edwin nibbled at Astra's bosom. She cradled him for a moment like he was a monstrous baby and then took him by the hands and led him inside the house. Jeff watched them go and wagged his tail. Once convinced that Edwin was no longer going to play with him, he picked up the ball in his jaws and offered it to Tommy instead but the old man was snoring like a pneumonic walrus.

*

The evening was balmy but still hot. Tommy, Astra and Jeff strolled up to their favourite place: A hill overlooking the Rochdale canal. They wandered amongst the clumps of wavy dark-green meadow, purple swathes of heather and the nodding heads of cotton grass and they listened to the gentle callings of Curlews and Lapwings who knew it as home.

'Good old Crooked Ned,' Astra affectionately patted a tall rock jutting out of the flora at the top of the hill. It was worn and pitted and padded with moss. She sat down and leant against it.

'Hello, Crooked Ned,' Tommy greeted the rock and sat down next to it too.

'I've got a sweat on,' said Astra, fluffing up her hair.

'You mean you're perspiring?'

'You what?'

'Men sweat. Women perspire.'

'You daft old twat.'

They sat in silence for a while and gazed down at the canal. It looked like a muddy brown streak cutting through the wonderful colours of the moor, like a spiteful child's attempt to ruin a more inspired infant's painting. Tommy took in deep lungfuls of warm air. Astra smoked a fag. Jeff circled about and snapped at insects and birds.

'I wish it was still going,' mused Tommy.

'You're talking about the canal?'

'Aye.'

'How did I guess?'

'Do I always say that when we come up here?'

'You always say something like it. Even if you don't say anything, I can still tell you're thinking it.'

'So I might as well say it?'

'Silence is golden.'

'So you want me to shut up?'

'Don't start!'

'So *you do* want me to shut up?'

'It would be nice if you could enjoy the canal without wanting lots of boats on it, that's all.'

'This was once a vein of industry. I'd give my right arm just to see one boat sail by, laden with goods for the mills of Manchester.'

'Why?'

'Because.'

'I don't know why you get nostalgic for the so-called good old days.'

'Why not? What am I supposed to love? Computers? Mobile phones? Blooming epods?'

'Most people had terrible lives back then, especially the children. You never think of that!'

'I suppose,' said Tommy with a twinge of melancholy after considering it. 'What about these rocks then?'

'We're not going to discuss that till later,' said Astra, sounding genuinely cross.

'There's no one here except us!' Despite his words, Tommy looked around. There were some heads bobbing up and down along a trail from behind the next ridge. 'It's just that if we're going far away, I want to know, that's all.'

'Crewe,' said Astra quietly.

'Crewe?' cried Tommy, his cheeks reddening and his moustache prickling.

'Keep your voice down!' Astra raised her hand as if to slap him. 'What's wrong with you? It's not that far!'

'But how will we get there?'

'We'll catch the train.'

'With whose money?'

'Yours, of course.'

'I thought so! And when will we go, pray tell?'

'First thing in the morning.'

'What about Edwin's water-polo?'

'What?'

'Edwin's got his big match tomorrow.'

'Well, he'll have to cancel it. We can't leave him here by himself.'

Tommy huffed and puffed, rolling around on his vast buttocks in objection.

Astra gave him a sharp look and hissed like a viper about to strike. 'This is very important, Tommy. Very important. Do you understand?'

Tommy sighed but did not answer and they lapsed into muted delirium, glancing sideways at each other or staring down through the haze at the boatless canal. Jeff tormented an injured fowl nearby, oblivious to their debate.

'I hope we can come back here afterwards,' said Astra after a long time. Her tone had softened and she sank her head on to Tommy's shoulder.

'Of course we will,' he chortled and wrapped a huge arm around her. 'It's our special place, isn't it, Jeff?'

By way of response, Jeff bolted over and licked his face. They laughed.

'Let's get back then,' said Astra, sounding reassured.

Tommy rose up and dragged her to her feet. They walked home hand in hand like young lovers and Jeff bounded after them. Tommy thought he saw someone in the distance watching them but could not be sure.

*

The sun revolved around the planet and came up the next day as scheduled with a promise of more heat later on. Tommy checked around his garden one last time with Jeff. He went into the shed and took something wrapped in an oily cloth. He locked the door behind him and tugged on it just to make sure it was firm. He could hear Astra and Edwin in the kitchen making their own preparations to leave. He strolled inside to look at them. They were piling up food on the breakfast table while Astra hummed an inventory like a mantra.

'Pork pies. Nuts. Scotch eggs. Penguin bars. Bananas. Fig rolls. Crisps. Cheese and onion pasties.'

Jeff trotted in and wagged his tail at her.

'Oh! I mustn't forget Jeff's eats.' Astra opened a cupboard under the sink and started passing tins of dog food to Edwin.

'They'll be a fair old weight for somebody,' observed Tommy.

'They can go in your pack then,' sniffed Astra.

'Edwin's as strong as I am.'

'He's going to take the rocks.'

Tommy looked at Edwin and smirked. 'Rock monitor!'

Edwin gave him a facial expression that he could not translate.

'The most important thing is tea,' stated Tommy.

Edwin held up a flask that was on the table.

'We'll need more than one. Just think about how much of the stuff we get through between us.'

Astra glared at Tommy and then shrugged her shoulders. 'He's probably right, put the kettle on again, Edwin. There's a good bunny rabbit.'

Astra crossed over to another cupboard and rummaged around inside while Edwin filled the kettle. She hauled out a pair of luminous jackets.

'We're not wearing them!' exclaimed Tommy, watching her.

'I don't want to lose sight of you both,' explained Astra and tossed one of the jackets at his feet.

'We'll look like lollipop men!'

'I don't want to lose sight of you both,' repeated Astra.

Tommy cringed and picked it up. 'What else do we need?'

Astra poked three backpacks that she had partially filled. 'We've got more food, spare clothes, some blankets, a torch, a first-aid kit, Edwin's tablets, your tablets, my tablets.'

'We'll be like a blooming walking pharmacy!' cackled Tommy but no one else laughed.

Edwin held up a trombone.

'I think we'll leave that here, my pixie,' said Astra to him.

'I'm taking this,' said Tommy, finally unravelling the cloth in his hand and revealing an ageing revolver.

Astra stared at him. 'What for?'

'Trouble.'

'Thing is, Tommy dear, you couldn't hit a barn door at ten paces with that contraption.'

'Yes, I blooming can! I could give The Duke a run for his money!'

'Who?'

'John Wayne, you soft cow!'

Astra's eyes narrowed dangerously. 'Watch it, Tommy Coomber!'

Tommy looked away, fondling the gun.

'I thought it didn't work anyway.'

'I've fixed it,' Tommy muttered and wandered back out into the garden. Astra watched him and shook her head. She turned her attention back to Jeff and Edwin and the expedition supplies.

*

They did well for time and got to Runcorn train station at that semi-deserted period between workers and shoppers. Tommy bought himself a newspaper and Edwin some chocolate. Their locomotive was punctual and before any of them had much time to think about it, they were on their way. Tommy quickly tore off his luminous jacket and sat down to peruse the tabloid. Edwin parked next to him and glanced at the headlines over Tommy's shoulder while munching on the chocolate. Jeff did not care for trains much and dived under the table to whimper and whine. Astra was the only one who watched their progress through the window. She sank back into a chair opposite the men, folded her arms and gazed solemnly at the urban sprawl of Greater Manchester as it passed, growing a smile as it gradually transformed into the rolling green fields of Cheshire. No words were uttered, only grunts and other vague communications. After a quick two hours, they were on Crewe station. It was much busier and they climbed off the train into a furious river of people, all seemingly trying to go in the other direction. Holding on to each other, they jostled through the throng and peered around for a way out of the madness. A handsome young man with a huge grin approached them. Despite the summer, he wore a long beige overcoat.

'You look lost,' he said, not really addressing any of them in particular.

'Yes,' smiled Astra. 'Do you know the way out?'

'The Lord can show you the way.' The young man's grin vanished as he adopted a more sombre tone.

'Pardon?' said Tommy, frowning with disdain at the pamphlets the young man was now thrusting towards them.

'God loves you and will show you the true way.'

Astra frowned too. 'Any god in particular?'

It was the young man's turn to look disgruntled. 'There is only one true God, madam.'

'No there isn't. There's loads.'

The young man's mouth dropped open but nothing came out.

'There was a whole variety of Gods thousands of years before your sanctimonious woman-hater showed up.' Poison dripped from Astra's tongue.

'Blasphemy.' The young man's face turned white.

Tommy stepped inbetween them and raised up his hands. 'You've really picked the wrong person to talk to, mate.'

It was then that they all noticed Edwin. He was looking back and up into the rafters of the station. He was terrified and murmuring the word 'jeebies' over and over. He had a tight leash on Jeff, who too was staring wild-eyed upwards in the same direction and growling. Tommy and Astra followed their gaze. Perched above the sea of people on a steel cross beam was a monstrous crow. It seemed impossibly big and swollen. It flexed its greasy feathers and fixed its stare down upon Astra. Its eyes were pus yellow. In a shrill voice that filled the entire station it pronounced: 'Whore! Whore! Whore! Whore! Whore!'

Astra looked at Edwin, fearfully. 'Is it one of them?'

Edwin nodded by way of response.

'Well I'll go to the foot of our stairs!' remarked Tommy, shaking his head in disbelief.

'Are you sure?' Astra urged Edwin.

Tommy glanced down at Jeff. 'Edwin might be wrong but Jeff never is.'

'Whore! Whore! Whore! Whore! Whore!' shrieked the bird again.

'They're onto us already,' cried Astra. 'Let's go!'

'Don't turn your hearts away from the love of Jesus,' pleaded the young man, tears welling in his eyes.

'Go nail yourself to a cross!' spat Astra and barged past him. She clung onto Tommy who, in turn, clung onto Edwin, who, in turn, clung onto Jeff.

'He loves each and every one of us.' The young man did not concede even as the procession filed past him but his voice was soon lost in the clamour. They chanced to look back as they found the exit at the opposite end of the platform but both the crow and the crusader were now gone.

*

The streets of Crewe were less manic and after racing for a few blocks, they stopped and huddled together. Edwin was still looking around, warily, but Jeff's tail was wagging again.

Tommy looked at Astra. 'Well, that was a bit of a do! Are you alright?'

She nodded and let out a deep sigh of relief.

'I should have shot him,' mused Tommy.

'Well, you can't persecute him just for being a Christian, I suppose.' Astra shrugged her shoulders and lit up a fag.

'I was talking about the bird.'

They glared at each other with furrowed brows and then burst into laughter. It was a few minutes before they stopped. They got bemused looks from Edwin and Jeff and anyone who walked by.

'Curb doable,' said Edwin.

'Right, let's get this blinking rock,' said Astra with fresh resolution and stamped out her fag. She shuffled her backpack to a more comfortable position on her shoulders and began striding down the street. The three males looked at each other and silently made a mutual decision to follow.

Despite Astra's initial determination, they soon relaxed into a more leisurely pace and actually indulged in a little window shopping. The shops, however, gradually thinned out, and they meandered instead through nondescript suburbs. They saw other people doing their gardens or just sitting in them or running or cycling or just strolling along, like them. The sun reached its zenith and with no clouds for competition, its heat became blistering. Jeff began panting and Tommy and Edwin had no choice but to remove their jackets. As the afternoon wore on, buildings became scarce and disappeared altogether. They found themselves wandering down a long straight lane fringed with fenced fields and, on one side, a river. They trudged after Astra like weary cattle.

'I thought you said it was in Crewe?' bellowed Tommy.

'It is!' Astra yelled back over her shoulder.

'I don't think we're in Crewe anymore,' barked Tommy.

'Nearly there,' said Astra and glanced back at them, looking a little exhausted herself.

Eventually the river widened out into a lake at the end of the lane. Astra came to a halt and looked out across the water, resting her elbows on the fence. Tommy and Edwin staggered up to her, red-faced and quizzical.

'This is it,' she said with a vague fleeting expression that could have been a frown or a smile.

The men gazed out across the lake. A flock of ducks sailed gently over to return their curiosity. Jeff stuck his nose through the fence and wagged his tail languidly at them.

'In the water?' asked Tommy.

'No, in there,' Astra pointed to a house on the far side of the lake. It was a huge place festooned with elaborate balconies and battlements. It looked more like a marble fortress. There was even a boathouse and a jetty rolling out onto the water.

'The rock's inside there?' groaned Tommy, his eyes scanning the stronghold with concern.

Astra nodded and lit up a fag.

'Castle hassle,' said Edwin.

'So what do we do? Just go up, knock on the door and ask for it?' Tommy scratched his burning bald patch.

'No, we'll just walk in and take it,' replied Astra with a lungful of smoke.

Tommy laughed but Astra kept a straight face. 'I think there's laws against that sort of thing,' he said.

'The rock is inside a glass cabinet in one of the rooms on the ground floor. The back door is left open during the day. I dreamst it last night. It'll be months before they notice it's gone.'

'Are you sure?'

'It's the only way.'

*

'Of all the harebrained schemes!' protested Tommy as he stubbed his toe on a tree root. The woods round the back of the house offered them a more discreet yet treacherous approach. They crept through the undergrowth nervously, striving to stay out of sight of the building's loftiest windows. Occasionally, there was a break in the tree line and they had to recede further into the gloom.

'We'll probably get arrested for being on private land before we even get chance to break in,' Tommy continued to grumble. 'These well-to-do Cheshire folk have gamekeepers and all sorts.'

No gamekeepers revealed themselves but the back way into the grounds of the house was barred by a gigantic wall, grown green and mossy with age.

Tommy looked up at the barrier and growled. 'Now what?'

Astra did not answer but calmly headed around the perimeter, beckoning the others to follow. They came to an arched wooden door with an iron ring set into it. Making a mockery of Tommy's trepidation, Astra turned the ring and quickly slipped through the door. On the other side was a flagstone yard and she waited for them there. Tommy and Edwin entered more hesitantly and gawped around like lost children in a secret garden. Dainty orchard trees grew up through the flagstones and offered them cover but the only sign of habitation was a wicker basket in the middle of the yard, overspilling with rotten fruit.

Tommy paused to put Jeff on his lead and handed it to Edwin. 'Keep hold of him,' he said.

Astra lead onwards to the back door of the house. She peered through its grid of tiny windows and tried the handle. As predicted, the door was unlocked. She turned to look at the others to make sure they were still following and crept inside. They found themselves in a kitchen. It was large and old-fashioned but well kept. A regimented tray full of sausage rolls had been left out to cool on a table. Edwin licked his lips and reached out for one.

'No, Edwin!' hissed Astra.

Jeff tried to leap up to claim one of his own.

'No, Jeff!' she hissed again.

They climbed out of the kitchen via a small set of steps into a plush hallway. They collectively inhaled the heavy fragrant scent that hung there. A much more enormous staircase with an oak banister continued upwards but Astra shook her head at it and took them further into the ground floor. They passed with wide eyes through a dining room that would have been fit for royalty. On the other side was an equally ornate study.

'It's in here,' whispered Astra.

They gazed around, daunted by the sheer amount of paraphernalia crammed into the room. There was more stuff in here than most people had in their entire house. It was up to Astra to lead again. She began to pace amongst the tables and shelves, frenetically shifting piles of books and objects as she went.

Tommy looked at Jeff and Edwin. 'You two stand guard.' He joined Astra in her search, taking the other end of the study.

'Here!' she shouted before Tommy had barely begun, perhaps a little too loudly.

Tommy stepped over and found Astra staring at a glass cabinet that rested on top of a squat leather stool. It was stuffed with geological specimens. At first, in the dimness of the room, they could not see their desired material, but as their eyes adjusted, a familiar crystalline lump seemed to reveal itself from one shady corner.

'Is that you, Gerald?' cried a voice from elsewhere in the house.

Tommy's eyes widened as he glared at Astra. 'We've been rumbled!'

'Not yet we haven't.' Astra sounded calm but her fingers frantically sought an opening to the cabinet.

Jeff began barking and Edwin tried to quieten him.

'Is there someone there?' wailed the voice again.

'Get a move on!' grumbled Tommy as he watched Astra struggle.

'Give us a hand then!'

Tommy grappled the cabinet but his lunge was clumsy and it toppled from the stool. Several panes of glass shattered and the rock samples spilled onto the floor in a heap. Jeff leapt and strained on his leash, his yapping becoming hysteric.

'You blooming nanna!' jeered Astra at Tommy, half panicking, half laughing.

'That's torn it,' he said with scarlet cheeks.

'There!' she proclaimed and reached down to seize a chunk from the pile on the floor.   'It's the same green colour,' said Tommy, peering at it as she held it up.

'Yep, it's the same aqua colour,' said Astra. She handed it to Tommy and he quickly shoved it in his pocket. She picked up what remained of the cabinet. She positioned it carefully back on the stool and began placing the geology collection back inside it.

'What in the name of John Wayne are you doing, woman!?' roared Tommy.

'I'm putting it back,' Astra explained.

'It's too late for that. Let's get out of here.' Tommy did not give her the chance to dispute, he grabbed hold of Astra and dragged her away.

'Mush splitting!' whimpered Edwin, still struggling to keep Jeff still and quiet. Tommy absconded him too as he passed and dragged them all back through the dining room into the hallway. Other objects were knocked over and broken in their shambolic wake.

'Who's there?' cried the denizen of the house. They could see the shadow of someone cast down the mighty staircase.

Tommy pulled and shoved them through the hallway and towards the stairs to the kitchen. There was a sequence of crashing and banging noises from behind them as the silhouette fell down the staircase like a human slinky. Astra tore away from Tommy's grip and ran back.

'Astra!' he yodelled in protest.

Edwin and consequently Jeff, were released too and they watched with Tommy as Astra attended the crumpled heap at the bottom of the flight.

'Are you alright, my bunny rabbit?' She helped the elderly woman to sit upright. Her floral nightdress did little to hide her frailty and she had a cotton wool pad over one eye.

'Say something dear.' Astra stroked the back of the victim's bony shoulders.

Shock gradually faded from the woman's face. It was replaced by bewilderment as she gazed around at her intruders. 'Are you the new nurse?' she stammered as her single eye came to rest on Astra.

Astra hesitated; '… yes, that's me.'

Tommy sighed. Astra flicked him a fierce glance. 'Are you in pain? Does it hurt anywhere?'

'I think I'm fine,' the woman chuckled slightly. 'It's my cataracts. The doctor said I would have no depth of vision with just one eye.'

'Let's get you up then,' said Astra looking at the boys. They swaggered over and helped Astra to lift her. The assistance of all three of them was excessive as the old woman was as light as a feather. They quickly swept her down to the kitchen and sat her in a chair.

'We'll make you a nice cuppa,' said Astra as she put the kettle on. Tommy and Edwin fussed over the woman with as many cushions as they could find.

'You're not really the new nurse are you?' asked the woman after a while, without looking up at any of them.

'What makes you say that?' replied Astra, fetching milk from the fridge.

'Well if you're a nurse, then who are these two and this dog? I might be over the hill but I haven't quite lost my wits yet, dear.'

'We're burglars,' explained Tommy.

'Tommy!' screeched Astra.

'Funny looking burglars,' said the woman.

'We're just taking one thing,' Tommy pulled up a chair next to her.

'Tommy!' Astra screeched again.

'We might as well tell her the truth,' he mused and stroked his moustache.

'What is it you want?'

'Just this.' Tommy produced the rock from his pocket.

'What is it?' The woman peered at it with her good eye.

Tommy turned to Astra. She walked over and placed a steaming cup and saucer into the woman's shaky hands.

'It's something that needs to be taken away. Something that needs to be destroyed.'

The woman was silent for a while. She sipped the tea. Edwin and Jeff had renewed their interest in the sausage rolls. 'Please have one,' she said, noticing them. They needed no further encouragement and tucked in. 'I should call the police.'

Astra bent down and took one of the woman's hands. 'You don't know us but you have to trust us. It's for the best.'

She nodded. 'There's truth in your voice and something special about you, I can feel it, but my husband wouldn't understand and he'll be home soon.'

Astra and Tommy looked at each other and then they both looked at Edwin and Jeff gorging themselves on the pastries.

'We best go then,' decided Tommy.

*

'Where next?' croaked Tommy the next morning. He strained his sleepy eyes into the dawn light lancing through the tree tops and struggled painfully to his feet. He paced around slowly, rubbing the small of his back.

Astra did not answer. She was still lying on the ground under an old bridge, cradled in Edwin's arms. Tommy turned round and inspected the ancient edifice. It did not seem to go anywhere or come from anywhere. Its purpose had long been lost.

'Ireland,' she muttered eventually.

Tommy just laughed, building from a quiet chuckle into a raucous baritone guffaw. Jeff trotted from out of the bushes and cocked his head curiously at him. 'Ireland, Jeff! Did you hear that one?'

'I dreamst it last night,' explained Astra.

'There's another one of these rocks over there I suppose?'

'Yep, out in the middle of nowhere this one. They'll still find it though if we don't first.'

'It doesn't happen to be anywhere near where your sisters live by any chance?'

Astra sat up and squinted at him. There were leaves in her hair. Edwin stirred as she left his embrace. 'My sisters. I'd forgotten about them.'

'So this isn't some elaborate scheme to get us to go and visit them?'

Astra sneered at him. 'What do you think?'

Tommy looked back at her and then down at his feet. 'Sorry.'

'You know I can't stand them.'

'Yes, I do, I said I'm sorry.'

'And you doubt my dreams, even though they've lead us this far?'

Tommy's cheeks grew red and he crouched down and put a paw on her arm. 'Okay, we'll go, but it will be the last of the money. There will be nothing to get home with.'

'We'll cross that bridge when we come to it.'

'They may be able to help Jeff.'

'Who?'

'Your sisters?'

They turned to look at Jeff. He wagged his tail at them.

'Maybe,' Astra shrugged her shoulders.

'At least we might get a warm bed. I'm not spending another night out in the woods. I barely slept a wink. Jeff was up and down all night too, weren't you, lad?'

'I don't think me and Edwin had any trouble,' Astra caressed Edwin's bald dome. He sat up and peered around, barely awake, his lips wet with slobber.

'No! You two can sleep anywhere.' Tommy got up and stumbled off through the undergrowth. 'I need to water the flowers.'

Astra rummaged in her backpack for a flask of tea and some fags. She jolted when Jeff suddenly started growling at something. Edwin began whimpering the word 'jeebies' and rocked back and forth on his buttocks.

Astra glanced from Jeff to Edwin and sighed. 'Oh no! Not again.'

'Whore! Whore! Whore! Whore! Whore!' shrieked a horrible and familiar voice from high up in the branches above them.

Astra got to her feet and saw the gigantic crow from the station flapping its oily wings. 'They've found us!'

'Whore! Whore! Whore! Whore! Whore!' it repeated with its diseased yellow eyes fixed on her.

'Why don't you just leave us alone!?' she shouted.

The crow seemed to cackle in mockery.

'You best be gone or I'll wail and then you'll be sorry!'

The creature ridiculed her again. Astra was reinforced by Edwin and Jeff who stood either side of her. Edwin threw stones at the beast and Jeff barked ferociously but the creature seemed impervious in its lofty haven.

'Whore! Whore! Whore! Whore! Who ...' there was a sharp crack and the bird exploded in a puff of blood and feathers.

They turned round and saw Tommy, his revolver raised.

'Tommy?' Astra peered at him.

'Couldn't hit a barn door at ten paces, eh?' he said proudly, blowing the smoke from the nozzle.

'You might have finished your wee properly though,' said Astra gesturing to the wet patch on Tommy's leg. She and Edwin sniggered.

Tommy ignored them, his thunder stolen, and holstered the gun.

'You won't be able to take that with you,' said Astra.

'What?'

'They're a bit sensitive about that sort of thing where we're going.'

Tommy glared at her angrily and then softened. He drew out the weapon again and stared at it. 'Then it shall stay here with the bones of its last victim!' He meandered over to the tree where the monster had sat. Jeff was there, sniffing at the pus and gore dripping down the trunk. Tommy cocked open the barrel and took the remaining bullets out. He hung the revolver on a branch and turned to look at the others. 'Let's get moving before some other bugger turns up.'

*

They stumbled through the wilds for the rest of the morning and got back on the road to Crewe. After a night in the woods, they looked dishevelled but startled glances were the worst thing waiting for them at the station. With the last of Tommy's finances, they booked a trip to Dublin, and with what remained of their provisions, they sat out the train journey to Holyhead. The weather changed dramatically in transit and they seemed almost to be in a different country when they got off the train. Holyhead's cold grey streets matched its cold grey climate. However, they did not have to bear it for too long. They had arrived just in time for the ferry. They boarded the ship and made straight for the comfy armchairs of the bar.

Tommy held out a handful of coins. 'Not even enough for a round of drinks!'

'We'll not be long now. I've rang Rona. She's to pick us up in Dublin,' said Astra.

'It might be a while in these conditions,' muttered Tommy gloomily, peering out the window at the heaving sea.

'Foisting oceanic blob,' spat Edwin, following his gaze.

'How about I stand yers all a round?' said an Irishman sat at the bar who had been watching them.

They turned to stare at him. None of them said anything.

'What'cha havin'?' he grinned, unfazed. A huge overcoat obscured his extensive frame and the stool he was perched on. His head was tiny and bare and his nose was beaked. He looked like an emu nesting in a tree.

'That's very kind of you but we couldn't impose,' said Astra.

'Nonsense! It's an honour to buy such a luvly lady a drink.'

Astra blushed and faltered for words. It was Tommy who spoke with defiance. 'We're fine, thanks.'

'C'mon! I'll get'cha all one,' he said to Tommy. 'This your wife? Yers a lucky fella.'

'She's not my wife.' Tommy bridled.

The pin-headed man cascaded off the stool and took a step towards them. 'Look, I'll make yers a deal. Any of yers a smoker?'

'I am,' replied Astra, showing him her packet of fags as proof.

'Well, so am I! And there's none to be found on this accursed tub. I'll stand yers drinks if you supply me out on the deck, how's about that?'

'Deal!' said Astra, quickly and excitedly, like an over-eager gameshow contestant winning a prize.

'So what'll it be?'

They all seemed unsure what to say.

'I know!' proclaimed the Irishman. 'A Guinness for everyone. When in Rome, eh?'

'We're not in Rome,' said Tommy, somewhat childishly.

'That sounds nice,' Astra beamed at the Irishman. 'But Edwin doesn't drink. Get him a lemonade or something.'

'Right you are.' The benefactor busied himself with the order.

Tommy glared at Astra.

She glared back. 'What?'

'We can't trust anyone.'

'He only wants to buy us a drink.'

Tommy opened his mouth to protest but the Irishman was upon them with the first two drinks.

'Here we go!' He placed them on their table and looked down at Jeff. 'What about yer hound?'

'That's alright, thanks, he can have some of mine,' explained Astra and much to the man's surprise, proceeded to pour some of the viscous black liquid into a bowl from her backpack.

He watched with raised eyebrows as Jeff lapped it up. 'Plucky fella!' He waltzed off to get the rest of the round.

Tommy regarded his Guinness with suspicion.

The man came back and smiled at Astra. 'Smoke then?'

She grinned and they left Tommy, Edwin and Jeff in the shadows of the bar.

*

'You're not on holiday?' observed the Irishman. He and Astra were forced to tango as they struggled to light up on the rolling deck.

Astra took a deep drag and narrowed her eyes. 'What makes you say that?'

'Shite holiday it'll be with no money. Especially in the country with the greatest boozers in the world.'

Astra fell silent, her grin had faded. 'We're going to visit my sisters.'

'Whereabouts?'

She regarded him with some misgiving. 'Kells.'

'I've got a second cousin in Kells!' the Irishman chuckled. 'I apologise for being nosy. Just trying to make conversation. I find it makes the journey shorter.'

Astra gazed out over the seething expanse of water. She was forced to grab the rail as the vessel dipped suddenly.

The Irishman was compelled to make the same manoeuvre. 'Sweet Jesus! I've never known such a rough crossing at this time of year!'

'Astra.'

'Rory.' He held out his other hand to shake with a somewhat pale face.

She shook it. 'No sea legs?'

'I've been on this tub three-thousand times but I must confess as to feeling a tad giddy. You seem okay.'

'I am.'

'Yer man's a tad frosty.'

'Tommy? He's just tired. Don't worry about him.'

'He's not your husband then?'

'It's a bit more complicated than that. Are you married?'

'I'm away home to see my betrothed. My sweet Mary.'

'Aw.'

'I know what it's like to be poor though. I was brought up on a farm in …'

Rory hurtled sideways as the ship tipped. Astra skidded after him.

'Feck! What the hell is going on!?'

Several things happened at once: A flash of thunder illuminated the heavens, it began to pour with rain, a door burst open and Tommy, Edwin and Jeff emerged. Rory cried out in horror and pointed into the sea. Astra looked down but saw nothing except the waves.

'What the feck was that!?' gurgled Rory.

'What?' asked Astra, almost laughing at him.

Tommy swaggered over. 'Astra?'

She turned to him.

'The boys have noticed that …' Tommy blushed.

'Something in the sea! Something in the fecking sea!' ranted Rory like a maniac.

'They've come after us,' continued Tommy.

Astra looked at Edwin, he was twitching and drooling and Jeff was snarling like a cornered wolf.

'It's best we stay inside.' Tommy staggered a step closer, wincing as the wind and rain lashed his face.

'It's just a storm,' said Astra without much conviction. She was desperately trying to finish off her fag.

'There!' shouted Rory, stabbing a finger at the depths.

The others stumbled over to the rail and looked down. Something vast and black broke the surface, a rack of spines cutting through the waves. An enormous rotting yellow eye rolled up at them. The ferry lurched violently in its wake and they all tumbled sideways. Edwin's head collided with a metal pipe and he dropped to his knees, howling in pain and clutching his bonce.

Astra looked at Tommy and finally tossed away the fag. 'I think you might be right, my bunny rabbit!'

They scooped up Edwin and broke for the door. Astra turned to Rory but he was flailing his arms like a demented air traffic controller and yelling. A young man in a ferry uniform ran over to him from the other direction and attempted a more forceful removal.

'C'mon, sir!'

'But ... the fecking sea monster!'

*

The ferry bounced into Dublin harbour like a toy in a bath. Its passengers screamed for their lives, found places to vomit or just calmly drank in the bar like nothing was happening. Crewmen ran here and there with purpose known only to them. Astra and the boys found their seats again and sat quietly, feigning ignorance of the situation. Astra tended the bloody gash on Edwin's head and they waited with grim fortitude while the ferry was moored and the gangplank lowered. They were among the last to get off. Others before them surged onto terra firma as one large mass of panic, like some single entity, twittering with alarm. Most paused to gawp and exclaim at the enormous rending claw marks in the metal on the side of the ship. The storm was no more and the sun bathed them in a reassuring brilliance. They saw no sign of Rory. Straggling behind, they let the other voyagers dwindle off to their respective destinations. They found a wall in the car park to perch on, putting as much distance between them and the sea as they could for now. Astra checked the rocks were still in Edwin's backpack while he sat and fingered his head injury.

'They must want this stuff badly,' commented Tommy as Astra looked into the murky confines of the bag. 'Have you seen them do anything like that before?'

Astra shook her head. 'No, but then I don't exactly spend much time at sea, do I?'

'Scream cream,' concluded Edwin.

An ancient Citroen 2cv stopped in front of them, its noisy engine reverberating. It was bright red but parts of it were rusty, eroded or discoloured pink. Its driver regarded them from within.

Astra waved faintly. The car reversed and parked next to them.

Tommy looked at Astra, enquiringly. 'Rona?'

Astra nodded as the woman got out of the car and looked at them. She was the exact duplicate of Astra but slightly younger, taller and slimmer. She had the mop of curly hair but it was a different shade of brown. She wore dungarees and Wellington boots.

'A more miserable bunch of wretches I've never seen,' said Rona and laughed.

'Hello, sister,' said Astra with considerably less humour.

They hugged and kissed but it was with false compassion.

'You look like shit,' observed Rona as she held onto Astra and looked her up and down.

'It's been a strange day,' she explained.

'No, I mean your hair, it's turning grey, and check out those wrinkles, and is that a wart?'

'Oh,' muttered Astra, self-consciously touching a slight lump on her cheek.

Rona laughed again and turned her scrutiny to her sibling's companions. 'You must be Tommy, and …'

'Edwin and Jeff,' explained Astra.

Tommy nodded, Edwin forced a smile, Jeff wagged his tail.

'Is everyone alright?' beamed Rona.

'We had a rough crossing. Edwin took a thump on the head,' replied Tommy.

'In this weather?' Rona glanced up into the clear blue sky.

'You didn't see the storm?' asked Astra.

'What storm?' Rona glared round at them all. Well, you'll be safe with us. Come on!'

Slowly, they got into the vehicle. Edwin was reluctant, he stood there and grimaced at Rona. The others looked at him.

'Edwin?' queried Astra.

Rona turned to her. 'Is he alright?'

'It's okay, Edwin, get in the car.'

*

With Astra in the passenger seat and the others crammed in the back, Rona drove her red Citroen 2cv at breakneck speed out of Dublin and through the unspoilt Irish countryside. The travellers peered through the windows at the passing trees, hills and houses as they blurred by. A silent hour passed, broken only by the occasional cackle from Rona but she did not share her joke. They left the road and kangarood up a dirt track. The route was broken and rocky but Rona barely slowed. Jeff, Tommy and Edwin were thrown about but this just provoked more hilarity from the driver. They approached an odd old house. It was fringed with tall and slender hedgerows which revealed the building gradually as they got closer. It seemed to be an amalgamation of various abodes. Sections of it were gabled, others were pebble-dashed, stone-clad or just left bare to reveal the bricks.

The whole place looked a little wonky, as if it was likely to fall in on itself.

'Home sweet home!' Rona said as the car rolled to a halt.

They all clambered laboriously out of the Citroen and noticed that the front door was open and an imposing woman was stood there, framed by the doorway.

'Hello, Magra,' said Astra without any joy.

'Your other sister?' Tommy's bushy silver eyebrows were firmly raised. Astra's eldest sibling looked nothing like the other two. She was big and lumpy. Her hair was long and straight and her face was sharp and pale like a hatchet. She wore a brown dress that sank to her ankles.

'Hail to you, sister,' said Magra loudly.

Jeff woofed and sprang at something lurking under the hedgerow. Everyone turned to look. A huge cat emerged from its hiding place. It hissed and waved a cautionary set of claws at Jeff. He leapt back, fur rising on his spine.

'Watch him!' Magra called out. 'It's a feral cat. It'll tear his nose off.'

Tommy rushed over to drag Jeff away from the creature but he needed no further encouragement, his tail was firmly between his legs.

'Come inside,' Rona chuckled 'You can get cleaned up and rested before dinner.'

*

'Nice place you've got here,' said Tommy, looking around the roomy kitchen. His hair and moustache were combed and his shirt was fresh but his grimy fingernails still betrayed him.

Astra's sisters did not answer. Magra stomped over and spooned stew into the bowl in front of him. Rona followed with a little more elegance and poured cider into his glass.

Astra put a fag in her mouth.

'After dinner, if you please, sister, and outside,' commanded Magra without looking at her.

'And get savaged by your blooming moggies?' Astra put the fag back in the packet. 'Since when has this been a non-smoking house?'

'Since mother died of lung cancer,' said Magra, filling Astra's bowl.

'Piggy espoused,' said Edwin, when it was his turn. He too was clean shirted and his head was now bandaged.

Astra's sisters took their places. Everyone looked at each other.

'Shall we say grace?' asked Magra.

'What?' Astra's mouth dropped open.

Magra sniggered mockingly and started wolfing down her stew.

'She's having fun with you, sister,' said Rona, tearing up some bread. 'She's seeing if you're still a dedicated iconoclast.'

'Oh,' muttered Astra, dragging her spoon around the edge of her bowl.

'This cider is the business,' remarked Tommy after a few awkward minutes of silence.

'We make it ourselves,' said Rona watching him take a swig. 'Careful now, big man, it's formidable stuff.'

'Certainly is!' beamed Tommy with satisfaction.

'It helps us to lure men up to our lair,' purred Rona and winked at him.

Tommy blushed and tucked into his stew.

Astra sneered at her. 'Still unmarried?'

Rona arched her eyebrows and giggled. 'You should know better, sister. Why buy a book when we've got an extensive library to borrow from?'

'Out here?' scoffed Astra, looking out of the window at the unpopulated landscape, dimming under the shadow of dusk.

'They come to us from all across the seas, sister,' Rona laughed. 'Drawn to our call like sailors to the Sirens.'

'Looks like you've a little collection of your own, sister,' said Magra.

'We're all just friends.' Astra scowled across the table, her meal still untouched.

'Alright, it was just a joke,' Magra chuckled.

'So you're all for separate beds then?' asked Rona.

'Under your roof, yes,' replied Astra.

'And why should our roof be different than any other?' Magra smiled, venomously.

'Because what we get up to in the privacy of our home is our business.'

'So it's true?' Rona twirled her spoon round in her fingers, playfully.

'Is what true?' Astra's face darkened with rage.

'That all of these men belong to you?'

'They don't belong to me! I care for them, that's all!'

'You care for them in that special way?' quizzed Magra. Rona giggled.

Astra stood up and stormed out, taking her fags with her. Tommy and Edwin were red-faced and concentrated on their stew. Even Jeff, who had been napping on the floor, shifted uncomfortably.

'Thanks for dinner,' said Tommy when the two sisters had finished laughing and his bowl was empty. He wiped his moustache with a napkin. 'It was delicious. You are, however, both very rude.' He then got up and left.

Astra's sisters were in hysterics.

*

'What do you want?' Astra exhaled a mist of fag smoke across the veranda. She did not look up at the two figures who approached her. She continued to stare at the Irish wilderness beyond the borders of the garden. It was now just a jumble of vague silhouettes in the night. Jeff sat at her feet, keeping an eye out for wildcats.

'You wanted us to take a look at the dog?' said Magra.

'His name is Jeff,' stated Astra.

'You'll have to leave him with us tonight,' said Rona.

Jeff whimpered.

Astra turned to look up at her sisters. 'If you hurt him. I'll kill you both. I swear.'

'Why the hostility, sister?' Magra folded her arms and shook her head, disapprovingly. 'We've not seen you for so long.'

'And now I know why,' said Astra, taking another puff.

'We were only teasing you about your men,' suggested Rona.

'Well, it's not funny. Our quest is very serious.'

'Still protecting your precious humans?' tutted Magra.

'Someone has to.'

'Tommy seems like a nice man but the other one seems … er … a bit retarded,' observed Rona.

'Well-built though!' remarked Magra.

Astra was on her feet instantly, snarling at them. 'You watch your filthy mouths!'

Magra stepped forward, towering above her sister. 'Astra! Calm down please! Are we not a family? Can we not speak our minds to each other?'

'Those men are more family to me than you two ever were!' Astra turned away and leant over the veranda fence like she was going to be sick.

'And they know you're a Banshee?' asked Magra.

'Of course they blooming do!'

'And both of them are your lovers?'

Astra whirled round and glared at them. 'Enough!' She took a deliberately menacing step towards them. 'Stop sticking your noses in! We have a purpose here in Ireland and we need shelter for the night. In the morning, we're leaving. Until then, leave us be!'

Magra and Rona glanced at her and then at each other as if exchanging some unspoken agreement.

'Very well,' said Magra eventually. 'Leave us the dog.'

'Thank you,' said Astra with a heavy sigh and walked towards the back door. She turned to them again before she went in. 'Remember what I said. If you harm so much as a hair on his head … if you harm any of them … you're dead!'

*

Astra returned to the garden in the morning to smoke again. The sky was cobalt blue and cloudless and the day was quickly growing hot. Tommy was out in the heat, inspecting the flora with his hands in his pockets.

'What are you doing?' she asked, preferring to stay in the shade of the veranda.

'Just taking a look at the garden,' he mumbled.

'We're out of here as soon as possible,' she said. 'I dreamst where to go next. It's not far.'

'Wonderful,' Tommy muttered sarcastically and vanished from her sight for a moment behind a shaggy willow tree.

'Too many sad memories here …' whispered Astra to herself.

Jeff trotted out into the garden suddenly and wagged his tail at her. Astra stared at him.

'Tommy!'

Tommy reappeared from the foliage and he too gawped at Jeff.

Rona and Magra came out into the garden. They were both dressed in colourful silk robes but they looked pale and tired.

'There's nothing we could do for him,' stated Magra.

'He's too far gone,' added Rona.

'Are you sure?' Astra peered at them with suspicion.

'How long ago was he changed?' asked Magra.

Astra shook her head and furrowed her brow as she struggled to recall.

Tommy strolled over and helped her out. 'Must be at least five years now.'

'The longer it's been, the harder it is to turn them back,' explained Magra. 'You should have brought him to us sooner.'

'Five years ago mother died,' said Rona, stepping out into the sunshine towards Tommy. 'You could have attended the funeral and saved your friend. Killed two birds with one stone.'

'Don't start!' hissed Astra.

Tommy ruffled the fur on Jeff's head 'Oh well! Perhaps he's happier being a dog anyway? Maybe we should change his name to something more appropriate? Rover or something? I always feel blinking daft shouting for "Jeff" in the park.'

'Let's just go!' said Astra decisively while stomping out her fag. She made for the back door.

'Astra?' Tommy stopped her.

She turned to him. 'What?'

He shuffled around, uncomfortably. 'I'm staying here.'

Astra glared at him, her mouth dropped open but no words came out.

'I thought I'd sort the garden out,' he reasoned.

'Have you finally lost your mind, you old goat?' Astra's look of disbelief turned into one of anger. 'Have you forgotten why we're here?'

Tommy fidgeted nervously. 'Magra and Rona have been kind enough to let us stay the night. I think it would be nice to return the favour by doing the garden.'

Astra noticed that Rona had stretched out a bare leg from her robe, seductively. Tommy glanced down at the flesh and licked his lips.

'You're coming with me, Tommy Coomber!' barked Astra with such wrath that the air around them seemed to seethe and ripple.

'Don't worry, sister,' giggled Rona. 'We'll look after him. She stretched out and her robe became slack, revealing even more of her nakedness beneath.

Astra shuddered with fury and turned to her other sister for support but Magra seemed equally amused.

Edwin stepped out on to the veranda. He was wearing stripy pyjamas and his bandages had fallen loose around his head and he looked like he was sporting some awful wig. He gawked at them all with a look of bewilderment. 'Turnip cropping,' he said.

Everyone laughed at him except Astra.

'Oh Edwin!' Tears fell down her cheeks and she ran to him, throwing her arms around him. They hugged and Astra pulled back to look at him. 'Come on, let's get you dressed.'

A frown crossed Edwin's face and he shrank from her arms.

'Edwin?' blubbered Astra.

Edwin crossed to the embrace of Magra. The large woman enveloped him and kissed his huge lips passionately.

Astra watched them with horror. 'What's going on!?'

'I think Edwin wants to stay here too,' sniggered Magra, mockingly.

Astra stared at them and then at Tommy and Rona, who were also frolicking. 'You hags! You've put a hex on them!'

'A lot went on last night when you were asleep, sister,' cackled Rona as Tommy gleefully slid one of his paws inside her robe.

'You promised me that you wouldn't harm them!?' Astra stamped her feet.

'We didn't!' laughed Rona. 'We were very nice to them!'

Astra shuddered like she was going to say something else but all she produced were more tears. 'Jeff?' she finally managed to say.

Jeff ambled away from her too and wagged his tail slightly.

'Not you as well?' croaked Astra.

The two newly formed couples congregated on the lawn and grinned at her like spiteful teenagers. Astra screwed up her eyes as if she could no longer bear to look at them. She gritted her teeth with fury and her cheeks burnt crimson.

'Isn't it about time you left, sister?' Magra asked her.

'We've got some serious gardening to do,' chuckled Tommy, his lips brushing Rona's neck.

'I don't believe this!' sobbed Astra.

'Go and collect your stupid rocks you sad old sack of shit!' Rona guffawed. The others burst into a chorus of cruel hysterics.

Astra left. She ran through the inside of the house, hastily snatching her rucksack on the way. She bolted from the front door and let out a shrill shriek of despair. Every window in the building exploded. The roaming wildcats responded with anguished cries of their own. Astra marched down the driveway as it rained glass.

*

'Curse them!' spat Astra for the hundredth time as she stumbled down a hill faster than her chubby legs could cope with. They buckled and she rolled the last few feet to the bottom. The rocks in her rucksack cut into her back several times as she revolved and all the air in her lungs jettisoned in one gasp of agony. She lay there and wept with self-pity again, her tears making fresh tracks down her burning jowls. She wondered if anyone had seen her fall. It must have been comical to see an overweight, middle-aged woman tumble like a log down a hill. Astra sat up painfully and peered around. She had nothing to worry about. Empty golden fields stretched away from her in all directions. Drystone walls were the only sign that anyone had ever been here at all. She decided to laugh at herself and stayed there for a fag. Filled with humour and reassuring chemicals, Astra clambered to her feet and squinted through the haze at her landscape again. Vague impressions of familiarity came to her as she struggled to recall her dream. She swung her head to a copse of trees on the horizon. They were so far away that they appeared to her as a dark green blob but Astra had the sense that this was her destination. She had not noticed the brown horse before. It was stood behind a wall far to her left. It had been absent from her vision. She shrugged her shoulders and began her march again. She worked her way like a steam train over another couple of shaggy hills, but took care not to repeat the same mistake and moved with greater care down the slopes.

Over the second hill, Astra was delighted to find a slender stream cutting through the land. It was nothing more than a trickle but it was clear and wholesome. She allowed herself to pause again and knelt at its side to splash cold water on her face. It eased the dryness and burning. She sank down and greedily slurped a few gulps to soothe her parched throat. She took off her rucksack and fished out the empty water bottle that was the only item it contained, apart from the rocks, and filled it. As one final comfort, she took off her socks and trainers and dangled her swollen feet in the water. Astra exhaled slowly and loudly.

After a few minutes, Astra replaced her footwear and advanced, this time determined not to be distracted. The way between her and the trees was just grass and walls. As she trampled along, Astra bent her head in concentration and gazed at the ground. She swiftly noted every detail as it sped past; each blade of grass, each tiny stone, each minuscule lump of muck, each labouring insect. She could feel the heat prickling on the back of her neck and became delirious. It was like she was back in her dream and she felt safe and happy there. She moved in a world where no harm could come to her, or so she thought. There was a sudden noise, something that sounded like skin flapping. It was unwelcome in her dream. Astra stopped, lifted her head slowly and scanned her surroundings. The tress seemed no closer but the brown horse was. The beast remained to her left but somehow it was now twice as near and in a different field altogether. Astra glared and her mind raced with possibilities. She considered that it could be a different horse and regretted not paying attention. Perhaps the creature was following her out of curiosity? It was not moving though, it stood still and returned her stare. Astra felt the instinct to call out to the horse but found herself moving on, turning her back. She focussed on the trees and bit her lip with resolution. After she had taken a few steps, however, she began to feel weak and dizzy, not like before when the delirium was agreeable and otherworldly, but a sense of vulnerability. Astra kept walking but glanced back over her shoulder. Her mouth dropped open; the horse was now on her side of the wall! She had not detected any movement or heard anything to indicate its transfer from one location from the other. It kept the same stance and looked like a cardboard cut-out that was being edged nearer to her by some invisible force. It seemed to have changed colour, it appeared darker, less brown, more black … and were its eyes now yellow? Astra quickened her pace and concentrated on the goal again but her legs felt feeble, like the blood was slowly being drained out of them. Her breathing became shallow as she laboured to keep mobile in the heat. She felt the hair on her neck stand on end as she finally heard the creature move. She could feel the thump of its hooves reverberate on the ground beneath her as it followed.

'Oh boys! Oh my boys!' she stammered and fought back fresh tears.

She almost collapsed as the horse neighed. Its whinny seemed to cut through the air and collide with her, almost knocking her down. Astra cried out and willed herself onwards. There was a wall not far ahead and she aimed for that. She needed to put a barrier between herself and it. The trees were too far away. She felt the earth tremble as the thing broke into a gallop and she ran. Astra did not dare to look back. She knew what she would see. She summoned every last scrap of vigour and grit she had left into reaching that wall. Her mind swirled with panic but she knew she had only ten paces left … nine … eight … seven … the ground shook … six … five … four … its breath was on her back … three … two … one … Astra seized the top of the wall and scrambled up, the stones cut into her hands, her trainers slipped. She dropped to the ground on the other side like a sack of potatoes. She looked up just as the animal crashed into the wall. Its hooves sent fragments of stone hurtling in all directions. She staggered to her feet, shielding herself with her arms and stumbled back. The thing had given up any pretence of being a horse. It was now unnaturally huge and its neck was elongated like that of a serpent. It had sprouted horns from its head. It sprang back from the wall and bounded around in frustration.

'Whore! Whore! Whore! Whore! Whore!' it shrieked.

Astra span her head around. She needed a better refuge. There was a small hillock nearby, crowned with ancient standing stones. It was just another short sprint away.

'Got you!' She almost laughed.

*

'There she is,' crooned Tommy as they approached the stone circle. Jeff ran ahead to inspect the figure crouched in the middle.

'Murmurs peas share,' whimpered Edwin as he squinted in the sunshine to see. He and Tommy halted on the boundaries of the ring. Jeff had reached the centre but the figure had not budged. They looked at each other. Jeff's tail drooped.

'Astra?' Tommy called, his voice almost failing.

Slowly her head raised.

Tommy and Edwin both sighed with relief.

'I destroyed it,' muttered Astra.

The men glanced sideways at a steaming puddle of black fluid on the ground.

'You were attacked?' asked Tommy.

Astra did not answer for a while, her head sank again. Jeff trotted over and sniffed at the patch of ruin.

'I used my wail. The sacred ground augmented its power,' she said from within her arms.

'Good for you!' praised Tommy, clapping his hands together. Edwin grinned with him. 'You were in fine voice back at the house too.'

'What do you mean?' mumbled Astra wearily.

'Every window, every piece of crockery, every bit of glass, bang! Your sisters were mortified!'

He and Edwin chuckled but Astra remained still.

'It broke the hex too,' Tommy hastily added. 'We were freed. We came to find you straight away, didn't we, Edwin?'

Tommy turned to Edwin for support and he nodded as compassionately as he possibly could.

'It took us a while to find you. It was Jeff who sniffed you out. It's a good job he's still a dog.' Tommy's expression turned from delight to concern as he stepped over to Astra. Edwin hesitantly followed. 'Have you been here all night?'

'What do you want?' she asked without looking up.

Tommy crouched down. 'We've come to help you, haven't we? You daft cow!'

'I don't need your help anymore.'

'Rona and Magra are wicked. Rotten to the core. We should never have gone there.'

'No, but at least it told me something.'

'What?'

'That you're weak. All of you! Too weak!' Astra rose to her feet violently and lurched. Tommy shot out a helping hand but she pushed him away. 'Don't touch me!'

'Astra!' Tommy stood back in shock.

Edwin let out a sob, equally dismayed.

She turned and looked at them both for the first time, her eyes were bloodshot and wild. 'I can't have you with me if you can't resist the smallest of temptations, can I?

'They did something to us, Astra!' pleaded Tommy.

'I'm sure they did!' She shouldered her rucksack and staggered away.

'Where are you going?'

Astra did not answer, she stumbled off like a drunk.

'You can barely walk, woman!'

Edwin chased after her like a needy child. She spun round and hissed. The air shimmered and pulsed. He winced with fear and pain.

'Your voice, Astra!' warned Tommy. 'Don't do it again, not to us! You want us to end up like that?' Tommy pointed to the liquefied monster.

'Leave me alone! Go home!' she squealed and wandered away.

'We can't give up on you, Astra! Not after all these years!' Tommy ran to the edge of the circle and he and Edwin stood there, watching her go. Jeff raced to catch her up and she turned again.

'Go back, Jeff!'

He stood there, wagging his tail.

Astra stopped and glared at him. 'Go back, Jeff, there's a good boy.'

Jeff continued to wag, his head cocked to one side in bewilderment.

Astra's face gradually softened. She looked up at Tommy and Edwin.

'You bunch of nannas!'

'Remember when we first met, Astra?' said Tommy, leaning on a stone and peering at her. 'I was on leave from the merchant navy? I met you in the bar at the Royal Oak? You were with that nitwit, what was his name …'

'Percy.'

'Well, I never gave up on you that night, did I? And I'm not likely to now and neither are Jeff and Edwin. It's not our fault that we fell foul of a pair of witches. You should have never led us to that nest of vipers.'

Astra scratched the back of her neck and puffed with frustration.

'Are we a team again?' Tommy urged.

Astra put her hands on her hips and said it quietly. 'I suppose so.'

He and Edwin laughed with joy.

'Come on!' ordered Astra. She waited for them to catch up and assemble in front of her. 'Anyone got any fags?'

Tommy looked at Edwin and he nodded and produced a packet from his coat.

'Where did you get those?' quizzed Astra.

'They were in Rona's car. In the glove compartment. We stole it.'

'You took her car?'

'Well, after what they did to us ...'

Astra sparked up.

'Where to next?' asked Tommy.

Astra pointed to the copse of trees on the horizon. 'Just over there.'

'And that's the last piece of rock?'

'No.'

The blood drained from Tommy's face. 'There's another?'

'I dreamst it last night.'

'Where?'

'Africa.'

*

'I guess this is it,' remarked Tommy.

'Is what it?' Astra frowned as she was forced to move out of the way of a family that were struggling to move a small mountain of luggage on trolleys. A loudspeaker incoherently announced some flight details.

Tommy waited for the confusion to pass. 'You said that Jeff can't get into the country and we can't leave him here in Dublin alone. Edwin can't look after him, nor himself. That means I have to stay. Stands to reason.'

Astra peered at him and then at the floor and then at Edwin and Jeff who were slumped nearby. 'We'll be fine.'

Tommy's moustache quivered. 'We won't be fine, Astra, and you know it! Jeff will be put into some quarantine centre for months. Even if they allowed him in, they probably eat dogs where you're going. Curse your sisters for not putting him right.'

'They don't eat dogs in Africa, Tommy, that's ridiculous,' Astra scratched her curly head. 'And can we stop talking about my sisters now? I'd be happier if we never mentioned them ever again.'

'Alright,' said Tommy. 'It doesn't change the fact that we all can't go.'

'I must go.'

'By yourself? Look at what happened yesterday.'

'Then I'll take Edwin with me.'

'What about me?'

'Like you said, you can stay with Jeff.'

'Here in the airport?'

'No! You daft old twat! Go home. Wait for us there. We'll not be long.'

'Astra, you're going to Africa with no money!'

'We'll be back by the time you've boiled the kettle, just you see.'

'It's a big place!'

'Stop fretting.' Astra put a finger on Tommy's lips and silenced him but he was now staring at someone else. The black man was dressed in an expensive suit and was looking at Astra, smiling expectantly. Even amongst the varied and exotic populace of the departure lounge, the man stood out. Astra followed his gaze.

'Is that him?' asked Tommy.

'That's one of his men, I think.'

'And he's giving you a lift in his private jet for free?'

'Stroke of luck, isn't it?' Astra looked back at Tommy and giggled.

'I'll say.'

'He's taking us to Namibia. The rock is much further north than that but it's a start.'

'It looks like he's come to fetch you already.'

'It looks like it.'

'Then as I said; I guess this is it.'

Astra took off her rucksack and handed it to him. 'Take these and bury them somewhere where the Jeebies won't reach them. You know where.'

Tommy took the bag with reluctance. 'A task for Tommy.'

Astra put her arms around his girth and smiled up at him, playfully. 'Is that alright, my bunny rabbit?'

'I guess so,' replied Tommy with less enjoyment. 'I'm not special like you or Edwin or Jeff.'

Astra kissed him. 'You're the most special man I've ever known, Tommy Coomber, and we'd have never made it this far without you. You've always been my knight in shining armour.'

Tommy noticed that hot tears were running down her cheeks and he opened his mouth to speak but faltered. The African man stepped closer and looked at his expensive watch, impatiently. 'Off you go then,' was all he could manage to say.

Astra let go and walked away. She beckoned Edwin to follow. Edwin yawned, got to his feet and strolled casually after her.

Tommy smirked. 'Edwin?'

He stopped and turned round, gurning.

Tommy walked over and took Jeff's lead from him. 'Me and Jeff are staying.'

'Lone bundle,' said Edwin.

'Look after her, mate,' said Tommy.

The two men shook hands.

Jeff barked as Edwin and Astra vanished into the crowd and Tommy crouched down to comfort him. 'It's just me and you now, lad.'

*

The big sun rose quickly and bathed the savannah in a lurid orange glow. Astra stumbled to a halt and squinted into the light. Edwin and the two bushmen stopped and looked at her with concern.

'Ma'am?' asked one of the Africans.

She glared all around, her gaze finally settling on a distant mountain range. 'That's it.'

The three men waited patiently for her to set the new direction. She moved again, limping painfully towards the peaks.

'You want rest, ma'am?' suggested the other bushman.

'No,' said Astra. Her face was contorted with pain but they politely followed. Edwin caught up with her and held her up with one of his brawny arms.

'My pixie,' she muttered, breathlessly.

They marched slowly and Edwin noticed a group of Giraffes that were trailing behind them. He whimpered.

'Just don't look at them,' said Astra.

The weird procession advanced across the grassland and the lofty creatures got closer and closer. The two bushmen sang and ate as they walked, ignorant of the danger. At the foot of the mountain range, Astra finally gave in, without warning, and collapsed onto the dirt. Edwin keeled over with her.

The two bushmen looked at each other and one of them said what they were both thinking. 'Ma'am! You are tired! You must let us take you back!'

'You can now,' stated Astra with triumph. She held up a piece of rock in her hand. It was covered in dust but a green glow shone through. 'This is what we came for!'

Edwin looked at the lump in her grasp and giggled but his joy was brief. There were two appalling screams. He and Astra looked up at the Africans and they were no more. The Giraffes had arrived and assumed their true forms. They were black and monstrous and yellow-eyed and they were tearing the men to shreds.

Edwin stared at Astra, his entire body shaking.

She gazed back calmly and smiled. 'Don't be afraid.'

*

Tommy and Jeff strolled up to their favourite place: A hill overlooking the Rochdale canal. They wandered amongst the clumps of wavy dark-green meadow, purple swathes of heather and the nodding heads of cotton grass and they listened to the gentle callings of Curlews and Lapwings who knew it as home. Tommy carried a shovel and a bag of rocks and as a consequence, had a red face.

'Hello, Crooked Ned.' Tommy greeted the ancient monolith at the top of the hill. He dug a hole at the base of the stone and buried the rocks while Jeff pranced around and snorted at the freshly dug earth, being absolutely no help whatsoever. Tommy did not mind and sank slowly to sit down afterwards. Jeff settled at his side.

They wandered back to the house after their rest. They waited for Astra to come home. There they waited until the end of their days.

What he saw on Knightsheath

Ray regained consciousness slowly. His head was not on a comfy pillow but on a hard shoe. He opened his eyes. The shoe he identified as one of his own and judging by its stench, had got a bit of doggy on it somewhere. He flexed in disgust and tossed the article away. It skidded across the floor, hit the skirting board and left a light brown splash on the white gloss. He returned his head to an equally cruel surface. His raw bonce was pounding like it was on the verge of splitting open and ejecting his booze-sodden brain like a ... *no! Best not to think about that. Best not to think about heads breaking .... think about something else ...* he could still smell the shit and even taste it.

    He gazed over at the sofa, mere feet away. In his drunken delirium, he had failed to reach its padded embrace, selecting the floor for his bed and some soiled footwear for a pillow. The sofa was an oasis of comfort amongst the carnage of his living room and it mocked him by being just another stumble away. A bottle of tequila seemed like a good idea the night before. Ray recalled the Mexicans he had seen in cowboy movies as a kid. No wonder the poor sods were always sat around in the dirt, shading their eyes from the sun with massive round hats. What were those things called again? He continued to lie on the floor for a while and tried to remember. He gave up and, like a paraplegic spider, scrambled to the promised land that was the sofa. A noise in the kitchen froze him mid-crawl and turned his blood to ice. It seemed he was not alone. He fumbled hastily for some defence but the only objects in his vicinity were a teddy bear and a packet of cotton wool. Not even a graduate from the school of hard knocks such as Ray could make weapons of those. *Damn it!* He should have kept the shotgun to hand.

    'Is that you, Princess?' As soon as the words left his mouth, Ray realised his folly; like the rest of his family, the cat was gone. He knew there were things the same size as cats. *Shhh! Shouldn't think about that now.*

    'I've never been called that before but if it turns you on.'

    Ray gazed up at the intruder. He was immaculately dressed; sporting a tweed suit and a bottle-green waistcoat. He wore a golden cravat and a pair of horn-rimmed spectacles on the end of his nose. His trimmed black hair was finely combed across his skull. The man seemed too young to bear his title.

'Professor?'

Cedric Hamilton Montague smiled. 'In the words of the butler Lurch: Youuuu raaaang?'

'How did you get in?' gawped Ray.

'The back door was open,' he explained.

Ray screwed up his face. 'Balls! Must have been pissed.'

The Professor nodded and carried on smiling.

'You didn't feel the need to knock?'

The Professor glanced around the room as if politely viewing a car accident. 'I did. There was no answer.'

Ray transferred to a more comfortable position on his buttocks. 'You're too fucking late.'

'Too late for what, old boy?'

'They've taken it back,' Ray looked away, brazenly.

'Taken what back?'

'It,' he sneered.

'The Angel of Fogwin?'

Ray nodded furiously, animated all of a sudden. 'They came back for it! The bastards! Not in the woods! Not in the graveyard! Here in my own home!' Ray clawed at himself and stared vacantly.

The professor put his hands in his pockets and flared his nostrils. 'Hell's Teeth, Ray! You've really been through it, haven't you?'

'My wife left me,' Ray hung his head, 'It was too much for her. Too much for her beliefs.'

The Professor stared around at the mess again. 'How long has she been gone? And what is that loathsome pong? Mind if I open the window?' he asked, going across and opening it before Ray could answer. His nose was pinched in disapproval and his spectacles slid even further down the piste. 'You could put some trousers on too, old boy, the sight of your unwashed and malformed underpants is bringing my splendid breakfast back up.'

'You love it really,' croaked Ray.

As The Professor pulled back the curtains he found that all the windows were nailed shut. 'What in the devil is going on here?'

Ray rocked backwards and forwards on his feet and chuckled. 'Can't be too careful these days.'

The tidy young scholar stared at him. 'You're beginning to frighten me, Ray. All this talk of angels and monsters. Quite frankly it's insane. And here I find you; squatting in your own filth with the windows nailed up. You're really letting the neighbourhood go.'

'Fuck them,' belched Ray. 'I thought you believed me?'

'I do, old boy,' sighed The Professor. 'But for every individual with a genuine case there's fifty madmen with a paranoid delusion. I've seen a few queer things in my time but what you're talking about is way beyond anything I've experienced and I barely know you.'

'But you put me under,' mumbled Ray.

The Professor shrugged his shoulders. 'I thought it would help. The truth of the matter is that hypnotic regression can sometimes retrieve false memories or images that are symbolic rather than literal. Perhaps you were ill-treated when you were young and, in your mind, your abusers have taken on the form of hideous dwarfs?'

'I know this is real!' snarled Ray. 'I held one of the things in my hands!' He clutched an imaginary miniature fiend. 'If you'd been here a few days ago you would have seen it for yourself!'

'This all seems rather convenient.'

Ray glared at him. 'What's that supposed to mean?'

The Professor shook his head briefly. 'You've been droning on about these creatures of yours and as soon as I arrive to examine the conclusive proof they suddenly vanish in a puff of smoke.'

'Okay,' said Ray, finding some fags and lighting one up. 'I admit it sounds a bit bonkers but I know I'm not ... what did you say? ... delusional. I thought you were here to help me but if you can't be arsed then piss off! I didn't know who else to call except you. I thought you were the only person left who I could trust.'

The Professor saw tears in Ray's eyes. He took a few deep breaths. 'I think you'd better tell me exactly what's happened,' he said.

'I've never wanted a cuppa so much in my life,' sobbed Ray.

The Professor helped him to his feet. 'Come on then, let's go and put the kettle on.'

They went through into the kitchen and The Professor kept his promise. Ray sat down on a stool and gazed miserably at his feet. It was only when The Professor put a hot steaming mug into his hands did the journalist become active again.

'Start at the beginning,' The Professor instructed.

Ray took a cautious slurp and looked at him with pools of red. 'Sombrero!'

*

I don't know what it was between me and Mark Lyons. We could and should have been mates. We both lived in the same town, worked at the same newspaper, came from working class backgrounds. We even shared interests, well, we played darts in the office nearly every lunchtime for four years. Yet, for some reason, we hated each other's guts. As far as I know, Mark is happy now. He still lives in creepy sleepy little Fogwin and edits the Enquirer. He even has a family. Back in the spring of 1980 though our rivalry came to a head and things got pretty ugly. Maybe it was because we were both in love with the same girl. Perhaps it was because he was a snivelley little twat.

Excerpt from the journal of Ray Weaver, volume one.

*

'Where the hell have you been?'
 Ray had no time to relax or take his coat off or even breathe. His editor was on his case straight away. Ray looked through into Archie's office and the moustache was annoyed. He saw it bristle like a satanic hedgehog.
 'Investigating,' stuttered Ray.
 'Investigating what? Your nob?' barked Archie.
 'My local history project.'
 'What local history project?'
 'The one we discussed last week.'
 'I don't remember discussing any local history project.'
 Ray shrugged his shoulders. 'Well, we did.'
 Archie stared intensely at him for a few seconds as if he was trying to see into his reporter's very soul. A lesser man would have been terrified but Ray had worked with the man for a while and was accustomed to his notorious glare. Dealing with the devil was a daily trial. His boss' ferocious scrutiny could be beaten only by that of his Glaswegian wife. Ray had grown somewhat bullet proof.
 'Why don't you come in here so I don't have to keep shouting?' shouted Archie.
 Ray nodded and ambled through into the editor's office.
 'Shut the door.'
 Ray closed the door behind him and shuddered. 'Look, Archie, I'm not really in the mood for this, Iris gives me enough earache as it is.'
 'Come and sit down.'

Ray was about to plonk himself him down when his boss did something that he did not expect: Archie stood up and gestured to his own chair.

'You want me to sit there?' Ray's eyebrows elevated in astonishment.

'Give it a try,' instructed Archie with an uncommon smile.

Ray was suspicious but did as he was told. He got up and walked round to the other side of the desk. Gingerly, he placed himself in the editor's huge leather chair. He gazed around with marvel. He had never seen the place from that angle before. He leaned back in the throne and there was a slight creaking noise as it cradled his weight. It felt magnificently comfortable as if every part of his body was being sustained and cared for. It made him feel important and reassured him that everything was going to be alright. Ray had never experienced seating pleasure like it and he wondered why Archie was always so grumpy.

'What do you think?' quizzed his boss as if anticipating Ray's delight.

'Nice,' said Ray.

'Cigar?' Archie thrust a box of stinky brown tubes in his face.

'Don't mind if I do,' replied Ray and put one in his mouth.

Archie ignited it for him with a gold lighter.

Ray leaned back even further back into the magic chair. The cigar tasted rank but it reinforced the impression of power.

'Comfortable?' enquired Archie.

'Very,' said Ray.

'Right! See you in two weeks!' Archie grabbed his coat and scarf from a hat-stand.

Ray scowled. 'Hang on! Where are you going?'

'On a cruise,' explained Archie. 'Doctor's orders.'

'And you want me to sit here for two weeks?' grumbled Ray.

Archie turned to look at him as he put his coat and scarf on. 'Well, it would be good if you could produce some newspapers while you're at it.'

'You want me to be editor?' shrieked Ray, a little too much like a hysterical woman for his liking.

'Just till I get back,' nodded Archie.

'I'm not qualified,' Ray protested.

'You've been working here for long enough. You know the score.'

'What about Mark? He's been here longer than me.'

'Lyons is an even bigger idiot than you are so it's the lesser of two evils as far as I'm concerned.'

'Have you told him?'

'Yes, he's locked himself in the toilet. Your first job is to get him out. He will be your one and only reporter, after all.'

'He's not going to be happy about this.'

'He isn't. He's crying his eyes out.'

'I don't know, Archie, what about my salary?'

'We'll sort something out when I get back.' Archie gave Ray a stern look. 'Don't take any risks. Stick to the usual format and print the usual small town crap and everything will be alright. Comprende?'

Ray gawped at him.

'Do you understand me, Weaver?'

Ray exhaled cigar smoke slowly and nodded. 'Send us a postcard then.'

The editor left with a blasé wave.

Ray enjoyed the chair for a while longer but stubbed out the cigar. He gazed out of the window. The morning sun was shining and he could see the town park stretching out in its golden glimmer. He realised that the editor had a better view of the outside world than anyone else. He pushed his superior seating to its limits; reclining fully and putting his feet up on the desk. On the opposite wall to the window, sucking in the light, was a gilt-framed portrait of the Prime Minister Margaret Thatcher and it made Ray restless.

'I'm not sharing with you for two weeks,' said Ray to the painting.

He swiftly left the embrace of the chair and took the portrait off the wall. He knew that Archie was fond of the article so Ray placed it carefully in one corner of the office, the offensive likeness of the new first lady turned inwards.

He put his hands in his pockets casually and wandered through to the general office where he usually sat and into the toilets where the first challenge of his temporary promotion awaited. Ray relieved himself. Behind him was a locked cubicle where someone sobbed and sniffed.

'Coming out of there, Mark?' asked Ray.

'Go fuck yourself,' he answered.

Ray chuckled and washed his hands. This was like all his Christmases and birthdays come at once. Resuming a relaxed demeanour, he returned to the general office. He was astounded to find someone there and even more stunned to find that it was the most beautiful woman he had ever seen in his life. She looked at him. His jaw dropped.

'Can I help you, luv?'

'Oh!' she exclaimed melodramatically. 'Sorry, I was looking for Mark Lyons.' Her blue eyes glittered as she spoke and her long curly blonde hair bounced playfully.

Ray tried to be cool. 'He's not here at the moment. Perhaps I can help?'

'And you are?'

'Ray Weaver. Editor of the Fogwin Enquirer.' He noted that it did not sound quite as impressive as he thought it would.

The woman, however, beamed and displayed a row of perfect white teeth. She extended a golden-tanned arm and Ray shook her hand. It was tiny and smooth and warm.

'Lucy,' she said.

'Lucy Springer? The Page 3 Girl?'

She nodded but corrected him. 'Glamour model.'

Ray trembled with excitement. He had seen those faultless breasts a few times in print and now they were there in front of him, hidden only by a skimpy white blouse. He tried in vain not to stare but it was like they were magnets and his eyes metal.

'It's alright,' Lucy giggled. 'You can look at them. I'm used to it.'

Ray blushed. Those words seemed to break the spell somehow. 'So you're here to see Mark?'

'I said I'd look him up while I was in town.'

'Well, he's … erm, engaged at the moment. Can I pass on a message?' Ray was instantly baffled by the mystery of why a woman as attractive and charming as Lucy would even give a loser like Mark the time of day.

She thought for a moment, rolling her sparkling eyes to one side in such a cute way that Ray felt helplessly in love just for that one quality alone. 'I'll be back later,' she said, delving into her handbag. 'I'll give you my Uncle's phone number. That's where I'll be staying.'

Ray waited patiently while she dug out a notebook and transferred the number to a scrap of paper. He seized the opportunity to drink in more of her heavenly form.

'Thanks, Ray,' Lucy handed it over.

'No problem,' he winked at her.

'Nice to meet you,' she said with a mischievous smile.

'Nice to meet you too,' he agreed.

Then she was gone. Ray stood there, his brain struggling to process the encounter. He felt like he had been slapped. He heard a sound behind him and turned to see Mark. His rival's eyes and cheeks were red.

'Alright, flower?' queried Ray, pocketing the phone number.

'Who was that?' snorted Mark.

'No one,' said Ray.

'I thought I heard somebody,' Mark peered around the room, suspiciously.

'Nope,' said Ray, slipping back into the editor's office. 'Come and see me when you're ready to start work.'

*

'So, tell me more about the legend that's Ray Weaver,' said Lucy, sipping her wine and licking her lips.

'Well, I wouldn't exactly call myself a legend,' explained Ray with a modest chortle. 'I'm more subtle than that; more like a crusader really, you know, like a ninja and that, a Jedi.' Ray was aware of the nonsense coming out of his mouth but he was powerless to stop it. There was something about the promise of an infinity of pleasure in the lady's eyes that was disintegrating his mojo.

'A crusader and a ninja and a Jedi? Wow!' Lucy laughed.

It made Ray's heart flutter. 'A bit like Chuck Norris.'

'Chuck Norris is sexy,' she added. 'Can you do all that kung Fu stuff?'

'Martial arts? Well, only when I have to.'

'Can you do some now?'

Ray glanced around the restaurant. 'Too dangerous,' he decided, even though it was empty. 'Besides, I'm smarting a bit from my last spot of bother.'

'Oh, you poor thing,' Lucy cooed with sympathy and reached across the table to touch his wrist. A few volts went up his arm. 'I hope they didn't damage you too much?'

Ray grunted. 'You should see the state of them.'

There was a peculiar pause while they eyed each other up. Ray was not entirely sure what was happening. He was having dinner with a famous Page 3 Girl and she seemed to be actually flirting with him. Or was she just toying with him? It was too good to be true and Ray suspected that he might wake up any moment now.

'So, being the editor of a newspaper, is that just cover?' she asked with a wry smile.

Ray shrugged his shoulders and smiled back. 'I've got to pay the bills somehow. Fighting the forces of darkness is strictly volunteer work. It means I've got to deal with more mundane stuff but it helps me to keep reality in check.'

'I see.'

'What about yourself? What's it like being … er … a glamour model?'

Lucy sighed as if describing herself was a chore. 'To be honest, it's dull. I have to travel up and down the country all the time and work very hard. I have to look after my hair and my skin and it's difficult when they're constantly being tampered with. I have to look after my figure too. I have to watch what I eat and drink.' She lifted up her glass of wine to emphasise her point. 'People are always looking at me. I'm more like an object than a person.'

Ray nodded. 'Sounds tough.'

'You don't see me as an object do you, Ray?'

'I suspect you have hidden depths, Miss Springer.'

'Very astute.' She peered at him for a moment. 'Can I confess something to you?'

'Sure.'

'I'm not what I seem.'

Ray felt anxious all of a sudden. The breathtaking smile had disappeared from the girl's face and she looked sad. He wondered if she was going to reveal to him that she was a demon or a mutant or a Tory. It seemed to be the fashion these days. He scanned around for exits.

'I've actually got a PhD in the history of art,' she said with a heavy sigh, as if letting go of some incredible burden.

'What?' Ray choked on his pint. It was not quite what he was expecting but astounding nevertheless.

'The bimbo thing is just an act,' she explained.

He stared at her. 'Serious?'

She nodded.

'Why for Christ's sake?'

'Having both beauty and brains makes men feel uncomfortable. I would never get anywhere in this business if they knew how clever I was.'

Ray took a few seconds to digest the revelation and the lager.

'It doesn't make you feel uncomfortable, does it, Ray?' she queried with genuine concern. 'You can handle it, can't you?'

Ray laughed. 'A bird with brains and smashing knockers? Sure!'

'I'm glad because I've had a really great time with you tonight.'

'Me too.'

'I wish that woman would stop staring at us though.'

'What woman?'

Lucy pointed outside and Ray turned to see a furious looking red-haired harridan glaring at him through the window.

'Who is she?' enquired Lucy.

'I don't know,' replied Ray, ignoring the fact that it was, quite clearly, his wife.

*

'I think I can tell where this story is going,' stated The Professor whilst poaching an egg.

'Yeah?' Ray put on some freshly-ironed trousers, also courtesy of his guest.

'Well, you've just been made editor and the power goes straight to your head. In walks a pretty girl and it's goodbye wife. You heterosexuals are so predictable.'

'She's gorgeous!' Ray closed his eyes as if to recollect the vision of Lucy. 'You should see her, Professor.'

'I don't think I could appreciate it, my boy.' The Professor shovelled the egg onto a piece of toast.

Ray snorted. 'She's so fit she'd even cure your gayness.'

The Professor issued him with his breakfast, shaking his head with amusement.

Ray stared at it. 'I don't feel very hungry, mucka.'

'You can't face evil on an empty stomach.'

Ray pushed the egg on toast around the plate a bit.

The Professor watched him. 'Was she worth it?'

Ray frowned and looked up at him. 'I miss my wife. She might be scrawny and pale and ginger and have crooked teeth. She's got an irritating laugh. She might be too strict with my kids and she constantly whinges and complains ... erm ... where was I going with this?'

'Was she worth it?'

Ray shrugged his shoulders and tried a mouthful of egg.

The Professor removed his apron and marigolds while he munched. 'I suppose you don't know what you have until it's gone.' He gazed out of the window as if recollecting some unhappy episode from his own life.

'You'd make someone a nice wife,' commented Ray.

The Professor ignored him. 'Well, Ray, I don't mean to be awkward but I am a paranormal investigator, not a marriage counsellor.'

Ray shook his head grumpily while he picked at the rest of his breakfast. 'I haven't got to the scary stuff yet, I'm just giving you the background.'

'I get the picture,' The Professor made himself comfortable on a chair and sipped tea from a cup on a saucer in an overly rehearsed fashion. 'Go on then.'

'Well, it all started back at the office again …'

*

'Busy?' Ray cocked an enquiring eyebrow into the office at Mark. 'Yeah,' replied his colleague, who was engrossed in the construction of an aeroplane made entirely of paper. 'Yourself?'

Ray rolled his eyes and climbed out of the comfy editor's chair. He put his hands in his pockets and strolled through to where Mark tolerated more barbaric furnishings. 'Aren't you supposed to be writing a newspaper or something?'

Mark shrugged his shoulders and continued plane building.

'What about the football results?'

'Done,' stated Mark and thumbed to a sheet of paper on the corner of his desk.

Ray picked it up. 'Town planning?'

'There isn't any this week.'

Ray stared at him while he beavered away on his origami project. He got cross. 'Are you going to behave like a spoilt kid for all of Archie's holiday?'

Mark finally ceased production and looked up at him. 'What do you want me to do?'

'I want you to go out there and get us some fucking stories!'

'There's no need to raise your voice,' said he. 'And how come you've started swearing so much?'

Ray exhaled through his nose so hard it blew the plane off the desk. 'Is this because Archie made me acting editor instead of you? I told him that he should have asked you. I didn't want the sodding job. If you want to do it then be my guest.' Ray gestured through into the boss' paradise.

Mark sulked. 'No, no, he asked you!'

'I knew it,' Ray nodded. 'You've got the monk on. You won't even play darts with me!'

Mark picked up his plane and fumbled with it. 'I've been working here loads longer than you have. It's not fair.'

'I know,' said Ray. 'That's what I told him. You should have it out with him, not me. I'm going to find this difficult enough without you being a dick.'

Impasse; they stared at each other.

'Haven't we got anything in?' Ray scowled.

Mark scratched his chin in thought. 'Well there is some weird shit going on. Might be your sort of thing.'

'What weird shit?'

'Mysterious goings on at the new industrial estate,' explained Mark, consulting his notepad.

Ray had to admit that he was curious. 'The Earthcom place?'

'Seems it's haunted,' Mark said. 'I was talking to a bloke who I went to school with in the pub. He got a job up there as a security guard doing nights and he's had to jack it in because he got so scared.'

Ray gulped. 'Scared of what?'

Mark read a list from his notepad. 'All sorts of nonsense; cold draughts, strange noises, lights in the sky, machinery breaking down, things getting moved around, etc.'

'Etc?'

Mark looked up at him and nodded. 'You know the sort of thing?'

Ray was confused. 'Do I?'

Mark chuckled. 'Look, it's just some beer talk, that's all. Brian's that sort of bloke. He likes to tell ghost stories, give us all the shivers before we walk home from the pub.'

'Yet it was enough to force him to quit his job and for you to write it down?' stated Ray.

Mark shrugged his shoulders. 'I don't know what the truth is. Brian likes to make stuff up. He probably just got the sack for drinking on the job. Wouldn't be the first time. I just thought you might be interested.'

'Have you checked it out?'

Mark shook his head. 'If I investigated every one of Brian Temple's tall tales I'd be a very busy man.'

Ray performed a little dance of frustration. 'I wish you hadn't told me that now! I'm fascinated! I knew there was something dodgy about that place. Knightsheath's got a lot of history.'

'I don't know, Ray.'

Ray sobered himself. 'Neither do I. The problem is that Archie told me to stick to normal stuff. He'd crucify me if I reported something like this. We'll have to forget about it.'

His colleague nodded in agreement. 'Besides, I went to the unveiling of that place myself and had a good look around. Seemed ordinary enough to me.'

'Yeah,' Ray wandered away and put his hands back in his pockets. As he reached the threshold of his office he stopped and turned back to Mark. 'Wouldn't harm to have a quick look though, would it?'

*

Knightsheath Road was long, straight and ancient. Antiquarians hypothesised that it had been built by the Romans but the ruins that it lead to were far older and their purpose more obscure. The remnants were no longer open to the inquisitive; a gate had been erected near the end of the road. A sturdy metal gate prevented entry and upon it a sign read "Danger! Construction site. Authorised personnel only."

'What now?' Ray whispered, even though the checkpoint appeared to be unattended.

Mark peered through the windscreen as if searching for an answer. The shadow of dusk had fallen, reducing the rolling countryside to dingy hues of purple, blue and grey.

'We'll park a mile back down the road and enter on foot,' Ray decided without his colleague's opinion and turned his brown Ford Cortina back down the road. He parked it under the cover of some trees about half a mile away.

The two reporters got out and marched back through the gloom to the gate.

'This is a bit strange,' commented Mark as they did so.

'What is?' mumbled Ray.

'You and me working together,' he clarified.

'We do work together.'

Mark smiled. 'Yeah, we work together but we don't work together. We're always locking horns, even at darts.'

Ray took the meaning of his confession and seemed annoyed with it. 'Don't get too gay with me. We're just going to look at something together, that's all.'

Mark went on. 'Archie wouldn't like it. He always tries to keep us apart. It's almost like he wants us to compete with one another.'

'Archie will be sunning himself in some far away port by now so let's just get on with it. Try to stay quiet.'

That was the extent of their conversation for now. When they got back to the checkpoint Ray instructed them to leave the road but that was all. For a while, they stumbled through wild thickets, ploughed fields and regimented crops in the dark, negotiating a vague circle around the estate. Ray seemed to trip over everything that could be tripped over. Mark waited for him to pick up the pace patiently. After a mile or two, they both suddenly bungled into each other. Ray had come to a sudden halt.

'What is it?' hissed Mark.

'There's someone over the next ridge,' murmured Ray.

They stared and sure enough the upper half of a gangly figure could be seen over an incline. They watched it sway in the wind for a while like some grotesque and lame puppet. Ray sighed. He picked up a stone and hurled it at the ragged sentinel with force. The projectile found its mark and bounced away into the night but the figure did not flinch.

'Scarecrow,' he concluded and stumbled onwards.

Reassured, Mark followed him. They walked past it but Ray gave the thing a wide birth, staring back at the straw man until it was out of sight.

'I hate scarecrows,' Ray revealed. 'Remind me of clowns.'

'You've got more to worry about than that, mate, if the stories are true,' said Mark, forebodingly.

They walked on for another mile and stopped again at the top of a steep summit. They could see down into a wide and shallow valley. On the far side of the basin was the skeleton of some vast man-made structure. The complex would have been hidden by the darkness if it had not been crowned by half a dozen lights. Bizarrely, one of the lights moved around slowly and menacingly; spearing the black and lighting up the wilds.

'That's the estate,' explained Mark, as if it needed saying.

'We'll work our way over,' retorted Ray. 'Take care not stray into that searchlight. I get the impression we're not supposed to be here, don't you?'

With silent agreement, the duo took a moment's rest. Suddenly, Mark started to walk away.

Ray turned to look at him. Where you going?'

'You don't need me,' said Mark, his voice trembling. 'I'll find my own way back.'

'Hang on!' growled Ray. 'I thought we were in this together? Like you said?'

'I've already seen it,' Mark sniffed.

'Don't give me that crap,' Ray glared at him. 'Where's your investigative spirit, man?'

Mark snorted and stomped around in the dark, as if striving to get something off his chest.

'What's up with you?' Ray prompted.

'I'm frightened,' declared Mark. 'Don't laugh! Okay?'

Ray pissed himself.

Mark sulked.

'Come on, you daft bastard!'

They descended into the valley, Ray virtually dragging his fellow reporter, and took an unclear course towards an unclear destination. They laboured now over muddy humps and dense scrub. They encountered no one in the realm of shadows. There was only the occasional flap of small wings or icy gust of wind to distract them. Several times, the baleful searchlight shone their way and they were compelled to stop and crouch for a few seconds until blackness resumed. Then they came across a feature that annihilated their progress completely; it appeared as an ordinary barb-wire fence no higher than the waist. Ray merely intended to stride over it. He scanned around just to make sure that he was not being watched and stepped across, shielding his crotch with one cupped hand. The satisfaction was quickly wiped from his face. A buzzing sound filled his ears. His brain jolted and he melted backwards over the fence. His vision blurred and his head span. The contents of his stomach erupted and soaked his shoes. Ray sank to his knees and puked more. He wiped his mouth and looked around like a wounded animal. The buzzing noise had ceased. He stood up, albeit a little shakily, and stared at the fence in horror.

'Fucking hell!'

'Are you alright?' Mark asked, somewhat unhelpfully.

Ray did not answer. Hesitantly, he walked over to the obstruction and touched it with shaking fingers. To his continuing amazement, there was no shock this time. He put his hands in his pockets and frowned. He needed a rational explanation but there was nothing forthcoming from his companion or from his own mind. His only reasoning was that he had taken an electric shock and somehow shorted the power out in the process. With a determined sniff, he stepped over the fence again, guarding the most precious parts of his anatomy as before. He was assaulted a second time. The dreadful buzzing filled his ears and the jelly inside his cranium quivered. He lurched backwards and had no time to vomit on the ground, splattering himself instead. A turd shot out of his arse too. His vision became white for a few seconds and Ray flailed and cursed amongst the undergrowth. His sight soon returned but the nausea remained for longer.

'You try,' he gurgled at Mark.

'No chance!' he replied. 'There's something not right here!'

'Go on!' ordered Ray. 'You might be alright.'

Mark faltered a little and then found some insane courage from somewhere. He took a few steps back and then hurled himself at the obstacle. Even if the reporter had the agility to succeed in such a feat he would have failed. It looked like Mark struck an invisible wall. He collided with the barrier in mid-air and slid back down to earth with a cartoonish thump. Mark became a crumpled ball on the ground, vomiting and defecating as Ray had done.

'Oh, God!' he wailed. 'Oh, God! Oh, God! Oh, God!'

For the second time that night, Ray laughed long and loud.

'What the hell was that?' groaned Mark when he had resolved himself.

'I don't know,' Ray wiped the tears from his cheeks and helped him to his feet.

'I think I've shat myself,' confessed Mark, unable to share Ray's humour.

'Don't worry!' Ray slapped him on the shoulder. 'That makes two of us.'

Mark looked at the fence. 'I'm not trying that again.'

Ray nodded. 'I hear you. Let's call it a night.'

The two soiled men headed back the way they had come or as close as they could find it. They clambered back across the shaggy hills and up the wall of the valley where the scarecrow awaited them.

'We don't belong out here,' Mark puffed and panted.

'It looks like the mysteries of Earthcom will remain thus for now,' added Ray as they climbed.

Ray was slightly wrong. As if on cue, the sky behind them lit up suddenly. A crack of what may have been lightning split the sky and, for a fleeting moment, the whole valley appeared as in daylight. There was no thunder to escort it; no sound at all. Ray and Mark were temporarily blinded and even when they could see again the air continued to flash and crackle with psychedelic discharge. They turned to peer at the industrial estate behind them and were amazed by the sight. Beyond the new structure was another; something that was far older and made of stone. The place would have remained hidden by the night if it had not been for the myriad of colours illuminating its rock columns. The phenomenon was hard to describe and in time to come, both writers put their notes together to come up with the description; *kaleidoscopic fireworks made of liquid and exploding in slow motion.*

'What the hell is going on, Ray?' whispered Mark, not daring to raise his voice any higher than necessary.

'I don't know,' his colleague answered, unable to tear his gaze away from the peculiar glow in the distance. 'I vote we beat a hasty retreat and find the nearest pub for a stiff one, disposing of underpants en route.'

'Sounds good to me,' agreed Mark.

In the vast shadow of Earthcom and its plume of strange colours, the two men scuttled away like insects.

*

'Some sort of automated sonic defence system?' The Professor sipped his tea thoughtfully.

'Come again?' Ray put a fag in his gob.

'The fence?'

'I don't know what it was, fruit, it was absolutely bizarre. I've never experienced anything like it.'

'The stuff of science fiction.'

Ray lit the fag with a lively match and squinted through a cloud of phosphorus. 'Considering that in the last few months I've been kidnapped by demons and a geezer with an extra eye, a sonic fence isn't a massive leap of imagination.'

'Quite.' The Professor arched his fingers and eyebrows in contemplation. 'I haven't actually seen any of these things for myself. What did you make of the lights in the sky?'

Ray shrugged his shoulders. 'Again I'm clueless. Another scientific experiment maybe?'

'How disturbing,' his visitor muttered.

'We haven't got to the maddest shit yet,' puffed Ray.

*

It was in the 70s that unidentified flying objects really took off, if you'll excuse the pun. Smart arse psychologists came to the conclusion that it was a cultural phenomenon rather than a scientific one. After all, the decade had seen a flurry of successful science-fiction films like Star Wars, Close Encounters of the Third Kind and Alien and it was no coincidence that nutters all over the world started spotting spaceships in the sky all of a sudden. They didn't see just UFOs but also reported abductions by slimy monsters and accused their governments of covering it up. The Cold War didn't help matters because any country worth its salt was conducting ultra-secret military experiments and these must have accounted for many so-called UFO sightings. I myself inhabited a strange limbo. Despite being a journalist, I was reluctant to proclaim any of my own experiences or get involved in any way at all. Ufologists, as they became known, were a legion of wild-eyed nerds in raincoats who had given up on the possibility of having sex with girls. I was not too keen to join them and get lampooned, locked up and shot at. However, Mark had witnessed the strange features of Earthcom with me so I was no longer alone. What happened next sealed my fate.

Excerpt from the journal of Ray Weaver, volume one.

*

In the dark of the car, parked under the canopy of a huge tree, under the black of a moonless night, lips brushed against lips. For a second they clamped.

Lucy recoiled. 'I'm sorry. I can't do this!'

Ray deflated and stared at her. He could not believe how close he had come to touching those famous breasts. A million men must have fantasised about being where he was now. Ray punched his steering wheel in frustration. 'I thought we were going to …'

'Don't be angry,' pleaded Lucy, looking away. 'What kind of woman do you think I am? Do you think that just because I take my clothes off for money that makes me a slag?'

Ray frowned and considered his answer carefully. 'Erm … well …'

She flicked him a glare.

Ray chuckled. 'Look, we've established that you're an intellectual. I like you because you're beautiful and you're clever. We've done the conversation thing. Now it's time for the hanky panky.'

'You've got a wife, Ray.'

'It's not what you call a happy marriage,' he explained. 'Iris loves Jesus more than she does me.'

'What did you see in her in the first place?'

Ray shrugged his shoulders. 'Someone who'd had the same shitty upbringing as me.' He fumbled for a smoke. 'I wanted to make her happy, take the pain away.' He offered one to Lucy.

'Ta,' she accepted and he lit them both up. They sat in silence for a while, smoked and peered out into the deserted road. It was a secluded backstreet that was quiet even during the day. Perfect for an illicit rendezvous, Ray had thought, though he imagined more kissing and less talk.

'Besides,' said Lucy. 'I'm supposed to be going out with Mark.'

'Why did you agree to meet me out here then?' groaned Ray, flaring up again.

The Page 3 girl exhaled. 'I don't know.'

'He's not good enough for you.'

'And you are, I suppose?'

'I like to think so.'

'You're an arrogant cock.'

There was another episode of hush while Ray tried to work out what was going on in that pretty head. He decided to tell her the truth.

'I really like you, Lucy, I'm not looking for just a quick thrill. I want out of this crap town and I want you with me. I'll leave Iris and you can leave Mark and we'll be together like we were meant to be.'

She looked into his eyes. 'You've got a silver tongue, Raymond Weaver. I want to believe you but somehow I can't. I've heard it a hundred times before. It always leads to the same thing.' With that, Lucy grabbed her handbag and got out.

'Lucy!' Ray exclaimed and pursued her. She was fast. She was half way down the road by the time he had climbed out of the Cortina and caught up with her. Angry women were swift even in high heels. 'Lucy! Please!'

She jolted to a halt and rounded on him. 'What?'

Ray almost barged into her. 'I don't want you to go. I'll make you a deal.'

'I'm listening.'

'If you don't believe me then I'll prove myself to you. Let's leave the sex for now. Let's leave it for a year … five years! Until we get married!' Ray could not believe the words coming out of his own mouth.

She stared into his eyes for what seemed like an age and then giggled. 'Okay.'

Ray adored that giggle. He was reassured; the promise was worth it.

'But we don't have to leave it that long though,' she added. 'I like sex.'

Ray was so delighted he nearly puked. He gazed into her eyes and grinned like an oaf.

'Is that all you wanted to say?'

'For now,' he answered.

She smiled and walked on. 'I'll see you soon, hero.'
Ray scowled. 'Don't you want a lift home?'
'No,' she said.
'Oh! That reminds me!'
Lucy turned round.
'Your Uncle Roger?'
'What about him?'
'Can you get me an interview?'
Lucy seemed cross again. She traversed the distance between them. 'Why?'
'Me and Mark were at his new industrial estate earlier tonight investigating ghost stories.' Ray sniggered, trying to make it sound like a caper. 'I just wondered if he had any insight for us. He's the head honcho right?'
Lucy nodded. 'Yes, but what do you mean ghost stories?'
Ray kept up the light-hearted façade. 'The place that it's built on is very old and Mark knows a geezer that works there. Had some strange things to say. We went to take a look ourselves but we couldn't get in. They've got a … erm … very unique security system.'
Lucy cocked her head to one side, as if contemplating something. 'My uncle is too busy to discuss something like that, don't you? He's a scientist and a businessman, Ray. The sort of man who makes a point of smashing mirrors and walking under ladders.'
Ray scratched his head. 'Of course. Just an idea. Forget it.'
'Besides,' Lucy sighed. 'He's not too well at the moment.'
'Nothing serious I hope?'
'Just stress I think. The project's been hard for him.'
'Well, I'm sure that having a niece like you brings some comfort to him,' Ray cringed at the bullshit flowing freely from his mouth again.
Luckily for Ray, Lucy saw the funny side. She giggled and, with a wave, attempted to walk away for a third time.
Ray put his hands in his pockets and watched her vanish into the night. Her blonde hair and long white coat made her look ethereal in the dimness and it was a fascinating vision. The angel glanced back at him a couple of times and he was graced with more of those sweet giggles. It was Ray's last happy memory of his second love.

*

He knew something was wrong straight away. Ray parked the car in the driveway, got out and locked the doors, all the time glancing at his house nervously. He fumbled with his keys and dropped them twice. A sickening panic was rising from the bottom of his gut and turning his fingers to butter. About two weeks previous, Ray had visited the home of Peter Stanley and discovered that the front door had been forced open and the man's most precious possession discarded onto the floor. There were no such obvious danger signs here, Ray just sensed something was amiss.

'Princess?' Ray greeted the cat as it slunk round the side of the house. She meowed in distress and he picked her up.

'Iris?' he called out his wife's name instinctively as he took the cat inside.

'In here!' she cried from the lounge.

Ray was now breathing laboriously and his heart was hammering in his ears. He marched into the room and saw his wife and kids huddled together on the sofa. He checked his watch, it was past midnight. 'Still up?' he enquired foolishly. The faces of his loved ones were stained with tears and it was obvious all was not well in the Weaver household.

'Where have you been?' Iris shrieked with such ferocity and volume that Ray winced and the children started crying again. Her words were barely discernible, it was little more than a scream.

'Working,' he stuttered. 'What the hell is going on?' Princess leapt out of his embrace and made good her escape. Cats are not known for their moral support in times of crisis and Ray's specimen was no exception.

He was dealt another mournful shriek. 'I know you haven't been at the office! The police have been trying to find you!'

'The police?' gawped Ray. 'Why? What's happened?'

'We had an intruder,' said Iris, sounding slightly more human.

'An intruder?' Ray was completely stunned. Already that night he had witnessed the peculiar goings-on at Knightsheath and been with Lucy. It was all getting too much. His brain was in meltdown. Words barely left his mouth. 'What? Here?'

She nodded at him vehemently and held Posy and William closer.

'When?'

'Earlier on,' she said, checking the clock. 'Just as we were getting ready for bed.'

Ray breathed out. He had been wandering the wilderness with Mark at that time, completely oblivious to the fact that his family were in peril.

'William saw something looking down at him from your room.'
'Something? My room? The attic?'
Iris nodded. 'You've brought Satan into this house!'
Ray stepped over and sat down next to them. 'Are you alright, William?'
The boy withdrew from the sanctuary of his mother's cardigan and regarded him.
'Are you alright, son?'
William shook his head slowly.
'Are you frightened?'
'Yes.'
'You know how I'm always telling you to be brave?'
Iris barked. 'He's only five, Ray! You should have been here.'
He turned away and rubbed his jaw. 'I know I should have.'
'You were with her, weren't you? 'That whore!' she wailed.
Ray scowled at her. 'Iris, not in front of the kids, luv. Let's not do this right now.'
He stood up and looked at them. 'You called the police?'
Her lips curled back with rage. 'I had no choice, did I?'
'What did they say?'
'They couldn't find anything.'
'They couldn't find anything? How long did it take them to get here?'
'They were quick.'
'And they couldn't find anything?'
Iris shook her red locks.
'Did you see anyone leave?'
'No.'
Ray half-laughed. 'Then it was the boy's imagination, surely?'
Iris glared at him for a couple of seconds and then softened. 'Maybe. The point is that we were scared and you weren't here.'
Ray relaxed a bit, his shoulders dropped and his respiratory and cardiac systems started playing along again. 'Alright, you stay here. I'll go and have a good check around and then we can all go to bed, okay?'
His family peered up at him with three pairs of sore eyes.
He gave them his best impression of a reassuring smile and left them in the lounge, closing the door firmly behind him. Despite his promise, Ray paced around in the hallway indecisively. It was true that his son had an overactive imagination and he was partly to blame because he had fuelled it with so many ridiculous bedtime yarns. He did not want to leave it to chance, however. Peering up into the uncertain gloom at the top of the stairs, Ray felt his bravery

ebb. His home felt horribly unfamiliar all of a sudden. Again, the cat was not helping matters; she was clawing at the front door, desperate to get out. This was unusual as Princess habitually stayed in after dark. As Ray stepped to the door to let the cat out the creature glared over its bony shoulder up the stairs and hissed. Ray shivered. He had never seen his gentle family pet so freaked out before. His mind was made up; there was no way he was venturing upstairs unarmed.

'Just going to get the gun, dearest,' Ray announced loudly to Iris in the lounge though it was more for the benefit of anyone who might be waiting for him upstairs in the shadows.

As he opened the front door, Princess shot out like a black furry dart across the road into the confines of his neighbour's hedgerow. Ray peered after the coward for a moment and then left her to it.

He marched round the side of the house and into the back garden where there was a small wooden shed. He unlocked the rusty padlock and stepped within. There was only a small lamp to illuminate this tomb of Ray's forgotten hobbies; pushbikes, tennis rackets, tool kits, fishing rods, golf clubs. A swirling length of dust glinted in the anaemic battery-powered light and he squinted desperately to locate his desired implement of doom. Ray was forced to become more animated as he could not see it. He held the torch with one hand and fumbled through the paraphernalia. Before long, he spied two rusty barrels sticking up from behind a wall of paint tins.

'Bingo!'

A few years ago Ray had tried his hand at shooting. He had harboured some fanciful ambition of becoming gentrified upon moving to the country. Like every other recreational endeavour, he became bored quickly and the trappings were relegated to the shed. Ray picked up the shotgun and released it from some thick white strands of spider thread. Positioning the torch on a shelf to use both hands, he gave the weapon a swift wipe with a cloth and loaded it with a couple of cartridges.

'Right!' growled Ray as he snapped the gun shut with a satisfying click.

Resolutely, the man of the house swaggered back inside. The door to the lounge was slightly ajar and inquisitive eyes peeped out at him from the gap.

'Get back inside,' commanded Ray as he mounted the stairs.

Iris stared with horror at the shotgun. 'What in God's name are you going to do with that?'

'Just get inside,' he scowled. He did not wait for the inevitable argument.

The darkness at the top of the stairs was no longer daunting. The shotgun had enough calibre to floor a rhinoceros, after all. With his jaw set firm and his chest puffed out, Ray switched on every light available and probed each room with his pointed gun. The house gradually became ordinary again. There was no interloper, just the mundane features of the home he had always known. He smiled and breathed more easily. He felt so relieved that he almost laughed. He was long overdue for his bed and the possibility was looking imminent. He just had his own chamber to examine; the location of William's supposed sighting.

He yanked down the wooden ladder and tucked the rusty shotgun under one arm so he could climb with the other. Gingerly, Ray ascended to where his eyes were level with the floor of his attic bedroom. He scanned around 360 degrees, unable to exhale until he was sure that his place was free of the boy's bogeyman. It appeared as intruder-free as the rest of the household. It was hard to be sure in the dark. He clambered up the remainder of the ladder and switched on a couple of lights. He propped up the shotgun in one corner and poured himself a stiff drink. Just as his lips touched the rim of the glass, he heard a slight scratch from under the bed but this did not perturb him; it was the spot where his cat always slept.

'Alright, Princess,' Ray greeted the creature and took a sip.

The hot liquor did not soothe his insides as normal though. They suddenly turned to ice. The cat had fled the premises ten minutes ago! Slowly, he put down the glass and turned. He stepped backwards, fumbling for the gun.

'Is that you, Princess?' he asked, knowing full well it was not.

As if in response, a tiny white hand swept out from under the bed, its slimy disproportionate fingers groping at the floorboards.

Ray glared with astonishment. His mouth dropped open. For a few seconds, he could do nothing except stare and shake his head.

'No!'

Despite a will to react swiftly and decisively, the journalist moved as if in slow motion. He crouched down at the same time as he brought the gun forward, hardly daring to breathe. A little face peered out at him from under the bed. Its glassy black button eyes betrayed no purpose or intent but Ray had an idea. He knew what this thing was and what its kind were capable of. The devils had taken away his best friend Magical Garry and they had haunted his nightmares ever since. Ray had discovered one in the local churchyard and surmised that they had come to take back their dead.

'Fuck you!' hissed Ray, pressing both triggers.

There was a deafening bang and a flash of light, as expected, but Ray found himself lying on his back staring at the rafters. He was dazed for a few moments and could do little except turn his head to one side to witness the unharmed creature scuttle out from under the bed and make good its escape. He saw now that it was not alone; several of the tiny white gnomes shifted like one entity across the floor towards the exit. They carried the dried lifeless husk of the one that he had hidden in his bedroom. The vision of his frightened and vulnerable family popped into his mind's eye and Ray was animated again. He leapt up and snatched the shotgun but its loading compartment was black and ruined. Briefly, he cursed himself for not keeping the weapon in good working order.

'Are you okay, Ray?' came the voice of his wife from below.

'Stay down there!' he shrieked.

Ray ran to the hole in the floor and could see the gang of pale goblins slithering down the ladder. Even though they transported the cadaver of one of their own they did so with remarkable speed and efficiency. Ray knew he could not equal their pace and chose to jump down instead. It was a good ten foot drop but wild abandon had seized him and he leapt. His landing was surprisingly soft. A bizarre high-pitched squeal was Ray's indication that he had landed on the last of the creatures. The noise was unlike anything on Earth and Ray was so shocked that he stepped off the thing. It stopped screaming and sprang up to join its brethren. They bolted single-file round a corner into the bathroom. Ray was glad that they were not heading towards his wife and kids but pursued them nevertheless. He had gone through hell to win that specimen and he was not about to let it go without a fight. He charged into the bathroom but was stunned to find it empty. He glanced at the window but it was shut. He whipped back the shower curtain only to find it devoid of demonic imps. Ray stood there for a second and scratched his head in bemusement. Seemingly, they had vanished. Had he imagined the whole episode? Was he cracking up that much? Then, he looked down into the toilet bowl and glimpsed a pair of minute white feet disappear round the U-bend. They had left via the sewage system! Ray was horrified but laughed; maybe due to shock or perhaps because their egress was genuinely comical. He slammed the toilet seat shut and sat on it.

Some amount of time must have passed but Ray was unaware. Reality had handed in its notice. It was Iris and the kids that snapped him out of his reverie. They stood in the doorway of the bathroom and looked at him, afraid.

'Dadda?' enquired Posy.

Ray sighed. 'Get your things. We're leaving.'

Iris screwed up her face. 'Where will we go at this time of night?'

'Somewhere else,' he replied.

'What's wrong, dad?' snivelled William.

'Nothing, son,' he explained, replacing his backside on the toilet lid with a large potted palm tree from the landing. 'Just a problem with the plumbing.'

*

Ghostly Goings On at Knightsheath
Story by Ray Weaver and Mark Lyons, published in the Fogwin Enquirer 23.4.1980.

For the last two years the residents of Fogwin have watched progress on the industrial development on Knightsheath Road. The 43,000 square feet estate was considered by Mayor John Dodge to be the linchpin for the regeneration of the town but it now seems that the project has been jinxed.

Several men in the employment of Earthcom have returned with stories of mysterious accidents and frightening phenomena. Brian Temple, a security guard said: 'It's like you're always being watched. There's a weird atmosphere. One night I checked on some fork-lift trucks and when I returned later they had all been moved, even though there was no one there except me! A week later an overhead crane came crashing down for no reason and almost killed several men.'

Knightsheath has long been the focus of local folklore and many of Fogwin's elderly long-term residents feel the need to warn the young to stay clear. Even as far back as 1835 there is a report in the local parish register of "cruel boggarts who prey on the unwary traveller at Knight Heath." Boggart is an old name for a ghost or fairy; the old wives' version of things that go bump in the night.

Building on the site attracted much controversy when it was first proposed three years ago with over five hundred signatures of protest. 'Hidden places on Earth should be left alone' wrote one Jean Clement. Launching our own investigation, the fearless reporters of the Enquirer have been unable to gain access to the accursed premises. Its high-tech barriers are extremely effective but not enough to prevent us from seeing bizarre lights in the sky from deep within the estate in the dead of night, like kaleidoscopic fireworks made of liquid and exploding in slow motion. Could there be a link between these secret experiments, the gloomy history of the place and the recent incidents? Management at Earthcom has so far declined to comment.

*

'What the flying buggery fuck is this?' roared Archie, hurling the paper onto Ray's desk.

Rudely interrupted from his mid-morning yoghurt, Ray solemnly gazed down at the article and then up at Archie. 'Newspaper?' he ventured.

'I thought I told you to stick to small town tittle tattle?' The editor continued at a volume which seemed to quake the entire building. 'Please tell me I told you that? I did, didn't I?'

Ray nodded. 'To be fair, Archie, yes, you did clearly say that.'

'Then how in the flames of hell does this constitute small town tittle tattle?'

Ray wondered if anyone had won a world record for shouting, either capacity or regularity. 'Always look out for the big scoop,' he explained; 'that's what you told me when I first started. I thought that directive would override this one?'

Archie shook his head in disbelief and looked a little bit like he was going to cry. The fearsome moustache was moist. 'This isn't a damn scoop! This is the plot of some absurd science-fiction novel!'

'It's all true!' protested Ray. 'I've risked life and limb to get that information. I swear to God, Archie, there's something going on!'

'All you're doing, Weaver, is severely taking the piss!' Archie turned red.

'I can back it all up, Archie, I swear!'

'This is going to cost both of us our jobs!' Archie turned purple.

'Just calm down a bit, eh?'

'We'll never work again! We'll be black balled! That two week cruise! All for nothing! I knew I should have left Lyons in charge!' Archie turned white.

'Archie!'

Archie went down like a deck of cards.

'Archie?

Archie?

Archie?'

Archie?'

*

'So that's how you've ruined your life?' speculated The Professor. It had grown dim outside, even though it was only mid-afternoon, and the academic's face became shrouded in shadow.

Ray peered at him, sighed deeply and nodded.

'And your boss?'

'Dead,' Ray sighed again. 'I killed him.'

'Nonsense!' snorted The Professor. 'If the dolt got himself all worked up over nothing and had a heart attack then it's his own fault. He should have never left you in charge.'

'Thanks,' groaned Ray. 'I think.'

'How did the story go down?'

Ray shrugged his shoulders.

'Do you want to tell me about Lucy?'

'I don't know,' muttered Ray. 'She's gone missing.'

It was The Professor's turn to sigh. 'I see.'

Ray burst into tears. 'I've lost everything! They even came to take this fucking house yesterday!'

The Professor rose to his feet. 'Oh, please don't cry, old boy. I can't stand to see a grown man in tears.' He crossed over the kitchen and offered Ray his handkerchief.

He took it and wiped his wet cheeks and snotty beak. 'Thanks.'

The Professor put his hand on his shoulder. 'There, there, we'll get her back.'

Ray looked up at him, a glimmer of hope emerging in his scarlet eyes. 'Lucy?'

'If she's the one you love, yes.'

'Do you mean that?'

'Yes, I do,' stated The Professor sternly. 'We shall find her and then we'll sort the rest of your life out, wretched and undeserving though you are.'

Ray felt like a child.

The Professor walked out into the hallway with purpose.

'Where you going?' asked Ray.

The Professor picked up Ray's telephone and looked at him. 'I'm calling in the cavalry.'

*

My time as a small town newspaper journalist was over and my reign as the world's leading paranormal investigator had begun.

Excerpt from the journal of Ray Weaver, volume one.

The Special Monster

Pluk moved through the woods with a silence that only a nimpeth could manage. Every fall of his long bony feet was slowly and methodically placed and so light that not even a twig would he break. His tiny black eyes pierced the gloom and every silhouette was regarded with suspicion, be it just a leaf twitching in the wind. The little creature's bulbous nose constantly twitched with a myriad of scents from the ancient rhododendron. His big fleshy ears picked up every miniature noise. So careful was he that even sparrows and squirrels were caught unaware. Pluk was a slight breeze through the bushes, a small force of nature finding a path where there was none. Just ahead, he distinguished the irregular trickle of flowing water. He paused for a moment to listen. He reckoned that this was the brook marked on the old map. He approached the water with added caution, conscious that its hubble and bubble could mask the sounds of those in wait for him. Cautiously, he slid out of the thicket and scurried to the top of a bank. He looked down into the water below and then all around, sniffing for danger. As soon as he was convinced that he was alone, he crouched to scoop up a sip of water but the brook was silty and foul and he spat it out. He decided to cross the brook quickly, springing up onto his bare feet, leaping across with a single bound and racing up the bank on the other side, all in one soundless flurry. The shadows welcomed him with open arms.

The top of the rise offered a view of a deep wooded hollow ahead but Pluk allowed himself to rest for a few moments. *Mustn't rush*, he reminded himself, *caution before haste*. The Forest of Starfel was difficult to negotiate and Pluk's talents as a pathseeker had been challenged. He sat with his back to an old ash tree and gazed back the way he had come. He peered down at the brook, cutting its way through the fading light like a vein of liquid silver, and then he gazed into the black jungle of rhododendron beyond. The woodland seemed ordinary enough but he had the vague feeling that something unnatural was at work here. The rotting stench that lingered in the air could just be mouldy vegetation, he told himself, and the faint vapour that snaked through the trees was probably just early autumn mist but he was not so sure. Starfel had a bad reputation and his attuned senses were tainted with a mounting dread.

To compose himself, Pluk breathed deeply and gazed up at the canopy of leaves above. The last vestiges of sunlight speared through the tree tops and formed a kaleidoscope of dancing lights before his eyes. He suddenly felt drowsy and closed his heavy lids. He allowed the sun to return warmth to his cold limbs. The fair features of his beloved Yhefi formed in his mind … she smiled at him … that smile … beaming warmth and hope … Pluk's ears twitched suddenly; there were fresh noises in the forest, some from the way ahead and others from the way behind. He sat up and shook the reverie from his hairy head. He listened carefully and tried to separate sound from sound. The activity from behind was doubtlessly that of his companions hurrying to catch up with him. He could even hear Oogar talking.

'Holy Mog!' cursed Pluk under his breath, what was the point in this legendary nimpeth skill if they just followed him like a herd of Grups?

The noises that came from the opposite direction were more worrying. He could discern low grunting and growling. Pluk was somewhere between his friends and something more unpleasant.

With a grumble, he got to his feet and hurried back down the bank to intercept the stragglers before they gave their position away. With another leap that belied his size, Pluk cleared the brook and vanished into the undergrowth. He quickly found the others; Oogar was crashing through the bushes and giving voice to his discomfort. Just behind the big warrior, Pluk could see light glinting off Damari's silver armour.

He pulled back his black hood and hissed at them. 'Quiet! You clumsy oxen! There's something just over the next rise!'

Oogar rolled his eyes at him but said nothing. He halted, set his huge stone hammer down on the ground and wiped the sweat from his brow, breathing heavily.

Damari walked past the barbarian prince and drew close to Pluk, clutching her sword and shield more guardedly. 'What is it, little one?' she asked, looking down at him.

'I don't know yet, I didn't get a chance to look,' whispered Pluk angrily. 'I had to come back here to stop you lot announcing our presence to the entire forest!'

Damari giggled at him, as the mindwalker often did. 'We got bored of waiting,' she explained.

Pluk frowned and looked around. 'Where the vack is Murgho?'

Damari pointed back into the rhododendron and after a few moments, the fat warmancer emerged from the gloom. Pluk saw the sweat shining from Murgho's forehead and could hear him panting. This terrain was not kind to an overweight man dressed in robes and sandals.

'What's going on?' he asked, plucking bits of the forest from his multi-coloured cloak.

Damari turned to answer him. 'The little one has found something ahead. We must proceed with caution.'

Pluk hated it when Damari called him 'little one'. He was certainly the tiniest but they would have all perished long ago without his skilled reconnaissance.

Murgho grinned sardonically. 'Isn't that what we're doing? Proceeding with caution?'

Pluk spat and cackled. 'Aye! The caution of an elephant circus!'

Murgho walked over to him but he was still grinning. Like the others he perversely enjoyed their lack of stealth. 'You do your thing, nimpeth, and we'll do ours. You do the sneaking about and we'll do the slaying.'

Pluk's temper was not improving. 'Just like you did with that Nettle Wraith last time?'

This wiped the grin off Murgho's sweaty face. 'That wasn't my fault, I couldn't find my spell book,' he mumbled.

Pluk bounced with agitation. 'And Yhefi was killed!'

Oogar suddenly picked up his hammer and stepped forward to assert his status as leader. 'That's enough!'

Pluk shrank back suddenly, his mobile phone went off. A shrill electronic version of 'No One Knows' by Queens of the Stone Age rang out through Starfel Forest.

The Referee appeared, striding out from his hidden place in the undergrowth. 'Time out!'

*

The Dragon's Heart Live Fantasy Role-playing Club stood around and lit up cigarettes while Pluk, or Dave, as he had now become, talked to his mum on his phone. When he had finished, Dave returned to the group somewhat sheepishly and apologised for the interruption to the game. He replaced a big pointy rubber ear over his own.

Jack, the Referee, gave him a stern look. 'You're supposed to switch it off, you know that.'

Dave shrugged his shoulders. 'Sorry. My Aunty Brenda's in hospital.'

Oogar the barbarian prince, who was actually Scott the computer programmer, turned to Jack. 'How do you think it's going?'

Jack nodded with approval. 'Good, but we could do without these modern interruptions.'

Murgho, or Barry, as he was known in real life, joined the persecution of Dave's crime. 'Yeah! Dave is always on about the stealthy approach. We're about to walk into the next encounter and your damn phone starts ringing!'

Dave looked sideways at Barry with belligerence. 'Christ! I said I'm sorry.'

Damari, whose actual name was Melissa, wiped some mud from her long slender bare thigh, getting the attention of her male friends. Melissa was a seamstress by trade and helped to make most of the costumes for the game. Her own mindwalker's outfit was immaculate. She wore silver armour, leg and arm greaves and a breastplate, all forged traditionally with real metal and carved into elaborate shapes and patterns. The rest of the costume consisted of a white chiffon tunic and knee-length soft white leather boots. It left little to the imagination. There was also once a helmet but Melissa had chosen to leave this at home when she realised that it limited her vision in combat. She decided to let her long raven-black hair cascade over her shoulders instead. She too scrutinised Dave. 'Did you have to bring Yhefi up again? I thought we established that wasn't Barry's fault? Not anyone's fault?'

Dave looked back at her. 'My character is meant to be callous and arrogant.'

Barry chuckled at him. 'You do it very well.'

Dave turned away from the group and fell silent. The familiar "let's pick on Dave" ritual had begun. How easily they had forgotten the many times he had saved their necks or the fact that he was a founder member of the club.

Jack decided to step in. 'There was nothing wrong with Dave's role-playing, let's just keep those phones switched off.'

Dave turned and looked at him. Jack passed him the second half of his fag and Dave accepted the gesture. He looked at his three fellow adventurers. 'I've got a bad feeling about this place and I mean to avenge Yhefi's death, so let's get through this carefully ... please?'

Responding to his plea, Scott practiced with his hammer. He swung the monstrous weapon through the air a couple of times with both hands and cleared some space. The weapons in the game were made from latex and foam. They appeared to be genuine articles but were not actually hard or sharp enough to cause injury, or, at least, not very often. Scott looked at Dave and became Oogar again.

'Don't let your thirst for revenge cloud your judgement, pathseeker.'

Dave smiled at his old friend. 'Have I ever let you down?' The smile was toothy and lop-sided and combined with the wig, beard and prosthetic ears and nose Dave was wearing, he really did look like an otherworldly denizen. Dave's return to good humour seemed to calm his companions down too. They finished their cigarettes and looked at the Referee.

Jack nodded. 'Time in!'

*

Dusk cast long shadows through the woods and Murgho fumbled with the leather satchel under his warmancer's cloak. He checked that his spell book was secure but easily reached. From what the nimpeth had said, it looked like he was about to need it. Murgho had developed a knack for misplacing the damn thing. He had been thrown out of the Guild of Sorcery once for his neglect and another time for getting drunk and ravishing the King's wife who was, of course, the Queen of all The Realm. Murgho the Magnificent, as he had once named himself, was a wizard of poor repute but as far as this lot was concerned, he was the only wizard and that made him feel important enough. "The Magnificent" part of his name would have to wait.

Oogar rested his hammer onto one shoulder and looked round at them all. 'Pluk leads the way. We go slowly. We go quiet. Don't talk unless you have to. We work as a team.'

The warrior was doing his leadership thing, Murgho decided. They had all been together long enough and his counsel was unnecessary but Oogar had to have his little ego parade. *If it made the barbarian swing that damned hammer with more confidence, then so be it*, he thought.

'There's the brook just ahead with a steep bank on the other side,' explained Pluk. 'At the top you can see into a narrow hollow, I think that's where the mine entrance is, but it's not unguarded, there's something down there.'

Murgho shuffled through the bushes, trying not to make too much commotion, as requested. The rhododendron continued to pull on his robes and he was soon left behind. *Serves them right if there's something out here and I get my damn throat cut,* he cursed, *they'll have to do without their warmancer then.*

The rotund wizard heard running water and was relieved to finally leave the thick bush and its hidden dangers behind. He was not so happy to see that his three companions had already jumped across the brook and that they were waiting for him to display his own athletic skill, of which he famously lacked. Murgho gloomily approached the brook and gazed down into its murky channel as if it was molten lava. He then looked across at the others. Oogar offered a helping hand but Murgho shook his head. He had his pride and refused to be treated like some dainty princess. He took a few steps back and then charged full pelt. The next thing he knew, he was up to his knees in freezing water with mud oozing up between his sandaled toes. He looked up and could see that his so-called friends were trying to restrain their laughter. With combined endeavour they pulled him out of the brook and dragged him up the bank. As they did so, Murgho chanced to look down to admire Damari's perfectly-formed thighs. They gleamed milk-white in the dusk and Murgho slobbered. How he longed to run his hands up and down those soft beauties. One day soon, he knew that Damari would fall for his incredible powers as a warmancer. She would easily forget the attentions of dull Oogar, and then those thighs would be his ... *focus, Murgho, focus* ... he scolded himself.

The four adventurers crawled the last few yards to the top of the bank. They peered down into the murk of the hollow below and could see several misshapen figures stood around at the bottom. Their hunched bodies and bulbous heads were illuminated grotesquely by several burning torches staked into the ground. The creatures were surrounded by bits of old crumbling wall. There had once been some sort of structure here but it had been reclaimed by the forest.

'Death Breed!' snarled Pluk with disgust. 'The lapdogs of Skarron!'

Oogar rubbed his stubbled chin thoughtfully. 'Don't let them touch you with their big right-hand claws or you'll become infected.'

Damari turned to Pluk. 'How many?'

The nimpeth peered down at the beasts for a few moments and held up four stubby fingers.

'Here's your chance, Murgho!' Oogar turned and grinned wolfishly at the warmancer. 'Prepare some magic!'

A sick feeling rose in the pit of Murgho's stomach. *Oogar was right, damn him.* These creatures were simple of mind and easy to enchant. Their retribution, however, should he fail, would be lethal. He drew out his spell book and in the last of the fading light, thumbed nervously through its pages to select a suitable hex.

'Mongo. Mormo. Mongo. Time to count some sheep. Mongo. Mormo. Mongo. Time to count some sheep. Mongo. Mormo. Mongo. Time to count some sheep.'

Murgho muttered the words of the slumber spell under his breath repeatedly as he crept after Oogar and Damari down a broken and pock-marked path into the hollow. Long and skeletal undergrowth clawed at them as they went. Pluk had chosen a different route of attack; skirting through the rock and scrub around the Death Breed to outflank them. This was their usual group strategy for dealing with multiple enemies. Sometimes it actually worked.

They reached the bottom of the hollow and were now level with the beasts. There were a few moments of uncertainty and anticipation. Murgho could feel his heart quicken and his mouth go dry. This was the moment they all lived for and would someday, die for. Murgho had a sudden swell of courage and strode boldly out into the light of the camp to confront Skarron's abominations. All four of the creatures turned their red pulsating heads towards him and hissed. Oogar and Damari took up position either side of him. Murgho cleared his throat and raised his podgy hands in the air to invoke his spell. It was at this point, Murgho made the error of looking down at Damari's majestic thighs again.

His concentration broken, he blurted out the wrong words. 'Murgho! Mongal! Morman! Go and kill some sheep!'

The Referee dashed forward from his hiding place nearby and yelled: 'The spell failed!'

Oogar and Damari looked at the warmancer together and cursed him. The Death Breed all shrieked in unison and raised their oversized right-hand claws that oozed and dripped with thick black venom. The things were supposed to be fast asleep but Murgho's sorcery had failed. He shrank backwards into the trees with shame. The biggest of the creatures was upon them in an instant and Oogar swung his hammer in a wide arc, its stone block crashing into the creature's mutated skull with a sickening crunch. Damari had to dive out of the way to avoid being hit by the hammer and fell onto the ground next to the lifeless form of the felled monster. One of its twisted kin leapt onto her from a wall and the mindwalker forced her shield upwards to keep its lethal claw at bay. They wrestled around on the ground for a few desperate moments, foul spittle from the creature's mouth dripping onto her fair face. The last two 'Breed closed in on Oogar before he could save his beloved Damari. The hammer was most effective when the barbarian prince had the room and time to swing it but now he was locked in close quarters and all he could muster was to push them away with it. The monsters swiped at him with their claws playfully and cackled with perverse glee.

Back in the shadows of the tree line, Murgho realised it was up to him to save his friends. There was no time to find a new spell. He would have to resort to more basic methods. Using his fleshy bulk, Murgho hurtled towards the 'Breed violating Damari like a meteor of robed fury. The wizard collided with the creature and knocked it flying. An instant later, he landed on top of it, evacuating all the air from its fetid lungs. Murgho pulled himself up and watched the 'Breed writhe around on the ground with a mixture of surprise and fascination as it struggled to inhale. He looked around and saw that Damari had got to her feet too. She looked furious and with a terrifying scream that echoed through the forest, she ran to Oogar's side and swung her sword savagely at the two creatures tormenting him. Her face looked demonic in the light of the flames. Suddenly, the 'Breed on the ground in front of Murgho found fresh vigour and sprang up. Murgho looked straight into its cold, soulless eyes as it drew back its massive claw. He fumbled frantically with the dagger tucked into his belt but it was trapped under the girth of his mighty stomach. He closed his eyes and waited for the inevitable strike that would end his pathetic existence but it did not come. Murgho heard a swashing noise and a curious gurgling. He opened his eyes to see that Pluk had opened the creature's throat with his long narrow blade.

The nimpeth winked at him and laughed. 'That's another one you owe me, big man!'

Damn, thought Murgho, *that was all he needed! Another debt to the little tree urchin! At least he had saved the girl.*

Murgho and Pluk turned around to help but the battle was already won. Damari had gone berserk. She hacked at the two remaining Death Breed until they were on the ground and became still, and then she hacked at them some more. The others watched her with alarm and wonder.

The four companions stood for a few moments, panting, and considered the ruin they had made. Damari let out a slightly deranged cackle, relishing the bloodshed. They went over to examine what the fiends had been guarding. There was a rusty metal hatch set into the ground.

'The Mine entrance,' stated Pluk with a worried glance at the others.

'I think we've got more immediate problems,' said Murgho and they all turned to see what he meant. He pointed to the black venom wound on Damari's thigh.

'Time out!' called the Referee.

*

Oogar or Scott, looked at the "venom wound" and shook his head with sadness. They all knew its lethal significance. A wound from a Death Breed that was not treated quickly meant fatality. Those were the rules of the game. The venom wound was, of course, actually paint. The players acting as the enemies would daub their weapons in the stuff before an encounter began, thus the Referee would have a clear indication of any injuries after a battle had been fought. Scott, Melissa, Dave and Barry were all experienced role-players and it had become rare for their costumes to be soiled by any paint at all, especially by such measly grunts as the Death Breed. It seemed that Damari or Melissa had been complacent in her fury. She gazed back at Scott. Her eyes sparkled as they always did when she looked at him but she frowned miserably.

'I'll use my healing magic,' said Murgho/Barry. He too looked gravely at the wound.

Scott turned to him and his eyes flashed with anger. 'You should have got it right in the first place!'

He put his arm around Melissa and tenderly led her away to a secluded edge of the hollow. Barry looked around for support but Dave shook his head at him and turned away. The "Death Breed" were removing their masks and finding somewhere to sit down. They too looked at Barry with some regret.

Jack the Referee, walked over to him and put his hand on his shoulder. 'Give them all a moment, Barry.'

The warmancer, who was actually a shelf-stacker at HMV, looked at him. 'I can use my healing magic though, right?'

Jack shrugged his shoulders. 'It will take a lot of your remaining power.'

'I don't care,' said Barry. 'I'm not getting the blame for the death of another hero.'

Jack smiled thinly. 'Why can't you remember the right words?'

A cool wind had accompanied night fall and Barry struggled to light a fag. Jack looked ponderously at him for a few moments and then went off to talk to the people in the monster costumes.

In the shadow of the trees, Scott hugged Melissa. They were lovers both in the game and in real life. She welcomed his affection and he was glad. He had been worried about her for a while. During the last couple of adventures, Melissa had shown unbridled ferocity and their encounter with the Death Breed was no exception. The aggression did not suit her character. Scott wondered if her lack of control in real life was affecting her performance in the game. Melissa had recently suffered a messy break-up with her last boyfriend, Phil, who was also a member of the club. He had played the Death Breed that had just viciously attacked her. Despite wearing a costume, Scott guessed that Melissa knew it was him. Everything seemed rosy enough in the pub the night before. All three of them sat together, drank together, smoked together, laughed and sang together, but Scott sensed an undercurrent of bitterness between Melissa and her ex. He looked over at the offender and found, to his surprise, that he was returning his stare.

'Alright, Phil?'

Phil sneered back. 'Actually no, I just got belly-flopped by a big, fat, sweaty man in a dress, would you be alright?'

This made the other "monsters" laugh but Scott did not share the humour. Phil, it seemed, was taking every opportunity to make life difficult for Melissa today. As an enemy in the game, this was actually his job and therefore difficult to begrudge. Scott wished Barry had broken the bastard's ribs. He was relieved when Jack ushered Phil and the rest of the monsters to their feet.

'Right, come on you lot!' he said with his usual authority and gestured towards the metal hatch. The monsters got up and Jack opened the mine entrance for them. One by one, they disappeared into the earth to get ready for the next stage of the game. Phil was the last to descend and he gave Scott and Melissa a final surly glance. Scott held his girlfriend tighter and gently kissed her forehead. Last night, Melissa had passed out in her own vomit on the bathroom floor. Scott affectionately scooped her up and wiped the sick from her face and hair and carried her to bed, then waited for a few hours to make sure she did not turn blue. He knew Melissa had a bit of a drink and drugs problem but he would not give up on her, not in this world or the other.

On the other side of the camp, Dave was rummaging through the Death Breed's scattered belongings. All he found were bits of mouldy fruit and gnawed bones.

'Anything?' asked Barry, walking over to him.

Dave looked up at him and tossed away a rotten morsel in disgust. He shook his head. Scott, Melissa and the Referee soon joined them.

'Nearly ready?' asked Jack, looking around.

Scott turned to the mine entrance. 'We're seriously going down there?'

'Cool, isn't it?' Jack smiled proudly. 'We're actually going underground.'

The four adventurers were not looking so enthusiastic.

'The mine has been here for ages,' explained Jack, undeterred. 'It's just taken me ages to get permission to use it.'

'I've decided to use my curing spell to heal Damari,' said Barry, pulling out his spell book.

'Okay,' said Jack, 'Do it as soon as I call time in.'

They looked at him.

'Time in!'

*

Oogar reluctantly watched Murgho work his sorcery. The warmancer ran his sweaty hand up and down Damari's thigh and recited words of power from his book. The venomous wound slowly closed and faded away. The barbarian prince had a deep-rooted mistrust of the forbidden arts, as did all his people. It was an unnatural practice and those that dabbled were doomed to become slaves to secret gods. The very sound of the incantation made him feel dizzy and sick and he turned away. Besides, he did not like the way Murgho was grinning and slobbering with obvious glee. Too long had that pompous oaf's eyes lingered on his woman. Despite being a wizard, it seemed to Oogar that the man had very ordinary desires. He gave his attention to Pluk who was looking down into the mine, pensively. He preferred the nimpeth's simple woodsmanship. Oogar walked over and he too looked into a narrow old shaft descending into darkness. They both contemplated potential terrors.

'This is new,' said the warrior, looking up at the nimpeth.

Pluk frowned in response but did not return his gaze, he continued to stare down into the shaft. 'The Forest is evil but at least its trees and streams are familiar to me. I'm out of my depth here, if you'll excuse the pun.'

'Same skills, Pluk. Your senses are as quick and as sharp as the blade you carry,' suggested Oogar.

Pluk bent down to the edge of the shaft and sniffed it. 'It smells damp and musty, but I hear nothing except drips of water.'

'Have we got light?' asked Oogar.

'I don't need it,' said Pluk but reached for a small knapsack under his cloak. He ferreted inside and pulled out three sticks wrapped with oily rag and a copper tinderbox. Oogar took a couple of the torches and helped the pathseeker to set them alight. He then went to the shaft edge and threw one of the torches down. He and Pluk watched as it fell. It bounced and sparked off the walls about thirty feet down, revealing the depth and landing to illuminate a small patch of damp floor at the bottom. A rusty old metal ladder ran all the way down.

Oogar grinned deviously at Pluk. 'Mind how you go then.'

Pluk was hesitant and looked up at his leader for an excuse but reason failed him. He pulled up his hood and sprang into the mine before Oogar could jest further. Pluk went down the shaft like a spider down a web. He was soon just a weird black silhouette, rapidly growing smaller as he climbed down into the flickering light. Oogar enjoyed watching Pluk's nimble and fearless progress, as he always did. He hoped that nothing nasty was waiting down there for his brave little scout.

As soon as Pluk got to the bottom of the shaft, Damari and Murgho joined him at the top. Damari was well again but had no smile to show for it, she still looked a bit upset. Murgho, on the other hand, was grinning from ear to ear, clearly more delighted with the experience. They waited a few moments for Pluk to look around below and he soon appeared to beckon them down. A cold wind had picked up in Starfel Forest and this was their only compensation for going down into the mine.

In turn they clambered down into the slender underground throat. Pluk had made it look easy and his three companions took more time and labour to follow him. The ladder was crumbling into dust and had become partially calcified over time. Murgho went down last and the shaft was only just wide enough to accommodate his immense girth. His companions sniggered as they watched him climb down. From where they stood, they could see up Murgho's robes. Two fat hairy legs and a huge pair of discoloured Y-fronts were there to greet them.

The humour went some way to diffuse the anxiety but as the heroes regrouped and looked about them, they realised their peril. They were in a long and low cavern which gradually sloped deeper away from them into the gloom. Piles of rock and rusty old mining gear were strewn here and there; long abandoned shovels, picks, buckets, chains and objects less obvious in purpose. The bits and pieces were stuck together with rust, like twisted metal sculpture, and the flames from their torches drew out a host of shadows. It was not clear for a few tense moments whether they were alone. The cavern roof seemed to be shored up by several wooden timbers spread out at irregular points. Worryingly, the timbers looked damp and rotten and even as the companions stood still and gaped about them, they thought they heard the wood straining and cracking, accompanied by an orchestra of dripping water and trickling rock dust. The air was ancient and cold and it soon stuck in their throats like clammy phlegm.

Oogar already felt the chill on his bare arms and the damp in his long red locks and he formed an instant dislike for the underworld. It was too easy for enemies to hide in and too enclosed for the swing of mighty Skullbreaker. He reminded himself that he was the leader of the group. He knew that any fear shown by him could break the resolve of them all, regardless of the obvious danger. He was their pillar of strength, like the ancient beams that held up the mine. The barbarian strode defiantly a few steps further in, holding up his torch with one hand and his hammer with the other. His eyes were drawn upwards to the roof of the cavern where a turquoise vein of copper ore twinkled back down at him.

'Have you checked around, Pluk?' he asked, still looking up at the vein.

'Not completely,' said Pluk. He darted forward beside him and began to sniff around the edges of their mysterious domain like an obedient hound. The nimpeth had no torch, like the others, and his cloaked and diminutive form was soon lost amongst the wreckage and murk. Damari and Murgho were more reluctant to give themselves to the unknown and merely lingered behind Oogar, saying nothing and darting nervous glances around them. Pluk emerged on the far side of the cavern with astonishing progress, calling out to them in the dark. They walked towards his voice until their torches illuminated the little creature by the far wall. Pluk looked at them and thumbed backwards over his shoulder to two tunnels leading out of the cavern. The one on the left was roughly triangular in shape and the one on the right was more of a rectangle.

'We're clear. Nobody here but us!'

As soon as Pluk said that, a black shape dropped from somewhere above and landed behind him, mocking his survey.

'Holy Mog!' screamed Pluk and dived forward, tumbling several times across the cavern floor and rolling to the feet of his companions. He drew out his sword and looked back, snarling like a frightened animal. The shape had now become a tall, thin and hooded figure.

Murgho let out a joyous belly laugh. 'That vacked you up, Pluk! That vacked you up good and proper! Nobody here but us you said!'

Pluk glanced back at the warmancer with disdain. 'Maybe you should lead the way?'

The hooded figure hissed at them and barred the way to the exits menacingly. It was unnaturally tall and there was a faint green light coming from within its hood. The companions could now see that there was a slight stone shelf near the roof of the cavern where the thing had been hiding. Pluk hardly ever got caught unaware like that. Oogar remarked to himself that the nimpeth's complacency equalled Damari's lack of care earlier. *What was happening to his friends? Had they all spent that little bit too long in the tavern the night before?*

'Speak monster!' bellowed the barbarian 'You caught my scout off guard and now you hinder our way. Speak or consider your life over!'

'It's already dead,' stated Damari, stealing her barbarian lover's thunder.

The others turned and looked at her.

'I've just walked its mind. It's not on the same plane. It's trapped between this world and the next.'

'A ghost?' suggested Murgho, peering at the thing with fascination.

'Of sorts' replied Damari. 'I think it *can* hurt us though.'

The others nodded. They were all accustomed to her talent to steal the thoughts of others. Their attention, however, was drawn back to the hooded stranger as it hissed again and some words became audible; 'the way forwards is to the left ... certain death waits for you to the right.' The green phosphorescence once again glowed from deep within its hood. Its deathly whisper made them all shiver.

'How do we know that you speak the truth?' commanded Oogar, determined to be valiant.

'It can't lie,' said Damari, stealing Oogar's thunder a second time. 'It's bonded to the truth.'

The phantom waved its skeletal claws at them, forebodingly: 'Tell me my true name and release me and I will tell you something you really need to know.'

The adventurers exchanged puzzled looks and Pluk voiced their mutual puzzlement. 'How do we know what its name is?'

Oogar suddenly laughed with realisation and took a defiant step towards the hooded thing. 'Your name is Sembir!'

The creature hissed affirmatively. 'You're not as stupid as you look, savage one.'

Oogar grinned. 'I'll take that as a compliment, even from a dead thing.' He looked back smugly at the others. He was supposed to be the muscle of the outfit, not the brains. Luckily for Oogar, he had a natural aptitude for both the fighting and the riddles.

'Very well,' hissed Sembir. 'You have released me from your world and before I go, I will tell you this: One of you is a traitor!'

These words seemed to resonate through the cavern and left all four companions dumfounded. The creature called Sembir vanished. It became part of the darkness with only a slight flicker of their torches to mark its passing. They looked at each other, distrust and accusation quickly growing in their eyes.

'It's a lie!' said Damari, her voice quailing a little.

'You said it was bonded to the truth,' scoffed Murgho.

'I must have been wrong,' she said.

'It was telling the truth, Murgho, and you know it.' Pluk sneered at the warmancer and slowly put a paw on the hilt of his sword. 'You've been acting strangely for a while now. Getting things wrong all the time?'

Murgho stared at the nimpeth with horror. 'What are you talking about? If anybody's been acting weird, it's you, tree lover!'

'Just like you to save your own skin,' added Pluk.

'When I get as craven as you, hairball, that's when I'll start worrying about it,' sneered Murgho.

Oogar watched the others and stroked his stubbled jaw thoughtfully. His mind was also swirling with the implications of Sembir's words but this was not the time for division.

'Hey! Come on!' the barbarian stepped into the middle of the group and looked around at them all. 'The creature's words were meant to vex us. Let's not give in. We're in a dangerous situation and we need to stick together. Let's leave the matter of treason for later.'

'And if the trap is about to be sprung, Oogar?' Pluk challenged him. 'A traitor could have lead us this far, into the jaws of death? This place seems to suggest such a horror, does it not, barbarian?'

'So what do you propose then? It could be any one of us,' retorted Oogar. He went over to Damari, who was looking a little shaken. He lifted her chin gently and gave her a reassuring kiss on the lips. *Surely his beloved would not betray them?* As soon as that terrible thought entered Oogar's mind, he swiftly rejected it again.

They took a few moments to compose themselves before moving on, taking deep breaths and checking their torches and weapons. Oogar saw that Pluk and Murgho were still regarding each other with suspicion but they kept their accusations to themselves for now.

'We'll take the left tunnel' he said. 'Pluk leads the way.'

The heroes took his orders and slowly filed out of the cavern into the triangular shaped exit.

'How did you know its name?' enquired Pluk as they left.

'It said on the map' grinned Oogar. 'Mine of Sembir!'

Deeper into the earth they went, their unease growing with every step. They had taken the phantom's advice to use the left tunnel but Sembir's second revelation was not so welcome. The mine had become nothing more than a narrow passage sloping deeper and damper into the unknown. The claustrophobia only heightened their anxiety that one of them was not as they seemed. They clustered together, whether it was for security or fear of turning their backs on each other, they were not certain. At least Pluk had become extra careful after his fright and now regarded every shadow with a sharp eye and the business end of his slim blade. They followed a broken old metal rail track and after what seemed like an age, stumbling and groping down the tunnel, their torches began to weaken and Pluk had only two more to replace them. Oogar chose to take one himself and gave the other to Damari who was on rearguard. Now Murgho grumbled along with no light of his own, mumbling not only about treachery but also about favouritism within the group. The warmancer eventually came to a halt and crossed his arms and stamped his feet like a spoilt child. The others stopped to look at him, somewhat wearily.

'I think I should go back' the warmancer said.

'What?' barked Oogar, clearly annoyed.

'You need someone back there,' explained Murgho. 'To make sure no one follows us down here. I've got some power left in me, just give me a torch and I'll shout if there's trouble.'

'We stick together,' stated Oogar. His patience with the warmancer was stretching thin. As Murgho launched into a multitude of other reasons to chicken out, Oogar found himself musing on the possibility that the warmancer was the traitor.

As if reading her leader's mind, Damari speculated. 'Perhaps you know something we don't, Murgho?'

The warmancer faltered, aware that his companions were glaring at him. He was unsure what to say next.

Suddenly Pluk hissed at something, shifting their attention. The nimpeth pointed into the darkness ahead. The others looked and they too saw movement in the gloom. Something was slowly climbing up the wall on their left and the group snuck closer to catch it in their light, breathing heavy with anticipation. What they saw made both Murgho and Damari scream, made Pluk yell 'Holy Mog!' and even bold Oogar recoiled and spat in disgust. The creature was not a big rat or a spider but an obscene hybrid of them both, and yet neither. It dragged its deformed bulk laboriously up the rock with a combination of legs, arms, tentacles and tails. They stared at it a moment too long, morbidly transfixed and the thing sensed them somehow. It turned its fleshy body towards them to reveal a bulbous sack which seemed to operate as some sort of head. An orifice twitched open like a huge quivering maw. It made a depraved slurping noise and a slow drool fell from its mouth. The companions looked at each other and exchanged mutual looks of bewilderment and revulsion.

'What the hell is it?' Oogar finally managed to say. Before anyone could offer him an answer the hideous being suddenly found speed and leapt. It hit the floor with a soft splat and its numerous appendages became a blur as it tore away into the darkness. The adventurers all sprang backwards in alarm even though it was running away in the opposite direction. By the time they found the courage to go and search for the thing, it had vanished. On closer inspection, the walls and ground were pock marked with fissures, many of which were big enough for the creature to disappear into.

'Whatever it is, it's gone,' concluded Pluk with a shrug of his shoulders.

'Whatever it is, it's vacking ugly,' said Damari and put down her shield and torch to hug herself. Oogar took his cue to go over and put a reassuring hand on her shoulder but their troubles were yet to begin; there was a mournful cry from behind them, the noise of a new threat. A mob of shambling monsters were hurrying to catch them up.

'You see! I was right!' announced Murgho haughtily. 'It's a trap!'

Pluk sneered at him. 'Aye and you'd have been butchered if you'd gone back alone!'

'Oh good, a fight!' Oogar ignored their squabbling and grinned perversely. He threw his torch on the ground between him and the newcomers. The creatures stalled for a moment. They hesitated at the sight of the naked flame and tried to cover their eyes as if the torch on the ground had the power of a sun. The barbarian had fought such fiends before and being the experienced warrior that he was, knew that all Gravelings were afraid of fire. Oogar recognised their rusting armour and pale, scabby flesh. Cowardly by nature, these carrion were once men that had forsaken their humanity for a depraved appetite. They lived beneath the ground, usually underneath cemeteries where it was easy to seek out and devour the flesh of the newly dead. Gravelings also salvaged the weapons and armour of warriors whose rite it was to be buried with them. Oogar was not sure what would drive such craven miscreants out to attack the living but proclaimed his knowledge to his comrades. They had precious few seconds to prepare themselves for the inevitable clash. Damari chose her torch instead of her shield on Oogar's advice and sprang forwards to meet their assailants with flame and steel. Pluk had only his short sword but also took the opportunity for a counter strike; he, Damari and Oogar charged the ghouls together. Murgho was not infected with the bravery of his friends and quivered in the shadows like a big jelly, struggling to get his get his spell book out.

'For the nimpeth!' cried Pluk.

'For Gormyr!' roared Oogar.

Damari just shrieked.

Despite their courageous dash, the thought lingered at the back of Oogar's mind that the enemy looked quite formidable. For starters, he could see four of them which meant they were evenly matched. The Gravelings were also well armed, even by the standards of their own kind; two of them had cleavers and large round shields which they used to form a crude wall and the other two had thick spears that they used to thrust out at them from behind. There was only one thing for it, Oogar would have to use a special combat manoeuvre practiced by his tribe called the panther leap. He jumped onto one of the spears and forced it down to the ground. The barbarian then used the spear as a spring board and propelled himself high in to the air. He somersaulted in mid leap to land on the rear side of their shield wall. Oogar had already started to swing Skullbreaker before he hit the ground. The Gravelings had no time to react. One of them was hammered into the rock wall and the others were scattered in panic. Now all hell broke loose. Damari and Pluk were equally astonished by their leader's athletic transfer and suddenly found that they had no one to swing at. There was some dancing around in the dark for a few wild moments while everyone found a space to fight in the confines of the tunnel. Pluk forced back a Graveling that had a spear. The pathseeker did not quite catch what the fiend said about his mother and neither did he care. The spear was a poor choice of weapon for the enclosed arena and Pluk skipped around its length to hack into the creature's throat with deadly precision. There were fresh groans from the other end of the tunnel as two more Gravelings approached from the opposite direction. The new monsters had axes and shields.

Murgho now found himself in the middle of the fight and his spell book was useless without any light to read it. He cried out in terror. 'It's an ambush! Help me! Help me! It's an ambush!'

The demented screaming of a woman filled the tunnel and all knew that Damari had gone berserk again. The mindwalker dashed to Murgho's aid, leaving her side of the melee to Oogar and Pluk. She pushed past them all and chopped and sliced at the two new Gravelings. They fended off her storm of blows for a few tense moments, waiting for an opportunity to strike back but Damari was too fierce. They cowered and hid behind their shields but the mindwalker's unrelenting storm of blows soon found gaps in their defence and they were felled.

Oogar could see Damari through the tussle and watched her skill with admiration. However, he and Pluk still had one more fiend to slay at their end of the fight and his attention was complacent. The final Graveling swung its cleaver round full circle and bit deep into the barbarian's forehead. He felt no immediate pain but his vision began to dim as he stumbled back. He felt warm blood drip thickly down his left temple. His hands went limp and his torch and hammer slipped from his grasp onto the ground. His knees buckled and he too slid down. As he dropped, the warrior saw Pluk drive his sword into the back of the monster that caught him. He was then vaguely aware of Damari, crying and charging back over towards him. She held him in her arms as he lost consciousness.

'This isn't how it was supposed to end,' thought Oogar and the last thing he heard was someone shouting 'time out!'

*

'Who's got the first aid kit?' yelled Jack as he ran over to Scott. Melissa was struggling to hold him up as the lad was nearly twice as big as she. The Referee helped her to ease Scott down to the ground and they leant him against the tunnel wall.

'Who's got the bloody first aid kit?' roared Jack a second time.

'I'll go fetch it,' said one of the role players who had been acting as a Graveling. The monsters had got to their feet and were removing their masks. In the dark and confusion, however, Jack could not see which member of his crew was the benefactor.

'Can I get some light?' cried Jack, panic trembling his voice. The Referee disliked his players actually getting hurt, especially in a genuinely dangerous place. His only consolation was that Scott was a tough sod and had suffered far worse before, laughing and bragging about it in the pub later. Jack hoped that Scott would be able to add this one to his repertoire.

Barry picked up the flaming torch off the ground where Scott had dropped it and held it up above them so they could see. Scott's eyeballs were rolling around in his head. There was real blood amongst the paint. Somehow, the wound to his forehead was genuine. He was mumbling and gibbering and clearly fighting off oblivion.

Melissa tried to bring her boyfriend round by slapping his cheek gently. He looked up at her, his jaw slack and his eyes still rolling. 'How many fingers am I holding up?' she asked, showing Scott all five digits of her left hand.

'Nineteen,' he replied, somewhat bizarrely.

Melissa and Jack exchanged worried glances.

'I love you, Damari,' added Scott, slumping his head against the rock.

'Oh my god!!' said Melissa, unsure whether to be pleased or concerned. 'He's never said that to me before. He must be fucked!'

'He just called you Damari,' chuckled Barry. 'He doesn't know if it's time in or time out.'

'Here's the kit,' said the volunteer, returning. He had also brought them a lantern which lit up the whole area more adequately than the two burning torches the party had been relying on. They saw that it was Phil, Melissa's ex-boyfriend.

'Good man,' said Jack, standing up and taking the kit and the lantern. He and Melissa attended to Scott's injury. They cleaned him up and bandaged the cut. All the others watched on. They had been monsters and heroes but they were now a group of friends again, rallying together with genuine concern. Another of the monster crew fetched a flask of hot tea and busied herself with distributing the refreshment. The injured man was first in line. Jack and Melissa dragged Scott back up onto his feet. They gave him caffeine and jump-started him back to life.

'Thanks, Phil,' said Melissa to him. Despite their previous issues, it seemed that her ex-boyfriend was eager to help.

'No probs,' said Phil and shrugged his shoulders. 'It was me that hit him.'

'What?' snarled Melissa, anger suddenly replacing her gratitude.

By way of explanation, Phil went and picked up the scimitar he had used as a Graveling. He showed her the offending weapon. Some of the foam protection on the blade had been torn away, revealing the wood beneath.

'You wanker!'

Jack held up a hand in between them. 'Calm down, Mel, it's my fault, I should have inspected the weapons more closely.'

Melissa glared at Phil for a second and then turned away. She went back to comforting her current lover.

Jack and Phil stared at each other. Phil looked a little dejected. The Referee took pity on him and put a reassuring hand on his shoulder but Phil just snorted and skulked off.

Jack joined Barry and Dave who had found a small alcove a little way back down the tunnel to smoke and drink tea. The monster crew were moving on to prepare for the next stage. Dave had removed his prosthetics and was gazing down at the floor, thoughtfully. Barry looked equally as glum.

'Six Gravelings down a mine?' said Dave, looking up at the Referee.

'You are level ten heroes,' replied Jack, trying to justify the unpleasant encounter. Jack not only oversaw the proceedings but had written the adventure in the first place. It was his task to engineer each phase of the game; organising the locations, the costumes and the weapons. He was therefore responsible for anything that happened. Pluk, Oogar, Damari and Murgho, however, were on their tenth adventure together. The challenges were meant to match their experience. They were nearing their final confrontation with their arch enemy, General Skarron. The evil one's nefarious plans threatened the whole of The Realm. He was also to blame for the deaths of two of their previous comrades. The group had initially embarked as six and now they were four, with Oogar threatened, possibly three. The death of a character was always a realistic possibility but never a welcome one, especially to a hero that had come so far.

'Is Oogar dead?' Barry voiced what was on their minds.

Jack shook his head. 'No, but Scott is actually concussed and I have to take him out of the action.'

'But what will we do without him?' whined Barry.

'It's time for you to rise to Murgho the Magnificent,' chuckled the Referee but the humour was lost. Barry and Dave just looked at him with dismay. Venturing into certain peril without their mighty hammer wielder was not funny.

'We're taking him with us,' said Melissa, striding up to them.

They all turned to look at her with surprise.

'I can't let you do that, Mel,' stated Jack. 'It's too dangerous.'

Melissa, however, had made her decision. 'I'll take care of him.'

Jack faltered, as if to make an argument but he looked into Melissa's eyes and saw her steely resolve. 'As you wish. Get ready and I'll call time in.'

*

Damari was shivering from the subterranean chill and her silver armour felt heavy and frozen and it dug into her skin like a suit of ice. Her limbs ached from the strain of the last two battles and her porcelain white skin was marred by scratches and bruises. She breathed slowly to compose herself. Her ample bosom heaved with determination and gradually her mind became sharp again. Her aches and pains diminished and Damari began to sense the thoughts and emotions of those around her. She sheathed her sword and swung her shield over her shoulder. She picked up one of the diminishing torches and took Oogar's hand. She looked up into the eyes of her dazed barbarian lover and saw that they were watery and dim with pain. There was very little going on in that head. She smiled faintly at him and then led him slowly down the tunnel, past where they had been ambushed and deeper into the mine of Sembir.

Murgho was a few paces ahead. The warmancer lit the way with the other torch which danced and flickered low, like her own. Damari tried to reject the thought that they would soon be in total darkness. She could hear Murgho whistling softly and pensively, an indication that he shared her fears.

Pluk led the way, as usual, with his extraordinary nimpeth talent to see in the dark but Damari could not see him past Murgho's gargantuan silhouette. They must be close now, she reassured herself. Skarron had not told her that the mine was so deep, nor had he indicated that the Gravelings would be so deadly. The ambush had been intended as a mere distraction. A distraction that had nearly cost them the life of their leader and most capable warrior. No matter, decided Damari, it would all soon be over and she in the arms of her true lover, Skarron.

Suddenly, Murgho halted and held up a hand to signal her to do the same. At that same moment, Damari noticed the wispy tendrils of smoke drifting down the tunnel to embrace them, like some ghostly giant octopus. This must be it, she thought, and her pulse quickened in response.

'What is it?' she asked Murgho, feigning ignorance.

Murgho turned to answer her but Pluk appeared from the fog next to him and beat him to it. 'There's a chamber ahead but it's filled with smoke and I cannot see. I fear that if I scout in, I won't come back out again. I've got a bad feeling about this this one.'

'Then we go in together,' said Damari decisively, casting down her torch and drawing her sword.

'So you're leader now, Damari?' sneered Murgho.

'No, but it's the only way,' she said, unfazed by his challenge. 'If we're going to die, we might as well do it together.'

Damari was in no mood for the wizard's pedantry but Murgho gave no more. He merely shrugged his shoulders and followed the others into the veil of smoke.

The tunnel became wider and taller and gradually opened out into a second chamber. It was much bigger and higher than the first cavern but the timbers holding it up were equally rotten. They stepped tentatively within and their torches caught the twinkle of copper ore veining the rock. More mining gear had been abandoned, partially claimed by the limestone, and there were half a dozen metal carts on the rail track, running alongside the mine face. Around the walls of the chamber were several metal braziers giving off the soporific smoke. Standing in the middle, amongst the wreckage was a sinister and familiar figure. He was a tall man dressed in the elegant uniform of the Queen's Guard. A cloak was swung casually over one shoulder, revealing a sheathed rapier. The man would have been handsome but half of his face was covered by an elaborate gold mask.

'Skarron!' spat Pluk with barely concealed hate.

'Hail to the brave heroes!' Skarron called out to them, his deep voice dripping with mockery.

'You murderous dog!' roared Pluk, brandishing his sword at the villain. 'Let's finish this, once and for all!'

'Wait!' pleaded Skarron, holding up a gloved hand 'Not so hasty little squirrel man. I have some surprises for you. Damari, my love?'

A ripple of confusion crossed Pluk's face and he and Murgho turned to Damari. By way of response, the mindwalker swung round and drove her sword deep into Oogar's heart. She held him there for an instant and looked into the barbarian's eyes one final time. She relished the horror and disbelief she found there. Damari drew out the treacherous blade and Oogar slid to the ground again but this time he really was dead.

'Damari!' screamed Pluk and Murgho in unison. Their shock was genuine but she just laughed and crossed the chamber to Skarron with a sickening indifference. She embraced and kissed him. The General felt solid and warm against her body.

'My fierce little vixen,' Skarron whispered into her ear passionately and she tingled all over with delight. She looked back at her former companions, giggling with the perversity of her deceit. Pluk and Murgho were still stood there, gawping. She would enjoy this now. Too long had she suffered the amorous groping of the stupid barbarian and the pathetic wizard. Then there was Pluk, always arrogantly striding ahead, like the quest was his alone. Their companionship had become stilted and pointless. It was time for them to die. It would be Damari that would decide the end.

'That's right, boys!' she called out to them. 'Skarron and I have become allies. We lured you into this trap and you followed us like good little lambs to the slaughter.' She turned to the General who was howling like a victorious wolf to ridicule them further. 'Shall I kill them?'

'No,' said Skarron, his eyes glinting with fiendish intent from behind the mask. 'I have a much more entertaining death for them.'

Damari nestled in his embrace as he began to mutter an incantation. She felt his mind become alive with complex thoughts. She watched Pluk and Murgho looking at each other, perplexed as to how to react. They too could hear Skarron's words of dark sorcery.

'Do something, Murgho, you oaf!' cried Pluk to the last of his companions.

By way of response, the warmancer turned and began to walk away.

'Where are you going?' shrieked the nimpeth.

'Over here,' replied Murgho, somewhat vaguely. 'Keep him busy.'

'Keep who busy?'

'The Demon that Skarron is summoning.'

'Demon?' Pluk's panic was now paramount. Damari thought that she could actually see him trembling. Murgho, however, was showing unfamiliar cool. *What was he up to?* Damari wondered. Either way, Skarron was right, this would be an entertaining death.

The Referee appeared. 'Time freeze!'

*

Big Jason entered the chamber, strongest and most ferocious player of monsters in The Dragon's Heart Live Fantasy role-playing Club.

The notorious giant was dressed head to foot in a new costume. The monster suit has been kept a secret from the party. Jack wanted it that way. It would be a nasty surprise for them at the end of their adventure. Big Jason filled the vast shaggy-furred costume perfectly. With the twisty demon horns and single eye, he looked truly terrifying. The Referee led him into the middle of the chamber, in between Skarron and Damari and Pluk and Murgho. "Time freeze" was called when the Referee wanted to bring in a new character. In this case, the appearance of a summoned demon. The players had to keep still and their eyes shut until Jack called 'time in!'

*

'For the love of Mog!' screamed Pluk as he looked up at the beast that had just materialised in front of him. 'A vacking Direclops!'

Twice his size, the brute seized him by the shoulder. Pluk felt its claws bite into him like knives as the Direclops swung him round. The nimpeth became aware that the ground was no longer beneath his feet and before he had time to do something about it, he bounced off something hard and metal and then off something hard and rocky. He felt his teeth jolt in their sockets with both collisions. Dazed, He looked around and saw that he had hit a rail cart and then the ground. There was a good fifteen feet between him and the Direclops. Bemused by his own ability to be thrown that far and numb with pain, Pluk shook his head. He had to get up. The demon was crossing the distance with a speed that belied its size. It roared with lethal purpose. The immediate possibility of death gave the nimpeth some vigour and he leapt up, picking up his sword in one move. The attempt was admirable but too slow. The Direclops grabbed him with both paws this time. Pluk closed his eyes and thrusted his blade but the beast had him gripped tight and the lunge was useless. Again, he felt the sensations of flight and collision with the floor. The air was knocked from his lungs this time and Pluk stared up, his eyes wide with the strain of drawing fresh breath. He found himself at the feet of Skarron and Damari. The mindwalker looked down and giggled at him as he writhed.

'Damari! You traitorous bitch!' Pluk managed to gurgle.

'Aww, bless him,' mocked Skarron. 'Perhaps the little squirrel man would like to see his beloved before he dies?'

'What?' winced Pluk, wondering what devilry Skarron could possibly conjure worse than this.

Damari pointed into a corner of the chamber. Pluk painfully sat up and looked. He could see someone chained to the wall. The corner was dark and obscured by the swirling smoke but as he stared he could make out a recognizable figure. She was tiny, hairy and barefooted like him but her once fine nimpess outfit was now ragged and soiled. Her face had once been bright and beautiful but it was now grimy and sad. Those big brown eyes used to beam with warmth and hope but that was now gone. Pluk felt a wrath building deep in the pit of his stomach.

'Yhefi!' he cried so loudly and mournfully that the sound echoed through the entire mine and the Forest of Starfel above. He screwed up his eyes with anguish and fell back to the ground, tears streaking down his cheeks.

'She was alive all along, Pluk,' explained Damari. 'The Nettle Wraith just paralysed her. We thought she was dead.'

'And I found her,' sniggered Skarron. 'A little pet for me!'

'You bastard!' Pluk snarled with fury and attempted to leap up with the murderous intention of seizing Skarron by the throat but the Direclops emerged to save its master. The demon grabbed Pluk by the ankles and dragged him away.

'No!' cried out Pluk, half in agony as his spine rolled over a variety of rocks and half in frustration as he was torn away from his revenge. The plea was futile, he stared into the thing's single eye and saw an inhuman intelligence staring back at him. Skarron's demon knew no remorse. A large foul tongue emerged from its loathsome maw and licked its lips.

'Oh Holy Mog!' muttered Pluk to himself hopelessly. 'I'm its vacking dinner!'

Suddenly, something blunt and heavy hurtled into the Direclops' face. Despite its size, the demon was taken clean off its hooves. It landed a few feet away, squirming and bellowing with pain. The hammer blow was clean and strong and Pluk knew only one man that possessed such skill.

'Oogar?' he murmured, gazing up in amazement at the barbarian's toothy grin.

'I reckon you could have beat him. Just thought I'd lend a hand,' chuckled Oogar.

'Is everyone coming back from the dead tonight?' asked Pluk, deliriously.

'I resurrected Oogar with the last of my power,' said Murgho walking over and standing next to the barbarian proudly. 'I just needed you to keep that demon busy for a while.'

'Glad I could be of service,' mumbled Pluk.

'I need to finish this,' Oogar looked over at the Direclops which was now shaking its shaggy bonce and trying to get back up onto its hooves. He raised Skullbreaker into the air and whispered a strange word of power under his breath. Old runes inscribed on the hammer head began to glow with a burning intensity. The barbarian had activated the terrible and secret force of his weapon. He had given it the power to destroy the indestructible. He strolled almost casually over to the beast, swung the flaming hammer in a vast arc and smote the creature with a bellow. Pluk watched and mused on which was the more terrifying; the demon or the barbarian with the magic hammer?

'Time freeze!' called out Jack.

*

Big Jason got up and left the cavern. He removed the head of the monster costume as he left and rubbed his own balding dome painfully.

*

'Time in!' announced the Referee.

Pluk, Oogar and Murgho opened their eyes and looked for the Direclops but it was nowhere to be seen. Oogar's hammer had dispatched the demon back to the hell from whence it came.

'My beautiful demon!' sobbed Skarron. The adventurers turned to look at him and saw that the villain was on the verge of tears.

Damari was furious. 'I should have killed them myself!'

'I wanted my pet to do it,' whimpered Skarron like a stubborn infant. The general had lost his looming stature somewhat. He seemed hunched and troubled, like an ordinary man on the edge of ruin.

'What now, genius?' Damari asked him, sardonically. Their former companion looked a lot less thrilled to be at Skarron's side now.

By way of response, the general whipped back his cloak and quickly drew out his long rapier. He snarled like a beast, forsaking his suave composure, and charged headlong at Oogar. The attack caught the barbarian by surprise and he hastily took on a defensive stance. Skarron was complacent in his fury, however. He failed to acknowledge the threat that was an angry nimpeth on the floor. Pluk took his opportunity. He sprang to his feet and drove his blade into the general's unguarded ribcage, cutting short his charge. Skarron was still staring at Oogar. His eyes bulged with horror and his arms went limp. His rapier fell to the ground with a loud clatter. Pluk held

Skarron in the lethal embrace for a moment and then let his corpse slowly slide to the ground next to his sword.

'The blades of the nimpeth always settle their score!' said Pluk, triumphantly. Despite his long thirst for vengeance, he did not linger on his victory. He dashed over to the gloomy corner where his beloved nimpess Yhefi was manacled and took her in his arms. The others looked on as the two little creatures embraced and kissed and wept with the joy of an unexpected reunion.

Oogar turned his attention to Damari. With a grim expression, the barbarian waded over to his traitorous lover. She raised her sword to strike him but Oogar did nothing. He merely stood in front of her and frowned.

'Are you going to kill me again?' he asked.

Damari's sword arm faltered and she looked into his eyes. Tears were there and she dropped the blade to the ground. She took a knife from her boot and offered it to him.

'No,' she said. 'I have betrayed you.' She hastily took off her breastplate and pulled open her tunic to reveal her white breasts. 'It is you that should slay me.'

Oogar looked at her for a few sad moments and then laughed; 'Nay! We have different ways of punishing an errant woman where I come from!'

Damari looked at him with mounting dread. The meaning of his words was unknown to her and she could not yet begin to imagine what horrendous fate he had in mind.

Pluk had removed the chains from Yhefi and tossed them over to Oogar by way of gesture. The barbarian understood and winked at his old friend. He transferred the manacles to Damari. She was silently compliant and Oogar said nothing more either. There was, however, a curious smile on his face.

Murgho watched his friends thoughtfully. He felt lonely. Pluk had found his Yhefi and even Oogar and Damari were now reunited in a peculiar sort of way. He stood alone in the middle of the chamber, his arms wrapped around himself. Now all the excitement had come to an end, he felt the cold again and it seemed to accentuate his isolation. Then, to his surprise, the others walked over. They all looked at him and for the first time in a long while, it was not with pity or ridicule. Infact, they were smiling.

'Murgho the Magnificent I presume?' enquired Pluk.

'What?' said Murgho. No one except himself had used his full moniker before.

'You saved the day, Murgho!' Oogar slapped a big paw on his shoulder like a proud father.

'I did?' Murgho scratched his head, finding the gratitude of his companions unfamiliar. They all nodded at him. 'I did, didn't I? Well, it was nothing really, I first came up with the idea just back there, I knew something bad was going to happen, it occurred to me that …'

'Time out!'

*

The Dragon's Heart Live Fantasy Role-playing Club waited for the van. Big Jason had gone ahead to fetch it and they stood huddled together beside the road. An icy faced full moon bathed them in brilliant white light, a touch of real magic to end the day. Though they created their own terrors, the woods behind them looked even more dark and foreboding than ever before. Frozen, damp and nursing various injuries, they were content to leave their not so enchanted kingdom for the comforts of the mundane. Their costumes and props were packed away. They smoked and drank and happily talked about the day's events but they were all eager for the heat of the pub's open hearth. The dramas acted out in the old mine had made for a tough end to the game and not one player had left the place unscathed. The adventure had told the end of a secret saga and though they now succumbed to fatigue, all knew that it had been extraordinary in many ways.

Many had complimented Jack on his design. Perpetually enthusiastic, the Referee proclaimed plans for more games; new places, better costumes and greater challenges. He jostled for attention with Barry, however, who was intent on discussing with everyone his new found success as the club's most powerful wizard with equal relish.

There was a buzz amongst the group like never before but two couples were more concerned with each other than the rantings of Jack or Barry. Dave and Emily who had played Pluk and Yhefi were back to their human selves but their affection for each other remained tactile. The game had not been so kind to Scott and Melissa's relationship. Damari had betrayed Oogar and Scott was genuinely hurt. Combined with his head injury, he was having difficulty understanding his girlfriend's controversial decision. The others watched them with some amusement.

'I just wanted to make things more interesting,' she tried to explain.

'Did you have to go that far?' grumbled Scott.

'I thought you might have noticed the changes in Damari's behaviour?'

'I thought that was because of …' Scott wanted to say 'Phil' but cut himself short when he noticed that the offender was listening.

'It was my fault,' Jack intervened; 'I wanted to do the traitor thing and Mel said she was bored with her character.'

'The end wasn't the scariest part,' suggested Barry.

Jack turned to him, intrigued. 'Oh no? What was the scariest part?'

'That thing that was climbing up the wall in the mine,' said Barry, laughing nervously as if recalling the experience.

'Oh yeah!' Dave nodded in agreement. 'That was way up on the grossometer!'

Jack looked at them blankly. 'What are you talking about?'

'You know,' said Scott. 'That rat spider thing?'

'Yeah,' agreed Melissa. 'It was just there, climbing up the wall in the tunnel and then it saw us and took off.'

Jack stared at them and slowly shook his head, his face turning pale.

Frozen

The pigeon cooed in the new dawn. Ronni Lethbridge listened to it for a while, drowsy and half-asleep. Its wobbly noises were curious but she ached from a cold sleepless night and it was too early for a song. Springing out of bed, she opened the window, wrath fueling her limp body. The December chill surged in and her nipples responded, poking through her white lace nighty. She persevered and encouraged the bird to go away.

'Cock off!'

The avian minstrel pecked at her, determined that its melancholy commotion should be heard. Ronni admired the creature's audacity but it was in no mood to entertain it. She picked up a shoe and launched a merciless attack. The pigeon took wing immediately, gone in a flurry of grey feathers. She slammed down the window and slid back under her duvet, smiling with triumph. The victory was short-lived. She slept for another minute until her alarm clock went off. She rose and revenged her second rude awakening on the timepiece. She trembled as she looked at herself in the mirror.

'My god!'

Her hair was almost completely flat on one side.

'Chuffing pigeon!'

She sought out clean clothes that were strewn about the house. Though she had been defeated, she dressed and washed with frantic efficiency, making her way gradually downstairs to the kettle. By the time the coffee had cooled down, she had sorted out her rebellious red mane. She noticed that the pigeon had returned. It was outside the kitchen window, menacing her once again. It stared at her with its tiny black eyes, its head twitching, its song resumed. She wondered if mum had made a habit of feeding the bird. It seemed very single-minded. She did not care now, it was time to go to work and the creature could croon all it wanted. Wrapping herself in one of her dad's overcoats, she left the house and gawped into the heatless rays of the sun. She felt the urge to return to the womb of her bed. She considered the realistic implications of such a crime and it took more ferocity to enter the day.

She hurried through the frozen streets. She was compelled to look at her reflection at every opportunity. Her hair was still looking sleepy and her complexion too pale. She passed all the tea shops, ice cream parlours and amusement arcades that were closed for the winter. Ronni's place of work, the town museum, looked dormant too. Her frozen fingers fumbled with the aging lock of the back door. It opened from within. She saw the round and friendly form of Reg, one of the museum attendants. Her saviour ushered her inside.

'Are you winning?'

It was an odd question that Reg would ask her up to twenty times a day. Ronni was never quite sure what the right answer was but Reg never stayed still long enough to hear one. Already, the little old man was away into the main hall of the museum, switching on lights and unlocking doors as he went. He whistled "We Wish You a Merry Christmas" cheerfully, as he did all year round. Ronni went in and closed the door behind her with less glee. She stood and shuddered for a moment. The place seemed no warmer than outside. Reg waited for her in the hall like a concerned dog. She mustered a nod of assurance and followed him through aisles of dusty glass cabinets.

'The Dragon's here,' he warned in a more serious tone.

'Already?' Ronni frowned.

'Not in the best of moods neither.'

Reg heralded her progress upstairs to her office, unlocking more doors and activating more lights. She could hear his whistling grow ever more distant as he marched off to bring life to the rest of the building, his small plump frame vanishing into the gloom.

'Chuffing museum.'

Ronni took off the overcoat and hung it up. An electric heater buzzed with industry and it was a little warmer in the office. She rubbed her hands together to encourage circulation. Her heart still longed to be under her duvet. Before she could contemplate a day's work, there was a shrill voice from the next room.

'Is that you, Ronni?'

A fresh shiver went down her spine, but this was no reaction to the December cold. Dolly was the curator of the museum and her name was one that suggested innocence and fun, like a childhood toy, but this disguised the true nature of Dolly.

'Good morning,' replied Ronni as politely as she could manage.

Dolly came through from her adjoining office and scowled at her.

'What would you like me to do today?' Ronni asked.

'Can't you organise your own work schedule? Do I have to treat you like a child?'

'I'd just thought I'd ask.'

The curator pondered for a moment, holding up her hand in a pose of feminine contemplation. Ronni could see her immaculately manicured fingers, they glistened like icicles in the pale morning light.

'I suppose you could carry on cleaning the vaults.'

The disappointment must have been evident on Ronni's face. It was a long and menial task for a young academic but she had to admit that the museum was well out of tourist season and the curator had to keep her staff busy.

Dolly looked at her. 'Have you got a problem with that?'

Ronni recoiled. Not only was Dolly's challenge laced with barely concealed belligerence, but she was now in striking distance of her halitosis.

'No, of course not,' she shook her head. She had only been working at the museum for five months but she had learnt not to mess with Dolly. Two other members of staff had been axed in that time.

'It gives you the chance to familiarise yourself with the collections,' croaked Dolly, attempting to justify herself.

'Yes, I'll just check my emails,' agreed Ronni but The Dragon had already wandered back to her lair.

*

Chris failed to unlock the door to the vaults. Reg watched him struggle with the old lock, like a father observing a child's folly. Ronni paced around in the frozen yard behind them, less patient with the young attendant's inexperience. Chris had only been with them for a week and a half. Reg grinned and took over. The veteran unlocked the wide metal door and swung it open with ease.

'You have to be gentle with it,' he explained.

Chris shrugged his shoulders and sniggered at his own incompetence. Reg led the way into the darkness, flicking on a multitude of lights with casual routine and ambling down a narrow staircase before most of the lights could respond. They came on slowly and sluggishly, accompanied by a chorus of fuzzy noise, as if they were complaining about being woken up. Ronni followed the gangly frame of Chris more cautiously. She became engulfed by the powerful odour of musty artefacts as she descended the stairs. The air was thick and it seemed to her not just a smell but an atmosphere.

It was tinged with the vapour of various chemical treatments that stuck at the back of her throat.

'Pongs a bit down here, don't it?' Chris wrinkled his nose up and turned to her.

Ronni looked back at him but was stuck for an answer. She had not attempted much in the way of conversation with Chris yet. She found something unsettling about his toothy grin and the way he always looked at her chest and not her face. Chris fumbled with his keys nervously in his trouser pocket every time they spoke. His nose was undeniably massive and despite his youth, he was as bald as Reg. The hairless cranium did little to improve his aspect. Ronni thought that he looked like an under-fed vulture. The museum had taken him from a school for students with learning difficulties. It was some sort of community scheme.

'I suppose you get used to it,' he mused, jangling his keys.

'Yes, I suppose,' agreed Ronni awkwardly, trying to be nice.

Reg poked his head round the corner and winked at them. 'Are you winning?'

They followed him around as he opened up the vaults and gave them light. Chris was wide-eyed at the multitude of skulls and stuffed animals staring back at him from the shelves.

'Will you be alright down here?' he asked Ronni.

'Yes, thank you, I've got lots of work to do,' she replied.

'Do you want me to stay down here with you?' Chris jangled his keys excitedly again.

'I think Dolly will have plans for you upstairs,' she said.

'Come on, lad, I'll show you how to empty the dehumidifiers properly,' said Reg. 'We don't want you getting a tongue lashing off The Dragon,' he added with a chuckle and led the novice away.

Ronni was suddenly alone amongst the bones, fossils, rocks and long dead beasts. She felt the chill and gave herself a hug. She listened to the two attendants and paced around until they had gone. She heard Reg's ceaseless march back up the stairs followed by Chris' more languid step. They shut the metal door behind them with an ominous bang that echoed around the bare stone walls and made Ronni shudder. The clang had a certain finality to it. She felt like she had just been locked up in a jail.

She gazed around at the objects crammed onto the shelves and racks. The skulls and stuffed animals were her silent companions for the rest of the morning. She had already cleaned and repacked some of the collections, as indicated by the new brightly-coloured boxes on the shelves. Most of the objects, however, were still loose or in old, grey cardboard containers and these represented the remainder of her chore.

'I'm chuffing Cinderella!'

With resolve, Ronni tied back her red locks, put on her spectacles and rolled up her sleeves. She switched on the lamp and the heater in the middle of the vaults where she processed each item. She plugged in her lap-top and it hummed into action. She crossed over to the corner where the ethnology section was kept and slid out the next box. There appeared to be some sort of beaded adornment inside. She moved the yellowed wrapping paper and a tiny puff of dust filled her nostrils. It looked like a tribal necklace of some kind but not one that had been worn for over a century. She removed it, dusted it carefully and checked its serial number on the computer. Perhaps she would see what it looked like around her own neck. After all, no one was watching her and it was a thing made to be worn. She was delighted by the object; a professional reaction followed by a more human response.

Ronni did not mind being left alone in the vaults so much. Most people felt uneasy about being left alone in this murky underworld but until the door opened again, she was her own boss and could work at her own pace. She had the opportunity to explore each artefact with her hands, unlike visitors to the museum who had to settle with looking at them behind glass. For Ronni, history was a tactile experience. Some of the collections were more appealing than others, of course. The ethnology section contained unique wonders from the far corners of the globe, brought together by Victorian curators, who, at that time, were little more than treasure-hunters. Something like the Neolithic section, on the other hand, was comprised mostly of bone fragments and had given her a long two weeks.

She darkened her computer screen so she could see her reflection. The African necklace felt heavy and uncomfortable. She bounced and turned slightly but its rainbow colours clashed with her white skin. She felt foolish and took it off. She found the necklace a new home in a plastic box. Perhaps it would be another hundred years before it was worn again. As the morning passed, more effects from the ancient world were boxed anew. Ronni handled a shrunken head, a blow-pipe dart, a leather shield, a voodoo doll, a petrified bird's nest, some bone earrings, a wooden death mask and a hand-basket made from an armadillo shell. Each was dragged from the cobwebs and shadows and brought into the illumination of the modern age. If she could get past Dolly's obsession with ceramics, it would make a wonderful display. After all, what would a visitor rather marvel at? Derby china or a dart coated with tarantula poison?

Ronni wandered into a section of the vaults that was much darker than the rest. Despite the sufficient lighting, it seemed curiously dim, as if the light itself was not welcome. This is where the art collection was stored and she browsed idly through some of the paintings. As much as she could see in the murk, most were depictions of local landscapes or portraits of long-forgotten dignitaries. She yawned and felt tired. She saw an object that she had not noticed before; a life-size statue of a bare young man. Despite his nudity, the youth showed no sign of shame. He stood boldly infact, proud of his muscular physique and rather adequate manhood. She took a step closer to the sculpture. She became aware that her mouth was open and that her heart had quickened. The sculpt looked remarkably like her ex-boyfriend. The mop of curly hair in particular resembled his. A wave of regret and melancholy suddenly overwhelmed her. The more she stared at the lithe figure, the more it seemed like that of her beloved Rupert. Astonishingly, the man had been carved from wood. There were no signs of the sculptor's tools. It was as smooth as …

'… real skin.'

Ronni touched it and stepped back. She fought back a squeal. She stomped out of the dark and back to her desk. Her mind was obviously playing tricks. She had not been the same, not since the accident. She reached for the intercom and asked the jailers to come and let her out.

'Quickly, please!'

*

'You look pale. Are you ill?' Dolly asked.

Ronni had not noticed The Dragon enter the staff room. She was too busy staring into her cup of coffee.

'I'm okay, thanks.'

'You should look after yourself properly.'

'Did you get a scare down there? Was it one of them rats?' suggested Reg with more authentic concern.

'No, really, I'm okay.'

Ronni tried to smile at both of them. Reg was constantly on guard against the vermin menace. He spoke of them daily but Ronni had never actually seen one of the critters. According to Reg, there was a secret war between the museum rats and the pigeons that inhabited the yard.

Chris looked up from his newspaper with a mouth full of sandwich. 'It's probably haunted down there.'

'Don't be so absurd!' Dolly hissed and stomped out, leaving the others to ponder what she had come in for in the first place. Warmth seemed to return to the room.

'It's not so daft,' whispered Reg. 'Some odd things have happened here over the years.'

'Yeah?' Chris' eyes boggled with curiosity.

'We found a pigeon up on the top floor once. Must have gotten in through the one of the holes in the roof. Set the motion sensors off it did.'

'That's not that odd.'

'It is when you consider that it was dead.'

'Well it probably got a look at Dolly and died of fright.'

The two men laughed and so did Ronni.

'What else?' urged Chris.

'You shouldn't encourage him,' said Ronni.

'Well, there was the Japanese family,' Reg leaned back in his chair and crossed his fingers like a seasoned raconteur.

'Yeah?'

'Long time before either of you were here we had some foreign visitors; a bloke, a woman and two little girls. They spent a long time in the shop, buying fossils and what-nots. Must have had a few bob and some time to waste. They went upstairs for a look round and the bloke comes back down after a while and says that he's lost his family so I went and looked round for them and called the other attendants to do the same but they were nowhere to be found.'

'Did you try the bogs?' suggested Chris.

'Of course but they weren't in there.'

'One of the fire exits?'

'Would have set the alarms off, wouldn't they? Anyway, later on still, long after the bloke had given up and gone, the woman and kids come wandering back down the stairs. I tried to tell her that her husband was looking for her but her English weren't too good and she had trouble understanding what I was on about. Turns out, according to her, that her husband had died years ago.'

'That doesn't make sense.' Chris looked perplexed.

'I know it doesn't. Still foxes me to this day that one.'

'You're telling us porkies,' Chris shook his head and guffawed.

'How about this one, then,' Reg seemed a bit put out. 'One year we had a call out. New Year's Eve it was. The ground floor was completely flooded. We were up to our ankles in it. Bits and pieces floating around in it and all sorts.'

'One of the pipes had burst then?' Chris attempted more logic.
'No.' answered Reg, defiantly.
'Heavy rain had got in?'
'Wasn't raining.'
'Come up through the floor?'
'No, the vaults underneath were bone dry.'
'What was it then?'
'No one knows, it's a mystery.'

Chris considered it for a moment and then laughed in disbelief.

Reg shook his head and seemed cross. 'It's odd this place, you'll see!'

*

Despite her fright and the old man's stories, Ronni returned to the vaults in the afternoon. She decided to focus on her work and not give in to distraction. Fuelled by caffeine, the rest of the ethnology collection was efficiently and rigorously processed. She was not quite sure what to do with some exotic beetles that she had found in a tin but this was only a temporary hitch. After consulting the curator, they were to be left as they were for now. The minute insects had, after all, already survived a hundred years in the tin.

It was not until the last hour, when the light of day no longer shone down from the skylight in the roof that her mind began to wander once more. She thought of the statue and tentatively stepped towards the art section to see it again. She could distinguish its outline in the gloom and felt that was close enough. She did not dare to touch it again or even gaze upon it fully. Ronni sat down on a pile of packing material and stared at its silhouette. It was miraculous that such a form could be carved so perfectly from a block of wood. The resemblance to her former lover, however, was surely mere coincidence. She came to the rational conclusion that touching the sculpture had brought back the memory of touching Rupert's body. In her reverie that morning, it had seemed real. Wrenching herself away, she returned to her computer and checked the museum files. There was only one record for a wooden statue of a man and this had to be it. Disappointingly, there was little information, only that the piece had been donated to the museum some three years previous by a Miss M. Bilk. The entry gave her address; a farm just a few miles out of town.

*

The Landrover thundered through the ice-coated wilderness. Its frozen innards chugged and spluttered, threatening to explode.

'Cocking engine!'

Ronni yelled at the aging machine but was angrier with herself for deciding to take this journey. The rest of the world looked dormant, as if the people had heeded the warnings of the weather man and decided to stay at home where it was warm and safe. As she turned off the road, the wheels skidded on the snow and she had to battle to keep the vehicle upright. Her heart danced as it lurched onto two wheels. This was the road where her parents had met their deaths a year before and for a horrifying moment, Ronni thought she was going to join them. She wrestled with the steering wheel, frantically trying to point the Landrover in the direction of the road. She reflected that perhaps it might be wise to go a little slower. Over the next ridge, she was relieved to see her destination; a small grey crump of buildings jutting out of the white horizon. She could almost make out the entire road between her and the village. Sunlight glinted from puddles where the snow had been cleared.

Arriving in one piece, Ronni decided to take a break. Her hands were completely numb from effort and cold and she needed to find out exactly where Miss Bilk's place was. Huddled down into her dad's overcoat, she left the Landrover in the village square and went to explore. There were a few people walking around to give directions but she felt like a pub would be a good place to find something to revive her, as well as glean information. She found one a couple of streets away. A huge stone fireplace roared with a well-kept blaze within. Ronni went over to the fire and returned the warmth to her hands, ignoring the curious looks of the toothless locals at the bar. When she could move her fingers again, she went over and bought a whisky. She asked the barman for the way to the farm. She had plenty of time to drink the whisky, it took ten minutes and the combined knowledge of all the barflies to establish its whereabouts.

A crooked mile was the true answer, along a road which was not so familiar with a snow plough. Despite the odds, Ronni drove on with determination. She knew it was foolish but she considered some of the glares of the natives and felt compelled to move on. She considered the notion of getting stranded in that place for the night and it made her shiver, facing the hills and the snow had to be the lesser evil. Up and down the machine struggled, as if speeding along the spine of some vast frozen serpent. When the Landrover went up hill, the engine chugged laboriously and the wheels screeched horribly in protest. When it went downhill, the vehicle did little more than slide, leaving twisted furrows in the snow behind it. She started to enjoy the battle in a perverse way. There was a wild unpredictable freedom about this trip that was far removed from the tedium of the museum.

The snow-coated sign at the side of the road was easy to miss. Ronni noticed it at the last moment and had to brake and reverse. If she had overlooked the turning she would have doubtlessly carried on into white oblivion. She turned in and discovered that she was at the top of an incredibly steep path. Miss Bilk's farm was in a valley below. If she did not wreck her dad's old vehicle going down the icy drop, she would certainly never get back up it. Ronni felt that she had tempted fate far enough and decided to leave the Landrover there. She climbed into the back, put on her Wellington boots and walked the rest of the way. The boots were red with white spots. She had bought them back in London and like most of her clothes, they made her stick out like a sore thumb.

She approached the farm, clouds of frozen breath billowing from her rosy lips. The valley itself was beautiful, but the farm was somewhat dilapidated and ramshackle. It looked like a Siberian mining outpost. She counted the rusting hulks of at least three different vehicles sticking out of the snow and there were countless tyres, spare parts and miscellaneous pieces of metal scattered about. There seemed to be no signs of habitation but Ronni noticed that the front door to the farmhouse was open. She went over and knocked and looked inside. Soon, a large man emerged from within. He wore oil stained jeans and a leather waistcoat that did little to conceal his bulging pink gut. The winter weather obviously did not bother him too much. He looked surprised to see Ronni, ruffling his ginger mullet and raising his eyebrows inquisitively.

'I've come to see Miss Bilk, I'm from the town museum.'

The man snorted, revealing a row of broken teeth. 'She's dead, luv,' he said, bluntly.

'Oh!' Ronni felt stupid. 'I'm sorry, are you a relation?'

The man shook his mullet. 'No, never knew her. I took on the place about two years ago. Want to see it?

Ronni blinked. 'See it?'

'Where she died,' explained the man.

She smiled and shook her head. 'I'm not sure …'

He did not wait for a definite answer. He stepped out and marched passed her, round the back of the farm, beckoning her to follow.

Ronni looked around. She did not feel safe. Despite her fears, she was compelled to follow him. The man's strides were long and she hurried to keep up with him as he led a trail through more ruined buildings and rusty wreckage. The place stank of manure. Glancing sideways into a barn, Ronni caught a glimpse of what looked like a dead animal, its hooves protruding from a pile of filthy straw. It did nothing to ease her anxiety. She was about to say something when he came to a halt. Ronni looked ahead; the track ended abruptly. Ahead was an old quarry filled with dirty frozen water.

'She drowned in there,' said the man, gazing out across the dark ice. 'Though they never found her body,'

Ronni stared with him for a few moments, the morbidity of his statement accentuated by the gloom of the location. She could imagine an old woman's hand sticking up from the water, desperately grasping for help. 'She's still in there?'

The man shrugged. 'They say Maggie Bilk was a mad old bag. Very unpopular with the locals. Not fit to be buried. Probably the best thing for her.'

She looked up at him, astounded. 'It doesn't bother you?'

'Not really,' he said, returning a vacant expression.

She could believe it.

'She's dead isn't she?' He grinned. 'Want to come inside?'

Ronni shook her head, very decisively. 'No, thanks.'

'Are you sure?' he said, scratching his belly. 'I'll soon warm you up, luv.'

She could no longer speak. She turned and walked away, her impulse to survive taking over. For a dreadful moment, she anticipated his grubby paw on her shoulder, but it never came. She walked as quickly as she could without actually running, not daring to look back, no less unpleasant images of a drowning woman in her mind. *What a horrible lonely death*, she thought.

She managed to find her way back through the farm and up the slope. There were no answers here. A simple phone call would have told her that. Ronni cursed her impulsive nature and clambered back into her vehicle. Feeling a bit safer, she chanced to look back down at the farm and the Neanderthal was there, staring up at her and grinning. For another horrible instant, the engine would not start and she had to contemplate being stranded out there with him. She almost cried out with joy when the machine shuddered into action.

She ploughed all the way back with a trance-like concentration, her survival instincts peaking. She was exhausted by the time she got home and it was dark. She wondered miserably about better ways to spend a day off. She had stopped to buy milk and sherry. The milk went straight in the fridge and the sherry straight in a glass. She kicked off the rubber boots and sank into her sofa, nestling in the skeletal shadow of last year's Christmas tree. She gulped the sherry down and smoked a cigarette. She was on one fag a day, just to relax with. Back in London, Ronni had been a twenty a day girl but she had been many different things back then. In her home town, life was a lot less gregarious and her habits had become more subdued. The combination of warmth, alcohol and nicotine was overwhelming and she felt drowsy. She was vaguely aware that she was thinking of the statue. There was a certain warmth in her lips, chest and groin that had not been there for a while. It was the first time in ages that she had not cried herself to sleep.

*

'Are you winning?' asked Reg in the morning.

'I don't think I am,' said Ronni with absolute honesty. She had overslept and her hair was a mess.

'You'll have to face The Dragon,' he said and led her upstairs to Dolly.

'There's lots of work to do,' stated the manicured tyrant. 'I need you to be dedicated.'

'It won't happen again, Dolly, I'm sorry.'

'Do you realise how many people would like to work here?'

'No.'

'There's not much employment in the town and competition amongst the peasants is fierce. This is a wonderful place to work.'

'It could be.'

'I beg your pardon?'

'Nothing.'

'Yes, well, just get on with it.'

Before Ronni knew it she was back in the dungeon. Reg and Chris took her down and seemed hesitant to leave her.

'You don't look well,' said Reg with concern.

'I'll be okay,' she reassured him though her limbs felt heavy and sensitive and she wondered if she had caught a chill.

'Just give us a call if you see any ghosts,' Chris sniggered.

They left. Ronni switched on her lamp, heater and computer but sat for a while to compose herself. She sipped some water from a bottle and tried to put the bad start out of mind. For a while, she worked hard. She cleaned and boxed artefacts like a manic robot. Inevitably, she meandered over to the art section. Deep down, Ronni knew that she was just delaying. The statue was waiting for her.

'Who are you?'

The muscled youth gazed back at her without an answer.

'You don't say much do you?'

Ronni took some slow yet deliberate steps towards him. His pupiless eyes regarded her every move and his lips betrayed a slight smile.

She bit her lip 'Not shy at all.'

Ronni reached out and caressed his perfectly formed torso. It was made of wood but it felt warm and fleshy. Her hand ran down his lean, muscled frame and back up again. This time, Ronni did not want to scream and run away. She felt a wild heat ripple through her. Her breathing became shallow and her heart quickened. It may have been her imagination but he seemed to be breathing too. His eyes began to glitter with life and his lips parted slightly. Ronni kissed him, hesitant at first and then lustful, sucking his mouth with a feral yearning. She stood back momentarily.

'What am I doing?'

But the last trace of reason was slipping away. Ronni could hesitate no longer. It had been too long. Her hands and lips were on him again. She closed her eyes and allowed the pleasure to consume her. She fondled and embraced and bit and ripped. She ran her hand down to his groin and shrieked in astonishment. The statue had changed even more. He had become erect.

'My glorious boy!'

Ronni tore off her clothes with lunatic abandon. She threw her legs and arms around the statue. The museum vaults echoed with her cries of rapture and were not silent again until she was done.

*

The door to the vaults opened. Ronni franticly dressed. She was just doing up her blouse as Reg and Chris found her. She looked at them, cheeks flushed, eyes sparkling.

'Feeling better?' asked Reg.

'Oh, yes,' she said.

*

It was February and the frost clung to the land like a veil on a corpse. The townsfolk were half asleep. They were pale and sunken-eyed and went about their business with lethargy. The sky above them was a perpetual blank canvas. Even the sun and the moon were strangely absent. It seemed to Ronni Lethbridge like a different world where life had almost given up. She, however, felt reborn. She had a real fire at home and it brought a new warmth and light to the house. The first thing to be burnt was the long-dead Christmas tree, then most of her parent's stuff and finally some more conventional wood and coal. She had accumulated a small fortune from her earnings and inheritance combined and she began to decorate the place in her own image. She sold the rusty Landrover and replaced it with a less treacherous contraption. She gave up smoking and drinking. She went back to London to see some old friends. She had even found her darling Rupert and discovered that she did not care for him anymore.

There was one further morsel of catharsis: The pigeon that woke her every day. The bespeckled nuisance stood on the driveway, eating a crumb. It looked at Ronni with its beady little eyes. She stared back at the bird. She turned on the ignition and gently released the hand-brake.

'Bye bye!'

Ronni floored the accelerator and shot down the driveway. She felt only a slight bump to mark its passing.

*

'Are you winning?' asked Reg, opening the back door to let her in.

'Yes,' said Ronni and gave him a peck on the cheek.

The old man blushed. 'What was that for?'

'It's your birthday, isn't it?'

'Well, it is now.'

Chris was sulking in the main hall. He jangled his keys as he watched Ronni walk in and licked his lips at her.

'Do I get one on my birthday?'

'No.'

Ronni skipped upstairs to her office. She did not have to see the look of disappointment on Chris' face. She could imagine it well enough and it made her laugh. Not even Dolly could dampen her spirits.

'Have we finished yet?' enquired the curator. She was lying in wait for her.

'Sorry?' Ronni was phased slightly. Dolly was sporting a new haircut. It had been chopped into a bob and highlighted. It was a style for a younger lady and Dolly looked like an unhappy bloodhound with a colourful wig. Ronni had to try hard not to laugh.

'The vaults?'

'Oh, yes, I just have the geology collection to finish.'

'I want it done by next week, ready for reopening.'

'Of course, Dolly.'

'We've worked very hard.'

Ronni noted her curious usage of the word 'we.'

'Yes.'

'Good.'

Dolly went to leave the room but Ronni stopped her.

'Dolly?'

'Yes?'

'Your hair looks nice.'

Dolly stopped, turned round and gawked at her. She touched her new hair-do self-consciously. It took a few moments for the compliment to filter through, as if Dolly was unaccustomed to such a notion. She then did something that Ronni had never seen her do before; she smiled. Her crone-like features stretched to accommodate the unfamiliar expression, so much so, that for one disturbing moment, Ronni thought her face might snap like an over-stretched elastic band. The Dragon said nothing more, however, and merely shuffled back to her office.

Ronni made her way down to the vaults as quickly as possible. This relied on the haste of the attendants, however, who did not know the meaning of the word. She found it hard to disguise her impatience. She stomped around the flagstones and folded her arms while Reg and Chris seemingly took eons to unlock the doors and switch on the lights. She ushered them out. Time was wasting. She spent two hours furiously processing the geology collection, as promised, but looked at her watch continually. Finally, when it got to the point where she felt like she was going to burst. She charged over to the shady corner where her beloved awaited.

'Morning, my love.'

It had become a familiar ritual but no less exhilarating, Ronni pulled up her skirt and pulled down her knickers. Half an hour later, she was lying at his feet, soaked and breathless. It always felt too long till the next time. For Ronni, that was two hours later.

*

She woke in the middle of the night. Her entire body throbbed with the urge. Ronni sat up and switched on her lamp. She briefly considered some alternative means of satisfaction but she knew that there was only one true way. Despite the maddening compulsion, she got up and dressed slowly. She would have to consider this operation carefully. It was one thing to get her kicks during the day but another issue entirely to visit the museum at night. She calculated the risks and tried to shut the frenzy out while she got ready. She would not give into her instincts until she stood before him.

Dressed like a ninja, Ronni rushed through the murky streets. The town seemed deserted and for a while she saw or heard no one. The barking of a dog made her heart skip a beat. On a corner, by the museum, stood a group of hooded teenagers with a hound. They watched her as she approached and Ronni realised that she was dressed a bit like them. Rather than risk any sort of misunderstanding, she took a long detour and approached the museum from the other direction. Again, the dog was baying and her nerves were getting frayed.

She scrambled across the museum yard and struggled to unlock the back entrance, as always. The door opened with a creak and she hesitated, almost expecting the alarm to go off. By some cruel coincidence, the town hall clock struck three. For a moment, she did not distinguish its dulcet tones from the anticipated clamour of the alarm. She panicked and whimpered. Logic returned and Ronni moved inside and giggled at herself. She switched on her pocket torch and fumbled around for the deactivation keypad.

'5 ... 9 ... 2 ... 9.'

She sighed for a long time with relief and laughed again. Thankfully, all was silent.

'Cocking town hall clock!'

Ronni allowed the shadows of the museum to embrace her like a welcoming family of spirits. She breathed deeply but felt little comfort. She considered turning back but her heart was still in her crotch. She dashed through the maze of cabinets to the kitchen. She kept one eye on the motion sensors high up in the ceiling. Their solitary eyes glowed red when they picked up her movement but gave no cry of distress. She had silenced the electronic sentinels and in theory, would now be free to do as she pleased. The taxidermied occupants of the main hall did little to put her at ease either. They stared at her with their slack glassy-eyed sockets and she did not dare to look back. Once inside the kitchen, Ronni took a mouth full of tap water. She considered making herself some tea but decided not to tempt fate with unnecessary delay. She opened the key box. Making sure she had the right set, she swept back out into the main hall. Another walk through the dead things and she was out.

She gazed across the monotone expanse of the back yard. Once convinced that it was clear, she bounced over to the door of the vaults. The metal monster would not open easily and when it did, the screech seemed to echo across the entire town. She had to inflict its din on the sleeping populace again to close it behind her. Ronni paused to calm down. The acrid stench of the underground storage chamber was stronger in the dark but its familiar tang was reassuring. She hugged and rubbed herself to encourage further consolation. Just as she felt in control of herself again, she heard a thump in the darkness.

'Hello?'

She continued to stare into the gloom but there was no response to her greeting. She grew cold.

'Is that you, my love?'

Her voice fell to a whisper. She deliberated for a moment and with fresh resolve, switched on her torch and descended the stairs. She told herself that the building was old and made peculiar noises. She had heard them during the day. In the blackness, such groans of protest seemed more intrusive. Despite this faith, Ronni stepped cautiously through the bays. After a few breathless steps her torch lit up a friendly figure in the corner. Her boy was waiting for her with his usual confidence. He seemed more real than ever. She grew warm again.

*

'It smells odd in here,' said Dolly, inspecting the vaults the next day.

'Yes, it always does,' added Ronni nervously at her desk. The curator had come for an impromptu inspection of her work. Luckily, Dolly had found her diligently cleaning a piece of quartz and not humping one of the art works.

'I mean through here.'

Ronni heard the curator's stilettos stamping across the flagstones. She got up and followed her. To her horror, she found Dolly sniffing around the art section.

'It smells ... fishy,' Dolly wrinkled her nose up in disgust.

'Oh?' said Ronni, putting a finger to her lips. Her cheeks were hot with shame.

'It's probably just decay,' the curator decided and Ronni exhaled slowly with relief. The respite was short lived, however, as Dolly approached the statue.

'Magnificent, isn't he?'

'Yes,' Ronni whimpered. She was panicking inside. This was too close for comfort.

'Would look good on display.'

She felt sick but managed a nod.

Dolly scrutinised her.

'Do you know anything about him ... it?' quizzed Ronni, annoyed with her lack of ability to change the topic of conversation.

'It belonged to a local lady called Maggie Bilk. A figure of some controversy.'

'Really?' Ronni was suddenly unsure if she wanted to know.

'She wasn't very popular with the community. She died and the man who cleared out her house brought us this.'

Dolly's hand stroked the statue briefly. Ronni felt a twinge of envy.

'We've never been sure what to do with it. It just stays down here, gathering dust.'

'Perhaps we can find him ... it ... a good home?'

'I think he's fine where he is', said Dolly with one of her infamous frowns and waddled off to look at something else.

A fantasy of the statue at home with Ronni quickly dissipated from her mind. It seemed absurd. It was also very peculiar that out of thousands of objects, she and the curator had ended up talking about that particular one. She looked into the thing's blank eyes before she left and there was a different meaning in its smile, though she could not tell what.

*

Ronni went back to the village near the farm. To get there, she needed to drive down the road where her mum and dad were killed. This time, however, there was no snow, nor was she in a knackered old Landrover. Her mortality intact, she parked on the village green and got out. She wanted answers but recalled the ignorance of the pub locals the last time. She instead found a hairdressers. She needed a trim anyway.

'Sit thee down, luv,' said the lady inside. She was getting on a bit and reminded Ronni of her grandmother. She gestured to a chair and began snapping her scissors in anticipation.

'Here's a pretty lass,' said another customer with a towel wrapped around her head. She was referring to Ronni but only glanced up from her magazine briefly to make the observation.

'She's got lovely hair,' stated a third woman, sat next to the one with the towel, filing her nails.

Ronni felt welcome and took the seat with a smile. She listened to the three women gossip while her locks were shortened. She gradually built up the courage to approach the subject.

'Have you heard of Maggie Bilk?'

The room went silent. The scissors stopped. Ronni had drained the parochial jollity out of the room with one question.

'She was born here,' explained the hairdresser eventually.

The scissors resumed. The shop became alive again.

'She was ugly.'

'Very ugly,' added the nail-filer.

'She was cast out of the village when she was young,' the hairdresser went on.

'When was this?' asked Ronni.

'Oh, a long time ago, luv, I was just a little 'un myself. She used to bring milk down from her parent's farm but they died, you see, and poor Maggie was left all alone. With her looking the way she was, folk just started ignoring her.'

'It wasn't just that, Bet, you know it,' said the nail-filer.

'I'm sure this young lady doesn't want to know about that nonsense,' said the hairdresser called Bet.

'No, please go on, I'm from the museum. She bequeathed something to us, well, her house clearers did and I'm trying to find out more about it.'

'Did they now?' Bet seemed startled. 'Well, there were certain allegations.'

The room went quiet with expectation.

'It was said that she had the mind of an adult since birth and that she refused the milk of her mother, preferring that of the farm animals instead.'

Ronni felt like laughing and was astonished that the room was still silent.

'She grew a vicious temper as she got older and some say that nothing grew or lived up near the farm. The pigeons were her only friends.'

'Oh yes, the pigeons,' repeated the nail-filer.

'Pigeons?' Ronni felt strange all of a sudden.

'She could send them to bother people and this one in particular she could send to turn a man's beer sour,' supplemented Bet.

'Just cruel stories surely? She was probably just lonely,' challenged Ronni.

'All witches have their familiars,' said the nail-filer.

'Now I never said she was no witch,' Bet sounded a bit cross and stopped cutting for a moment. 'It was the local Parson who was her biggest enemy and he had a lot of influence on the village, you see. He's dead now, God rest his soul. He noticed that Maggie Bilk never attended his church, unlike everyone else in those days and he began to speak out against her. The war went on for years. Poor

Maggie couldn't get near the village, even the kids would throw rocks at her if she tried. Then one day, the Roberts boy disappeared.'

'There was never any proof that she took him, Bet,' said the woman with the towel.

'One of the children?' asked Ronni.

'Nay, lass, he was a young man. Big, strapping and handsome. The fairest in the village.'

'He was proper gorgeous,' added the nail-filer.

'Such curly hair!' exclaimed the woman with the towel.

'What happened to him?' enquired Ronni.

'No one knows, luv, he just went missing one day. Some said that Maggie Bilk murdered him out of spite. Others reckon that she took him as a lover.'

'There was never any proof that she did anything with him,' said the woman with the towel.

'Well, something happened to him,' concluded the nail-filer.

'But wasn't she old and ugly?' said Ronni.

'Witches can have their way with the young and innocent,' suggested the nail-filer.

'I'm not sure if I believe all of this,' Ronni felt dizzy.

'Well, like you said, luv, they're just cruel stories.'

The haircut was finished and Ronni paid in haste. There was some fuss from the women and Ronni had to show some token satisfaction. Her hair had become a mundane concern.

'What about that Japanese family, Bet? That was queer!' she heard the woman with the towel say as she left.

*

Ronni did not notice the drive home. She found herself stood in her dad's shed with a monstrous hatchet in her hand. It was now dark and only the pale light of the rising moon illuminated the shiny blade.

'Chuffing witches!'

It was too early and Ronni went back to the house. She created a fresh fire and paced around. The waiting soon became unbearable and she dug out a hidden packet of fags to ease her anxiety. She smoked the lot and as the clock eventually chimed ten, Ronni decided it was late enough. She changed into her ninja outfit and wrapped the hatchet in a cloth. She got in her car and drove to the museum. There were more people around than she expected so Ronni parked a few streets away. She tucked the hatchet under her hoody and ambled round to the back of the museum, looking around to check that she was unseen. As she crossed the yard to the back door she noticed that the door of the vaults was slightly ajar. She stood there for a few minutes, staring at it. It was unlike Reg to be complacent. Slowly, she walked over and pushed the metal door open a little wider. It creaked slightly. It was black inside. Ronni stepped in and she could hear a slight rustling or murmuring from deep within. The museum professional inside of her reasoned that there was an intruder on the premises and that she should raise the alarm. But how would she explain her own presence? Dressed in black with an axe? Recklessly, Ronni drew out the weapon and plunged down the stairs. After all, this was her territory and she could settle this. She switched on the lights and illuminated a terrible sight.

'Dolly!'

The old crone was working herself up and down the statue, croaking with unbound pleasure. Her white wrinkled body juxtaposed with that of the tanned muscular youth.

'Get off him!' Ronni snarled. She seized The Dragon by the hair and dragged her back.

'He's mine! He's mine! He's mine!' squealed Dolly like a spoilt child in a tantrum and collapsed on the floor, a clump of her hair still in Ronni's clutch.

'You disgusting old bitch!' spat Ronni.

'I love him!' cried Dolly desolately and looked up at her with tears in her eyes.

'This thing is evil, Dolly,' stated Ronni with a twinge of compassion. She turned and swung the hatchet at the statue.

'No! No!' sobbed the curator.

To their mutual astonishment, the blade bounced off the statue like it was made of rubber. Ronni hacked at the thing again with both hands but her blow left not even a scratch.

'No! No!' wailed Dolly again and leapt up onto Ronni with the speed and ferocity of a wounded cat.

Ronni was not prepared for such a feral retaliation and fell into the rack of shelves behind her. There was the cacophony of thousand ceramic artworks smashing to pieces as the rack hit the flagstones. Ronni was pinned down on top of it by Dolly's gnarled and sinewy form. The Dragon's fingers wrapped around her neck like snakes and she began to squeeze. Her nostrils filled with fetid breath as Dolly hissed with murderous intent. Ronni struggled to free herself but the old woman's grip was unnaturally strong. Her vision became speckled and dim as her windpipe was crushed. She felt the blood draining from her limbs.

'I hate you pretty young whores!' snarled Dolly in a voice that was barely human.

Ronni's fingers found something; a broken piece of plate. With what remained of her resistance, she jabbed the fragment into the back of Dolly's neck. She felt porcelain penetrate flesh and hot blood splatter her fingers. The naked old woman screeched horribly. Her grip weakened and she fell away. Ronni gagged and choked her way back to her feet. Dolly was writhing on the floor, scraping and clutching at her neck. Ronni watched with horror as the crone's eyes rolled white and her body twitched with agony.

'Are you winning?' enquired a familiar voice.

Ronni looked up as Reg walked into the room. Chris was close behind him.

'The alarms went off. We had a call out,' the older attendant explained.

They looked down at the pitiful figure struggling on the floor.

'Bloody hell!' said Chris. 'Is that Dolly?'

'It's a long story,' said Ronni, breathlessly.

They watched with morbid curiosity as The Dragon became still and thick black smoke began to curl out of her nose, mouth and vagina.

'Bloody hell!' said Chris again.

'Let's out of here!' cried Ronni and the three of them made a dash for the door. Behind them, Dolly's corpse combusted into flames. The dry wood of the shelves and the paintings instantly caught fire.

'I'll get the fire extinguisher!' yelled Reg.

'Screw that!' Ronni urged him onwards. 'It's too late! Just get out!'

Chris was the first to reach the metal door but it was closed. He franticly tried to open it, fighting with it like a rabid gibbon.

'Let me! I've told you before, you've got to be gentle with it!' shouted Reg, his usual composure replaced with panic.

Chris made a peculiar shrill whooping noise to indicate his own rising terror. He stepped back to let his mentor in but Reg could not budge the door either.

'It's jammed!' he bellowed and looked wild-eyed at the fire that was swiftly eating up their space. There was a strange clamour from outside, like a chorus of pigeons.

'The skylight!' exclaimed Ronni, pointing up at the only other method of escape.

'How do we get up there?' shrieked Chris, gazing up at the glass pane in the ceiling.

'The stepladders?' suggested Ronni calmly, gesturing to the apparatus propped up against the wall.

'Oh, yeah,' Chris giggled.

'Come on!' roared Reg and snatched hold of the ladders. It was a heavy piece of equipment and Chris and Ronni both had to help the old man shift them into position. Foul black smoke engulfed them as they did so and they coughed and choked.

'You first!' Reg shouted to Ronni.

'Hang on!' protested Chris.

'Beauty first!' justified the older man.

'I don't know if I can break the glass!' cried Ronni, looking up with dread.

'Right!' Reg resolved himself and clambered up the ladder. Without hesitation, he punched upwards with his fist and showered the others below with broken glass. The ladder did not quite reach the full height and Reg had to leap up slightly to grab the edge of the skylight. It was an awkward and desperate manoeuvre and for one horrible moment, he swung by his arms like some geriatric circus act. He managed to pull himself up and out into the night. His sweaty terrified face soon reappeared to encourage the others to do the same.

'Go on then!' said Chris to Ronni.

She ascended as quickly as she could. She was taller than Reg and did not have as much trouble to climb out, especially with him there to grab her arms and virtually lift her. Ronni found herself out on the roof, the chill of the night air replacing the heat of the furnace below.

'Come on Chris!' Reg yelled down.

Ronni looked into the pit of flame and smoke but could no longer see the bottom.

'Chris!' bawled Reg again. He waited a moment and then wriggled back down onto the top of the ladder.

'Reg, no! Don't go back!' hollered Ronni but she was too late. The old man had vanished into the inferno. As she peered over the edge, a plume of flame erupted from the broken skylight like a volcano. She tumbled uncontrollably backwards, head over heels, and off the edge of the roof.

*

Ronni awoke. Every part of her body hurt. She painfully turned her head from side to side. She realised that she was hanging in a tree. There was smoke and sirens everywhere.

'I'm going back to London,' she said to herself.

Devourer of Men

She saw them first as glints of light bobbing on the horizon but, as they got closer, Mary McDoon could tell that they were men clad in shining steel. The vision quickened her heart and she looked around for her daughters; only Agnes was visible, pulling weeds from the ground.

'Find your sisters and go inside!'

'Why, mam?'

'Just go!'

With one terrified glance at the approaching strangers, little Agnes did as she was told.

Her mother took a deep breath and turned back to them. A thousand fears raced through Mary's mind. She tried to remember where she had put the axe and when was the last time she had sharpened it.

It was only the call of the leading man that gave her any hope. 'Fear not, good lady! We are men of God!' His voice was stout and loud enough to panic the sheep.

Mary stared at him. He was not dressed like the metal men that followed him. He wore mere robes and wore a cross. As the procession reached her curvaceous walls, they drew to a halt and the priest tried again to put her at ease. 'Fear not, my highland rose, we mean you no harm.' He did not have to shout this time and his tone was more tender, accentuated with a broad smile.

Mary did not trust smiles. She opened her mouth but was too afraid to utter a word. She could see into the eyes of the four men in helmets. From within those iron masks glittered predator's eyes. She had seen that hungry look before and her hand flexed for the feel of her axe handle.

The priest's eyebrows arched in anticipation of a response. 'Can you understand what I'm saying?'

Mary managed a nod.

'May I speak with your husband?'

She shook her red curls and gazed solemnly towards a grave on a hill beside her croft.

The men looked at the hill and took her meaning.

'We are sorry for your loss,' said the priest. 'A Christian burial?'

Anger found Mary a voice. 'The men that killed him had crosses!'

The priest looked again upon the man's grave and noticed that it was marked by a sapling with a cloth tied to it. The smile vanished from his face as he turned back to her. 'You are pagans?'

'Like I say …' she snarled, twitching from foot to foot with brewing wrath.

'Very well, good lady,' the priest nodded and held up his hands. 'We come in peace, I give you my word.'

Mary crossed her arms. 'What do you want?'

'We seek the loch,' he explained.

'It's that way.' She jabbed a finger in the right direction.

'Thank you,' said the priest. 'Is it far, pray tell, bold maiden?'

Mary shook her head. 'You can hear the water, can't you?'

The priest turned to his four warrior companions and barked something in a bizarre tongue.

One of them addressed him with a reply in the same musical dialect.

The priest nodded and looked at Mary. 'We shall trouble you no longer and bid you good day, kind lady of the glen.' He bowed his head slightly and led the strangers away.

Mary watched them go with gasps of relief. She had hardly dared to breathe. She drank in more details of the dazzling armour of the outlanders and caught her own astonished reflection gleaming back at her. Each suit was different and yet the same, finely-wrought steel plates hanging over cascades of dripping mail, like a …

'… dragon!'

Mary blurted the thought out aloud.

The strangers froze and glared back at her.

'Dragon,' one of them repeated. Though they were from a far flung land the men in metal clearly understood the word and they bristled like huge steel peacocks.

The priest peered at her. 'You know of it?'

Mary shrugged and blushed. 'Everyone knows of it.'

The priest gave her a joyous little chortle. 'Of course! And it lives in the loch I suppose?'

'Aye,' said Mary. 'But I wouldn't go down there if I were you.'

'Why ever not?'

'No one who goes looking for the kelpie ever comes back.'

The Priest relayed the warning to his friends in their language and, much to Mary's surprise, they burst into laughter. So merry did they become that they danced and capered and slapped each other's ironclad shoulders.

The priest too enjoyed the good humour and felt the need to explain to the poor woman. 'I say to you again, fair flower of the mists, fear not! For these are Northmen and they are monster killers!'

It was Mary's turn to laugh. She bounced down the yard towards them, no longer so fearful. 'Aye! There's many who have claimed that before!'

'And where are these noisome geese?' the priest sneered, inspecting his fingernails.

'Lying at the bottom of the water,' she hissed and narrowed her eyes. 'Their bones picked clean by the kelpie!'

Again the priest changed her words for the Northmen and again they laughed.

The priest nodded and smiled at Mary. 'You've a stout heart, lass, and it pleases our visitors.'

She grinned back at them and thought for a moment. 'There's an empty barn a little way down the path. It's mine. There's a well next to it. You're welcome to rest and drink. Monster killing is hard work.'

'God bless you,' said the priest. 'We have walked for many days across the glens. We have been trapped many times. Twelve was our number when we set out. Now we are five. The people of your country have shunned us, tricked us and beguiled us at every step. We have been led into the jaws of wolves and murderers, but there is something in your manner that tells me you mean us no harm.'

'Times are hard,' sniffed Mary. 'There's no damn country here.'

The priest turned his watery grey eyes away from her and gazed down the path. The Northmen had grown impatient and strolled on without him.

'I want something in return,' pleaded Mary.

The priest looked at her.

'Promise that you'll leave my daughters be?'

'Of course,' he said. 'We are men of God.'

'Then why look for a dragon?'

'Satan has many forms,' the priest announced earnestly and rushed off to join his companions.

Mary watched them until they disappeared. Best find the axe and sharpen it.

*

'Fjord!' concluded Runolf as he surveyed the scene before him.

The priest corrected him. 'Loch.'

'Pisshole,' was the interpretation of Ulfric Fishface.

It was a desolate cut into the earth this water, long and thin and curvy like the formidable serpent it was believed to contain. The undulating surface reflected the grey clouds above. Tortured crags crowned its shores, clumped together as if fearful of the gloomy depth.

'God has forsaken this place,' the priest drank in its misery.

The forest that formed the ghostly borders of the loch was dark and alarming; a seldom used path snaked through thick wild trees and jagged boulders that dwindled to make way for a more barren descent into another gloom.

'We've come all this way for this?' Asger removed his helmet and shook his yellow locks in disbelief.

'Doesn't look like there's much to eat,' said the biggest of the Northmen, patting his belly. It was a more mundane concern but Runolf was right, they had not seen any animals since entering the forest. It seemed that the Almighty was not the only one to desert this land.

Magnus shook and growled with laughter. He did not share the qualms of the others. He just advanced onwards, using a furrow in the rock to climb down the last steep drop to the shore. He was the leader of the Northmen and set the level of their courage. Within the time it took for a few grey clouds to pass, all five men had wet feet. They stood on the edge of the water and gazed evenly across its expanse as its tide kissed their toes. They could see to the opposite shore but the loch's ends to either side of them were lost in the murk. If someone had not told them otherwise, they would have thought it some colossal river.

Magnus shouted so loudly that his voice echoed. 'Where are you, dragon?'

This provoked hilarity in his men.

The priest did not always understand the humour of the Northmen. Cheerful and frequent were their jests but sometimes a little too primitive for his tastes. He scanned the waves all the same. Like his companions, all he saw were those made by the breeze.

'Doesn't look like he's in,' sniggered Asger.

As if to mock his words there was a huge and sudden commotion in the water only a stone's throw from where they were stood. Within the blink of an eye, the Northmen reflexed and drew out their huge weapons.

'Come on then, you big scaly bastard!' roared Magnus, froth jetting from his bearded maw. He unsheathed an extraordinary broadsword from his back.

The priest was dumbstruck. The warriors from the north hardly seemed fazed at all. Something was rising from the depths of the loch and they were ready. The priest had never seen a monster before. His foreign friends told him that they had never seen one either. Perhaps it was a question of faith. Not holy faith like his but a belief that their crude myths could actually be given form. It was the first time the priest had gazed upon the chief's broadsword too and it was the most majestic object he had ever seen. Its blade glimmered like a mirror and the hilt that wove around the Northman's fingers was a miniature procession of writhing figures. The holyman had witnessed Magnus fight several times already but not with the broadsword. He had kept it sheathed for the entire journey. It seemed this king of weapons was reserved for dragon dicing. The priest was as amazed by the blade as he was by the fuss in the water. He took a deep breath and said a quick prayer, muttering whatever plea came into his mind. He found himself glancing back up the crags, looking for a way out, his voice dwindling.

White spray gushed up from the loch and there was a splash and a great snort like that of a vast beast. The Northmen strained on the banks like a pack of wolves but, in just a few heartbeats, the turbulence ceased. The ferocious bubbling descended to little more than docile circles on a pond. The Northmen staggered to and fro and glanced at each with puzzlement.

'I saw its scales!' proclaimed Ulfric Fishface.

'I saw its tail!' added Runolf.

The Northmen stared for a time, unable to tear themselves away from what they had just observed, though none truly knew what it was. It was long enough for the sky to dim and the priest to regain his courage.

'Pray tell, brave men of the north, when shall we rest and make camp?'

Magnus tore his eyes away from the water and frowned at him.

'I'm sure the monster will return,' urged the priest. 'It's probably just having a look at you. Sizing you up. It's gone back to the depths to plan its moves.'

Magnus scrunched up his beard of many hues in consideration and then nodded. 'The holyman is right. Let us find shelter.'

They put away their armaments and worked their way round the shoreline but every man kept one eye on the water. It was not long before they stumbled upon a rocky peninsula, jutting out into the loch. There, they found the ruins of a once majestic stronghold.

'A fort!' stated Magnus, coming to a halt and kicking at some timber.

'*It was* a fort,' suggested Asger, gazing around at the remnants.

'Nothing stays whole for long in these parts, explained the priest, wearily. He was pale and breathless and quickly found a spot to sit. 'The clans are always at each other's throats. They reject the love of Christ.'

'When food and women grow scarce, men will fight, Christ or no Christ,' Asger stroked his yellow forked beard, thoughtfully. 'This land seems to have little of either.'

'And what women they do have look like the backend of a cow!' added Ulfric Fishface, which was a bit rich coming from him.

Everyone guffawed manically, except the priest.

'And don't let us mention the food either,' grumbled Runolf. 'A sheep's stomach stuffed with meat and barley!? What in the name of Thor was that all about?'

While his men recalled their adventures, Magnus ran up a spur of rock and looked around. Whether the stone platform was natural or man-made was not certain but it served the purposes of the chieftain. He squinted into the distance. 'We shall rest here,' he announced eventually and took off his helmet to emphasise his point.

The priest frowned at him. 'Shouldn't we seek somewhere further inland, my lord? We're very close to the water. Perhaps we could go back to that kind lady's barn?'

'But the dragon is here!' barked Magnus, sounding cross and glaring at him from under his eagles' nests of eyebrows.

The priest looked down at his sandaled feet and mumbled. 'Yes, that's what I mean.'

'Any of that goat left?' Runolf asked, planting his mighty frame down, opposite the priest, resting his back against a lump of blackened wood.

'No,' answered Asger, joining their huddle. 'Some fat bastard's eaten it all.'

Ulfric Fishface sniggered and started to gather firewood.

'And the wine?' slobbered Runolf.

'Gone,' replied Asger.

The big Northman almost wept. The rumbles of his stomach were audible, even above the incessant lapping of the loch on the banks. 'What are we going to eat and drink?'

'Let the learning of the Apostles fill you, my son,' the priest drew out his book.

Runolf gazed up at the heavens in despair. 'Great!'

*

The sky waned from light grey to dark grey and then to black, tinged with an ethereal purple. There were no stars, only clouds that churned with unrest and the Northmen and their divine cohort cowered beneath them, sheltering from the wind and drizzle as well as the broken stones could afford them. They understood little of the words the priest read out to them and with the advent of nightfall, he gave up, the blank and drowsy expressions of the warriors offering no endorsement. Only Asger's bright blue eyes reflected any sentience and they glittered with contemplation, even in the worsening gloom. Magnus had yet to sit with them. He had taken a stance on the shore with his broadsword resting on his shoulder, staring out across the dreadful loch even though little could be seen.

'He's not going to give up, is he?' the priest asked Asger.

The Northman smiled. 'Magnus believes it's his destiny to slay a devil, the end of his saga, or the beginning of a new one. In our country, each man believes it's his right to become what you would call a saint.'

'Even at the cost of his men?'

Asger stopped smiling and flicked the holyman a look of contempt. 'Do not say that to the chief! The loss of his kinsmen is a terrible weight on Magnus. It drives him onward so that their deaths are not in vain.'

'My apologies,' muttered the priest. 'I'm just starting to think that his obsession is going to get us all killed.'

'Your words of wisdom are always welcome, holyman,' said Asger, sternly. 'But you should watch your pretty tongue around an old Northman like Magnus. He was born in the shadow of the raven and his quest is in his blood. He tolerates you, that is all.'

The priest shivered at the warning. He drew his robes tightly around him and gazed out at the powerful figure standing on the shore. 'And what about you, Asger?'

The blonde Northman stirred the campfire with a stick and glared into the encouraged flames. 'What about me?'

'You would follow your Uncle to your death?'

Asger shrugged. 'Of course. I'm here, aren't I?'

The priest sniffed and looked at him. 'But you are young, my friend. You have a beautiful girl that wants to wed you. Do you not want to see Hilda again? Have children? We could have spent the night in that barn where it was dry and safe. Where does this madness end?'

'It ends when Magnus cuts the head off that beast,' sighed Asger as he reclined back into the furry embrace of his bear-pelt cloak. 'We Northmen do not fear death and nor do your people, or so you claim anyway. It comes when it comes. Now I must beg your silence, holyman. I do not wish to think of my Hilda on this black night.'

The priest stared at him but Asger closed his eyes. Despite his words, the Northman was fingering the stones on his necklace his bride-to-be had given him. The priest turned his scrutiny to the other warriors on the opposite side of the campfire but Runolf and Ulfric Fishface were nodding off, propping each other up like pieces of the collapsed fort. It seemed conversation was over for the night. The priest could not give himself to exhaustion so easily. Certainly, he was tired and starving but the memory of the clamour in the loch was still fresh and frightening. He considered the reality of a monster in the water and wondered how the foreigners could be so calm, resting on its edge in the dark. There was something in the deep. Not only had the priest witnessed it but he now felt it; the sense that they were being watched by malevolent eyes.

Eventually sleep took him but, as it turned out, his fears were not unfounded. He was awoken rudely, the light of day had not returned completely, rather the first few rays of dawn were spearing through a bank of purple clouds but the Northmen were up and in distress.

Before the priest had even fully opened his eyes, Ulfric Fishface seized him violently by his collar and barked into his face. 'Runolf! Have you seen Runolf?'

'No!' the priest shook his head and recoiled from the disfigured Northman's rank breath. It was not a pleasant way to wake up. He had been dreaming about giant serpents but that was heaven compared to his rotting mouth.

Fortunately for the priest, Ulfric Fishface released his grip and stormed off. He rose to his feet and rubbed the cold ache from his bones, his features screwed up in a scowl of rage. He hated Ulfric Fishface and he hated it when the uncouth imbecile ruffled him like that. What gave him the right to lay so much as a finger on a man of God such as he?

He looked around for the others with a view to protest but Magnus and Asger were some distance away. He could just about make out the shape of the young fork-bearded Northman climbing the rubble at the bottom of the crags. Magnus was more visible, splashing around in the shallows of the loch. It appeared that both men were searching for their lost kinsman. He had to wait some time before they all returned. That is all except Runolf.

'Where is the big dumb ox?' grumbled Asger as they rejoined the priest.

'I think he got up in the middle of the night,' confessed the priest, recalling a vague episode from his troubled slumber.

'When?' growled Magnus.

'I don't know,' the priest shrugged his shoulders. 'Were you not on watch, my lord?'

'I was,' Magnus groped his beard. 'And I heard one of you stir when the moon was at its highest but I did not move my eyes from the water. I fear that it was Runolf and I fear that our friend has not returned.'

'Idiot!' Asger put his hands on his hips and glared around into the distance, flummoxed.

Ulfric Fishface just laughed and sat down to warm his hands on the smoking remains of the fire. 'He's probably gone off to find something to eat! You know what Runolf's like.' Despite his jest, there was something in the Northman's deformed features that betrayed his true thoughts.

All of them were considering the same horrific possibility but no one wanted to say it. For a while, none of them could find words of any kind.

'We'll split up!' Magnus broke the silence. 'Asger! You and I will head this way down the shore. Ulfric! You and the holyman go the other way and we'll meet you half way round. Arm yourselves! Make the call of the hawk if there's trouble!'

The three Northmen sprang into action, spurred on by Magnus's bold decision, and pulled on their armour. The priest, however, was a little more cautious. He raised a finger in meek dispute but it was enough for the warriors to stop and stare at him.

'A few problems there, chief. Firstly, I don't want to be paired up with Ulfric Fishface; the man is a godless brute. Secondly, I do not use weapons, I am a priest. Words are my weapons. Lastly, I have not the faintest notion what a call of the hawk sounds like.'

Magnus regarded him with fierce eyes that sparkled from deep pits within his helmet. 'Very well, go with Asger then. He knows our signals. May your words protect you from the beast!'

The Northmen chuckled at this and walked away. The priest paused to check that his book was safe before he hurried to catch up. Normally, he would put every faith into his revered tome but right now, all things considered, it seemed the better choice was a suit of armour and a huge sword.

*

The sky was dark with pregnant clouds and it soon began to pour with rain. The priest drew his robe about him but it was poor defence against the driving wet. He muttered and cursed from within his hood and tried to remember where the nearest chapels were located. Perhaps he could pay one of them a visit while these obstinate Northmen were busy getting themselves killed? However, before he had time to put his scheme in motion, his companion spotted the missing man, or what was left of him.

'There!' cried Asger.

The priest looked up. They had almost returned to where they had entered the boundaries of the loch the previous day. He could see the black woods atop the crags, blurred though they were by the veil of damp in the air. Asger shifted further inland and the priest strived to keep up with him, slower even without armour. Resting between two jagged boulders in the shadow of the crags was a leg. The limb was big and white and hairy, bare except for a leather shoe. The priest winced and looked away, his stomach venting what little was in it. He urgently made the sign of the cross.

Asger copied his gesture then cupped his hands, raised them to his mouth and made a shrill bird call. There was a faint but unmistakable reply from the distance and Magnus and Ulfric Fishface covered the ground so rapidly that the priest was agog.

The Northmen stared down at the gruesome find together.

'So it's true!?' the chief's voice dripped with awe rather than any regret for his kinsman. 'The dragon exists!'

'Why do you say that?' The priest scowled at him.

Magnus bent down, seized Runolf's leg and waved it at him, his sudden rage making a mockery of the priest's mild despondency. 'Can you not see for yourself, holyman? Tis' Runolf's shank! The beast has devoured him!' Blood pumped out of the severed limb as he shook it and splashed onto the ground, peppering the grey mud with scarlet.

The priest turned green and dry retched again but spat and quickly righted himself to confront the Northman. 'Nonsense! Where, pray tell, are the creature's footprints?'

Check mate. Magnus glazed over. The leg became still.

The warriors looked about them and realised the priest's wisdom. Sure enough, there was no sign of any beastly footprints to accompany the murder.

To the priest's surprise, it was the most dim-witted of the foreigners who found an explanation. 'Perchance the dragon has wings?' suggested Ulfric Fishface. 'And it dropped the leg whilst flying to its nest?'

'Yes! Yes!' Magnus nodded, overjoyed with his reasoning. 'It must have wings! Runolf must have gone for a piss last night and the monster plucked him from the ground before he even had time to cry out. Poor bastard!'

The priest was unconvinced. 'This thing lives in the water like a fish yet flies and nests like a bird?'

'Tis' truly a monster!' proclaimed Magnus, the unlikelihood failing him.

Asger shrugged his shoulders. 'Could it be that the rain has merely washed the footprints away?'

They all stared down at the quagmire beneath their feet and none could find dispute with his theory.

The priest conceded. 'More likely than wings!'

'We must find more of Runolf!' ordered the chief. 'Spread out!'

The others did as they were told and searched to each point of the compass. It seemed, however, than Runolf's leg was the only morsel the beast had spared from its loathsome jaws. They came back together and gazed upon it once more.

'We shall fish for the beast!' Magnus decided. 'We will put what's left of Runolf to good use. Let us build a boat!'

Without question, the Northmen reacted.

'Wait!' The priest halted them. 'Are you suggesting what I think you're suggesting?'

Magnus glared at him. 'We use the leg as bait!'

The priest shook his head violently in protest and almost laughed at the preposterousness of it. 'No! No! No! No! No!'

'What's wrong with that, holyman? You're trying my patience!' Magnus threw down the leg in anger.

'He should have a proper burial,' answered the priest, sternly. 'Just like all the others.'

Ulfric Fishface blinked at him. 'Even though we only have his shank?'

The priest nodded.

'Odin's bollocks!' snapped Magnus. 'The leg will be reunited with the rest of Runolf in the belly of the beast! I shall cut it open after I have slain it and we can bury him as one piece.'

'That's not going to happen, Magnus,' the priest frowned.

The chieftain stepped in and put his helmeted face right up to the holyman's. 'If I say it's going to happen then it's going to happen! Do not mock my words!'

'I'm not mocking them,' said the priest, taking a step back and wiping the spit from his face. 'It's my job to translate the will of God for you and I'm saying that a man must be buried in the ground as quickly as possible after death.'

'It's just his stupid leg!' Magnus shuddered with fury and picked the body part back up again. 'Runolf will be making himself useful like this. He would have wanted it this way.' He looked at his kinsmen for support.

Ulfric Fishface nodded. 'More useful than he was in life.'

The three Northmen laughed.

The priest was appalled by their callous wit but at least it seemed to calm Magnus down a bit. The priest was aware of the fine line he was treading with a warrior chief who was fierce even at the best of times, never mind when pushed to his limits. He realised that his buttocks were firmly clenched. He decided to appeal to Asger instead. All he had to do was look at him.

'It seems a good way to catch the creature,' pondered the blonde Northman. 'But perhaps the holyman is right? Runolf was an oaf but he was a man of good heart and he was one of us. He deserves to be recognised in the eyes of God.'

Magnus stared at them all, inhaled very slowly and then exhaled equally as deliberate. 'As you wish,' he said quietly.

'One thing's for sure,' added Asger.

The others looked at him.

'The grave won't take long to dig.'

*

And so it came to pass that the left leg of Runolf Gudriksson was buried in the shadow of a bleak crag far away from the land where he was born. It did not feel right or just and the heavens wept in sympathy. The men gathered round a muddy stain of a grave and their priest strived to find some meaning in his death.

'Amen,' he said finally.

'Amen,' chorused they.

The priest glanced around at the Northmen. They had replaced their helmets and the rain fell so hard that steady streams of water dripped from their metal faces. 'What now?'

'Revenge!' growled Magnus. 'We'll build a boat and find this dragon even if I have to swim to the bottom of the fjord and drag the coward up by myself!'

The chief's last two men grunted in affirmation and followed him away.

'I was afraid you were going to say that,' the priest muttered to himself and shook his head. With one final look at Runolf's pitiful burial place, he sank back into his hood and stumbled through the sludge after them, freezing mud oozing up between his sandaled toes.

They climbed out of the valley into the forest. The priest's heart lifted slightly at the prospect of shelter but the woods were just a different sort of misery. He sat beneath a vast tree and hugged himself while the Northmen cut down some of its smaller cousins and began crafting them into a vessel. The air was trapped beneath the canopy of leaves and it was damp and thick with foul sap and rotting scrub. The holyman contemplated building a fire but there was nothing dry in that awful realm. He even considered helping the Northmen but his resolve was too weak. The outlanders had stripped to their waists and had put their lean muscular forms to great purpose. They built a boat as one creature, hardly needing to speak, so rehearsed were their people in sea craft. The priest was not invited to participate, nor even acknowledged. His job was done. A tumultuous storm gave tempo to their labour. The strike of their pagan god's thunder hammer competed with the din of their hacking and chopping.

The priest leaned back against the bark and tried to think about a nice chapel but he was so dreadfully cold, wet and hungry that he soon became delirious. The comforting visions of a well-ordered interior of a house of God slipped away and were replaced by glimpses of hell. He passed in and out of consciousness and bore witness to toiling demons, their leering visages lit by flashes of lightning. He no longer knew what was real. Northmen and devils became one. The sight of Runolf's severed leg mingled in, along with all the other unpleasant apparitions he had acquired on this ill-fated journey. The priest had forgotten why he had come. Some hazy heroic aspiration still lingered but it was almost gone. The Northmen had promised him glory but in truth, he was just following an idiotic barbarian with childish delusions to a premature demise. There was no turning back now though. He would never make it home by himself. The full realisation of his folly shone through his feverish nightmares and fuelled Satan's mirth.

'Holyman!... Holyman!... Wake up!'

The priest came back from the void. He looked into the bright blue eyes of Asger. Certainly more agreeable than Ulfric Fishface's ungodly mug.

'You do not look well, my friend.'

'I ... do not feel well,' croaked the priest, his voice a mere rasp.

'Perhaps this will make you feel better?' Asger gestured to the boat that he and his kinsmen had built. It was little more than a raft but it looked sturdy and impressive considering the circumstances.

The Northmen beamed at him like sons awaiting a father's approval.

It took all of the priest's strength just to smile. It felt like there was no blood in his veins, just ice.

Asger was undaunted. 'We are going fishing!'

*

The priest turned his nose up at the boat as the Northmen pushed it into the water. 'You must be mad if you think I'm getting onto that!'

'I'm not asking you to,' spat Magnus without looking at him. 'Asger and I are going out. You and Ulfric can stay here.'

The priest looked around with no less objection. They were back in the shelter of the ruins but he did not want to be alone with the Northman he disliked. The possibility that Magnus and his nephew would not return alive from the loch crossed his mind. He would be left with Ulfric Fishface for good. However, before he could raise a dispute, Asger spoke.

'Ulfric is not so keen on water, are you, Ulfric?'

The man in question shook his head briefly and turned away. 'I kept some dry kindling over here, under a rock,' he said and stomped off.

Asger sniggered at the priest. 'He had an accident.'

'Go on,' urged the holyman.

'The first time Ulfric got into a boat, he was leaning over the prow and an almighty salmon leapt from the water and delivered a blow to his face with its tail, breaking his nose.'

The priest chuckled and forgot his fever for a moment. 'You do not jest?'

'Nay, I do not jest! It is how Ulfric got his name.'

'I presumed he was called Fishface because he looked like one.'

Asger shook his blonde mane. 'He is Fishface because a fish changed his face.'

The priest and the Northman laughed together.

Magnus did not share the joke. 'Let us be gone! Before the light fails!' he grumbled. His eyes glimmered like a hungry wolf.

Asger sobered rapidly and stepped onto the vessel with him.

'It will be dark soon. When will you return?' the priest asked.

'We'll be back before you know it,' Asger reassured him. 'With the head of the kelpie!'

They rowed gently away. The priest watched them drift out onto the smoking surface of the loch. Seeing two large, fully-armoured men floating on such a flimsy craft made the priest fear for them. He gripped the cross around his neck and prayed. He could not decide if they were brave or just plain stupid. Surely just the tiniest of commotions in the loch would tip them over and send them to a watery grave, anchored down by all that steel. He had the feeling that he would not see them again. He sat and tried to come to terms with the inevitable consequence of being left with the most repellent and vulgar of the foreigners. Knowing where Ulfric Fishface had gotten his name made him slightly more cheerful but it was of little consolation. As the fishermen vanished like ghosts into the murk, the priest made himself as comfortable as he possibly could and passed into reverie again.

*

His third and final day in the realm of Satan began slowly and dreadfully. He heard a noise not unlike that of a gigantic serpent slithering slowly from the shore to devour him. Before he had even opened his eyes, the sounds of scales grinding on pebbles filled his ears, accompanied by the rasps of its vicious breath. His heart quickened and the priest awoke, a scream on his lips. It did not come. He saw the Northmen clambering out of their vessel. They looked cold and wet and miserable but it was them and not the beast.

'You have been out all night?' the priest quizzed, regaining his senses.

'Aye,' Asger nodded. 'We saw no sign of our prey.'

The priest looked at Magnus and the chief's dour expression echoed the younger man's disappointment.

'That is probably because it does not exist,' groaned the priest.

Magnus bared his teeth as if to make some angry retort but none came.

'Unless this is the fabled dragon of the loch?' ventured Asger, dragging a carcass from the raft. He tossed it at the feet of the priest and it hit the rocky ground with a soft wet splatter.

The holyman gazed down at the article with disgust. It appeared to be some sort of dead dog or cat thing with a slick paddle-like tail. Blood dripped from a rend in its neck where the Northmen had hooked it. The stench of its damp fur and fresh blood assailed his disapproving nostrils. 'What in God's name is this?'

Asger shrugged with playful amusement. 'Well, it's not a dragon. Breakfast perhaps?'

'I'm not eating that!' sniffed the priest, even though his empty belly rumbled with the prospect of eating anything.

Magnus cut short the caper. 'Where is Ulfric?'

The priest stared around. The Northman he had been left with was nowhere to be seen. There was not even a fire to indicate that Ulfric had returned to the old fort. He had not seen him since Magnus and Asger had departed the previous evening. In his sickness, he had slept right through. His mouth dropped open with horrible realisation.

'You have not seen him?' barked Magnus.

'No,' said the priest.

'Thor's hammer!' roared the chief, his fury bouncing off the crags. 'Can you do nothing, holyman?' He glared at him.

The priest had yet to move. His limbs were paralysed from cold and now he was rooted in place for fear of his mortal life. The leader of the Northmen had emerged from the boat with his broadsword in hand and he had yet to sheath it. 'I …'

Asger interjected. 'Come now, Uncle! It was not the holyman's place to guard Ulfric. Our kinsman was the warrior of the two. If he has wandered off and gotten himself killed then it's his own fault.'

Magnus stomped around and swung his fabulous blade in agitation. The sense of Asger's words slowly penetrated his wrath and tamed it. 'You are right.' He turned towards the priest. 'Forgive me.'

The man of God found some vitality in his limbs and rose to his feet though he stumbled slightly with the effort. Asger shot out a gauntleted hand to help steady him. 'I share your despair, Magnus. I did not like Ulfric but I hope no harm has come to him. Perchance he has fallen asleep somewhere else?'

Asger nodded in agreement. 'Ulfric has a taste for the womenfolk. Could it be that he has returned to the place up the road to sate his appetite?'

'I hope not!' said the priest. 'Given his vow to God and my promise to the lady that lives there.'

'It's worth a look,' Asger sniffed. 'Don't you think, Uncle?'

The chieftain sighed and nodded. 'Let us hope that he has broken his vow and ruined your promise, holyman, for if this monster has claimed another of our kind then I fear I shall not be able to contain myself. Our twelve will have become just three.'

'I shall go and look for him,' the priest stretched his arms with resolve.

'Asger, go with him,' ordered Magnus.

'And leave you here alone, my lord?' objected the priest.

'Aye,' said Magnus. 'This dragon is the most cowardly of creatures and takes us in the dark, one by one. I shall remain and see if my solitude tempts it out of its hiding place. Once it does ...' The Chieftain held up his sword to emphasise his point. '... I shall take its head and this nightmare will be over.'

The younger Northman and the priest stared at him for a few moments and nodded their understanding. They commenced their errand, Asger having to support his learned friend as they walked.

'Holyman?'

The priest stopped and looked back at Magnus.

'However this ends, you will record my deeds with your writing?'

The priest attempted to smile but his mouth drooped limply from his pale face. 'That was my promise to you, my lord.'

Magnus exhaled sharply as if with some kind of relief. 'Then Valhalla I am come.'

There was nothing more to be said. The priest and Asger stopped once to look back at their leader before their climb out of the valley. The fearless warrior was stood on the edge of the loch, still like a statue, gazing out across the water with his blade on his shoulder, daring his opponent to reveal itself.

'May the wrath of God be with him,' commented the priest.

'Magnus is the wrath of God,' muttered Asger.

*

Progress was slow and painful. By the time they reached Mary McDoon's croft, the priest was dripping with sweat, so much so that his robes were damp. His breath came in shallow gasps and he had to halt every few steps to vent the liquid from his lungs. Asger's grip had failed him once and the priest had taken a bad fall. Dark blood seeped from a gash on his forehead. The Northman was virtually carrying the priest's shuddering frame as they arrived at the stone walls of the croft. The two men scanned the scene before them. The glow of fire coloured the windows of the house and wisps of smoke snaked up into the air from the chimney. They could hear the dull thud of an axe chopping wood from somewhere within. It seemed like heaven after spending two full days in the wet and gloom.

'We are here,' stated Asger, unnecessarily. 'Even if Ulfric is not, perhaps the lady will show some mercy and care for you?'

The priest regarded him with rheumy eyes. 'Perhaps.'

'Stay here a moment and I shall approach,' suggested the Northman. 'My charm on the ladies has yet to fail.' He leaned his companion against the stone, transferring his support to the structure.

The priest clutched hold of the wall and wheezed, striving to regain some rhythm to his breathing.

Asger took off his helmet to reveal his golden locks and good looks. He placed it on the wall next to the priest. Despite the hopelessness of their predicament, he wore a cheeky grin. 'Magnus for the monster-slaying. Asger for the woman-pleasing. Each to their own.'

'Try not to frighten them,' whispered the priest without looking up.

'I'll try!' sniggered Asger and leapt over the wall. His armour jangled and a dog barked.

'Asger! Wait! You do not speak their tongue.'

'I've picked up a few of your words along the way,' said he. 'I shall let my handsome face do most of the talking.'

The warrior bounded across the yard to the house like a youth on his way to a feast.

The priest watched him with amusement, forgetting his discomfort for a moment.

What he saw next happened so swiftly that the priest could have dismissed the vision as a figment of his tortured imagination. He could do nothing except stand and stare, still desperately grasping the rock to stop himself from keeling over with the shock. No sooner had Asger reached the walls of the house than Mary McDoon appeared to greet him with an axe. There was a flash of light from the blade as it was swung into the Northman's head. In a heartbeat, his friend was reduced to a lifeless heap on the ground, blood jetting across his shining armour, his corpse twitching. And that was that. A warrior from the lands of the north, so full of joy and courage and spirit, became just meat.

'No!' cried the priest, though his protest had the volume of a dormouse.

Four of Mary's daughters joined their murderous mother and wasted no time in dragging Asger's body inside. They laughed and squealed and so great was their delight in their terrible deed that they did not notice the robed man hugging their wall. Even their dog was oblivious to his presence, the creature caught up in the jubilation of its matriarchs.

The priest was left alone, his abused senses struggling with the reality of what had just happened. He froze for a long time, swaying like a diseased sapling in the wind. He then clambered over the wall. It was a clumsy effort and the priest knocked Asger's helmet from its perch. It clattered onto the stone. The dog barked and the women emerged from the house to see him. Somewhat idiotically, the priest glared down at the youth's helmet and wondered if it would have saved him from the ghastly assault. Probably not.

'We have another visitor, girls!' announced Mary, her tone cruel and mocking. 'My! How we shall feast this winter!'

As if drawn to his fate, the priest stumbled towards the women. His vision had grown dim but he could see that they were all flame-haired and beautiful, like their mother. They smiled at him poisonously, like serpents.

'Have you come to join your friends?' asked Mary.

The priest dared to peer into the confines of the house. Just beyond the doorway, lit by fire, three lumps of meat hung on large hooks, swinging and dripping.

Three familiar lumps of meat.

'There's not much flesh on him, mam,' observed little Agnes.

'He'll do for the dog,' said she.

The Perfect Gift

'A drink for everyone!' announced Benedict White, raising a robust wallet into the air and slapping it down on the bar.

Despite the charitable offer there was a meagre show of enthusiasm from the other punters.

'I'm feeling generous today,' he explained, undaunted. 'It feels good to be alive, after all.' He turned to the two workmen perched next to him. 'What the French call joie de vivre, eh?'

The dusty duo returned blank expressions. They tried smiling and said "cheers, mate" as their pints of lager were poured but that was all.

The other couple in the corner of the pub accepted the offering with muttered thanks. The woman was old and took her half-a-Guinness with a shaky liver-spotted hand. Her male companion was much younger, probably her son, Benedict surmised, and wanted only orange cordial. His big round shiny face hinted learning difficulties. They both looked like they had been planted there for decades. The same thin layer of dust coated them and the couch they sat on. He took their tipples over to them and considered conversation but one glance into their glazed eyes told him he would not get very far. His expensive suit, perfect teeth, manicured hands and lust for life had erected a social barrier between him and the entire establishment. His best bet was the landlord. There was more cheer and sentience in the features of the old walrus than those of his lunchtime clientele.

'One for yourself,' Benedict nodded at the change.

'Thank you, sir,' said the landlord, shovelling the coins back into the till with his oversized hands.

'It's gloomy out there,' ventured Benedict, thumbing out of the window. He meant the weather but realised that he could have been referring to the place.

'Aye,' agreed the landlord. 'It's supposed to brighten up later.'

Benedict took a sip of his whisky and ice and smacked his lips together in satisfaction, somewhat theatrically.

The landlord polished some glasses and glanced at him. 'Not from round here, are you, sir?'

'Actually, I am,' he smiled, pleased with himself. 'Sort of.'

The two workmen to his right nodded with approval, seemingly more comfortable knowing he was a fellow native.

'I boarded at St. Edward's.'

'The posh school?' enquired the landlord.

'Yes, I suppose you could say that,' said Benedict.

The workmen were disappointed. He was not one of them after all. They shifted their attention back to their newspapers, finding more comfort in naked teenage girls, murder and scandal.

'My cousin went there,' remarked the publican.

'What year?'

He peered into thin air while he worked it out, as if the answer was being spelt out by the trails of dust that floated through the atmosphere. 'Long time ago now; the early sixties I'd say. No! Hold on, late sixties more like.

'I would have been a few years his junior,' concluded Benedict. 'What was his name?'

'Jack Moss,' replied the landlord. 'Dead now.'

'Sorry to hear that,' said Benedict.

'Don't be,' sniffed the landlord. 'He was an arsehole.'

The workmen laughed at this.

Benedict did not understand the humour.

The landlord went away to serve an impatient customer in the lounge and Benedict contented himself with gazing through the window at the shop across the road.

When he returned, Benedict asked 'do you know what time that place opens?'

The landlord stared out at the shop as if he had never seen it before and shook his head. 'I'm not sure it ever does,' he replied, unhelpfully.

Lunchtime meandered into afternoon and Benedict gave up trying to fit in. The two workmen soon stumbled off back to their labour anyway. He sat in silence and eased his way through more Scotch. The light in the taproom changed several times and Benedict kept glancing from his watch to the shop over the road. A couple of times he chanced to glimpse over his shoulder at the couple in the corner, just for something else to look at. He noticed that the young man's hand was resting on the old lady's knee, under the table, and it made him shiver. Perhaps they were not related or perhaps they were. Incest was probably not a taboo around here. The place had always given him the creeps. For decades, it seemed to be a refuge for people that society had left behind and, in turn, they gave birth to others who would be left even further behind. It was strange that his old school was just up the road; an institution that groomed its occupants for success. It was unfair, of course, but if he had to reflect on England's social divide he would rather do it from the upper crust.

It was not long before the odd couple left too and Benedict allowed himself a smirk as the elderly woman led the boy out by his hand.

Mummy's special boy he thought.

So preoccupied was Benedict with this perverse notion that he almost missed his signal. A small, thin man in an oversized raincoat appeared over the road, outside the shop. The man fumbled with his keys, unlocked the door and virtually disappeared inside before Benedict noticed.

As if by magic, the shopkeeper appeared.

'Lacey!' he immediately drained the golden contents of his glass. He hurried on his own raincoat, raced out of the pub and shot across the street, almost barging into the odd couple who were leaving the pub at a snail's pace.

The owner of the shop turned his "closed" sign to "open". His eyes narrowed with suspicion at Benedict. At first, there was no recognition. The penny dropped slowly. 'My apologies, old boy! I didn't recognise you.'

'Has it been that long?' chuckled Benedict, shaking his hand warmly as he stepped inside.

Lacey examined him up and down. 'You look different somehow.'

'I've lost a little weight perhaps?' suggested the visitor, patting his gut. 'Or maybe it's my tan? I've just got back from Brazil.'

'That could be it.' Lacey gurned. 'South America, eh?'

'Yes, I've got a house over there now. A large one.'

The shopkeeper nodded in approval. 'You've done very nicely for yourself, Benny.'

'I've tried my best. And how have you been, Lacey?'

He shrugged his bony shoulders. 'Same as ever.'

'I was beginning to think that you weren't going to open today. I've been waiting in that dreadful pub for over an hour.'

'I'm sorry about that. These days I tend to open when I like and close when I like.'

'But you knew I was coming?'

Lacey scratched his flaky scalp. 'Must have slipped my mind. Again; my sincere apology.'

'I will accept your apology,' said Benedict. 'I've had to endure some of the local residents. What a bunch of zombies!'

'Yes,' agreed Lacey with a solemn nod. 'This area has gone to the dogs, I'm afraid, not that I have much to do with it anymore. I just deal with my customers and most of those are outsiders. It's strictly import and export and I prefer it that way, to be honest.'

'Good,' agreed Benedict who had started to glance around the shop.

Lacey slapped him affectionately on the shoulder 'You have a good look around while I open up.'

The proprietor scuttled off and swiftly vanished amongst the crowded aisles of stock. Benedict advanced a great deal more tentatively, peering around at the merchandise with wide eyes like an astonished owl. Lacey's shop tended to have that effect on its customers. There was no order to it; the place was piled high with every piece of junk known to mankind and it was bewildering to look upon. Only Lacey had grown accustomed to its chaos. Next to Benedict, a ceramic Chinese dog sat happily next to a gas mask, a toy fire-engine, a box of rusty springs, a book about rivers, a multi-coloured umbrella, a mouse-trap, a tiny brass bell, some war medals, a telescope and a pair of shoes that seemed too big for any conceivable human being and that was just one shelf of thousands. Benedict inhaled sharply and the stench of old things filled his nostrils and made them twitch. He mooched around, browsing idly, drowsy from the flood of lunchtime whisky. He wanted to sit down in a corner of the shop that housed a selection of random furniture. Benedict fancied a purple chaise in the shadow of a vast antique gramophone but just as he aimed his buttocks, Lacey reappeared.

'Sorry, Benny, this isn't the stuff you want to see, is it?'

'I want to see the special things,' concurred the customer, straightening up.

Lacey nodded. He had changed out of his raincoat and into his shopkeeper's coat that looked very similar. 'By all means.'

Benedict grinned and found some fresh vigour.

The shopkeeper led him through the labyrinth of jumble to a plain and unassuming wooden door in a plain and unassuming wooden wall. It was almost indistinguishable and Benedict suspected that the subterfuge was intentional. Lacey drew out a mighty ring of keys and unlocked the door at the top, then at the bottom, then in the middle, in a well-rehearsed ritual.

Benedict licked his lips with anticipation.

Lacey looked back at him, smiled and opened the door. He led him up a set of wooden stairs that were as nondescript as the entry. Their shoes echoed on the bare timber.

'Anything new?' probed Benedict.

Lacey briefly faltered in his ascent. 'Since you were last here? Probably, yes! I've acquired some very unique oddities lately.'

The two men climbed to the first floor. It was the same size as the one below and the odour of age lingered but it was cooler, darker and far less crowded. The items for sale on the ground floor jostled for space but in the secret chamber above, everything was granted plenty of room. Objects were hung on the walls or set out carefully on tables or on pedestals or displayed inside glass cases. Benedict allowed himself a few moments to take it all in and Lacey stood and enjoyed his customer's reaction, glowing with pride.

'Lacey's Cornucopia of Wonders!' expressed the customer.

'I like that, yes,' the shopkeeper nodded with approval.

Something caught Benedict's eye; a slender metal artefact that glinted in the light from the room's solitary window. He strolled towards it, his brow furrowed in fascination. Lacey trailed after him and peered over his shoulder as he crouched down to examine it.

'This looks old,' Benedict hissed. 'A broadsword? Saxon?'

'Viking,' Lacey corrected him.

'Is it authentic?'

'Of course,' sniffed the shopkeeper. 'Or else it would be downstairs with the rest of the tat.'

'It's a bit battered.'

'So would you be if you were a millennium old. It was found on the banks of Loch Ness, sticking out of the mud.'

Benedict turned to him with an incredulous expression. 'Are you sure?'

Lacey shrugged his shoulders, a gesture almost lost in the immensity of his oversized coat. 'That's what I was told.'

'I didn't know the Vikings ever went that far inland.'

'I don't think anyone else did either.'

'You could be sat on an important archaeological discovery, Lacey.'

The shopkeeper scratched his bony nose. 'I have frequent visits from museum curators. They're welcome to bid for it, same as anyone else. A man has to earn a living.'

Benedict stood erect and smirked. Lacey obviously stung with guilt. Benedict imagined the room full of frustrated museum curators, all bidding for the remarkable sword. In reality, he had never seen anyone else in Lacey's shop, despite regular visits for decades. He always felt like the establishment existed just for him though it was an arrogant notion; the objects came and went and other patrons must have visited.

'I'll probably leave them to it. It's not what I'm looking for.'

'What are you looking for, Benny?'

'The perfect gift,' said he, elusively, and strolled off to another part of the room to inspect the statue that stood there. 'This fellow is rather spectacular.'

Lacey pulled out a dented tin of tobacco from the depths of his coat and began to roll a cigarette with fingers that were stained with too many previous constructions. 'Isn't he!' he agreed without looking up.

Benedict stood level with the muscular wooden man and gazed into his pupiless eyes with delight. 'This might be more appropriate. Who's the artist?'

'I can't tell you anything about it, I'm afraid. I acquired it from a small museum and they had no information to go with it.'

Benedict looked at him. 'More disgruntled curators?'

'I should think so, the whole place burnt down to the ground!' explained Lacey with a perverse snigger. 'They lost everything.'

'Except for this?' the customer turned back to the statue.

'Quite,' Lacey nodded. 'A miraculous survival.'

Benedict shivered and took a step back from the figure. 'Hmm. I'm not so keen all of a sudden.'

'Gives you the creeps, doesn't it? There's something not right about it. I mean; you would expect it to burn. It's made out of wood.'

'Perhaps it was in the grounds as opposed to the actual building?' Despite his logical conclusion, Benedict continued to put distance between him and the statue.

'Perhaps.' The shopkeeper lit his roll-up, filling the chamber with anaemic blue smoke.

Benedict turned his nose up at him. 'Are you allowed to smoke in here?'

Lacey turned red. 'It's my bloody shop! I'll do as I please!'

Benedict laughed at his reaction and went to look at some green rocks in a glass case. 'You had these last time I was here.'

Lacey took a deep drag on his cigarette and then stubbed it out with his shoe. 'The meteorite fragments? Yes.'

Benedict laughed at him again. 'I was only teasing you about the smoking, you know.'

'This talk of things burning down has put me off,' said Lacey.

'Can't find a buyer then?'

'For the fragments? No. I was told they were very rare and much sought after.'

Benedict's amusement continued. 'You've been in this game long enough not to fall for the patter, Lacey.'

'Seemed reasonable enough to me.' The shopkeeper came and stood next to him. 'I did have some potential customers but they didn't want to pay for them. They said the rocks were dangerous and that I should just hand them over.'

'Maybe they're radioactive?'

Lacey shook his head. 'These people didn't look like scientists. There were three of them and a dog. They were knocking on a bit and they were dirty and scruffy. One of the old boys just talked gibberish at me.'

'Sound like scientists to me,' Benedict giggled.

'If you want to buy them, I'll do you a deal.'

'No, thanks,' said the customer and wandered off with his hands in his pockets.

Lacey gazed at him and scratched the white stubble on his chin, thoughtfully. 'How about a Sasquatch scalp? I got one sent over from America. What was the place called again? That's it; Devil's Creek, Oregon.'

Benedict turned round and watched him whilst he fetched the article from a shelf. It looked like half of an enormous coconut with orangey-brown hairs sprouting from it. 'What the hell would I do with that? It's disgusting!'

Lacey squirmed, desperately searching for a reason. 'Why don't you give me an idea of what you're looking for?'

'I'll know it when I see it. In a rush are you?'

Somewhat exasperated, Lacey scanned his chamber and laid eyes upon a knackered old rowing boat hanging from the ceiling. 'Ah!'

'What?' quizzed Benedict, following his point of focus.

'An offer you can't refuse,' explained Lacey. His lips contorted in what passed for a smile on his scrawny features. 'I won't sell this to any old Tom, Dick or Harry, you know.'

Benedict stared up at the boat. 'Your suggestions are getting worse, Lacey, I'm a hopeless sailor.'

'It's not the boat I'm selling. It's the words that have been etched into it.'

Benedict took a couple of steps closer and peered into the dark confines of the rotten craft. Sure enough, crude letters had been scratched into the timber. He glanced at Lacey for enlightenment.

'The final testimony of a pirate,' muttered the shopkeeper in a hushed melodramatic tone. 'He carved his story into the boat before he died in it.'

Benedict glared at him blankly for a moment. 'Have you read it?'

'I've tried,' said Lacey. 'My eye sight isn't what it used to be. And these damn glasses they've given me are no use.'

His customer, however, was not listening. Another of Lacey's commodities had caught his eye and he was drawn towards it as if mesmerised.

The shopkeeper followed him and he too gazed at the picture hanging on the wall.

The two men stood in silence for a while. So long in fact that Lacey turned to stare at his client and wondered if he had become catatonic. 'Benny?'

'This is it!'

'I don't know if I can sell it to you,' Lacey decided immediately.

Benedict turned to him, looking cross. 'Why ever not?'

'It's cursed.'

The customer glared at him and then laughed. He switched his attention back to the painting. It was a portrait of a young boy in a Victorian suit, yellow hair poking out from beneath his little cap. It was far from being a spectacular piece of art but there was something in the youth's tear-stained face that was expressive; a raw kind of anguish.

Lacey went on; 'At one time, The Crying Boy was a common feature of many a terraced household, like those flying geese.'

Benedict nodded. 'I recall seeing it somewhere before.'

'Trouble is that anyone who owns a copy seems to befall some bizarre and horrible demise. They're quite rare now. If you ask me it's hard to see why anyone would want a miserable looking child on their wall anyway.'

'Perhaps there's some pleasure to be found in the folly of youth?'

Lacey frowned at the picture. 'And the punishment of it? The poor lad looks like he's been abused.'

'And that's why I want it,' snorted Benedict. He drew out a handkerchief and wiped his sweaty neck.

Lacey's frown deepened. 'You want a cursed portrait of an abused child?'

'It's a damn sight more appropriate than a bloody yeti head and a pirate's boat!'

The shopkeeper grunted and stepped away. He found the cigarette he had stubbed out on the floor and felt the need to resurrect it.

'It's for Hayes,' the customer explained.

Lacey glanced back at him. 'Who's Hayes?'

'Our old geography master.'

'Good god! Is he still alive?'

'Yes,' replied Benedict with a regretful sigh.

Lacey lit up and shook his head at him through the pale blue smoke. 'He must have been pushing forty when we there. Christ! What a sadistic bastard! I remember when he punched Wiffy Carter and broke the poor little blighter's nose. Some of us got splattered with his blood. Why didn't he get the chop for that?'

'They just covered it up,' Benedict said quietly.

'How the hell could they? The lad's nose was ruined!'

'I don't know. Somehow they did. They wanted to protect him. I'll never understand why.' The customer had taken on a strange manner. He stood still, with his arms limp at his sides and his head low.

Lacey peered at him with concern. 'Are you alright, Benny?'

Benedict nodded but clearly was not alright.

'Did he hit you too?'

'Not exactly,' he muttered and screwed his eyes up.

Lacey chuckled but out of discomfort. 'I don't understand.'

Benedict kept still and struggled to find the words. 'He …there were things going on at that school …things most people don't know about …'

'Like what?'

'Hayes … he took me to his room … he … had sherry on his breath … his hands …'

It took a long time for his customer to say very little but Lacey understood. He backed off slightly, his mouth agape, his cigarette burning, untouched. 'No need to spell it out. I get the picture.'

Benedict recovered slightly. He opened his eyes. 'It only happened once or twice but that stuff never leaves you.'

'I can't imagine,' said Lacey. 'You never told anyone?'

Benedict shrugged his shoulders. 'Who could I tell? My father? My mother? Bless her. Half of the teachers at our school were at it. Who could I trust? To be honest with you, Lacey, it was a long time before I could even talk to myself about it. Do you understand?'

'I understand. What I don't get is why on earth you want to buy him a painting?'

Benedict became fully animated again. 'Look at it!'

Lacey was forced to stare into the distraught cherub's tearful eyes again.

'It's the perfect symbol,' explained the customer. 'A reminder to an old man of the dreadful things he's done.'

Lacey took a couple of drags and thought about it. 'If you say so.'

'The curse is just a bonus,' added Benedict. 'Let's hope it finishes the devil off.'

The shopkeeper looked at him. 'It's a little strange, Benny. Plus I can't guarantee the curse. I've had it in my shop for nearly a year and I'm still breathing.'

'I'll give you a thousand for it,' said Benedict, trying a language Lacey could understand better.

The shopkeeper guffawed and looked around as if to appeal to an audience that was not there. 'Bloody hell, Benny! You can have it if you want it! A hundred will suffice.'

Benedict grinned and walked over to slap the proprietor's bony shoulder. Some colour had filtered back into his cheeks. 'A thousand I say!'

'You're the worst haggler I've ever known.'

The customer laughed heartily and fully resumed his jolly self. 'Let's call it a contribution to your retirement, Lacey. An investment even. We could be neighbours in Brazil!'

'The lunchtime drink has got to you, Benny. I suspected it, now I'm convinced!'

'Get it down and wrap it up for me before I change my alcohol-sodden mind,' smirked Benedict as he pulled out his cheque book.

'There's other ways, you know?'

Benedict glanced at him. 'What do you mean?'

'You could just bury the past.'

'This is what *I am* doing. Burying the past.'

Lacey busied himself and unhooked The Crying Boy from the wall and took it over to the counter to wrap it in brown paper and tie it with string. 'Do you know where he lives?' he asked as he did so.

'It took me a long time to find him but, as it turned out, he didn't move too far away.'

'Are you going to deliver it to him in person?'

'I'll probably just leave it on the porch.'

'Then I wish you the best of luck with it.'

There was nothing more to be said between the two friends. Reminiscing about old times or musings on the recent weather could not follow such a terrible revelation. Lacey wrapped the article. Benedict paid for it. They shook hands and he left.

Out on the street the sun had grown fierce and low but the brilliance was lost in the shade of the pub. Benedict had to squint as he carried his purchase round the monolith to where he had parked his car. As he crossed from the gloom into the hot sunlight of the car park his head swam suddenly and his mouth felt dry. Outlined by the astonishing white light, he could make out two figures who were made giants by their shadows. They were stood by his Jag. Benedict hesitated. He had to lift his arm up to see them properly.

'Wallet and car keys!' demanded the closest of the two apparitions.

Benedict saw the two workmen he had bought drinks for in the bar.

'Wallet and car keys, nobhead!' growled the closest again, louder and more urgent. These men did not seem so friendly now. It occurred to Benedict that they had not been too sociable in the first place. The one furthest away seemed to be inspecting the Jag and laughing at what his amigo was saying.

'Give me your wallet and your car keys!' came the request a third time. The ape was bunching his fists and bulging his eyes with anger. He stepped right up to Benedict and began to thrust his dusty face at him.

Benedict stepped back and looked around for help. He saw the landlord in the pub but the old walrus merely glanced through the window at them and then closed the curtains like there was nothing going on. There was no one else.

'Are you fucking deaf?'

Benedict fumbled. He tried to get the requested objects out of his pocket and dropped the painting under his arm in the process. It tumbled onto the ground. He suddenly found his courage. 'I'm not giving you anything, barbarian! Get out of my way!'

The other man laughed again.

The aggressor drew out a blade. 'Give me your shit, old man, or I swear to God I'll fucking cut you up!'

For some reason unknown to him, Benedict said 'Go on then! Do it!'

And he did it.

The next thing Benedict knew he was lying on the ground, his white suit gradually turning red. Curiously, it did not hurt. He just felt tired and cold. He laid there and watched as the two men took his money and keys and drove away in his car. The wheels kicked up a cloud of dust and Benedict had to wait a few moments before he could see anything again. When the maelstrom cleared, all he saw was the painting, lying next to him. The robbers had not bothered with it. It was a while before anyone found him and a great deal longer before anyone found him who felt the need to call for an ambulance. The Crying Boy was his solitary companion. By the time he heard the sirens, it was too late.

Jellyhead

'I suppose this is it,' said the man called Mark Lyons.

'I suppose it is,' agreed the man called Ray Weaver.

'Civilised handshake?' suggested Mark.

They performed the social ritual. It was followed by a brief episode of silence while both men glanced around the car park, as if searching for more to say.

Mark found inspiration first. 'It's going to be a lot more normal around here without you.'

'I'll take that as a compliment.' said Ray.

Mark laughed. 'Remember that article you wrote about the rock that could sing?'

'Yeah,' Ray laughed too but without any genuine mirth.

'Turned out it was a nearby gas leak?' Mark's ample frame juddered with hilarity.

'Good times,' said Ray with a generous measure of sarcasm and melancholy.

'Do you remember that charity cricket match when you knocked out that kid in a wheelchair with the ball?'

'At least he was already sat down. And it scored us a few runs.' Ray waited politely for Mark to stop guffawing like an asthmatic buffalo.

'Well, Ray, I don't think it would be unfair to say that we've never really been friends.'

'No,' concurred Ray. 'It wouldn't be unfair to say that.'

'I think I'll miss you though, in some strange way. I just hope I never work with anyone else who thinks it's hilarious to superglue me to the toilet seat.'

'Sorry about that.' Ray noticed that Mark had a tear in his eye, though he was not sure if it grew from joy, sadness or humiliation. 'I'm not one for big goodbyes, Mark. You're the editor of the paper now. You can do what you want. There won't be any wankers like me or Archie making your life a misery.'

'No, well, you'd better be getting off.' Mark slapped him awkwardly on the shoulder.

Ray smiled thinly and nodded. 'I've got a present for you.' He fetched something in a carrier bag from the back seat of his car.

Mark accepted the offering, pulling the object out of the bag with amazement. 'Your dartboard?'

'I was going to take it with me but I want you to have it,' explained Ray. 'Besides, there's a mark on the office wall where it used to be. It's a choice of keeping it or getting the place redecorated.'

'I shall treasure it,' said Mark, nodding and grinning with authentic approval.

Suddenly, there was a muffled racket from the car, like someone was trapped in the boot.

Mark's eyes bulged. 'What was that?'

'Nothing,' said Ray and got in the driver's seat. 'Good luck, Mark.'

'Yes,' he replied. 'Good luck to you too.'

Ray took one last look at his former colleague as he shut the door. He ignited the engine, found first gear and took off the handbrake. He was about to pull away when Mark knocked on his window. Ray indulged him.

'Ray?'

'Yeah?'

'Do you think she'll be alright?'

'Maybe.'

'I think I loved her.'

'Yeah, me too.'

Ray drove off and caught one last sight of Mark in his rear view mirror. The idiot was waving. Ray shook his head and smirked slightly. He had one last stop to make before he left Fogwin for good.

*

Out of all the terrible and horrific experiences that I have endured as a paranormal investigator it is Jellyhead that haunts me the most.

Excerpt from the journal of Ray Weaver, volume one.

*

Ray tossed what he could find in a suitcase. He was baffled by a lack of underpants and wondered if his wife had destroyed them as a final act of retribution. The absence of his favourite Dr Who Y-fronts was a particular mystery. Just as such mundane trepidations began to trouble him he spotted The Professor in his bedroom doorway, shadowing him like a camp ghost.

'Leaving?' the enigmatic scholar enquired with both hands in his pockets.

Ray stared at him and nodded slowly. 'When all this bollocks is over, yeah. There's nothing here for me anymore, is there?'

'Where will you go?'

'Back to London I suppose.'

'I thought you hated it?'

'I do but not as much as I hate this place.'

'Want to come downstairs and meet the gang?'

Ray abandoned the packing and followed his guest to the ground floor. He was alarmed to discover that his house now contained other freaks: A sweaty spherical-shaped man was busy cooking himself a full English breakfast in the kitchen whilst a woman sat on a stool and watched him, nursing a cup of black coffee. She was easier on the eye than the globular cook but her long black hair, long black dress and long black stare made her look like a Goth who was old enough to have left that phase behind. He stared at them both.

'The famous Ray Weaver!' commented the breakfaster, turning round briefly and revealing a cast-iron mullet.

Ray was stunned. 'You've heard of me?'

'No!' the man sniggered. 'I'm taking the piss, like.' There was a smattering of Geordie in his accent.

'Oh,' Ray tried to laugh.

'Don't mind if I help myself to some nosebag, do you?'

'Knock yourself out,' said Ray.

'This is Billy Briggs,' explained The Professor. 'He's a photographer from The Tribunal.'

'The Tribunal?'

Billy swung round again and tossed a few squares of toast onto a plate. 'It's a new rag. We started up about six months ago. We specialise in weird stories, like.'

Ray frowned and put his hands in his pockets. 'You've invited another journalist?'

The Professor shrugged his shoulders. 'Billy is the country's leading paranormal photographer.'

Ray smirked. 'You mean he's the country's *only* paranormal photographer?'

'Gathering visual evidence is crucial in this line of work, Ray,' stated The Professor, sounding slightly cross. 'And this man is the best.'

'My partner would be here,' added Billy. 'Only he seems to have mysteriously vanished whilst investigating mysterious vanishings; the ironic bastard!'

'I see,' mumbled Ray and turned his attention to the woman. 'And you are?'

'Maeve Dubois.' She extended a slender pale hand enigmatically.

She meant Ray to kiss it but he felt silly and opted to shake it instead.

Maeve jolted as he did so, as if she had suffered an electric shock.

'Alright, luv?'

'You poor man!'

The Professor intervened. 'Maeve is an accomplished psychic.'

Ray stepped back and looked at them both. 'You're pulling my pisser now?'

They shook their heads at him like the amused parents of a foolish child.

'American?' enquired Ray.

'Canadian,' she corrected him.

There followed an awkward silence or, at least, it was for Ray. The Professor and the woman just smiled calmly while it all sunk in.

It was Billy who broke the intermission. With well-rehearsed agility he transferred the separate parts of his breakfast from the cooker onto the platform of toast; bacon, sausages, black pudding, eggs, beans, mushrooms, tomatoes, hash browns. 'Sure you don't want some, beautiful?' he asked Maeve as he did so.

'No, thank you,' said she, sipping her coffee, contently.

Ray turned to The Professor. 'Can I have a word?'

They strolled through into the living room and gazed through the front window.

'I'm not being funny but when you said you were calling in the cavalry this isn't quite what I had in mind.'

'What do you mean?' The Professor growled.

Ray scratched the back of his neck. 'A heart-attack-waiting-to-happen and a fortune teller?'

'These people have unique skills that can help you, Ray. What did you expect? Knights in shining armour?'

'You just sort of got my hopes up and that,' he grumbled.

The Professor looked into his eyes. 'You need to trust me, old boy. Billy and Maeve are powerful allies of mine. In addition to their remarkable talents they have experience. Like you, they have seen things.'

'Alright,' Ray conceded. He looked like he was about to say something else when a mechanical racket from outside broke his attention. He and The Professor peered out into the front yard where an old fashioned motor bike and side car appeared, trailing enormous clouds of grey smoke.

'My chariot arrives!' The Professor beamed.

A man got off the antique wheels and removed his helmet.

'Who's this geezer?' Ray was stunned again.

'The fifth and final member of our little consortium,' said The Professor.

They watched as the bike rider crossed the yard and let himself into the house. He swaggered in his black leathers and darted glances to either side of him as if he was crossing a war zone. His dark skin and curly black hair signalled his origin unmistakably as that from the Middle-East or somewhere equally exotic. Ray could tell straight away that this was not a man to be messed with. There was something in his panther-like gait that suggested a trained and fearless killer. His complicated beard was equally as impressive.

'This hombre is a bit more like it,' whispered Ray, in awe.

'Kaleef,' The Professor smiled. 'My manservant.'

Ray burst out laughing. 'Your what? Your manservant?' What is that? Some kinky gay shit?'

'No!' snapped The Professor sharply and immediately. 'You must never say that! Not in front of him!'

'Alright,' Ray composed himself. 'Don't get your knickers in a twist.'

'Kaleef has yet to come to full terms with his sexuality,' explained The Professor, grabbing Ray's wrist to emphasise his seriousness.

The Arab biker entered the room bowed his head at them.

'Kaleef Ashanti Kalaleur,' The Professor returned the greeting.

Ray lit up a fag and giggled.

*

A cool breeze blew up the silk sheets and woke The Professor pleasantly. The fresh draught felt nothing less than ecstatic as it caressed his sweating genitalia. The first feature to grace his eyes as they opened was the smooth dark skin of the well-formed young man sleeping next to him. Even without his glasses on, The Professor laid there for a while and admired the youth's perfect back. He lifted his head slightly and glanced at the windows. They were open and golden sunlight streamed into the room. Saffron curtains billowed playfully in the breeze. From beyond came the early hubbub of the streets; close enough to be heard but far away enough to be unobtrusive. The wind brought hints of cinnamon, mint, paprika, ginger and other spices. Heavier scents of hashish and liquor hung in the room too and went some way to explaining why he could recall little of the night before. Judging by his throbbing head and coating of dried seamen it had obviously been a riotous evening. The four-posted bed was in the middle of an ornate bedroom fit for an Arabian king. He had no idea where he was but it was like a perfect dream. In his sleep he had revisited the streets of Cambridge and capered with his fellow scholars again. They were places and people he knew but they seemed oddly alien and unreal, as denizens of dreams often do. The Professor's grubby life at university juxtaposed with his new fairytale surroundings. He had come a long way. As he laid and contemplated, his bedfellow stirred.

'Hello there,' he croaked as the man turned and looked at him.

The Arab nodded slightly and scratched his head in bemusement.

'I thought you said no meat for Ramadan?' The Professor grinned.

The quip failed his companion. 'Professor?'

'You can call me Cedric if you like. Professor seems so formal and a tad seedy, considering our circumstances.'

'Kaleef,' he extended a hand.

'Please to meet you, Kaleef,' The Professor shook his hand; his plea for informality lost. Here they were in bed, naked, after all. At least the Arab had not asked him for any money yet. Considering the opulence of the chamber, perhaps the arrangement was the other way round.

There was a silence as they stared at each other, both wondering what to say next. The decision was taken away from either of them: From behind the bedroom door came an almighty clamour. It sounded like a large group of people running and shouting in their direction. The rumpus was accompanied by what sounded like swords being drawn.

'My father!' exclaimed Kaleef, sitting up and staring with horror at the door.

The Professor up righted himself too. 'Your father?' Kaleef did not have to explain. The Englishman knew that homosexuality was a dreadful crime in Morocco. They had been rumbled.

'You hide!' screamed Kaleef.

The Professor tried to get out of the bed quickly but he was still dizzy from the intoxicants that he had consumed and he stumbled wildly. His head span as he scanned the room for a suitable hiding place but, apart from the magnificent bed, it was virtually bare.

'Too late! We go!' yelled his panic-stricken lover just as the door burst open and a murderous mob poured in. They shouted in a language that The Professor could not understand but their outraged expressions and large curved swords gave him the gist.

Before The Professor knew it he was being dragged through the window and out onto a balcony by Kaleef. Momentarily, he glimpsed the insane height that they would have to jump to land in the river below. It was uncertain how many storeys they were up but the water appeared little more than a tiny brown ribbon. He was suddenly conscious that he was outside and nude in broad daylight but there was no time for any shame. Again, choice was not required of him. His new friend seized him by the neck and together they leapt. After all, a chance of death was preferable to certain death. As they dropped, the Professor realised that, should they survive, it was going to be an interesting day.

*

Top Model Missing
Published in the Fogwin Enquirer 30.4.1980.

Lucy Springer has been missing for over a week and was last seen in this area whilst visiting her family. Police are urgently appealing for any information and can be contacted on the telephone number at the bottom of the page. Lucy is twenty-three years old, about 5'10" in height, slim build with blonde hair and blue eyes. She is a professional model and has appeared in several national tabloids and on the television programme Sale of the Century.

*

'Don't worry, we'll find her,' Maeve placed a reassuring hand on Ray's shoulder. He was clearly anguished, sitting with his head in his hands.

'People round here go missing all the time and no one ever sees them again,' groaned Ray, his voice muffled by his fingers.

The clairvoyant sighed and turned to The Professor for support.

'This town does have a bit of a worrying history,' he explained. 'Ray's friend Magical Garry disappeared last year; abducted by alien creatures, a traumatising experience that Ray is able to recall only under hypnosis. A local resident knew where one of these things was hidden but he and the cadaver have also vanished. Ray suspects in the involvement of a very bizarre and powerful authority. Maybe even the new Tory government itself.'

'Seriously?' Billy Briggs scoffed.

Ray glared up at him through watery eyes.

'Alright!' Billy held out his palms in a gesture of defence. 'I believe you, mate. It's just ... this is big. What we've been waiting for. Right, Prof?'

The Professor nodded in agreement. 'Quite. That's why I asked you all to come here.' He peered round the kitchen at his assembled team. 'But you must understand the gravity of the situation. If what Ray suspects is true then we could all get into some very serious bother. If you have any reservations then I suggest you leave immediately.'

'Count me in,' Billy said after a few moments of silence. 'This is my line of work, like. Exposing the truth.' He held up his camera to emphasise his point.

The Professor turned to Maeve.

She just smiled back at him, her serene features conceding no doubt or fear. 'It's like Billy says; it's what we've been waiting for.'

'Good!' The Professor approved.

'What about matey?' Billy jabbed a thumb in the direction of Kaleef. He was sat in the darkest corner of the room, sharpening his scimitar, seemingly lost in his own world.

The Professor almost laughed. 'We don't need to worry about Kaleef.'

Billy nodded. 'So where do we start?'

The Professor turned to Ray. 'Mr Weaver?'

Ray glanced back at them all and scratched the neglected stubble on his jaw, thoughtfully. 'I don't know but I think all this shit revolves round this new industrial estate on the edge of town but, so far, I've not been able to get in to take a gander. My girlfriend's uncle owns it.'

'This is the missing girl?' asked Maeve.

'Yeah, it's built on a place called Knightsheath. The locals think it's haunted though I must confess that every bit of wood or patch of moor round here seems to have some sort of legend attached to it.'

'Then let's go and have a look,' Maeve decided.

'It's probably best if we go at night,' said Ray. 'It's well guarded.'

'Time for a pub lunch then?' Billy beamed and patted his vast stomach with potential delight.

'You've just had your breakfast!' Maeve pointed out.

The photographer shrugged his shoulders. 'By the time we've got there and had a few pints ...'

'Can you get us into this Knightsheath place, Ray?' enquired The Professor.

'I'll see what I can fix up,' nodded Ray, getting to his feet with some renewed determination.

'Then I think Billy is right; a tipple or two is in order,' The Professor clapped his hands together. 'Such a clandestine operation requires Dutch courage.'

*

'Will you get that fucking thing out of my boat race!' Ray swatted aside Billy's intrusive lens.

The rotund Geordie withdrew his camera. 'Sorry, mate. I was just taking yers picture for the Tribunal, like.'

Ray gave him his hardest glare. 'Perhaps I don't want to be in your stupid paper?'

'There's nothing stupid about the Tribunal, cockney,' Billy sniffed. 'Yers want to check it out some time. Might be an opening if yers interested.'

Ray glanced around the pub but its dim rustic interior was devoid of life. Occasionally the landlord would step through and regard his unusual lunchtime guests with weary barefaced suspicion. His dog appeared a couple of times with the same haggard look but that was all. It was a quiet old Edwardian place on the edge of town and its usual clientele consisted of workmen and farmers. Ray thought it would be discreet enough for their purposes. He took a deep swig on his pint. 'You what?'

'Like I said, my usual partner, Liam Allerdice, has gone missing. If he doesn't show up soon, we'll be advertising his job. Yers might have what it takes.'

'I'll see if we get through this mess first.' Ray stared deeply into his beer like it was a pint-shaped crystal ball that could reveal his destiny.

'Yers don't look too good though, mate,' commented Billy.

Maeve, who was sat next to Ray, intervened. 'Leave him be, Billy.'

'I didn't even drink or smoke till a year ago,' said Ray, offering his cigarettes around the table. 'Now I can't seem to stop.'

'It's a slippery slope,' grunted Billy, accepting one.

Maeve watched the two men with concern as they lit up. 'You've just lost your way, that's all.'

Ray turned and looked at her. 'Yeah, maybe.'

'We'll find your bonny lass,' said Billy, choking slightly. 'Then you come and join us big boys in the city. You've outgrown this one-horse town, Ray.'

The beleaguered publican approached them with a steaming roast dinner.

Billy's eyes lit up. 'Ah! Me lunch! Cheers, sunshine.'

The landlord scuttled away again.

Ray expected the photographer to stop smoking while he ate but Billy managed both at the same time; wolfing down gravy-drenched blobs of meat and veg and dragging on the fag in between mouthfuls like the world was about to end.

'So what's your excuse?' Ray felt the need to ask him.

'What do you mean?' Billy munched without pause, impressing Ray not only with his ability to eat and smoke but also to form coherent words.

Ray scratched his head. 'Well, the horrors I've seen …'

'No trauma for me,' explained Billy. 'I'm just a natural hard-drinking, chain-smoking bastard. I love it.'

'Fair enough,' said Ray.

Billy laughed raucously, revealing a gob full of half-chewed lunch.

Ray was compelled to look away. Oddly, The Professor and his so-called manservant were silent. They were perched at the other end of the table with solemn expressions and barely-touched drinks. Perhaps Cedric and Kaleef both had more understanding of the gravity of the situation, Ray surmised. Maybe Billy was just making enough noise for everyone. The unmistakable creak of the front door opening diverted his attention. Two men walked in. The shorter of the two wore a cheap suit and an expression of perpetual imprudence while the tall one was dressed more casually but so thin and drawn that he looked in danger of slipping out of existence at any moment.

'Ray,' the man in the suit nodded.

Ray introduced him to the others. 'Ladies and gentlemen, this fine figure of a man is my fellow reporter Mark Lyons.'

'Alright,' said Mark, looking around at them with a raised monobrow.

They returned vague greetings.

Mark turned to his colleague. 'Who are these people?'

Ray sniggered slightly. 'You wouldn't believe me if I told you, Mark, trust me.'

'This is Brian Temple,' Mark gestured to his skinny companion. 'He used to be a security guard at Earthcom and he reckons he can get you in.'

'Keep your voice down!' snarled Ray, peering around. 'Sit the fuck down!'

Mark and the man called Brian Temple hesitantly took seats with the collection of colourful strangers.

'You know a way in then, Brian?' queried Ray.

The former security guard nodded. 'It'll take you straight into the middle of the place though I'm not sure you really want to go there.'

'Let us worry about that, sniffed Ray. 'You're coming with us, Mark.'

'I am?'

'Yeah, I need some journalistic back-up in case I don't make it out alive, you savvy?'

'Okay, sure,' agreed Mark though the anxiety in his eyes betrayed him.

'You want a pint?' asked Ray.

'Go on then.'

'Brian?'

'Yes, please.'

'Billy?'

'Count me in'

'Professor?'

'Port and lemon juice.'

'Kaleef?'

'Nothing, thank you.'

'Maeve?'

'I'll come with you.'

She and Ray strolled over to the bar. They rang a little brass bell and waited for the publican to appear.

'Can you trust them?' asked Maeve.

'Who?'

'Those men.'

'Mark and Brian?'

'I sense fear in them.'

Ray rubbed his chin and looked into the Goth's green eyes. 'Well, I've been working with Mark for years. He's too much of an idiot to be any danger to anyone. I don't know his friend.'

Maeve put a dainty hand on his wrist. 'I sense doubts from you too, Ray.'

'Me?' he chuckled. 'I'm scared shitless, luv, I'll gladly admit it. But just stay out of my head, okay? I don't need another woman in there. That's what got me into trouble in the first place.'

She sighed and then smiled. 'I understand.'

'What's your poison?'

'I'm not sure,' said she, scanning the bottles on display behind the bar. 'I was a Bloody Mary fan but I've gone off that stuff recently. Reminds me of someone I don't want to think about right now.'

*

Maeve Dubois was rarely caught unaware by anyone. One evening in particular came her greatest defeat.

'Ms Dubois?'

The voice rumbled from behind her suddenly like an avalanche. The tone was baritone deep. Maeve almost screamed. She span round with wide eyes.

The man who was stood there bowed his head. 'My apologies, it was not my intention to startle you.'

Maeve scowled at the stranger. 'Startle me? My heart skipped a beat! How …?'

The man tried to smile through his shame. 'I'm so sorry. I'm a complete buffoon!'

She scrutinised him. He was plain to look upon; average height, average build, ordinary brown hair, equal features, yet there was something mysteriously individual about him too. Perhaps it was the antiquated air of grace in his courteous manner, the wisdom in his grey eyes, the thunderous voice or a combination of all.

'I caught your show tonight,' said he.

Maeve glanced around her dressing room. She felt no more at ease. The theatre was ancient and there was not a floorboard within its musty shell that did not creak. Not only had her sixth sense failed her but her more mundane wits had too.

'I saw you in Edinburgh last weekend and I thought you were great but this evening you were nothing less than sensational!'

Maeve could hear the intruder's words but she was not taking them in. Inwardly, she was still panicking and desperately trying to understand how he had approached her undetected. There was only one answer. She composed herself.

'Are you alright?' the aficionado asked.

'Yes,' she giggled, fanning herself. 'It's these stage shows, they exhaust me.'

'Of course,' the man nodded. 'Talking to those on The Other Side must be a huge strain.'

'Yes, it is.'

'As I said though, you were quite wonderful.'

'You're too kind,' Maeve blushed slightly.

'I've watched many clairvoyants and I could tell that they were charlatans but it is plain to see that you are the genuine article, Ms Dubois.'

'Thank you,' said she. 'Call me Maeve, please.'

'Very well, Maeve, I am Doctor Malcolm Selinger.' He kissed her hand with another slick bow.

'Pleased to meet you, Malcolm.'

'Did you receive the flowers I sent?'

Maeve scanned the array of flora adorning her dressing room table.

'The black roses,' he specified.

She looked at him. 'Oh, so it's you that's been sending me the black roses?'

He nodded excitedly. 'I've caught your last three shows actually. It's taken me a while to find the courage to talk to you.'

'I've been wondering who's been sending me those,' she cooed.

Malcolm stood there and fidgeted like a shy schoolboy.

'Well!' Maeve slapped her knees. 'It's always nice to meet a fan but I am very tired ...'

'That's a pity,' said Malcolm. 'I was going to ask if you would do me the honour of joining me for dinner?'

Maeve sighed. 'These shows really drain me. I'm sorry.'

'A quick drink in the theatre bar perchance?'

She shook her head and tried to keep smiling.

He was obviously disappointed. 'That's a pity. I fly to Prague later tonight. This may be my last chance to talk to you.'

There was an awkward pause. He kept staring at her with anticipation. It was obvious he was not going to take no for an answer.

'Alright,' Maeve conceded. 'Just one drink.'

Malcolm bounced and grinned with barely contained glee. He danced around a bit and punched the air with his fists.

While her devotee was distracted, Maeve opened her handbag and drew out a flick-knife. Without any remorse or hesitation, she sprang up and plunged the blade deep into the man's heart. At once,

Doctor Malcolm Selinger imploded and became a puddle of gore on the floor. Scarlet ran between the floorboards and dripped from her dress.

'Fucking vampires!' she spat.

*

Obituary of Archibald Deakin
Published in the Fogwin Enquirer 30.4.1980.

Mr Archibald Deakin of Lamplighter Drive died aged 59 of a fatal heart attack on April 25. Born in Norwich, Mr Deakin lived in Fogwin for over twenty years. He is survived by his wife Gillian and two sons Jason and Justin. Mr Deakin was educated at the London School of Journalism and, after cementing his craft on Fleet Street, became editor of the Enquirer in 1960. He was devoted to his work but also very well-known and involved with activities at St. Mary's church, most notably the choir. He also loved cricket and crown green bowls. Mr Deakin will be missed by his colleagues who found him to be a wise and patient mentor, issuing the dictum 'that a reporter should seize a story by the throat.' The funeral will take place at St. Mary's on Monday afternoon. Arrangements will be made by Pope and Morley.

*

'Archie would have our balls for earrings if he knew we were doing this again,' Mark commented as they followed Brian Temple through the gloom.

'Archie's dead,' sneered Ray. 'Now shush!'

The former security guard led them across a boggy patch of wasteland in the fading light of dusk. They were close enough to Knightsheath to discern the mechanical hum of Earthcom but far away enough to be concealed by the shadow of the setting sun. The guide came to a halt outside a group of ruined buildings. Their roofs had long since failed and the windows were smashed. It was little more than a collection of stone walls fought over by mosses and weeds. 'This is it,' Brian proclaimed nevertheless.

Ray and Mark waited for the others to catch up. Kaleef marched towards them silently, his dark eyes darting from side to side. The Professor and Maeve sauntered over to them in a more casual manner whilst Billy bungled behind them, laden with camera equipment.

Brian looked around at them all with bulging eyes. 'Follow me.'

He then scuttled inside one of the ruins and waited for them all again. They filed in and formed a vague semi-circle around him. Somewhat ceremoniously, Brian descended a narrow flight of stone stairs below the level of the ground where a rusty metal hatch was set into a damp crumbling wall. With a violent tug, he dragged open the hatch and it protested with a brief yet shrill metallic screech. Behind it, some sort of subterranean entrance was revealed. There came from it a blast of icy wet air like the final breath of a drowned corpse. The visitors shivered in unison.

'What's this?' Ray vocalised what they were all wondering.

'Secret passage,' explained Brian, looking up.

'You're taking the piss?' snorted Ray.

The thin man shook his head. 'It's an old drainage tunnel. You can follow it for about half a mile and it will take you straight into the middle of the industrial estate, bypassing all the fences and guards.'

'I'm a bit claustrophobic, like,' confessed Billy, gazing down with disgust.

Brian shook his shoulders. 'It's up to you. It's the only unofficial way in that I know of.'

Ray regarded him with suspicion 'Are you sure about this?'

'To be honest with you, Mr Weaver, I've never been into the central part of the estate before but from what I've seen and heard that's where all the special stuff goes on.'

The Professor did a little cough. 'Special stuff?'

'The secret experiments and what not,' Brain answered him. 'Most of the estate is just for normal business but it's all a front for something much more sinister. I'm sure of it. The outer section hides the central section and that can only be accessed by a chosen few. The security guards in there are not like us normal blokes; they're outsiders. We never mingled or chatted or anything. These blokes are serious; they've got weapons and stuff. Paramilitary you might say.'

'Sounds like fun,' said Maeve, flippantly.

'I hope it's not the bloody IRA,' added Billy.

Ray straightened his overcoat and tie with resolve. 'Well I'm going in! You lot can stay here if you want to. I'm getting to the bottom of this shit.'

Brian pulled a couple of torches out from his coat as he mounted the stairs. 'Here; you can take these.'

'Cheers, nice one,' Ray rubbed his hands together and took one.

'Kaleef will take one of those and lead the way,' instructed The Professor.

Without hesitation, the Arab took the other torch, sprang down the stairs and vanished, his colourless silhouette indistinguishable from the black of the tunnel.

'Good luck.' said Brian.

'Cheers, mate,' Ray got out his wallet handed him a tenner. 'Get yourself a few pints.'

'Bless you, Mr Weaver.' Brian looked delighted with the offering.

The Professor was next to venture into the passage. He did so a little more gingerly than his manservant.

'I'm going to leave you to it,' Mark decided suddenly.

Ray glared at him. 'We've discussed this already, Mark! This is a Fogwin Enquirer *team* investigation!'

His colleague groaned and puffed and sighed. 'Alright! But I'm holding you responsible for anything that happens to me!'

'Ladies first,' Maeve said with a great deal less fuss.

Mark hovered impatiently whilst the Canadian clairvoyant descended into the earth. He followed her with a face like a persecuted stepchild.

'Your mate doesn't seem keen,' commented Billy to Ray.

'He just needs a bit of gentle encouragement,' said he. 'And he's not my mate.'

'I must admit that I was happier in the pub,' Billy scratched his mullet. 'Good company, nice food, plenty of booze, like. Could have been a classic session. Now I'm taking a secret underground passage into what sounds like a shitstorm. I'm definitely out of my comfort zone.'

'Welcome to my world,' said Ray. 'You want a hand with some of that kit?'

'I think I'll leave some here,' Billy said and discarded a tripod and a couple of satchels.

'I'll bring up the rear.' Ray slapped the photographer on the shoulder, urging him towards the hole in the ground.

Billy bumbled down the steps intrepidly but paused before he stepped into the tunnel. He took a couple of deep breaths before he ducked inside like he was about to swim the Channel. Ray tagged behind and watched him with an amused curiosity. He glanced back before he stepped into the darkness; only Brian remained. The narrow man was stood at the top of the stairs, motionless and not a little odd. Ray nodded at him and departed.

He switched on the torch but its beam only illuminated the small distance between him and the massive Geordie who was making slow progress ahead. Billy seemed to fill the whole space and the passage was revealed to Ray one step at a time. It was arch-shaped and about six feet high. This meant that anyone taller, like Ray and Billy, had to stoop slightly. Ray felt the strain on the back of his neck after just a few strides. As he walked he examined the stone work. It was not certain how old this construction was but some of the rock had fallen away, creating a carpet of rubble. Emancipated puddles of black water made conditions under foot even more unpleasant. It was dreadfully cold and damp too. Every lungful was uncomfortable. It felt to Ray like he was no longer breathing natural air but a substance much more malign and ancient and not fit for humans. The sequence of wheezes coming from Billy's chest indicated that he was equally uncomfortable. Apart from that, there was little noise from up ahead and Ray wondered how the others were getting on. Suddenly, there was a loud bang from behind him. It shook the crumbling stone and reverberated in his guts. His arsehole flared.

'What the …?'

Billy froze and turned his head to one side. 'What the bloody hell was that?'

Ray swung round and shone his torch back down the tunnel. There was no light at the end. 'The hatch has closed!' The reporter charged back down to confirm his suspicions, banging on it with one fist. 'Brian!? Brian!? What the fuck are you playing at?' There was no answer from the other side, however, just the ominous drone of the icy breeze blowing down the passage. Ray exhaled and shambled back up to Billy, who had now been joined by the others. He could see their worried faces beyond Billy's bulk. They were illuminated by the pale torch light and they looked like ghostly disembodied heads, floating about in the tomb-like gloom.

'What the devil is going on?' enquired The Professor.

Ray shrugged his shoulders at him. 'Search me! Brian must have closed the hatch behind us. Unless the wind blew it shut.'

'Great!' blubbered Mark. 'Now we're stuck down here!'

Ray narrowed his eyes at him. 'Don't blame me! He's your mate!'

Maeve shook her head. 'I thought there was something not quite right about that man.'

'You read his mind?' asked Ray.

'No,' replied she. 'I can only do that if someone is willing or caught off guard.'

'Fat lot of good that is then!' he scoffed.

'Why would he want to trap us down here?' wondered Billy. 'It must have been a gust of wind, like.' Despite his words his eyes were wild and worried.

The Professor held up the palm of one dainty hand to appeal for calm. 'Take a deep breath everyone. Let's not ask ourselves such questions just yet. This passage must have another end. Let's keep going.'

The scholar's plea seemed to do the trick. The companions kept still and quiet for a minute and composed themselves. They exchanged glances but kept any more apprehensions to themselves for now. The Professor turned to Kaleef with expectancy and the Arab nodded in response. In the low light, Kaleef's features almost looked satanic. He just needed a pair of horns sprouting from his skull, mused Ray. Little more than a shadow, The Professor's special friend led the way and they fell into line in the same sequence as before. Of course, as soon as Billy turned his back Ray could not see the others in front of him anymore. There were a few minutes of trudging along the stygian subway before they came to another snag. Ray heard a slight commotion from up ahead and Billy ground to a halt.

'What is it?' he hissed.

Billy turned side-on and backed up against the side of the tunnel so he could see. 'Bit of a blockage,' he explained.

Ray shone his torch up at the rest of the group. Beyond them the passage looked like it had come to an abrupt end. They peered back at him.

'Now we're screwed!' wailed Mark with despair.

'End of the line?' enquired Ray with a tad less horror.

The Professor addressed him. 'There's been a cave-in, that's all. No need to panic. We just need to clear a few rocks.'

'Let's hope so,' Mark quipped. 'This could be a grave for us all! It'll be a hundred years before they even find our skeletons!'

Ray rolled his eyes at him. 'Shut your cakehole, will you? People like us don't die like this. Well, maybe dickheads like you but not me.'

'Right!' Let's form a human chain,' instructed The Professor. 'We'll pass each rock back one at a time. Let's go!'

Again, no one was able to resist The professor's irrefutable logic. He was becoming a leader to them of sorts. Each rock, stone, boulder and more indefinable fragment of obstruction was handed from Kaleef to Professor to Maeve to Mark to Billy to Ray, who lobbed it behind him into the shadows. It kept them busy for almost an hour but, like some perverse team building exercise, they managed to shift the obstacle. They rested briefly afterwards, the sweat of their labour turning cold and their hands caked with dust. Breathing was becoming almost impossible.

'I think I've broken a nail,' murmured Maeve, inspecting her fingers.

'Hmm, last orders has just gone,' supplemented Billy, checking his watch.

'This is fun isn't it?' Mark's tones dripped with venomous sarcasm. 'A night out with Ray Weaver! You too can spend your evening digging yourself out of a grave!'

Ray's nostrils flared. 'If you keep moaning, Mark, I swear I'm going to belt you one!'

'I didn't want to come!' screeched his colleague.

'And I'm starting to regret asking you!' Ray's fists bunched.

'Now, now!' crooned The Professor, as if he was the beleaguered guardian of some reprobate youths. 'Let's cool it down, shall we? Perhaps a little tipple will help.' He removed a metal flask from inside his tweed jacket and passed it around. No one refused the gesture and drank like their lives depended on it. 'Now let's get out of this hole,' he sniffed and took a gulp himself.

After ten minutes of shuffling through the dark the procession were all relieved to see that the tunnel came to an end. The narrow confines widened out into a lofty rectangular chamber which must have extended upwards back above ground. The group filed in and instinctively gazed upwards where light filtered in through several damp grills in the ceiling. It was a thin ailing light but light nonetheless. On the far side of the wall, a rusty metal ladder indicated the only way out. At its summit was a round metal hatch. The companions said nothing but each hoped that it was not bolted shut. Mucky water dripped from above and down the walls and the floor became distinctly sludgy. There were indescribable objects in the mud and the air was no less rotten. There was a hint of faeces.

'Thank God for that!' groaned Mark.

Ray glanced at him. 'Have you shat yourself?'

His colleague opened his mouth to retort when a peculiar snuffling noise drew his attention back up to the roof. The others were compelled to look up too. A large wet black nose snivelled at them through the gap in one of the grills. It was followed by a growl and a flash of white fangs. The team collectively receded back into the shadow of the tunnel. The nose and the fangs promptly went away.

'Did anyone else just see that?' appealed Billy.

'There's some kind of dog up there,' whispered Maeve.

'Fucking big dog,' observed Ray.

The Professor scratched his chin. 'It seems the drainage system might not be as defenceless as our friend Brian claimed.'

'What are we going to do?' whimpered Mark. 'We can't go back.'

The Professor turned to his Arabian ally. 'Kaleef?'

The quiet man nodded and pounced across the chamber to the ladder. Most humans would have made a racket crossing all that sludge and detritus but Kaleef was not most humans. His companions could only witness the skill as he crossed the distance without making a sound and scaled the rusty old ladder equally as quick and silent. He nudged open the hatch at the top and his spectators exhaled with relief at the revelation that he could do so. Kaleef grabbed the rim above him and hauled himself out all in one manoeuvre. There followed a few tense moments. There were no sounds of a commotion as expected. All that happened was a large ball of black fur dropped back through the hatchway and landed with a soft splat in the quagmire.

Mark stared with disbelief. 'Is that …?' He was too astonished to finish his question.

Maeve obliged him. 'The dog.'

'Is it …?' Again, Mark had difficulty forming words.

'Dead?' Maeve continued to assist.

'Kaleef does not kill,' explained The Professor. 'He has merely subdued the hound.'

A second limp form fell through the hatchway. This was one was also unconscious but more man-shaped. Kaleef sprang down a second later and inspected his victims. He propped them up against the wall and checked the pulse of both beast and man. The others trudged over to him.

'Good work, my friend.' The Professor smiled with approval.

Kaleef looked up at him and nodded.

'It's a good job you're here,' added Ray.

'What the hell is that bloody thing?' Billy gestured to the comatose dog.

The others looked and understood what he meant; the canine appeared to be a cross between an Alsatian and a Rottweiler but bigger, uglier and hairier than either breed.

Ray was especially troubled. 'I've seen one of these critters before,' said he.

The Professor turned to him. 'What do you mean?'

'When I got taken to that mansion a few weeks ago. The one that belonged to that old freak with three eyes. He had one of these beasts in the front yard. If it hadn't been for a fateful sandwich I would have come a royal cropper.'

'Then perhaps this place belongs to him too,' surmised The Professor.

'That would explain a lot,' said Ray. 'We need to be careful.'

'Look at this!' Mark pointed out the pistol in the holster on the belt of the dog's human cohort.

'Guns and dogs,' mused Ray. 'Like I said.'

'I think I spot a photo opportunity.' The chamber lit up with a sequence of flashes as Billy snapped indiscriminately.

Ray turned to his camp intellectual friend. 'What's next, Prof?'

'Onwards and upwards,' said he, exhaling stoically. 'I'm not sure how much further we will get without being caught but I for one refuse to stay a minute longer in this cesspit.'

Whatever weirdness Ray and his collaborators expected to see above ground could not compare to the bizarre panorama that awaited their bleary eyes. At first glance it looked like a football pitch, it was roughly the same size and shape and illuminated by flood lights. The turf was not surrounded by seats, however, but by squat concrete buildings that hinted at practicality rather than beauty. More guards and dogs patrolled the perimeter. The focus of the place seemed to be on the ancient structure in the middle of the grass. It resembled Stonehenge but time had not been so kind; its rocks were crooked and black and broken.

'Bloody hell!' exclaimed Billy. 'What's all this about?'

None of his companions could offer him an answer.

*

He could not see what Liam Allerdice was doing in the fog. He stared as hard as he could through the grey vapour but only a brief pocket of clarity gave him the impression that his partner was bent over and poking at something on the beach with a stick.

'What you doing, man?' shouted Billy Briggs in that vague direction.

There was no answer, just the gentle return of the tide and a deathly bell clanging somewhere in the distance. Billy shivered; it was freezing but this place also gave him the creeps. His apparent solitude was no comfort.

'Liam!' he bellowed again.

This time there was a reply; 'over here!'

Billy grunted some wordless disapproval to himself and plodded down the steps to the beach. As soon as his shoes crunched pebbles he felt the need to zip up his coat. The fog seemed to hang heavier on the shore and its icy caress was more acute. Billy shambled over to the spot where he thought he had seen his colleague. His camera bounced on his belly as he did so and it was a loss to him why he had even bothered to bring it. Even the most accomplished of photographers would fail to get a snap in this soup.

'What are you doing, man?' he repeated, hoping that the spectral shape he addressed was actually Liam and not a piece of driftwood or something. 'I'm starving!'

'This will challenge your appetite, Briggs,' said Liam with some degree of menace. It was indeed him.

'What? Yers found another one?'

Liam nodded with somewhat perverse delight. He leered up at him, his narrow bony face dripping with moisture.

Billy's eyes had not deceived him; his partner was poking at something on the ground with a stick. 'Is it ... a man's?'

'Thank, God, yes.'

Billy peered down at the article of Liam's morbid fascination. All he could see was an Adidas trainer. That was enough. He did not need to see the dismembered foot that he knew was inside it. 'Left?'

'Just like all the others.'

'So what's that now?' Billy pondered. 'Eight?'

'Nine if you include the one in '78,' stated Liam. 'But yeah, eight in the last three months.'

'This is totally weird, like.' Billy shook his damp mullet. 'Why nothing except the left foot? And why always this beach?'

Liam scratched his sharp chin in contemplation. 'The work of some crazed individual, no doubt. Maybe even a cult.'

'Perhaps they got eaten by a shark?'

'Come on, Briggs!' Liam scoffed. 'It's too much of a pattern! Plus there's no bloody sharks round here. You'd be lucky to find anything alive on this coast, it's so damn polluted.'

Billy moped and they stared at the ownerless foot for a few moments in mutual thought.

'Well,' said the photographer, 'as much as I'd like to stand here all night ruminating on this mystery I can hear my pint and steak and kidney pie calling me. Let's ring the police and let them deal with it, like.'

'You go on ahead,' said Liam. He put his hands in his pockets and stared out to sea, his eyes glazed.

Billy frowned at him. 'Yers can't stay out here alone, Liam, man. Not with a potential killer on the loose. Yers catch yer death of cold if nothing else.'

'I'm gonna take a mooch over there.' The reporter pointed a slender finger into the gloomy yonder.

The Geordie followed his intended direction but could see nothing except the rotating beam of a lighthouse. 'That island? Aw, Liam! There's nothing out there, man! It's just a rock with a lighthouse on it. There isn't even any people; it's automated, like.'

Liam sniggered. 'Aye! Funny how the feet always wash up within eye sight of that place though, don't you think, Briggs?'

Billy peered through the haze for a while. A fog horn sounded suddenly and made his heart skip a beat. 'How yers gonna get over there anyway? Swim?'

'I'm going to take this,' said Liam, strolling over to a nearby rowing boat.

'Yers joking? That's not even yours.'

'I'll just borrow it. Coming?'

Billy watched him untie the boat and just for a couple of seconds, actually contemplated joining him.

'I'll do anything to get a story, Briggs, that's how I got this job in the first place,' Liam explained with a slightly insane chuckle.

The Geordie shook his head. 'You've been obsessed with these bloody feet since that girl disappeared, man. And she's probably got nothing to do with it.'

The reporter was no longer listening. He was dragging the boat across the pebbles down to the water. Billy advanced after him for a dozen steps, hoping in vain that some sense would return to his colleague. He watched him long enough to see him get into the vessel and go bouncing through the first few waves. He opened his mouth like he wanted to say something more but words failed him. Instead, he just turned around and went home.

Billy never saw Liam Allerdice again. Not all of him anyway.

*

After sneaking around in the shadows for a while and finding a few locked doors, they took sanctuary in what appeared to be a laboratory of some kind. The dim interior was spacious, like a warehouse but much to the surprise of Ray Weaver and his assembly of misfits it was decked out with scientific equipment. The vast chaotic display of apparatus was perplexing to the eye. A hundred different machines bleeped and whirred at them from the walls. There was only one previous occupant; a bespectacled man in a white coat. Kaleef had gone ahead to make sure there was no resistance to their trespass.

'He's quite good at that, isn't he?' remarked Ray, nodding at the Arab and the unconscious scientist.

'Kaleef is a consummate professional,' agreed The Professor. 'However, I fear that we may be on borrowed time.' He peered outside through the gap in a blind. 'There appears to be something going on.'

'What do you mean?' quizzed Mark, shadowing him.

'Well,' replied The Professor whilst checking his pocket watch. 'It's eleven-thirty on a Saturday night. With the exception of the security guards, one would expect the place to be deserted but it's a veritable hive of activity out there, don't you think?'

Mark had a sneaky peep out of the window and shook his head. 'It's like they're getting ready for something. We shouldn't be here.'

'Is he moaning again?' Ray sighed. He, Billy and Maeve had started nosing around.

'Have you seen this, Cedric?' The Canadian called out.

The Professor strolled over and joined them. The far wall was coated in maps, charts, diagrams and schematics.

'Looks like a big project,' Maeve commented, gazing at it all with wide eyes.

Billy's camera got busy.

The Professor squinted through his glasses at some of the drawings. 'There's an emphasis on that stone monument out there. But why all this bother over some old rocks?'

Maeve turned and pouted at him. 'You know as well as I do, Cedric, that there's still power in some of these stones.'

'Just take a gander at this lot,' said Ray.

He shifted the attention of the team to some illustrations of what appeared to be animals yet the zoology of the creatures was not recognisable. The subjects were warped and alien.

The Professor examined them and shivered. 'By the gods! What are these madmen up to?'

'I told you, didn't I?' Ray hissed at him, his eyeballs bulging with conviction. 'I told you there was something fishy going on!'

The Professor chuckled with mirth and put his hand on Ray's shoulder. 'Raymond, old boy! I think that was a massive understatement!'

'Look what I've found!' screeched Billy suddenly, as if he was trying to steal Ray's thunder.

Everyone turned to look at him.

The photographer was stood in a dingy corner, holding up a kettle. 'Anyone fancy a cuppa, like?'

'Jesus, Mary and Joseph, Billy!' Maeve glared at him. 'We've just stumbled upon Doctor Frankenstein's lab and all you're interested in is the damn kettle!'

'I'm thirsty, lass,' he protested. 'That bloody potholing was hard work. And there's biscuits! Chocolate digestives no less.'

The Professor frowned. 'I'm with Maeve on this one, Mr Briggs. You should be taking photographs of absolutely everything in here. We may not get another chance.'

'Alright, alright,' grumbled the Geordie. A fresh sequence of clicks and flashes signalled his compliance.

Ray noticed that his fellow reporter from the Fogwin Enquirer was hovering in the middle of the lab, looking pale and twitchy. 'You alright, Mark?'

'We should get out of here,' answered he, tugging at his shirt collar with distress.

'Yeah, alright,' Ray allowed him some uncommon compassion. 'We'll shoot off in a jiffy. Don't get yourself worked up. That's what finished Archie off.'

'It's just all of this!' he squawked. 'It's not right!'

Ray lit up a cigarette. 'I know.'

'Remember the last time we were here, Ray?' That fence? Those lights? I think we saw that stone circle. We caught sight of it in the distance?'

'I remember,' Ray nodded. 'That was the night Lucy disappeared.'

Mark frowned at him. 'Lucy? My Lucy?'

Ray shrugged his shoulders. 'Your Lucy. Sure.'

'You've been seeing her haven't you?' said Mark suddenly and sharply.

Ray rolled his eyes at him and puffed. 'Yeah, sorry, mate. It just sort of happened and …'

'You left your wife?'

Ray glanced around, uncomfortably. 'Can we do this later?'

'I'm not angry or anything,' explained Mark. 'I just want to know the truth.'

'Me and Lucy met up a couple of times, that's all. Iris found out and naffed off with the kids. Well, there was a bit more to it than that …'

'I never expected a Page 3 girl to fall for me anyway, a short balding newspaper reporter with B.O. and a beer belly. How ridiculous! With you, it makes more sense. You're smart, Ray, you're brave, you're sexy ...'

Ray sniggered. 'Mark! You're making me blush. What's got into you?'

Mark regarded him with moist eyes. 'I just wanted to get things cleared up. Just in case we don't make it out of here.'

'Mark!' Ray slung a comforting arm around him. 'We'll get out of here, mate. Get a hold of yourself. Let's just find Lucy together, eh?'

The dawn of a smile returned to Mark's face. 'Okay.'

The two journalists adjusted their attention back to their surroundings. The Professor and Kaleef were inspecting a large metal door; the only apparent way out apart from the way they had come in.

'What's up, gaylords?' Ray asked.

The Professor turned to him. 'It's locked with one of these new-fangled key-card things.'

'Perhaps this man can help us,' suggested Maeve.

Everyone span round to look at her. The clairvoyant was hovering near the comatose scientist like a predatory raven. She stared at the man in the white coat for a few moments with her head cocked to one side. She then reached inside his pocket and pulled out a black plastic card.

'That mind reading thing finally coming in useful then?' Ray belched.

Maeve ignored him and held up the key. 'Shall we?'

'Do we want to know what's behind the next door?' stuttered Mark with apprehension.

'Your killer journalistic instinct is overwhelming,' Ray sneered at him, sarcastically. He snatched the card from Maeve's fingers and swaggered over to the door like he was making a point. With one swipe, a light turned from red to green and the mighty door swooshed aside. 'Open sesame!' he proclaimed and ventured into the black void beyond.

The others followed somewhat more hesitantly. The chamber was of an equal size and crammed with more machines and scientific endeavour though it was much darker. Their eyes were immediately drawn to the two-dozen pillars of light running down both sides. They extended from floor to ceiling and they looked like giant test tubes. They were the chief source of illumination and the investigators could see clearly that the containers were filled with a pale-yellow viscous fluid. Within some of the tubes, floating within the amniotic fluid, were misshapen objects that twitched and bubbled and cast a variety of obscene shadows across the floor and walls. It was like the work of a shadow puppeteer gone mad. The companions stopped and stared for a while, faces agog and eyes blinking. Even Ray, who had entered the vault of horrors boldly, was halted in his tracks. The cigarette fell from his lips and lay smouldering at his feet.

'Shit the bed!' he said.

Slowly, each member of the group found some courage or curiosity and approached the containers for a closer look. Those nearest to them accommodated what appeared to be babies but upon closer examination, they were more like tiny men. The skin of these humanoids was snow white and their pale long hair was so wispy that it moved around, tendril-like in the bubbling goo. Their little faces were ugly and though they appeared to be asleep or perhaps dead their expressions were cruel and malignant.

Only Ray had any idea what they were. 'Well, well, well! It's my little friends!'

'Are they real?' questioned Mark, his features scrunched up in disbelief.

Ray looked at him. 'Afraid so.'

The Professor peered at the specimens through his spectacles. 'How extremely fascinating! I'm deeply sorry for ever doubting you, Raymond.'

Ray turned to Billy, who was frozen in astonishment. 'If there was ever a good time to take a photo it would be now.'

Billy stayed on pause.

'Billy!' snapped Ray.

'Aye!' the Geordie responded suddenly and began to adjust his camera to his new surroundings.

'I thought you were the world's leading paranormal photographer?'

'Christ!' profaned Billy as he fumbled. 'It's all a load of bollocks, man! I've taken pictures of weird stuff before but nothing like this!'

'Interesting,' purred The Professor. 'No genitalia or nipples.'

'Nor do they have any thoughts,' added Maeve, touching the glass, gingerly.

'Are they alive?' quizzed Mark.

'I can't tell,' answered she.

'They don't appear to be breathing,' remarked The Professor. 'But who the devil knows?'

Ray wandered away to examine something else and left his companions to marvel at the creatures like infants in a zoo. After all, he had seen them before. Even beings from another world were slightly old hat after several occasions. Ray spotted something a bit more hardcore towards the back of the lab. One of the rearmost tubes was home to something more freakish.

'If you think that's crazy you should blow your minds on this,' he said, tempting the congregation over to him.

The specimen was not a giant rat or a spider but an obscene hybrid of them both, and yet neither. Its deformed and lifeless bulk dripped with a combination of legs, arms, tentacles and tails.

'I feel sick,' was the only audible reaction and that was from Mark. His companions anticipated melodrama but when the reporter rushed over to a corner and ejected the contents of his stomach into the gloom they realised he was serious.

'Alright, sunshine?' Ray called out to him with a mixture of concern and amusement.

Mark could not answer except with a sequence of retching, grunting and choking.

'Not feeling too good myself,' confessed Billy, staring at the thing.

Ray beamed at him. 'Put that on the front page of your fucking newspaper!'

'What is it?' The photographer prepared his weapon.

'You've got me there,' sniffed Ray. 'This ugly wanker is new to me.'

The Professor took a cautious step towards it. 'It rather looks like something that's been torn inside out.'

Kaleef shook his head and turned away. He stepped over to the corner opposite to where Mark was vomiting.

'Is he going to throw up as well?' Ray asked The Professor.

'He's probably gone to pray,' replied he. 'We all have to deal with this in our own way, it seems.'

'How do you feel?'

The Professor shrugged his shoulders. 'Flabbergasted! I've been waiting a long time to see something like this.'

'We all have,' added Maeve. She bravely reached out to touch the glass.

'Think I could have lived my life quite happily without it,' said Ray with some melancholy.

Billy raised his camera and took a shot. The flash blasted the occupant of the tube and it suddenly sprang into life; its many appendages lashing against the glass. Maeve leapt back and screamed so loudly that they were all deafened for a few moments, as well as blinded by the flash. Once they regained their senses, Ray,

Billy and The professor all found that they too had receded quite a distance. They glared at the abomination. It was very much reanimated.

'This one isn't dead then?' giggled Ray, amused and breathless with shock.

'I think I've shat myself,' Billy exhaled and also found some humour in the situation. 'Sorry about that.'

'Are you alright, my dandelion?' The Professor took his Canadian friend in an embrace.

Maeve accepted the comfort. 'Caught by surprise twice in as many weeks,' she whispered. 'I must be losing my touch.'

Mark emerged out of his corner, his lips wet with puke. 'What's going on?'

Ray addressed him. 'Igor! It lives!'

Mark glanced at the thing dancing in the container and turned green again. He span round and returned to the shadows for a fresh spew.

'What do we do now?' was Billy's question once he had photographed his unearthly subject from every conceivable angle.

'Shall we let it out for a play?' joked Ray though no one laughed.

'We've seen enough,' decided The Professor. 'It's time we left.'

Maeve looked at him. 'I think you're right.'

'Suits me,' Billy nodded in agreement.

'Okay,' grunted Ray. He fetched Mark from the shadows and they made for the door. As they did so, a screen on the wall flickered into life and they bungled to a halt. The image of a peculiar face materialised. Once more, the investigators were collectively stunned.

'Decided to gatecrash another of my parties, journalist?' The old man's face on the screen was withered and deformed. The left portion of his features looked like melted candle wax and there was a lumpy growth in the middle of his forehead. It throbbed and pulsed like the Mount Vesuvius of all boils.

Ray put his hands in his pockets and chuckled at the screen. 'So! The ringmaster of this twisted circus finally reveals himself?'

The old man croaked. 'Brought some friends this time?'

'Oh, yes!' Ray lifted a dainty hand to his chest in a gesture of faux embarrassment. 'How rude of me! Everyone; this is the creepy old bastard with three eyes who kidnapped me and stole my alien. This is Cedric Montague Hamilton, also known as The Professor, Miss Maeve Dubois, Billy …'

'I know who they are!' shrieked the old man, his enraged voice almost detonating the speakers apart.

'Nice place you've got here.' Ray continued to mock him. 'I thought your mansion was something but I'm really liking the whole secret lab thing. I like what you've done with the armed guards and the mutant dogs and that's before I get onto your simply divine menagerie ...'

'Silence!' the voice screeched again. 'You have crossed me a second time, journalist! I should not have let you escape!'

'Please call me Ray. Let's not be so formal. You did nearly succeed in killing me. I'd like to thank you for that. I'd also like to thank you for sending your little mates round to my house.' Ray thumbed over his shoulder to the white gnomes in the tubes. 'I really appreciate you putting my wife and kids in danger. Why don't you get off that telly and come down here so I can thank you in person?' Ray's voice descended from sarcasm to murderous intent.

'You are all trespassing,' explained the old man. 'My guards are on the way. I suggest that none of you move until they arrive. They are armed and will shoot if instructed to do so.'

'Hey!' snarled Ray, his lips curling back like an animal. 'I was just being friendly!'

'I've had enough of you, journalist!' the ancient creature retorted with mutual loathing. 'You think you can just walk in here and do what you want and you think you're so pissing funny ...'

'Augustus?' It was the old man's turn to be interrupted. The Professor had been staring at the screen with intense scrutiny.

The furious fiend drew silent and regarded him with his two natural eyes.

The Professor took a step forward. 'Augustus Peck? Is that you?'

The old man seemed surprised.

Ray glanced sideways at The Professor. 'You know this twat?'

He nodded. 'I believe so, though he has not aged well. How long has it been, Augustus?'

There was a sudden clap of what sounded like thunder from outside. It startled everyone. Even the man on the screen was distracted for a moment.

'Something's not right,' hissed Maeve, half to herself.

'What in God's name has happened to you, man?' probed The Professor, readdressing the screen.

The old man, whose name it seemed, was Augustus Peck, opened his slit of a mouth to speak but it was a few seconds before he dribbled a reply. 'I have become powerful, Cedric, very powerful.'

'You look dreadful, old boy,' The Professor snorted.

Peck ceased to scream like a maniac. His tone had become much more civilised. 'One cannot attain great power without a few physical side effects.'

'A few physical side effects?' The Professor scoffed. 'You look barely human!'

'You two at school for posh gay weirdos or something? Ray scratched his head.

'We were in the same magical circle at Cambridge,' explained he.

'What?' smirked Ray. 'Card tricks and that?'

'Ritualistic magic. We were just messing about really but Augustus here had more ambition. He wanted to raise demons and devils to do his bidding, didn't you, Augustus?'

'Science is the key,' he answered. 'Though the ancient people regarded anything that they could not understand as magic. Science and magic are one and the same. It has taken me many years to fully understand that.'

The Professor almost laughed. 'And that's what you're doing here, is it, Augustus?' Using the knowledge of the ancients?'

'Indeed,' gurgled Peck. 'And I have succeeded.'

'A union with your precious demons?'

'They have taught me much!' Again the old man's voice grew shrill with anger.

'You want to calm down a bit, man,' Billy chipped in. 'We're British press and our readers have got the right to know about this lot.'

'They are not ready for this!' cried Peck. 'Not until I decide!'

Ray shrugged his shoulders. 'He's got a point there. This is a bit much in one go. Well the hell would we start? Perhaps we can do it in instalments? Ease them in gently?'

'You will tell them nothing!' barked Peck. 'Your camera will be confiscated and I will see to it that your memories are wiped!'

The sound of booted feet became audible. 'The guards!' announced Mark, who was stood nearest the exit.

'Quick everyone! Follow Kaleef!' ordered The Professor.

The Arab had darted back to the dim corner where he had made his prayer and began to climb up the wall. The others could see that there was a ladder of some sort leading up to a hatch in the roof.

'Come on! Let's go!' urged The Professor.

No further prompt was needed. They fled back into recesses of the lab.

Peck realised their intention. 'No! Stop! Stop where you are!'

Ray laughed and waved at him. 'Bye, handsome!'

Peck continued to wail and shriek but from his remote view he was powerless to do anything. His protests became wordless noises and the dreadful third eye in the middle of his forehead began to wake; pushing open the ravaged flesh around it.

A dozen security guards and a monstrous dog burst into the room but most of Ray's companions were already scaling the ladder like a procession of unusual insects.

'Keep going!' Ray shouted over his shoulder. 'I'll deal with this lot!'

The guards aimed an assortment of firearms at them and the dog bounded forward to tear out Ray's throat but he just laughed. 'Come on then, you wankers!' Defiant in the face of certain death, Ray grabbed a metal stool and hurled it with all the force he could muster at the glass container containing the feisty multi-limbed beast. The glass shattered and a tsunami of amniotic fluid gushed across the floor. Seemingly not prone to the laws of gravity, the spider-rat-octopus- thing rippled with astonishing vitality. It took no time to recover or think. It just began to kill.

The dog was the nearest victim. The thing snatched it and tore it limb from limb in one second, showering nearby Ray with bone, blood and fur. The dog did not even have time to realise its doom. Ray, his comrades, the guards; all watched with amazement and horror. They had no time to contemplate the sickening efficiency of the creature's ability to slaughter. Everyone just knew that they had to get out of its way. The security guards panicked and bumbled into each other, each deciding on a different course of action; some wanted to stop and shoot, some felt the urge to run away, some thought that pushing someone else towards the monster would give them time to escape. The thing actually went for Ray but he was quick with another stool. *All those years scrapping in Eastend boozers were not entirely wasted after all*, he mused briefly. He thrust the piece of furniture forward like an impromptu ram, shoving the monster towards the shambolic mob of guards. 'Go get 'em, boy!' he managed to shout, even though he was as terrified as they. Fortunately for Ray, it seemed to get the message. It rounded and span towards the guards with the fury and power of a combine harvester. Ray spared no time to look. He turned in the opposite direction and made for the ladder. A couple of bullets dented the wall as he reached it but then there was some awful screaming and the shooting stopped. He glanced up and saw that his allies had got out. He could even feel the cold night air on his face from the open hatch. Only the obese form of Billy Briggs remained between him and freedom. Billy was struggling to make progress, panting with the effort of the climb.

Ray offered the photographer some gentle encouragement 'Move your fat arse, Geordie!' he squealed and sprang up and punched him in his ample buttocks.

'I don't like heights, man!' came the pathetic reply from above.

In desperation, Ray punched him again. 'Move it or else we're both fucked!'

The softly-softly approach seemed to work and the half-man half-potato shape that was Billy Briggs began to haul ass again.

Ray felt the urgent need to put as much space between him and the freshly-birthed super beast as possible. He yelled at Billy some more, he was moving but not anywhere near as fast as Ray would have liked. 'Come on, damn it!'

He chanced to look back and it was not a pretty sight. The guards who did not have the sense to run away were being systematically minced by the specimen from hell. Not only was it killing them but it had also now started to feed. Some of its endless array of appendages were busy destroying flesh whilst others were being used to consume it.

'Billy!' Ray quickly looked away. He had seen enough. There was no way he wanted to be dessert. Death would be welcome. Just not like that. Anything but that. 'Billy!' Ray noticed the shadow of the photographer's bulk lift from above him. He glanced up and saw that Billy had reached the top of the ladder and he was being assisted through the hatch by the others. Suddenly, an object fell, smacked Ray in the face and then crashed onto the floor below.

Ray was momentarily stunned. 'What the …?'

'Me camera!' screeched a Geordie accent.

Ray blinked and gazed down. Billy had indeed dropped his camera and it had landed in several pieces.

Ray grunted and descended a couple of rungs on the ladder with the intention of retrieving it. He had one eye on the unearthly killer, however, and the noise and commotion caused by the falling camera had redirected its attention. The monster dropped what was left of Augustus Peck's guards and slithered back over to Ray. The thing was either extremely annoyed or hungry; Ray did not know or care which. He quickly changed his mind and began to climb the ladder again as fast as he could.

'Me camera!' cried Billy from above.

'Fuck your camera!' panted Ray.

All Ray had to do was move his legs and arms but such basic motions were failing him. He was gradually freezing up with fright and exhaustion. His clothes were soaked through with cold sweat and his lungs wheezed with the labour. Ray felt like the ladder was coated in glue.

'Move it, Ray!' shouted a different voice from above.

Ray thought it was The Professor but he could not be sure. He did not have the energy to look or reply. He just tried to keep climbing, gritting his teeth and willing his limbs to respond.

'Come on, old boy!'

Eventually Ray felt the cold night air on top of his head. He glared upwards and saw the hatch just a few more rungs away. The opening was fringed with friendly faces, all willing him to join them. Just as he ascended the last few feet, something from below snatched his ankle. The expressions of his fellow investigators changed suddenly. Some of them screamed or cried out in horror. Ray did not have to look down. He knew what had happened. The beast had caught up with him. The slimy tentacle coiled around his sock and shoe like a snake. It burnt too, as if the very touch of the creature was corrosive. Ray wanted to scream, his mouth opened but nothing came out.

'Grab him!' ordered The Professor and he, Kaleef and Maeve all reached down and seized hold of Ray's arms. They heaved him upwards with all their combined might.

Now Ray was stuck in a bizarre tug-of-war. From below, some powerful demon that should have never been on this planet was pulling him down. From above, a homosexual expert of the paranormal, his Arabian lover and their psychic collaborator were pulling him up. Ray felt his jacket began to tear with the effort, or perhaps it was his flesh and bones. He could not be sure. It seemed that the monster was winning though. Ray's friends were slipping away, inch by inch. The thing was just too strong. It hauled on his leg with the force of an articulated lorry. He was staring up at them and tears started to roll down his cheeks. He barely knew them but they would be the last human beings he would ever see.

Ray managed to enunciate one last plea. 'Tell my wife and kids I love them!'

Just as he gave up hope and resigned himself to becoming the creature's next snack, it suddenly lost its grip, Ray's shoe and sock came off. It had many other appendages to resume its hold but The Professor and company were dragging him the other way so hard that he virtually shot out of the hole like a Champagne cork. He and the others exclaimed their surprise victory wordlessly. They wasted no time in closing the hatch. Apart from Billy's camera and Ray's sock and shoe, they had escaped intact.

Ray sat on the stone roof of the lab for a while and blinked.

Billy was stretched out next to him, gasping.

The Professor was the first to congratulate them. 'Well done, gentleman!' He turned to Ray. 'That was close, Mr Weaver!'

'Tell me about it,' he whispered without looking up.

'You have probably just released something terrible on an unsuspecting world but never mind,' he added.

'It's Peck's animal,' growled Ray. 'Let that bastard answer for it.'

'Sadly, it seems that it's a case of out of the frying pan into the fire,' said The Professor.

Ray glared around to see what he meant. They had escaped from the zoo of horrors, it was true, but planet Earth was not as he remembered it. The night sky was no longer black, it flashed and seethed with a kaleidoscope of fantastic colours. The ground too shook with protest and the top of the building they were perched on wobbled like a vast jelly.

'What now?' groaned Ray.

*

No one knows for certain the true purpose of these ancient stone circles. As well as astronomical and religious theories, there was a time when these monuments were thought to have a more sinister intention. Primitive people believed that they were gateways to other worlds. If conditions were right, you could exit this dimension and enter another just by stepping within the boundaries of the ring. More alarmingly, there is a belief that this process could be reversed and that beings from these other places could find their way into ours too. Is it coincidence that wicked and mischievous creatures from myth are sometimes associated with stone circles and some of them are even sometimes called Pixie Church, Fairy Ring or Goblin's Gate? Modern opinion generally regards this hypothesis as mere pagan superstition and, as stone circle theories go it is the least popular and most ridiculed. Yet one has to admit that the consistency of the association is intriguing.

Cedric Montague Hamilton
Myths and Folklore of the British Isles 1983

*

Maeve was on her knees with her hands clasped over her ears. Her eyes alternated from screwed-up to wide and staring. Her skin was pale and clammy. The red had drained from her lips.

'What's wrong with her?' asked Ray.

'I don't know.' The Professor shook his head. He crouched down in front of her and put his hand on her shoulder. 'Maeve? What is it?'

'They're bringing something through!' she squealed.

Ray heard her, even above the roar of the tempest. He realised what she meant. He stumbled over to the edge of the roof, where Kaleef and Mark stood. He glanced at both of them, they were staring down at the stone circle, seemingly mesmerised. Ray stared too. The monument was at the core of the unearthly maelstrom. The cracks and ravines of its rocks were aglow. The brilliant light splintered out into the air and made it crackle with torment. The earth beneath the stones pulsated, rhythmic like the beat of a drum.

'It's a gateway!' proclaimed Ray.

'Of course!' The Professor joined them. 'The creatures in the lab must have come from ...' Uncharacteristically, words failed him.

'Somewhere else?' suggested Ray.

The four men surveyed the scene. Maeve, who was obviously more sensitive to the disturbance, and Billy, who was still recovering from his frantic climb up the ladder, were left to their own devices. There was some activity around the stone circle, a crowd of people had gathered although they appeared as little more than vague black silhouettes in the dazzle of the aurora. It was difficult to tell who they were and what exactly they were doing.

Mark turned to Ray. 'I think I saw Lucy.'

Ray glared at him. 'What? Where?'

'Down there.' Mark pointed at the throng around the circle.

'Are you sure?'

Mark shook his head. 'I'm not sure of anything anymore.'

Ray peered hard into the display of phantom light but it was no use, the figures were indistinguishable. Suddenly, a hole materialised in the middle of the circle, like a vent had torn open in reality. The storm became even more furious. A peculiar shape began to emerge. It began just as a fuzzy black dot but as it floated forwards it grew in size and revealed a more solid shape. An egg shape.

'It's them!' screeched Ray, his eyes wide with realisation.

'Who?' demanded The Professor.

'Fucking dwarfs from hell!' explained Ray. 'That's their ship! We've got to get down there! We've got to stop this!' For a second, Ray teetered dangerously on the edge of the building.

The Professor snatched his arm. 'Ray! No!'

Ray brushed him off. 'Let me go! Lucy's down there!'

'We don't know that!' pleaded The Professor.

But it was too late, there was a wild madness in the journalist's eyes. He growled something which none of his companions heard and leapt. At first, Ray dropped the thirty foot height like a sack of potatoes but, by some miracle, managed to right himself in mid-air and got away with a slight bounce and a roll. He got up and kept going, charging towards the eye of the storm like a man possessed.

'Ray! Don't be a bloody fool!' cried The Professor from the roof.

Even if Ray could have heard him above all the commotion he would not have stopped. There is, after all, only so much that a man can take.

*

Transcript of a radio interview from late night show The Witching Hour between presenter Mick Makepeace (MM) and guest Ray Weaver (RW) 12 January 1994.

MM In his book, your friend Cedric Montague Hamilton, makes the astonishing claim that you entered a stone circle and actually crossed into another dimension?

RW It's not something I like to talk about.

MM Hamilton's story does seem a little crazy.

RW There's nothing wrong with The Professor's theories ...

MM The Professor?

RW That's what we call him. His theories on stone circles have a sound basis. It's just a very unhappy episode from my life and I don't like to talk about it.

MM But if it did happen, if you did find a way into another world, wouldn't that be something important? Something worth telling people about?

RW   I wouldn't be so sure, Mick. Sometimes I think the human race is better off living in ignorance. If there are other life forms out there they might be vastly superior in terms of their intellect or their ability to hurt us. Would we really want to meet them? Would we even want to know about them?

MM   You've got a point but are you speaking from experience?

RW   Look, the truth of the matter is; I'm not sure what the hell happened that night. It was fourteen years ago and it was very strange and traumatic. If I had gone somewhere then I have no clear recollection of it. Plus the location in question doesn't exist anymore. There's a lot of other cases from my career that I can remember and would be happier to talk about.

MM   Such as the case of the Lancashire Death Snail?

RW   Such as the case of the Lancashire Death Snail.

*

It was early in the morning when Ray got home. He was cut and bruised and his clothes hung in tatters. One of his shoes and the sock inside it were distinctly absent. Even more shocking was the appearance of the girl he was with. She had once been beautiful but she was now damaged and had only Ray's grubby coat to wear. Fortunately, it was the time of morning just before the majority of his neighbours got up. Their façade would have undoubtedly caused mass suburban outrage. Probably phone calls to the police.

    'What's for breakfast?' Ray asked as he opened the back door, jocular yet weary.

    The Professor was drying the dishes. 'Raymond! You're alive!'

    'Of course,' Ray brought Lucy inside. 'You can't get rid of me that easily.'

    The Professor embraced him. 'We thought we'd lost you, old boy.'

    Ray grinned, sheepishly. 'It was a bit hairy back there, wasn't it? I thought I was a gonner when that beastie got hold of me. Everyone alright?'

The Professor gestured to Maeve and Mark, who was sat at the kitchen table. 'A few bumps and scrapes perhaps. We had to dodge a few bullets on our way out.'

'Where's the Geordie?'

'Sleeping.' The Professor nodded through into the lounge where a snoring lump had taken over the sofa. 'He's a little upset about his camera.'

'Shame about that,' agreed Ray.

Mark stood up and looked at the girl with a gloomy expression. 'Lucy?'

There was no reaction. Her eyes were glazed.

Ray frowned. 'She's not too good, mate.'

Maeve stepped over and took her by the hand. 'Here, come and sit down.'

Mark gawped at her as Maeve assisted her to the table. 'Lucy?'

'She's not responding, Mark.' Ray rubbed the stubble on his chin, uncomfortably.

Maeve sighed. 'She's catatonic with shock. She needs to go to hospital.' She looked up at Ray with equal concern. 'You do too.'

'I need a drink first,' Ray growled.

The Professor nodded. 'Tea?'

'Something stronger.'

'It's seven in the morning, my dear.'

'I don't give a toss. Give me a fucking drink.'

'Fair enough,' The Professor inhaled sharply and fixed him a whisky.

'Jellyhead,' commented Mark, still staring at Lucy.

Ray turned and glared at him. 'What?'

'Jellyhead,' repeated he.

'Jellyhead?'

'Lucy,' Mark shrugged his shoulders. 'She's become a jellyhead.'

Ray shot across the kitchen so fast and violently that none of his guests had time to blink. He tore Mark out of his seat and pinned him up against the wall by his shirt collars with such force that his feet left the ground. 'Jellyhead!? Is that all you've got to fucking say?'

'Just an observation,' his colleague stammered.

Ray turned red with fury and soaked Mark's face with his spit. 'I ought to take your head off for that! You've got no idea what I've just been through to save this girl! And all you can to do is give her a stupid name!'

'Ray! Leave it!' cried The Professor. He and Maeve tried to drag him away. Kaleef appeared from somewhere to assist, no doubt alerted by the racket.

Mark stuttered, his eyes wide with fear. 'I'm ... sorry.'

Urged by the others, Ray let go.

Mark was returned to terra firma. He straightened his collar. 'I wasn't thinking. I'm tired too.'

Ray lurched over to the door and opened it. 'Just go!'

Mark looked at him but Ray could not return his scrutiny.

'Get out of my fucking sight!'

Mark glanced at the others for support but was offered none. He left in shame and silence.

Ray slammed the door behind him. 'Moron!'

The Professor handed him his drink. 'You overreacted, Ray. You need some sleep.'

'I should have never got Mark involved.' Ray knocked back the golden contents of the glass. 'He made no contribution whatsoever. Four years I've worked with that twat and not for one second have I felt any benefit. Jellyhead! I'll never get that out of my mind!' He paced around and glimpsed at Lucy with remorse.

'It's not your fault, Ray,' said Maeve.

'Isn't it?'

The Professor shook his head. 'You're being too hard on yourself, old boy. Her uncle owns that infernal place, doesn't he? She must have been involved somehow.'

Ray looked at Lucy with tears in his eyes. 'I guess we'll never know.'

'She'll be alright,' soothed Maeve. 'She just needs some proper care.'

Ray handed The Professor his empty glass. 'Hit me with another one of those bad boys and we'll go to the hospital.'

Maeve nodded in agreement. 'I'll fetch my coat and come with you.'

She wandered out of the room and Kaleef followed.

Ray sat down for a minute.

The Professor passed him another drink.

There was a pause.

'I should thank you,' said Ray.

'What the devil for?'

'For helping me out of this mess.'

The Professor put his hands in his pockets and stared at him. 'Well, don't say thank you. Let's call it a debt.'

Ray took a slug of his second whisky. The ice cubes clashed. He looked up at him. 'What do you mean?'

'I may need your assistance one day.'

'This isn't some gay thing, is it?'

'Of course not!' The Professor grew cross. 'Can we please get over the fact that I'm a homosexual and move on?'

Ray laughed. 'Yeah!' Then laughed some more.

The stern expression on The Professor's face softened and he chortled too. 'That's better! You should never give that up, you know.'

'Give what up?'

'That laugh of yours! That Ray Weaver defiance.'

Ray finished his second drink. 'I'll try.'

With silent consent, the two men shook hands.

*

When I was a family man living out in the countryside, I attempted several hobbies. The most successful of these was fishing. It wasn't because I was good at catching fish, nor was it because I actually enjoyed hooking and killing the poor blighters. It was more to do with the location. I stumbled across it by accident one day. Iris and I had an argument and I just to get out of the house for a bit and let things simmer down so I wandered across the fields. It was there that I discovered the pond. I say a pond but it was almost big enough to constitute a lake. Perhaps something mid-way between a pond and a lake. It had a few fish in it and, on countless occasions, I returned with my tackle and indulged myself. I'm not sure if the spot had a name. I never saw anyone else there and it wasn't on any map. I knew a few other fishermen in the town but I never divulged my secret to them. It became my pond. Ray's pond. It was the most peaceful place I've ever known. No sound nor sight of mankind could be heard nor seen. It was just me and nature. Coming from the eastend of London, I could really appreciate it. Sometimes, when things get stressful, I go back there, not physically but just in my head. After all, it's probably a bloody supermarket now or something, knowing this country. If it is I don't want to know. I want it to remain my special place of solitude.

Excerpt from the journal of Ray Weaver, volume one.

*

He half-carried and half-dragged the bag across the ground. Sweating and breathless, Ray was nonetheless determined. His fishing tackle bag was the largest piece of luggage he owned. Despite its capacity, it was not particularly heavy, just stubborn.

'Let me out! Let me out! Let me out!' squealed the bag.

Ray ignored it until he reached the edge of the pond. It was a fair mile between where he parked his car and the water. The bag had struggled and screamed all the way yet he felt no urge to respond apart from the odd kick or ten.

'Let me out! Let me out! Let me out!'

Ray did not want to leave for London without saying goodbye to his pond. Besides, he had one last need of it. He finally unzipped the bag and peered within. 'Alright in there?' quizzed the cockney.

'You are an utter bastard,' came the reply.

'Only to those who wrong me,' explained Ray. 'And you have so very wronged me.'

From inside the bag, Augustus Peck attempted his special trick; the third eye began to throb and peel open but Ray was ready for it. He had fallen for it once already. Once bitten, twice shy. With a swift and powerful punch down into the bag the unnatural peeper was closed.

'Ouch!'

Ray delayed no longer. He zipped up the bag, took a moment to summon some strength, lifted it up by its handles and hurled it into the middle of the pond. It splashed perfectly on target though the momentum of the action nearly took Ray in with it. He steadied himself.

'Toodle pip.'

Ray then sat on his favourite rock. He smoked and waited for the last bubble of air to rise to the surface of the pond.

In the bushes, a drunken clown laughed.

Made in the USA
Charleston, SC
09 January 2015